Don't Let Me Go

Susan Lewis is the bestselling author of twenty-nine novels. She is also the author of *Just One More Day* and *One Day at a Time*, the moving memoirs of her childhood in Bristol. She lives in Gloucestershire. Her website address is www.susanlewis.com

Susan is a supporter of the childhood bereavement charity, Winston's Wish: www.winstonswish.org.uk and of the breast cancer charity, BUST: www.bustbristol.co.uk

Praise for Susan Lewis

'Expertly written to brew an atmosphere of foreboding, this story is an irresistible blend of intrigue and passion, and the consequences of secrets and betrayal.' *Woman*

'A multi-faceted tear-jerker.' *heat*

'Utterly compelling.' *Sun*

'Spellbinding! You just keep turning the pages, with the atmosphere growing more and more intense as the story leads to its dramatic climax.' *Daily Mail*

'One of the best around.' *Independent on Sunday*

'Sad, happy, sensual and intriguing.' *Woman's Own*

Also by Susan Lewis

Fiction
A Class Apart
Dance While You Can
Stolen Beginnings
Darkest Longings
Obsession
Vengeance
Summer Madness
Last Resort
Wildfire
Chasing Dreams
Taking Chances
Cruel Venus
Strange Allure
Silent Truths
Wicked Beauty
Intimate Strangers
The Hornbeam Tree
The Mill House
A French Affair
Missing
Out of the Shadows
Lost Innocence
The Choice
Forgotten
Stolen
No Turning Back
Losing You
No Child of Mine

Memoir
Just One More Day
One Day at a Time

Susan Lewis

Don't Let Me Go

arrow books

Published by Arrow Books 2013

2 4 6 8 10 9 7 5 3

First published in Great Britain in 2013 by
Century
Random House, 20 Vauxhall Bridge Road,
London SW1V 2SA

www.randomhouse.co.uk

Addresses for companies within The Random House Group Limited can be found at: www.randomhouse.co.uk/offices.htm

The Random House Group Limited Reg. No. 954009

ISBN 9780099550839

A CIP catalogue record for this book is available from the British Library

The Random House Group Limited supports the Forest Stewardship Council® (FSC®), the leading international forest-certification organisation. Our books carrying the FSC label are printed on FSC®-certified paper. FSC is the only forest-certification scheme supported by the leading environmental organisations, including Greenpeace. Our paper procurement policy can be found at www.randomhouse.co.uk/environment

Typeset in Palatino 11.5/13pt by Palimpsest Book Production Limited,
Falkirk, Stirlingshire
Printed and bound by CPI Group (UK) Ltd, Croydon, CR0 4YY

To James, for everything we've shared,
and more to come

Chapter One

Never, in all her twenty-nine years, had Charlotte Nicholls imagined life being this good. OK, she didn't have the right partner, nor was there even the glimpse of some dashing Romeo ready to charge over the horizon, though it had to be said that her horizons these days were truly gorgeous to behold. Surrounded by calmly floating islands in shimmering blue seas, enchanted by dazzling red sunsets that took the breath away, she was actually living in paradise. And this shady cove where she stood now, tucked like a precious secret into the southerly shores of New Zealand's Te Puna Bay, was home for her and three- (soon to be four) year-old Chloe – along with a rowdy jabber of parrots, a lively orchestra of cicadas, and a whole host of marine life that flopped and skimmed and dived about the waves like circus performers.

Charlotte was becoming quite skilled now at easing memories of the past aside and allowing the joy, the promise of her new life to eclipse all she'd left behind. Gazing out at the bay and reminding herself of how lucky she was to be here usually did it. Not always, it was true, but if it didn't work then a single glance at Chloe and how happy she was here, how transformed from the silent, traumatised toddler she'd been a few short months ago, was enough to convince her they were in the right place.

Charlotte had yet to find herself a job. However, she'd resolved not to stress about her future until she'd explored the best ways for her various talents to be put to use.

'There's no rush,' her mother kept assuring her. 'Time is on your side and money isn't an issue.'

What a strange concept that was for Charlotte, not having money – or the lack of it – as an issue. A definite first in her life, and long might it last.

Long might all of it last, though she knew only too well that it could fall apart in a heartbeat.

But that wasn't going to happen.

They were safe here with her mother and stepfather, Bob, who lived in the big house on the point of the headland at the far end of the bay's southern shore. Their exotic stretch of white sandy beach joined Charlotte and Chloe's cove when the tide was out, so they could walk through muddy puddles across to the lodge. When the tide was in, or the weather was rough, they'd walk up the sun-dappled incline from their cove to where Charlotte kept the car, beneath an old puriri tree, and drive through the citrus orchards and vineyards to the main house.

Bob's grapes were Pinot Gris, Chardonnay and Shiraz – his wines, according to Rick, his irreverent son, were 'bloody undrinkable', but Bob was more bothered by a recent infestation of hares on his land than he was by his son's uneducated palate.

Charlotte's mother, Anna, had helped to design the exquisite Cape Cod-style lodge with its pale grey wooden walls, white shutters and balustrades, while Bob, a semi-retired dentist-cum-property developer, had built it. The land around, all sixty or more acres of woodlands, orchards, rambling hillsides and vineyards, comprised the impressive estate. And the quaint beachfront dwelling at the heart of Charlotte and Chloe's cove, known as a bach – short for bachelor pad – was where Rick, Bob's son, had lived and partied during his student years. These days Rick was an advertising executive based in Auckland, though he still found time to visit his father's rambling idyll out here on the magical Bay of Islands.

Charlotte and Chloe loved it when Rick was around. Already he was like the brother Charlotte had never had, and seeing the way Chloe had taken to him, even calling him Uncle Wick, was so sweet that it made Charlotte's heart sing like a bird. Rick's too, if his beaming smiles and overindulgence were anything to go by.

That Chloe could relate so well to a man after all she'd been through was the greatest source of joy for Charlotte. However, the damage was far from healed, and since they'd escaped the nightmare Rick was really the only man in whose company Chloe seemed able to relax. It pained Charlotte to see how withdrawn she became if Bob spoke to her, especially when he was so gentle and kind. Of course, he understood about her past, and though it must surely sadden him not to be able to swing her up in his arms and rough and tumble her the way he did his other grandchildren, he never tried to force her.

How awful it must have been for him to be likened in Chloe's mind to her monster of a father, but he never let it show, nor spoke a single word about the pain this caused him.

For the most part, however, both Charlotte and

Chloe were loving getting to know their new family, which also included Rick's older sister Shelley, her husband Phil, and their children Danni and Craig. Until seven months ago, which was when Anna, Charlotte's mother, had come back into Charlotte's life after a *twenty-six*-year absence, Charlotte hadn't even known that any of these people existed. Now, after four months of being here, she was already feeling as though she'd known them for most of her life. She felt so much easier with them than she ever had with her adoptive parents, though if the truth were told she knew that something inside her still couldn't quite forgive her mother for abandoning her at the age of three. Of course she understood why her mother had done it – anyone would understand if they knew the story of what had happened back then. However, Charlotte only had to look at Chloe, who was currently paddling and poking about in the surf as it swirled and foamed around her chubby ankles, to doubt whether she could ever have done the same.

She mustn't be judgemental. It would get her nowhere and what she really wanted, more than anything, was to bond with her mother in the way so many daughters did with their mothers. It would take time, she understood that, and they had time now – and once she'd managed to fight off the demons inside her she felt sure a close and loving relationship would follow.

She'd never been close to the woman who'd adopted her. Myra Lake, wife of Douglas, the rector, had never been cruel or neglectful, but nor had she ever really wanted her. It was the rector who'd rescued three-year-old Charlotte from the terrible tragedy that had struck Charlotte's birth family and taken her home to his wife. Myra and Douglas were both dead now, but their natural daughter and Charlotte's adoptive sister, Gabby, was very much alive.

It always hurt to think of Gabby, so Charlotte inhaled deeply the tangy salt air that embraced her with warmth and the fragrance of flowers, as though the very essence of her new world could stifle the old one. She listened to the music of the waves and chirrup of cicadas, and let her thoughts drift around the bay along with the terns, shags and occasionally a gull. When the tide was in, as it was now, a stream of water curved around the back of their cove like an arm, creating a translucent blue brook between their bach and the beach. A swing on ropes dangled over the far side of the brook, while a white wooden footbridge connected their garden to the shingly sand. There were eighteen stepping stones leading across their lawn to the bach, and Chloe could count ten of them in Maori.

She was starting to blossom at the Aroha Childcare Centre in Waipapa; she had friends now and projects to complete. She was even allowing Charlotte to leave her there for three mornings a week, though Charlotte was always anxious during those hours in case Chloe suddenly blurted out something about her past.

Smiling as Chloe emptied her toy bucket into the surf, Charlotte shouted out, 'Find anything?'

Chloe's pixie face looked troubled as she shook her head. A lazy sea breeze was tousling her wispy dark curls and her tender limbs, thickly slathered in sunblock, were speckled with clumps of stony sand. She was wearing her favourite red swimsuit and the dearest little pair of yellow Crocs. Standing as she was in the shade of what she called a pokwa tree, being unable to pronounce pohutukawa, she looked like an exotic little butterfly. Up until a month ago, the branches of the tree, which hung out over the shallow depths of the surf like a ballerina, had been shrouded in vivid red flowers. It was known as the New Zealand Christmas tree. Only a few of the vibrant blooms remained now, shedding their crimson needles over the beach like tiny shreds of confetti.

This past Christmas had been their first in the sun, with dinner served on a shady veranda of the lodge and nothing but their laughter and clink of glasses disturbing the still of the bay. Both Charlotte and Chloe had received so many presents – more than either of them had had before – that they'd been unable to carry them all home to the bach. Rick had driven them in one of the estate's old Jeeps, calling it a summer sleigh. Afterwards Chloe had helped to row their blue boat back to the white sandy beach where they swam and waterskied and played ball with the rest of the family until the sun went down.

It was unsettling to think of how close they'd lived to the sea in England – a very different kind of sea – and yet Chloe had never been allowed to play in it, or ride the donkeys, or bury her father in the sand.

She could swim now, albeit in a haphazard doggy-paddle way, and she loved to go out on the dive boat with Nanna and Bob when they went to bring up lobsters and scallops. It was her job, with Shelley, or Rick, or Danni to look out for other boats and make sure theirs didn't drift. She'd come back full of tales about naughty crayfish and their feelers and the dolphins that had spun and leapt around them like they wanted to play.

'Look at me!' Chloe suddenly yelped. Her face was glowing with delight as she waved her hands and wiggled her tiny hips back and forth, side to side and round and round.

'I'm looking at you,' Charlotte called back, putting pebbles on the corners of a tablecloth to stop it flying off in the breeze. Chloe had collected the pebbles and Charlotte had helped her to paint on funny faces. 'Are you ready for your tea yet?' she asked.

Receiving no reply, she glanced up to find Chloe on her hands and knees performing a strange forward, backward crawl and though Charlotte couldn't make out the words she could tell she was singing. No doubt this was another of the little Maori rituals she'd learned at childcare. Though there weren't any Maori children at Aroha she was still being taught *tikanga* – the Maori customs and traditions. And she adored Maya, Bob and Anna's housekeeper, who lived on the settlement that curved like a boomerang from the eastern shore of the bay. Over the years Maya had taught her ancestors' songs to Bob's children and grandchildren, and now she was teaching Chloe too.

When it came to learning Chloe was like a sponge, soaking everything up until she could take no more, though still she kept trying. Everything fascinated her, from why the clouds changed shape and colour, to how dolphins could jump when they didn't have legs, to why Mr Kingfisher kept coming to perch in their pokwa tree. She loved to help Nanna plant vegetables, or bake cakes, or fold napkins, almost as much as she enjoyed fishing with Rick, or horseback riding with Danni. On the way to school she'd recite some of the names of the wild flowers they passed, kaka's beak, bedstraw, harebells, and when she brought a mangled bunch into the bach as a gift for Charlotte her curly head would tilt curiously to one side as though she couldn't quite believe how thrilled Charlotte was to receive them. She was like a flower herself, continually blooming and blooming, bringing so much joy to everyone's lives that it simply wasn't possible to imagine that she'd ever been anything but the excited and engaging little sprite she was now.

Knowing she could trust her not to go any further into the waves than the depth of her knees, Charlotte stepped back into the kitchen to retrieve a tray of coconut bread from the oven. This was one of Chloe's favourite after-school treats, though Charlotte suspected it was the sifting, whisking and mixing of it that she enjoyed the most.

The kitchen of their bach was efficiently compact and yet wonderfully airy, thanks to the floor-to-ceiling glass doors that opened out on to the bay. At the heart of the space was a square mosaic-topped table that was never without something the intrepid explorer and archaeologist, Chloe, had discovered in the garden or the waves. The fridge, with its impressive display of Chloe's artwork, was decorously lit from above by the seashell lamp Nanna and Chloe had made and given to Charlotte for Christmas. The cupboards, shelves and work surfaces along the back wall were made from sand-coloured Tawa wood, as was the bach itself, though the walls and window frames were painted a creamy white. To one side of the kitchen was a door that led into a natural stone bathroom where Chloe's toys, shells and fossils cluttered up the old-fashioned roll-top bath, and Charlotte's hairdryer was joyfully plugged in next to the sink. How much easier life was with electricity in the bathroom.

Since the main living space was open plan, it was an easy flow across the brushed-granite floor from the kitchen into the sitting room, furnished with a deep comfy sofa, two basketweave armchairs and a large pine chest for the TV, with more French windows on to the bay. Behind the sofa an oriental-style screen and giant potted palm created some privacy for Charlotte's sleeping space. The elegance of her bed with its sumptuous plum and ivory linens, the built-in wardrobe and hand-carved driftwood lamps never failed to delight her. Chloe's room had been added on to Charlotte's just before they'd arrived in New Zealand, and was full of everything a little girl and her cherished teddy bear could wish for. Boots, the bear, even had his very own bed, though he'd yet to sleep in it, because he got lonely without Chloe.

There was no door between the two bedrooms, only a jangling bamboo curtain that meant no one could pass through without making a noise. This was a precaution that probably wasn't necessary here, on the Bay of Islands, but Charlotte felt happier to have it there. Besides, it woke her when Chloe came padding through after a bad dream.

After depositing the coconut bread on to a rack to cool, Charlotte flipped the oven gloves over her shoulder and reached for a band to tie back her hair. During these past four months it had grown to below her shoulders and the sun had bleached it to a silvery blonde. Her tan – Chloe's too – was as golden as a honey-baked bun, and surprisingly, given all the scrumptious food Anna kept serving up, plus the lavish dinners Bob treated them to in restaurants of nearby vineyards, neither of them had gained much weight. This could only be thanks to the swimming, rowing, bicycling, gardening and ball games they went in for, not to mention all the handstands, cartwheels and roly-polies Chloe regularly performed for her doting family audience.

'Mummy! Mummy! The ducks are here,' Chloe shouted, bursting in through the door. 'Look, look,' and grabbing Charlotte's hand she dragged her outside on to the patio. Sure enough, paddling out of the waves was the raggle-taggle collection of ducks that lived on the pond behind the bach.

'It must be five o'clock,' Chloe declared knowledgeably. Nanna had told her that they could set their watches by the ducks' evening constitutional – though Chloe couldn't say that word, so she called it their 'shall'. 'Have we got some crumbs?' she pleaded, looking up at Charlotte.

'Of course,' Charlotte smiled, and going back inside she dug out the bag she made up during the day especially for the evening ritual.

'They're nearly here, they're nearly here,' Chloe cried excitedly, and grabbing the bag she ran down to the footbridge where they were already starting to gather.

'No, that's naughty,' she chided, holding the bag high as a particularly impatient Appleyard tried to stick its beak inside. 'You have to wait your turn.'

Since Charlotte already had countless photographs and videos of Chloe at the centre of her greedy duck club, she resisted the urge to reach for her camera again and was about to stroll down to the footbridge to join them when the phone rang inside the bach.

'Great, you're in,' a cheery voice declared as she answered. 'Everything OK?'

'I think you could say that,' Charlotte assured her stepsister, Shelley. Though she was still getting used to the idea of even having a stepsister, it was easy to think of her as a friend when Shelley was so relaxed and undemanding.

Charlotte hadn't spoken to Gabby since she'd left to come here, and she wasn't sure if they'd ever speak again.

Don't think about it now. It's too late to change things, so put it out of your mind.

'Where are you?' she asked Shelley.

'On my way to collect Phil from the airport. He was supposed to be staying overnight in Auckland, but I think he got wind of Dad's barbie tonight. They caught some amazing crayfish when they were out yesterday, did you see them?'

'Bloody awesome,' Charlotte answered in her best imitation of Bob. 'Is your brother gracing us with his presence too?'

'Rick? I'm not sure, I forgot to ask. Did he say he was coming this weekend?'

'Not to me, I haven't spoken to him since he left last Sunday. In fact, didn't he say something about going to Sydney for a couple of days this week, so chances are he's not even in the country.'

'Well, I'm sure we'll find out when we see Katie later. Did you two get together earlier?'

Feeling a twinge of awkwardness at the mention of Rick's fiancée, Charlotte said, 'No, I had to cry off. They needed some help at Aroha, so I've been doing my bit for childcare today.'

11

With a teasing wryness to her tone Shelley said, 'And I bet Chloe loved having her mum around so she could show off to all her friends.'

As Charlotte's eyes moved to where Chloe was watching the ducks waddling off to their pond, she felt such a rush of tenderness that she had to fight the urge to go out and hug her. She was such a good little girl, never wandering out of sight, even when the temptation to follow the ducks must be almost overwhelming. 'It's true, she does seem to enjoy it when I'm there,' she conceded, 'but she's on her third week without me now *and* she's mixing quite happily with the other kids, so great strides are being made.'

'She's a little sweetheart and we all love her to bits,' Shelley declared fondly. 'Now, before I ring off, I'm taking Molly to the vet tomorrow so I was hoping, if you're going to be in town too, that you might join me for lunch.'

Thrilled, Charlotte said, 'I'd love to. I'm picking Chloe up at midday so we can be free any time after that.'

'OK. Let's do twelve thirty at the Fishbone. I know her little highness loves it there and we can always put Molly under the table if we eat outside. Meantime, I'll see you at Dad's in about an hour. Shall I pick you up on my way down the drive?'

'Thanks, but I'll take the car so I can bring Chloe back in it if she falls asleep, which she undoubtedly will.' Her heart gave a sudden jolt as Chloe let out a shriek. 'What the . . . ?' she gasped, dashing outside.

'What's happening?' Shelley demanded.

Charlotte's fear was already dissolving into laughter. The shriek, she realised, had been of

12

delight. 'Danni's just turned up on Diesel,' she told Shelley.

With a mother's long-suffering groan, Shelley said, 'I knew that girl would bolt straight out of the door as soon as I left the house. She should be doing her homework, not riding her horse, but hey, when did she ever listen to me? Tell her I'll want to see her essay when I get back and it had better be finished – and good.'

'Is Craig with you?' Charlotte asked, referring to Shelley's eight-year-old son.

'No, he's already at Dad and Anna's. He walked down all by himself again, which is making him feel very grown up, especially as he gets to take Danni's mobile in case he falls.'

Since Shelley and Philip had built a house on a neighbouring plot of land, it meant that Craig was only ever on family property as he made the half-mile descent to his grandfather's home. Nevertheless, the thought of him being alone in the pine woods, picking a lonely route through the tangled Chardonnay vines, wasn't an easy one for Charlotte. Clearly she still had a way to go before she could get past her inherent fear of danger lurking on every corner.

'OK, I've just pulled up outside the shack we laughably call a terminal,' Shelley was saying, 'and I can see the plane waggling its way out of a cloud so I'll love you and leave you.'

After ringing off Charlotte wandered down to the beach where Danni was sliding off her beloved chestnut to land plop in front of Chloe, who was gazing up at her adoringly. Danni was a striking-looking girl with long wavy blond hair, tanned, gangly limbs and vivid blue eyes.

13

'Hey you,' she cried, ruffling Chloe's curls. 'Thought I'd come and find out how you got on at school today.'

Chloe clapped her hands in glee, then launching forward she began patting Diesel's silky legs and reaching for his reins.

'Do you want to sit on?' Danni offered, holding the horse's head still so Chloe could stroke his nose.

Chloe's eyes shot eagerly to Charlotte.

'OK, for a few minutes,' Charlotte agreed, and after lifting her into the saddle she immediately wanted to laugh at how proud Chloe looked of herself all the way up there on the stationbred's back.

'Swim?' Chloe asked Danni.

Danni's eyes twinkled as she glanced at Charlotte.

Knowing she wanted Danni to take Diesel into the water and swim him round to the main house with her, Chloe, clinging on behind, Charlotte said, 'Not right now. You have to get dressed before we go to Nanna's and I thought . . .'

'We're going to Nanna's,' Chloe told Danni. 'She's got crayfish and a barbie . . .' She caught her breath. 'Can we do pipi dance?' Her leg was already coming over the saddle so Charlotte quickly reached up to catch her.

'You do the dance too, Mummy,' she urged, as Charlotte set her down, and grabbing Danni's hand she began dragging her into the waves.

Realising now what the odd little contortions had been about earlier, Charlotte stood stroking the horse as she watched Chloe and Danni digging their bare feet into the shingle while waving their arms until Danni suddenly dropped to her knees and Chloe followed suit.

'We've got one!' Chloe shouted triumphantly. 'Mummy, we've got a pipi.'

'Well done,' Charlotte laughed, and leaving them to their search for cockles, or pipis as Danni had taught Chloe to call them, she returned to the bach to freshen herself up for the evening ahead. No doubt Chloe would want to build a fire on the beach before they left in order to poach the pipis in seawater till they opened, but this evening they'd have to give them to Bob to pile up on the barbecue.

By the time they were ready to leave there was an impressive basket full of pipis to take to Nanna, all found by Chloe, Danni insisted, which made Chloe beam and Charlotte want to hug Danni for how ready she always was to make her young cousin feel special.

'You found some too,' Chloe insisted generously, and Charlotte couldn't have felt prouder of her as she swept her up in the air and landed her on the horse in front of Danni.

'Put the hat on,' Charlotte told her, as Danni unclipped it from the saddle. 'And no taking it off. No trotting or galloping either. Or swimming. I'll be in the car, right behind you, so I'll have my eye on you.'

Chloe broke into a mischievous giggle and began kicking her feet into Diesel, trying to urge him forward.

Danni pressed in her heels and off they went. 'We'll wait for you at the top of the slope,' she assured Charlotte.

'I guess I'm bringing the pipis,' Charlotte replied drily, and after going back for the coconut bread and a napkin to cover the cockles, she climbed the incline behind them, having to admire the picture they made amongst the towering canna lilies and manuka trees at the top.

'Did you know,' Danni said, as she reached them, 'that Captain Cook and his crew made tea and beer out of the leaves of these trees? I just learned that in school today.'

'No, I didn't know,' Charlotte replied, feeling the pleasure of their shared history stealing through her as warmly as the heady fragrances wafting up from the bay. 'In England we call it the tea tree, so I guess that makes sense.'

'I've never been to England,' Danni said, easing Diesel aside so Charlotte could put the basket and her bag on to the car's passenger seat. 'I think we're going to go though, one of these days. Dad wants to visit where his parents grew up.'

'Go now,' Chloe demanded impatiently.

Though Charlotte considered reprimanding her for being rude, it was so rare for her to speak or act out of turn that in truth it was a relief to see it. So, giving her leg a playful squeeze, she went round to the driver's side to begin following Diesel's magnificent rump through the fruiting Shiraz vineyard.

As they reached the main drive she was just reflecting on how all children should grow up free to roam the outdoors and feel at one with their world, when her attention was caught by a car coming up behind her. At first she thought it was Shelley with Philip and was about to wave, but as the silver BMW drew closer she felt herself sink.

What was it about Katie, Rick's English fiancée, that she couldn't quite warm to? Everyone else seemed to love her, and it wasn't as if she'd ever done anything to make Charlotte dislike her. Actually, dislike was too strong a word; it was more

16

that she found Katie's manner slightly off-putting, even dismissive at times, as though she wasn't too thrilled about Charlotte being there. Charlotte had never mentioned it to anyone, nor would she when the last thing she wanted was to cause trouble.

However, given the chat she'd had with Rick over a bottle and a half of wine at the bach last weekend when he'd come very close to confessing a truth Charlotte had already guessed at, Charlotte very much feared that trouble was closing in anyway, and there wasn't going to be much either she or Katie could do to stop it.

Chapter Two

By the time Bob carried a platter of sizzling crayfish from the monster barbecue to the candlelit table on the veranda, the kitchen and decks were crowded with guests. Though Charlotte had met most of them before, as always with her mother's and Bob's parties there were newcomers swelling the numbers and this evening's contingent, the Bowlams, had arrived on a twin-masted yacht, currently anchored close by in the bay while their tender bobbed alongside Bob's rigid inflatables at the end of the pier. Apparently the Bowlams were long-time friends from Russell, a pretty resort town on the island that sprawled across Te Puna's horizon. Like everyone else they'd been totally charmed by the greeting they'd received from Chloe and Craig, who'd offered them fresh pipis from a basket while Danni had taken their order for drinks.

Shelley and Phil had long since arrived from the airport and were busily catching up with everyone while making sure the wine flowed, and Sarah, Anna's oldest friend and Katie's aunt, was at the oven checking the garlic and rosemary potatoes she had baking there. Anna herself was stirring lemon juice into the vermouth and tarragon sauce she'd whipped up for the crayfish, while Charlotte was tossing a salad in the balsamic dressing Katie had made.

The kitchen was vast, with a fourteen-seater wooden table down the middle, two ice-making fridges at one end and two entirely glass walls which, when open, as they were now, seemed to join the house to the sun-dappled bay.

'Ready when you are in there,' Bob shouted out.

'Coming,' Anna called back. 'Where's the tarragon I chopped . . . ? Ah,' and grabbing a handful she sprinkled it over the sauce as she carried the pot to the table. With her fine blonde hair, twinkly eyes and girlish figure she appeared much younger than her fifty-one years, and might even, at a push, have passed for Charlotte's sister. They really were very alike in looks, and during the short time they'd been getting to know one another they'd discovered, to their delight and occasional embarrassment, that they had many similar mannerisms too.

As for Bob, his thick silvery hair, cobalt-blue eyes and luminous smile that seemed etched into every line of his face made him an extremely handsome man who didn't look his age of sixty either. Though Rick resembled his father quite closely, it was Shelley who was most like him. In fact she'd turned out to be far more glamorous on meeting than Charlotte had expected from the video footage she'd seen before coming here. She was taller and more shapely than the film had allowed, and her hair, which had been shoulder-length and mousy back then, was now a rich honey blonde and cut into an attractively wedged curly bob that Katie, the hairdresser amongst them, had created at her salon in town. Katie herself had spiked, platinum hair, soulful brown eyes and an exquisite heart-shaped mouth that even Charlotte found fascinating to watch.

'How are the potatoes going in there?' Anna called out to Sarah.

'On their way,' Sarah called back.

'I'll take the salad,' Katie declared, and easing the bowl from Charlotte's hands she turned and almost tripped over Chloe.

'You're in the way there, sweetie,' she told her, irritation seeping through her smile.

Chloe immediately pressed in closer to Charlotte. 'Nanna asked me to get the lemons,' she said quietly.

Putting a hand on her head, Charlotte shouted, 'Mum, what are the lemons for?'

'The finger bowls,' Anna shouted back. 'They're already quartered. Is the plate too big for Chloe?'

'It's OK, I can help her,' Danni offered, skidding up alongside them.

'I'm getting the apple juice,' Craig announced on his way through to the fridge.

'More wine?' Phil held up two bottles, one of white, the other red.

'White for me,' Charlotte answered, searching for her glass.

'House Pinot Gris,' he told her, using the bottom of the bottle to scratch his balding head. His clean-shaven face was an endearing contradiction of studiousness and humour, with his brown eyes appearing constantly startled behind their owlish spectacle frames, while the upturned corners of his mouth made him appear forever on the brink of laughter.

'That's great for me,' Charlotte smiled, holding out her glass. 'Go steady with the plate now, Chloe.'

'She's fine,' Danni assured her, keeping close to

Chloe as she carried the artful tower of lemons out to the table.

Charlotte turned back to Phil as he finished filling her glass, and taking a generous sip she said, 'How was Auckland?'

'Worth the trip, as ever,' he replied. 'I ran into Rick at the boat show. Have you met his business partner yet, Hamish . . . I can't remember his surname.'

Charlotte smiled. 'No, but I've heard a lot about him.'

'They're doing well with that agency of theirs, only six years in and already one of the big-shot agencies from New York, or is it London, is showing interest in buying them out. They're heading for great things, those two. Just watch this space.'

Having heard the same prediction from Rick and Bob, Charlotte readily toasted the prospect. 'So, did you buy anything at the show?' she wondered wryly, knowing he'd only gone for a longing look round.

He chuckled. 'Afraid my scientist's cheque book doesn't stretch that far, but hey, I can always dream.'

'Time to eat,' Bob boomed across the general burble of chat.

'We need extra napkins,' Katie called from the table. 'Can you get them, Charlotte? They're in the drawer . . .'

'I know where they are,' Charlotte interrupted, going to fetch them.

'I wonder what her last slave died of?' Shelley teased as she came to refill a water jug.

'Don't worry, it wasn't fetching napkins,' Katie shot back.

Charlotte glanced at Phil, whose eyebrows were raised expressively.

Reflecting the irony, she took the napkins to the table, saying to Katie, 'So, Rick's not joining us tonight?'

Katie flashed her a look. 'Actually, he's in Sydney, so it would be difficult.'

Charlotte was about to tell her that Phil had seen him in Auckland earlier when she thought better of it. For all she knew Rick had boarded a plane later in the day and so could indeed be in Sydney by now – just.

'Sweetie,' Katie said to Chloe who'd climbed on to the empty chair between her and Danni, 'why don't you go and sit next to Grandpa?'

As Chloe stiffened, Charlotte's eyes turned flinty. Katie knew her suggestion would cause a problem, so why on earth had she done that?

Jumping in quickly, Bob said, 'You don't want to sit next to smelly old me, do you? This is the boys' end – but I'm sure Craig will swap if you'd like him to.'

Chloe shook her head and slid off her chair to press against Charlotte. 'Sit with Mummy,' she said shyly.

'Of course, come on darling,' Charlotte said, and hiking her up, away from the nasty lady, she carried her to the other end of the table where Anna was already making room for them.

'OK, bon appétit, everyone,' Bob declared as Sarah brought out the potatoes. 'Anna, my darling, you've prepared another royal banquet.'

'Not without help,' she insisted, raising her glass. 'To the fishermen, Bob, Phil and Rick.'

'Hey! What about yours truly?' a cheery-faced man in an All Blacks shirt and wraparound shades piped up. Recognising him as the local police officer

22

who'd become a firm friend of the family since bringing a very drunken teenage Shelley home from a concert in town, Charlotte found herself marvelling all over again at how easily and readily people mixed out here. 'I was on the dive last weekend too,' he reminded Anna.

'Sorry Grant, sorry, sorry,' she winced. 'To you too, with knobs on.'

As everyone laughed and raised their glasses, he removed his shades to treat her to a playful glare.

'You out with us again this weekend?' Bob asked him, helping himself to a gigantic crayfish and passing the platter on.

'Sure, if the missus will let me.'

'Let you?' his wife retorted. 'I'll be happy to get rid of you.'

As the banter continued and spread around the table along with the food, Charlotte tucked a napkin into the neck of Chloe's T-shirt and served her a forkful of lobster.

'Where's Boots?' Chloe asked in a whisper.

Glancing over her shoulder to check the bear was where she'd left him, on one of the veranda's sofas, Charlotte said, 'He's just over there. Do you want him now?'

Chloe nodded.

Knowing she was tired, and that large gatherings could sometimes unsettle her, especially when someone suggested she should go to sit with Bob, Charlotte was about to get up and fetch the bear when Anna said, 'Don't worry, I'll go. Just make sure she has something to eat.'

'I think she might have filled up on pipis,' Charlotte replied, 'which probably won't have done this tummy much good, will it?'

Chloe giggled as Charlotte poked her belly, then hid her face in Charlotte's arm.

'I think you're absolutely shattered, young lady,' Charlotte told her.

Chloe nodded and grabbed Boots into a fierce embrace as Anna handed him to her.

'Just eat this little bit of crayfish and two potatoes,' Charlotte said, 'then you can curl up on the chair behind me.'

Obediently Chloe opened her mouth for the food to go in and closed it again as she chewed. Her table manners were good, even if her confidence was as fragile as a sparrow's egg.

Therapy was the answer, of course, but it couldn't happen yet. She was too young, the past was still too fresh in her mind and the last thing she needed was someone forcing her to relive it all. Better, for the time being, to carry on as though nothing bad had ever happened, that she had always been here with Mummy and Nanna and that her terrible, evil daddy was never going to be in her life again.

Did she think of him at all? Was there a part of her that actually longed for him even after what he'd done? She never asked for him, and Charlotte never spoke of him so it wasn't possible to tell.

Catching her mother's eye, she wondered if Anna's thoughts were running along the same lines. She'd be as horrified as Charlotte would if Chloe ever did express a desire to see her father, but they'd have to deal with it somehow if the time came, though please God it never would.

'The shoot I'm doing over at Kauri Cliffs next week?' Anna said. 'I could do with some extra assistance, if you're free.'

Charlotte lit up. 'Count me in,' she declared,

thrilled to be asked. Ever since Te Puna Lodge had been featured in *Design Folio* some ten or twelve years ago, Anna had found herself with a new career as a stylist for some of the country's more upmarket home wares and clothing catalogues. Charlotte had already assisted her on a couple of occasions since arriving, and had enjoyed it so much that she was definitely up for doing it again, especially if it was going to be at one of the world's most exclusive hotels. 'Who's the client?' she asked. 'The hotel itself, or is it just being used as a location?'

'A location,' Anna confirmed. 'The client is Owens Lifestyle, an Auckland-based company who're hoping to expand through mail order. They've got some gorgeous linens, I'll show you the portfolio they sent through. It's only two hundred dollars for a pillowcase, or five hundred for an embroidered throw.'

Charlotte gave a choke of laughter. 'So we'll be buying it all up then,' she retorted drily.

Laughing, Anna nodded for her to look at Chloe, whose head was lolling towards the table.

Pushing back her chair, Charlotte said, 'Come on sweetheart, let's lie you down, shall we?'

'And Boots,' Chloe mumbled sleepily as Charlotte carried her to the pillowy sofa behind them.

'Yes, you hold him nice and tightly now.'

'That's great! Did you hear that, Charlotte?' Shelley called across the table. 'Katie's free to join us for lunch tomorrow.'

Glad her back was turned, Charlotte raised a hand with a thumbs up and stooped down closer to Chloe. 'Off you go to dreamland,' she murmured softly. 'Mummy's here.'

Chloe smiled and put a hand up to Charlotte's face. 'Love you,' she whispered throatily.

'I love you too,' Charlotte whispered back, feeling herself melting with the sheer force of it.

As Chloe's eyes fluttered closed Charlotte stroked her hair and swore silently to herself that no matter what, she would never, ever let anything bad happen to her precious little girl again.

It was past ten o'clock now and Charlotte had carried Chloe upstairs to the room they usually shared when they stayed at the lodge. Though Bob had offered to drive them over to the bach and help carry Chloe down the incline and over the foot-bridge, Charlotte had decided against it. Chloe was still too nervous around him. It was the same with the other men – apart from Rick. She was mostly fine provided they didn't single her out for attention; if they did, or, heaven forbid, if they tried to touch her, it was tragic to see. She didn't become hysterical, never that, she merely seemed to collapse from within, hanging her head and shoulders, or turning to Charlotte with terrified eyes, proving that the horror inside her remained as livid as the fear.

It was heartbreaking, devastating even, which was why leaving England and bringing her here to Te Puna had been so important. Charlotte could take care of her now in a way that hadn't been possible before. She could make her feel safe and loved and gradually, she felt sure, Chloe would come to trust every member of the family and believe that the horrors in the past were well and truly over.

Though Charlotte had her mother and Bob to thank for making this new start a reality, the unexpected windfall she'd received just before leaving

Britain meant that, thankfully, she didn't have to depend on them completely. In fact, she was able to cover all of her and Chloe's expenses and had even bought a small car on arriving without noticing much of a dent.

'This is for you,' her sister, Gabby, had said as she'd pulled an envelope from her bag on that last day. They'd been outside the vicarage where they'd both grown up, with tears shining in their eyes as they looked at one another for what they knew could be the last time. 'I always meant to give it to you,' she'd continued, 'perhaps I should have said so before now, but it's yours and I want you to have it.'

Charlotte had looked at the envelope, not understanding what it was.

'It's half the money from the sale of the house,' Gabby had explained shakily. 'It's been as much your home as it has mine, so it's only right . . .' She'd been unable to go on as Charlotte had started to break down too.

'You don't need to do this,' Charlotte had told her. 'It wasn't what your mother wanted.'

'It was what Daddy wanted, and it's what I want too.'

It was a huge sum of money, at least by Charlotte's standards, and would definitely be enough for her to buy somewhere here in New Zealand – when the time was right.

She wondered if she would know when that time had come.

'Is she OK?' Anna asked, glancing up from wiping the table as Charlotte came back into the kitchen.

'Out for the count,' Charlotte assured her. 'Lucky I remembered to bring Boots, or I'd have had to go back and get him.'

27

Anna smiled. 'As if she'd ever go anywhere without him,' she commented. Then, 'Fancy a nightcap? There's still some limoncello in the freezer.'

'That you made?' Charlotte asked teasingly. 'From the lemons in the top orchard?'

'Actually, they're from the trees next to the veranda,' Anna corrected, 'and it isn't half bad, even if I do say so myself.'

'You'll have to show me how to make it,' Charlotte declared, going to fetch a bottle and two shot glasses while Anna dried her hands and rubbed in some cream. 'There are two trees behind the bach that should come into fruit I guess around July, August time, given everything happens at the opposite time of year here.'

'It might be a little earlier than that, we'll see. And you should have some oranges over there too, so we could make mandarincello – or marmalade. I'm sure Chloe will want to be involved in that, given it's Boots's favourite.'

Having no doubt of it, Charlotte smiled as she filled the two glasses, and passing one to her mother she wandered out to the veranda where clouds of sandflies were ready to close in on the ankles and the last track of Bob's jazz medley was fading into the night. The bay was shrouded in darkness now, with random sprinkles of light glistening from Russell in the far distance and the Maori settlement that was much closer to home. Though a slight chill was crisping the air, the scent of jasmine, mingling with citronella burners and salt water, was no less evocative of summer nights as it wafted up over the gardens, nor was the throaty whistle of a kiwi lost in the breeze.

'I think she's settling in very well, don't you?' Anna

said, as she came to join Charlotte on one of the pale grey and white striped sofas overlooking the bay.

Understanding she meant Chloe, Charlotte nodded as she gave a gentle sigh. 'She's like any other little girl of her age, healthy happy, full of energy . . . It's only the issue with men that sets her apart.'

Though Anna couldn't disagree, she said, 'She'll get over it, eventually.'

Charlotte didn't respond, she simply hoped in her heart that it would be sooner rather than later.

'I was wondering,' Anna said carefully, 'if you ever call her by her real name now.'

Charlotte glanced at her in surprise. 'No, never,' she replied. 'I'm afraid if I do that it'll bring it all back. Why? Do you think I should?'

Anna quickly shook her head. 'No, not at all. I think she's very happy being Chloe. Very happy indeed.'

Charlotte sipped her drink and turned her gaze to the translucent sliver of moon hanging over the bay. 'Why did you ask?' she said.

Anna shrugged. 'I'm not sure. I guess I just don't ever think of her as anything but Chloe now, and I wondered if it was the same for you.'

Charlotte's gaze stayed on the moon. 'Yes, it's the same for me,' she said. Then, 'We did the right thing, bringing her here. I've never been in any doubt of it, but if you . . .'

'There's no doubt in my mind either,' Anna interrupted, putting a hand on hers. 'Though I have to admit I was being selfish when I suggested it. After missing out on so much of your life, I couldn't bear the thought of missing out on any more. I also do happen to think it was the best thing for Chloe.'

29

Charlotte wasn't going to argue with that, but nor could she bring herself to say any more about it right now.

Anna glanced at her, and seeming to sense the turmoil inside her, she said, very gently, 'You're doing fantastically well, you know. I feel very proud of you.'

Forcing back a bitter laugh, Charlotte took another sip of her drink. Maybe she was doing well; maybe she should start telling herself that and believing it, instead of allowing her happiness to be so weighted with guilt and dread.

'I'm not sure whether now is a good time to bring this up,' Anna went on tentatively, 'but I feel . . . Well, I feel you resent me for what's happened, and I don't just mean recent events. I mean for the way I left you when you were young . . .'

'Actually, now isn't the time,' Charlotte told her, getting to her feet. 'But for the record, I don't resent you.' It was a lie, but what good would it do to admit it? 'I'm glad you came to find me,' she pressed on, meaning it. 'I never felt as though I belonged before, and now I . . . Well, I can't say I do, exactly, but I'm getting there.'

Anna stood up too and took Charlotte's hand. 'How would you feel about us having some counselling together?' she asked. 'It might help us to talk things through with someone . . .'

Stopping her, Charlotte said, 'I'm not refusing to, but just not yet, OK?'

Anna regarded her closely and eventually nodded.

Feeling bad now for being difficult, Charlotte said, 'I want you to know how much I appreciate . . .'

'Sssh,' Anna interjected, putting a finger to her lips. 'You don't have to thank me for anything. I'm your mother, I want what's best for you and I want to be there for you. I would have been a long time ago if . . . Well, if things had been different, but we can't change the past, so I guess there's no point pretending we can. At least not tonight.' She smiled gently. 'It's the future that counts now.'

Charlotte glanced away.

'And there's nothing to be afraid of.'

Astounded that she could say, or even think that, Charlotte turned back to her.

'You're thinking of Chloe's father, aren't you?' Anna challenged. 'Well don't. There's nothing he can do now. He won't be coming to find you.'

Charlotte's eyes went down. No, he wouldn't be coming to find them, thank God, because he'd received a life sentence for what he'd done. So right now, even as they spoke, he was over there in England finding out how other prisoners treated those who harmed young children, particularly their own.

So she had nothing to fear from him.

Nothing at all.

If only it was as simple as that.

Chapter Three

A jumping-off ceremony at Aroha Childcare Centre was always anticipated with great excitement by the children old enough to understand it; for those at the heart of it, it was one of the true highlights of their young lives.

Today Bevan Greengrass was the star of the show.

Because it was a special occasion for one of Chloe's special friends Charlotte had been invited to watch the ceremony this morning, along with Bevan's parents, grandparents, two of his aunts, and his very important Uncle Grant. At his nephew's request, Grant had turned up in his policeman's uniform while his wife, Polly, was in her white doctor's coat complete with toy stethoscope to test everyone's hearts.

Tomorrow Bevan was going to be five, which was the reason he was jumping off today.

It still seemed odd to Charlotte that children started school on their fifth birthday, rather than at the beginning of the school year, however that was the system here, and she wasn't about to fault it. Why would she, when everything she'd seen of childcare so far was as good as anything she'd ever come across in England, in fact in some ways it was better. Certainly the learning rituals were impressive, as were the outdoor activities as well as the embracing of native culture. Plus – and this was a huge plus for any parent – there was far less risk of predators prowling the vicinity than there was in Britain.

What a blessing it was to have Chloe here. If only it was possible to bring all the children who'd suffered the way she had and help give them a fresh start too.

Dream on, Mother Teresa, and mind your halo doesn't slip.

'He hardly slept a wink last night, he was so excited,' Bevan's mother whispered from the next seat.

Not surprised, Charlotte said, 'I'm sure he'll make up for it tonight after all the fuss, which can only be a good thing with such a big day ahead of him tomorrow.'

Ellie Greengrass nodded agreement as she leaned back to hear what her brother, Grant, was saying.

Their adult group was seated to one side of the circle the cross-legged children had formed around a gaily painted cardboard throne, which in turn was sitting grandly beneath the all important jump-off ring. This prized artefact was rather like a large coolie hat strung with vibrant ribbons and streamers and edged with dangling tags that sported the names of all the children who'd jumped off from its inspiring auspices in the past.

As they'd already sung the songs Bevan had chosen – 'Wheels on the Bus', 'Tufa Tafa Reach up High', and 'We're Going to the Zoo', and played his favourite games, Farmer in the Dell and Doggy, Doggy Where's Your Bone – it was time now for the big event. The large hall with its colourful building blocks and playhouses pushed to far corners, and game-painted floor, ignored for once, was in a stage of expectant hush as its excited occupants waited. When the group leader's office door finally opened and one of the assistants banged a drum, the apprehensive but proud freckle-faced Bevan in his cherished Indian feather headdress and cowboy chaps appeared. The other children quickly leapt to their feet, thumping tambourines, hooting on horns and stamping their feet.

Charlotte's heart melted as she watched Chloe desperately trying to keep up with the others as she struck her triangle and tried not to trip over her own feet. Bevan made a stately walk to his throne, at which point the playroom fell quiet again and Charlotte had to stifle a sob of laughter as Chloe dropped her triangle and whispered sorry – whether it was to the triangle, or the room at large, wasn't possible to tell.

Bevan climbed up on to his throne and at a nod from Celia, the group leader, the other kids sank to the floor. During the poem that Celia read out in praise of Bevan's character and achievements Chloe's eyes were like saucers. She simply couldn't have appeared more rapt.

'She's right into it,' Grant Romney murmured to Charlotte as the children rose to their feet again.

'Just a bit,' Charlotte whispered back wryly.

'OK, everyone, time to create the way,' Celia announced.

With much scuffling, pushing and whispering, they eventually divided into two columns to create an avenue from the throne to Bevan's family.

Bevan was now standing on the throne.

'So Bevan, who have you chosen to jump off to?' Celia asked.

Bevan's colour rose as he cried, 'My Uncle Grant.'

As the children applauded Grant stepped to the end of the avenue, clearly more than a little pleased.

'How many claps would you like?' Celia asked Bevan.

'Five,' he replied, holding up a hand, the fingers splayed.

Celia nodded approvingly. 'OK. So, if you're ready, it's time for your *jump-off*.'

'Jump off,' everyone cheered.

'Jump off,' Chloe echoed, adding a leap of exuberance.

Smiling so hard it hurt, Charlotte clapped and counted along with the others as Bevan made four jumps down the avenue, and with the last hurled himself straight into his uncle's arms.

'Well done, Bevan,' Celia applauded. 'You've successfully jumped off to your Uncle Grant and everyone here at Aroha, which means . . .' She put a hand to her ear.

'Love!' the children shouted.

'. . . we wish you good luck in your new school, Bevan, and we hope you do as well there as you have here with us.'

As everyone crowded around Bevan to pat his back or shake his hand, Chloe beat a path straight to Charlotte.

'Please can I do a jump-off?' she asked, her voice trembling with hope.

'Oh darling, of course you can,' Charlotte replied, scooping her up. 'When you're five and ready to go to school, you'll have a jump-off too.'

Chloe's face dropped with disappointment.

'You don't have long to wait,' Charlotte reminded her. 'In less than a month you'll be four, and think how lovely having a birthday's going to be. We'll bake cakes at home to bring for your friends here . . .'

'Celia said I can bake a cake here,' Chloe told her.

'Absolutely, you can do that too.'

'And I can have candles that I blow out.'

'Of course. It'll be *your* birthday, so you'll be able to do lots of lovely things like choosing the games you play . . .'

'And I can make a wish too.'

Charlotte showed her intrigue. 'Have you decided what you're going to wish for yet?'

Chloe frowned as she thought.

'There's no rush. You can take your time to think about it. Now, what about going to say good luck to Bevan?'

As she wriggled down and pressed through to her friend, Charlotte was curious to see how unaffected she appeared by the fact that Bevan wasn't going to be at the Centre after today. Maybe she hadn't taken it in yet – or more likely, Charlotte realised, as long as she, Charlotte, was around that was all Chloe needed.

'So how does it feel to be the chosen one?' she teased playfully as Grant and Polly came to join her.

With a waggle of his eyebrows, Grant said, 'The last time it happened I got myself a wife. I think this time's going to come with a lot less strings.'

'Will you listen to him?' Polly groaned. 'Don't you just want to smack him?'

'Assaulting an officer of the law could get you into trouble,' he warned.

Polly looked at Charlotte, rolling her eyes.

'She's after me putting her in handcuffs, that's what's really going on here,' he informed Charlotte.

'Shall we just ignore him?' Polly suggested,

36

linking Charlotte's arm and turning her away. 'We're taking Bevan to the Pear Tree on the edge of town for lunch if you and Chloe would like to join us,' she offered.

'That's lovely of you,' Charlotte replied, 'but I've arranged to meet Shelley in town at the Fishbone . . .'

'Then let's call her and see if she fancies the Pear Tree instead.'

'Katie's joining us too.'

Polly stopped reaching for her mobile. 'I see. Well, love her as I do, I know Katie's not mad about kids so maybe we'll leave things as they are.'

'Thanks for asking,' Charlotte said. 'I'm sure Chloe would have loved it . . .'

'Why don't we take her anyway? You know she'll be perfectly safe with us, and she and Bevan get along really well. We'll have her home by three, or later if you think you won't be back by then.'

Feeling torn between the need to keep Chloe in her sight at all times, and the urge to encourage her independence, Charlotte said, 'Why don't we ask her? If she wants to go, then that would be lovely.'

To Charlotte's amazement it turned out Chloe was all for it, until she realised Charlotte wasn't going to be there too, and just to cap it Grant made the big mistake of stooping down to her level and saying, 'If you're very good, you and Bev, I'll take you for a ride in my police car after.'

Immediately Chloe shrank back against Charlotte, turning her face away.

With a reassuring hand on her head, Charlotte said, 'Sweetheart, everything will be all right. Polly's going to be there, and Bevan's mum and Bevan would . . .'

'Want to stay with you,' Chloe muttered, turning her face up to Charlotte.

Feeling both regretful and protective, Charlotte said to Grant, 'I'm sorry, it was a lovely thought . . .'

'No, it's me who should be sorry,' Grant insisted, standing up again. 'I totally forgot I wasn't supposed to do that.' Though Grant wasn't aware of Chloe's full history, Anna and Bob had told their closest friends enough to make them aware of the problem so they wouldn't take any rejection from Chloe personally. 'Hey!' Grant laughed as Bevan leapt on him from behind. 'Is that my jump-off buddy?' he cried, tipping Bevan over his shoulder and dangling him upside down.

As Chloe giggled, Polly put a hand on Charlotte's arm and turned her aside.

'When you're ready for her to talk to someone,' Polly said, 'I'll be happy to make a recommendation.'

Swallowing, Charlotte said, 'That's really kind of you, thank you.'

Polly smiled. 'You're welcome. Just don't leave it too long, eh?'

The centre of Kerikeri was a colourful, bustling stretch of a palm-lined thoroughfare with a jaunty little one-way system that looped around Mitre 10, the DIY store, and various other furniture and kiddicare shops. Along the main street an assortment of fashion boutiques, florists, delis and cafés spilled out over the wide pavements, lending an air of conviviality and sophistication to the historic town, while the inevitable banks, estate agents and pharmacies provided a more commonplace tone. It was as easy to park a car as it was to find a seat in one of the eateries, though on a hot February day like today the tables with shade sails soon filled up.

As Charlotte drove in through the speckled sunshine, passing the newly opened police station on the right with its arty Maori columns outside and the supermarket on the left, she was enjoying waving out to familiar faces. They might not all be friends, exactly, but for the Kiwis in this town recognition was enough to lead to a greeting, or sometimes even to stopping and passing the time of day. And no trip into town was complete for Chloe without a visit to Paper Plus, who always carried an excellent stock of books to suit both their tastes.

After making it their first stop and delighting Chloe as much with the earning of more Fly Buy points as with the purchase of another Hairy Maclary adventure, they popped the parcel back to the car and skipped along to the Fishbone, where Katie was already waiting at one of the outside tables.

'Hi,' she cried effusively as Charlotte and Chloe reached her. 'It's so lovely to see you and I love that top, Charlotte. Did you get it here?'

Dutifully air-kissing both her cheeks and not taking the compliment seriously, since her top was a simple coral-coloured polo shirt, Charlotte quipped, 'Oh this old thing.'

'And look at you, sweetie,' Katie gushed over Chloe. 'You're such a pretty little girl. Have you had a lovely morning at the Centre?'

Chloe regarded her uncertainly. Clearly she felt no more at ease with Katie than Charlotte did.

Sitting Chloe down on a chair next to her own, Charlotte was about to ask Katie how her morning had gone when Katie dug in her bag saying, 'I have a little surprise for you, sweetie,' and pulling out a pink, heart-shaped box she presented it to Chloe.

Chloe glanced at Charlotte, seeming unsure of what to do.

Smiling at Katie as she took the box, Charlotte put it in front of Chloe. 'Shall I open it for you?' she offered.

Chloe's hands immediately came up to do it herself.

'You're going to like what's inside,' Katie told her, seeming quite excited. 'A rep brought it into the salon earlier,' she explained to Charlotte, 'and as soon as I opened it I thought, I know who would like this. So there you are, sweetie, they're all for you.'

As Chloe tipped up the box a fountain of feathery clips and hairbands tumbled on to the table, and Charlotte gave a cry of surprise. This, she reminded herself, was the side of Katie that made everyone love her. 'What do you say, Chloe?' she prompted, as Chloe held up a purple scrunchie for her to see.

'Thank you,' Chloe said to Katie in her whispery voice.

'They're lovely,' Charlotte said warmly. 'Are you sure, Katie? There's so much here.'

'Of course I'm sure,' and reaching for a daisy-chain bandeau she slipped it around Chloe's head and fluffed out her hair. 'Oh, you look so adorable,' she exclaimed, clasping her hands to her chest. 'Doesn't she, Charlotte?' she insisted.

Charlotte had to agree, but then Chloe always looked adorable to her.

'Here, I have a mirror in my bag,' Katie declared, and whisking it out she opened it up for Chloe to view her reflection.

40

Apparently pleased with what she saw, Chloe gave a breathy little laugh and punched out her hands. 'And Boots,' she cried, reaching for a butterfly clip and attaching it to one of her tatty bear's ears.

'Are these all yours?' a waitress gasped, stopping at the table to take their order.

Chloe looked up at her anxiously, as though afraid it was all about to be swept away.

'Her Auntie Katie's just given them to her,' Charlotte jumped in. 'Isn't she a lucky girl?'

'I'll say,' the waitress agreed. 'I wish I'd had something like that when I was little.'

Immediately Chloe picked up a yellow rose slide and offered it to her.

'Oh, bless your heart,' the waitress laughed, clearly touched. 'You're an angel, but it'll look much nicer on you.'

Chloe inspected it, and tried to capture a few strands of her hair, while the waitress pulled out her pad.

'Should we wait for Shelley?' Charlotte suggested, as Katie picked up the menu.

'She said not to,' Katie replied. 'She's had to take the dog home, so she's going to be late.'

Deciding this was a perfect opportunity to try and establish a better rapport with Katie, Charlotte said, 'In that case I'll have a feijoa and apple juice.'

'Nothing stronger?' Katie prompted.

'I have to drive,' Charlotte reminded her.

'Don't we all, and remember the limit's a lot higher here than it is in England, so one glass won't do any harm.'

Though she didn't much fancy a glass, having had too much the night before, Charlotte wanted to appear friendly so she changed her order to a

Sauvignon Blanc, which Katie promptly dittoed before deciding they should go for a bottle since Shelley would be sure to want some too.

'And for you, little angel?' the waitress asked Chloe.

With her fingers bound up in her new treasures, Chloe said, 'Please can I have a fluffy?'

Making a note, the waitress said, 'A fluffy it is – and maybe you'd like a little dab of ice cream with it?'

Charlotte almost felt Chloe's mouth water as she whispered, 'Yes please.'

'Remind me what a fluffy is again,' Katie said, as the waitress went on her way.

'It's frothy milk that's supposed to look like a cappuccino,' Charlotte explained, glancing at Katie's mobile as it started to ring.

'Rick,' Katie declared happily. 'I'd better take it. Won't be long,' and clicking on the line she got up from the table saying, 'Hey you, did you get my message?'

As she moved out of earshot, Charlotte found herself wondering, not for the first time, just how strong her relationship with Rick actually was. For an engaged couple they didn't seem to see much of each other, with Rick being away all week, and even when he came home at weekends – which certainly wasn't every weekend – Charlotte rarely saw them together. This didn't mean they weren't together, obviously, since she was hardly party to their every move, but there had been a couple of occasions lately when Charlotte had wondered if Rick had spent more time with her and Chloe at the bach than he had with Katie. Of course, she'd never ask; apart from anything else it was none of her business.

Deciding not to concern herself with it now, Charlotte sighed luxuriously and stretched out her bare legs as she let her head fall back from the shade of the umbrella. The sun on her face felt blissfully soothing, and suddenly the prospect of a glass of wine followed by an afternoon with her mother going over plans for next week's shoot felt decidedly good. She must try not to say anything to spoil it for Anna, as some demon inside her often seemed overly compelled to do.

How lovely it was getting to know her mother, but it was difficult and complicated too. One minute she felt closer to her than she had to anyone else in her life; the next she was pushing her away as though she were a stranger. She knew Anna wasn't finding it any easier, but at least she, unlike Charlotte, was willing to seek therapy to help them, and delving back into the past was going to prove far more difficult for her than it could ever be for Charlotte.

Perhaps it was best just left. After all, Anna often admitted that they couldn't change what had happened, so what was the point in making her suffer the memory of it all over again? Instead of this, Charlotte decided, she herself must try harder.

'Hey Charlotte, hey Chloe,' a voice called out, and looking up Charlotte spotted one of the childcare assistants pedalling by on her bike and gave her a wave.

'That was Cindy,' Chloe told her.

Charlotte smiled and dropped a kiss on her head. 'You've got lots of pretty things there,' she commented, poking around in the assortment of accessories. 'Maybe you could share some of them with Danni.'

Chloe turned to her as though this was the best idea she'd ever heard. 'Danni likes hair things,' she said earnestly.

Suspecting that Chloe and Danni had never even had the conversation, Charlotte laughed to herself and cleared a space on the table for their drinks.

'Sorry about that,' Katie sighed, sinking back into her seat and putting down her phone. 'It was about the house we're supposed to be viewing on Saturday.'

Charlotte's eyebrows rose with interest. 'Where is it?' she asked, glad to know that Rick was planning to come for the weekend.

'Opito Bay,' Katie answered. 'Bob put us on to it – you know how he always gets first wind of what's coming on to the market. Apparently he was interested in buying it himself, but then it occurred to him that it might work for us. So we're going on Saturday. Chloe, careful you don't spill your drink, sweetie.'

Turning to check on her, Charlotte moved the fluffy out of harm's way and picked up her wine. 'Here's to the house being a dream home,' she declared warmly, raising her glass.

As Katie smiled her eyes sparkled with happiness. 'Thank you,' she replied. 'I must admit I have high hopes for it, considering who's recommending it, especially when I'm sure Bob would rather see us settled out on the peninsula close to him and Anna.' She sipped her drink and gave a playful roll of her eyes. 'He's got so much land out there . . . You know he's offered to give us five acres as a wedding present *and* to help us build a house.'

Since Bob's generosity knew few bounds, and not only where his family was concerned, Charlotte said,

'I'm amazed you're not taking him up on it. Or does it feel too close?'

Katie nodded. 'A bit, I guess, but it's more of a problem for Rick than for me. He gets on with his dad brilliantly, but he's keen to make it on his own – and the way things are going with the agency he's doing a pretty good job of that.'

'So I hear,' Charlotte responded. She smiled and nodded to one of the other mums from the Centre as she sat at the next table, and said, 'So have you set a date for the wedding yet?'

Katie sighed as she gazed down at her wine. 'We're supposed to be talking about it this weekend, but with things being so crazy in Auckland, you know, possible buy-outs and new clients coming on board . . . I don't see anything being decided until it's all settled down there.' Her eyes turned suddenly anxious, even angry. 'If that Hamish Sinclair gets his way we'll end up never setting a date.'

Having sensed Katie's dislike of Rick's business partner on previous occasions, Charlotte asked, 'Why do you say that?'

Katie's face tightened. 'Don't get me started on that man. I mean, he's so . . . I don't know, *jealous* is what I want to say, or possessive. Honestly, it's like he wants Rick all to himself, and what I want to know is why he doesn't just go out and get himself a life? He's totally sad, doesn't think about anything except that agency, and if he had his way Rick would never come back here at weekends at all. It would be nothing but work, work, work and we know what that did to Jack, whoever the bloody hell Jack is. Anyway,' she ran on, waving a hand as though to brush the irritation away, 'that's enough about me.' She staged a quick smile. 'I'm so excited to be having this little chat with you. Honestly, I feel terrible I haven't been able to give you more time since you got here, you know, help you settle in and everything, but we've been so busy at the salon. And then I'm flying down to Auckland the weekends Rick isn't here . . . It's all go, go, go, it never stops. But now tell me, how are you liking Kerikeri so far? You seem to have settled in really well, and don't you just love the bach? Rick and I weren't together when he was living there, but I went to some of the parties and I can tell you they were pretty full on, if you get my drift.' She frowned. 'No, Chloe, you mustn't interrupt when grown-ups are speaking.'

Though Charlotte didn't approve of it much either, since Katie was proving a bit of an unstoppable force she said, 'What is it, sweetheart? Do you want to go to the loo?'

Chloe shook her head. 'I'm hungry,' she said, her eyes following a large bowl of fries and a burger as it went by on a tray.

'Auntie Shelley'll be here soon,' Katie told her. 'We'll order then.'

Chloe looked up at Charlotte.

'It's OK, you don't have to wait,' Charlotte said, stroking her face. 'Would you like fish fingers?'

'And fries,' Chloe added happily.

'So where were we?' Katie wondered as soon as the order was placed. 'Ah, that's right, we were talking about how well you're settling in here. I expect you're finding it a big change from England though. I know I did when I first came. I'd never go back though, would you?'

'I don't think so,' Charlotte replied. 'I don't have any reason to.'

'Mm, I don't suppose you do, with your mother being here. I think it's lovely, the way you two have found each other again after all these years. Everyone was so pleased for Anna when it happened. She'd been wanting to fly over to England and find you for ages. I always wondered what stopped her, but I suppose she's so busy and you no doubt had your own life going on over there with a different family and everything. Where was it you lived? Somewhere by the coast, wasn't it?'

'Kesterly-on-Sea,' Charlotte told her, a swell of unexpected nostalgia seeming to dry the words in her throat.

Katie looked incredulous. 'No way!' she declared. 'That's down on the edge of Exmoor, or Dartmoor or somewhere, isn't it? I've got a cousin who lives there. Maria Mitchell. I don't suppose you know her? She's about our age.'

'I don't think so,' Charlotte replied. 'What does she do?'

Katie shrugged. 'No idea these days. She used to teach yoga and Pilates. Maybe she still does. What did you do when you were there?'

Having the answer off pat by now, Charlotte said, 'I worked for the local authority.'

Katie pulled a face. 'No wonder you were keen to get out. What about Chloe's dad? What did, or does he do?'

Surprised, but glad, that no one had ever told Katie the truth about Chloe's father, Charlotte willed Shelley to turn up now as she said, 'I'd rather not discuss him in front of her, if you don't mind.'

'Oh God, I'm sorry,' Katie gasped. 'Have I put my foot in it? You didn't hear what I said, did you?' she asked Chloe.

47

Luckily Chloe was engrossed in wrapping more hairbands and scrunchies around Boots.

In a whisper Katie said, 'Bit of a b, was he?'

'You could say that,' Charlotte muttered.

'You know what I find weird,' Katie ran on pensively, 'is that Anna never mentioned anything about . . .' she nodded towards Chloe, 'before you came here. We knew all about you of course . . .'

Spotting Shelley rushing towards them, Charlotte broke into a smile of welcome. 'Here she is,' she said, getting up to greet her. 'How's the dog? Is everything OK?'

'Oh, she'll be fine,' Shelley assured her. 'I just didn't expect them to give her an op this morning. It was only to remove a fibroid, she'll live. Hi, Katie, how's everything? And how are you, my little angel?' she said, stooping to give Chloe a kiss. 'Oh my goodness, what have you got here? Is this all yours?'

'From Auntie Katie,' Chloe replied, swinging her legs. 'But we're going to give some to Danni.'

Shelley looked delighted. 'She'll be thrilled to bits,' she declared, 'but you make sure you hang on to your favourites, won't you? And is this your lunch coming?' she added as the waitress began hovering. 'I'm so glad you didn't make her wait,' she told Charlotte. 'Poor little mite must be starving. I know I am. Have you guys ordered yet?'

'No, but we're definitely ready to,' Katie informed her.

After they had made their selection Shelley reached for her wine, saying, 'Just what I need. So now what are we talking about?'

'Oh nothing much,' Charlotte quickly replied.

'Actually,' Katie corrected, 'I was just saying how

strange it was that Anna never told us anything about . . .' again she nodded towards Chloe, 'before she and Charlotte came here.'

Shelley was amazed. 'What are you talking about? She hardly stopped telling us. And why else would Dad have put an extra room on the bach and gone out to buy all that extra little-girl furniture?'

Katie flushed. 'I didn't realise he did that before they got here,' she said. 'Sorry. I guess I just got my timings in a muddle.'

'No harm done,' Shelley told her kindly. 'You probably didn't talk to Anna as often as I did on the phone while she was in England, or you'd have heard nothing but Chloe, Chloe, Chloe.'

Looking up, Chloe pointed her fork as she said, 'Auntie, Auntie, Auntie.'

Laughing, Shelley leaned across to pinch her cheek. 'And how did Bevan's jump-off go this morning?' she asked her.

Chloe nodded, up and down, up and down. 'I can have a wish,' she told her.

'Oh?' Shelley responded.

'For her birthday, when she blows out the candles,' Charlotte explained.

'Of course you can,' Shelley agreed. 'And what will you wish for?'

Chloe turned to Charlotte, and putting down her fork she climbed up to whisper in her ear.

Charlotte started to laugh. 'You crafty little minx,' she chided.

'What is it?' Katie asked.

'She's going to wish for a jump-off,' Charlotte confided, 'but I've already told her she has to wait until she's five before she can have one of those.'

Shelley frowned. 'Well, there's no reason why we

can't practise in advance, is there? We'll get Grandpa to make us a throne and see if Celia at Aroha will let us borrow the ring. So who are you going to jump off to? Have you decided that, yet?'

Chloe pursed her lips as she thought. Then, suddenly brightening, she said, 'Uncle Wick.'

As Shelley clapped her hands in approval, Charlotte couldn't help noticing the light fade in Katie's eyes before she was able to make herself laugh too.

Chapter Four

The early morning mist over the bay was drifting like a silvery gauze in the sunshine, shrouding the Maori settlement in its ephemeral mass and rolling like whispers into the trees. The tide was out; the sun was starting to burn in a milky white sky and over on the far hillside next to the water tank a family of pukekos was foraging about in the dirt. Spotting them, Charlotte felt tempted to wake Chloe since she adored the bright blue birds with their cherry-red beaks and white tail feathers, but they were often there and as she'd woken from a bad dream in the night it was probably best to let her sleep on a while.

She was sprawled out in Charlotte's bed now with Boots clutched in one hand and a single sheet wrapped around her legs.

'No tiger, no tiger,' she'd sobbed when Charlotte had gone in to get her around two a.m.

'No, darling, there's no tiger,' Charlotte had assured her, holding her close. 'Everything's all right. Mummy's here. Nothing bad is going to happen.'

'Don't want to see the tiger,' she'd choked.

'It's OK, it's not here. It's never coming here, so you don't have to worry.'

It had taken a while for her little body to stop shuddering and even longer for her to relax her grip on Charlotte, but after a lot of cuddles and a few pages from her new Hairy Maclary she'd finally drifted off again. It wasn't until Charlotte had woken a few minutes ago that she'd realised that she too had managed to go back to sleep. Usually, after one of their broken nights, she lay awake for hours afterwards worrying and fearing the worst, though God knew what could be worse than the ordeal Chloe had already been through.

I should have saved you sooner. You should never have had to go through what you did.

Ride the tiger, child. Come on, ride the tiger.

In her entire life Charlotte knew she would never forget those words, nor the horrendous images that had gone with them. She wished with all her heart that she'd never seen them, and yet, if she hadn't, she wouldn't have had the proof she'd needed to put Chloe's father where he was now.

Don't think about him. Don't let him into your mind to soil it. Just forget he exists.

If only that were possible, for Chloe, even more than for her.

As she put the kettle on and downed a refreshing glass of water she was wondering if the fact that she'd slept as soon as Chloe had after the nightmare meant that she was finally starting to let go of her fears. Or had she, once again, drunk too much wine last night? Her mother and Bob had come over with some scallops they'd brought back from a dive to add to the cook-up she, Chloe and Danni were having on the beach. Then Phil and Craig had wandered down to join them, shortly followed by Shelley. Another happy family occasion with nothing serious being spoken of, no visible signs of faltering heartbeats, or guilt draining the laughter dry.

'Are you OK? Would you like me to stay?' her mother had offered when Charlotte, carrying Chloe, had staggered against the footbridge on her way back into the bach.

'I'm fine,' Charlotte had told her. 'Don't fuss. She's just heavy, OK?'

She'd seen the look her mother had given Bob, and had wanted to shout at her to leave her alone, but of course she hadn't. What was the point in hurting her mother, trying to make her feel even worse than she already did? She'd been through enough, for God's sake, had suffered in ways Charlotte could hardly begin to imagine, so to try and reject her now would be giving in to the demons she had to learn to control.

Resolving to have a wine-free day today, she made some tea and carried it to the bedroom to check on Chloe. Finding her still out for the count she listened for her breathing, and feeling the relief of hearing it she decided there was still no point in waking her. It was Saturday, so no rush to get to Aroha, and all they had planned for the day was a ride on Diesel with Danni this morning and a waterskiing lesson for Charlotte later on. She wasn't sure yet who was going to drive the boat, Bob or Phil, it might even be Rick since he was due back around lunchtime, though she guessed that was unlikely given his reason for coming. She wondered what he was going to make of the house, if it would turn out to be as perfect as Katie hoped.

He wouldn't buy it, Charlotte felt as certain of that as she did of the fact that he'd be in touch with her at some point today. However, for now she was going to focus her mind elsewhere, and opening up her laptop she plugged in the T stick to make an Internet connection. At least two weeks had gone by since she'd last checked her emails, or, as she sometimes put it to herself, since she'd stepped back into her previous life. She rarely enjoyed the experience, since it usually left her feeling shaky and unsure of who she was supposed to be. However, it had to be gone through, and thankfully the contact from old friends and colleagues was becoming less frequent the more time went on. This was largely due to the fact that she almost never answered their questions, which was hard in many cases, but the need to keep herself and Chloe safe had to come first.

As always, as she watched the emails downloading, her eyes searched for Gabby's name, but there was no sign of it again today. There had been no exchange between them since the day Charlotte had left, and though it broke Charlotte apart to feel the gulf widening between them she knew it had to be this way. She wondered if Gabby found it any easier, and felt sure she didn't.

Better not to think about her and get on with making sure the closing-down of her old life was going to plan. She'd been Alexandra back then, or Alex, which was what everyone had called her. It was the name her adoptive parents, Myra and Douglas, had given her, even though for the first three years of her life, when she'd been with her real mother, she'd been Charlotte.

Myra and Douglas hadn't been able to keep her name, for much the same reason as she'd been unable to keep Chloe's.

She began deleting the endless junk mail and

birthday reminders, feeling as bad about not sending cards, electronic or real, as she had about ignoring her friends at Christmas. What must they think of her now? Did they feel hurt and offended, or perhaps even worried? No one had said so, there had been no recriminations at all, so it seemed they were simply getting on with their lives. She doubted any of them knew that she'd changed her name back to the one she'd been given at birth, nor would they have any idea that Chloe was no longer called Ottilie.

If only changing Chloe's name could be as easy as changing her own, which had happened within a matter of weeks. She even had a new passport and a copy of her original birth certificate now. To make Chloe's change official she'd have to seek her father's permission and that could never happen. Not ever.

However, Bob had assured her they'd work it out somehow, and if these past few months had taught her anything, it was how readily Bob rose to a challenge. She guessed he hadn't found a solution for this particular issue yet, but knowing him he'd be working on it, and as soon as he could make it possible Chloe would never be known as anything other than Chloe again.

Coming across a message sent a week ago from her old boss, Tommy Burgess, Charlotte felt a wave of sadness coming over her. Tommy had been more than a boss; he'd been a good, dear friend and loyal supporter, especially at the end when their bosses at the local authority had washed their hands of her.

Tommy was one of the few people who knew for certain that she wasn't coming back.

Hi Alex pet, how's tricks down there in Kiwi-land? Can't tell you how much I envy you all that sunshine and good living, especially when we're bang in the middle of winter – and a godawful recession – over here.

As I told you in my last email the Kesterly social service hubs have merged now, so we're working out of the swanky new offices the local council stumped up for – and needless to say we're still in chaos. Your favourite person (not), Wendy, is still the department manager and I remain team leader, but I have news, my lovely friend. Jackie and I have decided to move back north. Her mother's not getting any younger, nor is my dad, and we want to spend as much time as we can with them before the dreaded Alzheimer's or the Grim Reaper kick in. Obviously we'll miss all our friends here in Kesterly, but we're planning to stay in touch and we've already been bombarded with offers of places to stay for our holidays.

This leads me to your little car, pet. I know in your last email you insisted you didn't want anything for it, but we've talked to a dealer and he reckons you could get at least three grand. So please let us send you this sum. I know you've closed down your bank account here, but I'm sure you have a new one in NZ by now, and the transfer should be easy enough to make.

Jackie wants me to tell you that we were in Mulgrove village the other night, and thought while we were there that we'd drive up the hill to take a look at your old home – and what did we find but a building site. Whoever bought it is really going to town on fixing up the interior, but looks like they're keeping the integrity of the old vicarage intact. Seemed funny that you weren't there, but I'm sure you're very happy to be where you are out of all this doom and gloom.

Don't forget to keep me up to speed with your plans for a job. You said last time that you were 'exploring

*various possibilities' but didn't say what they were. I
know it's going to be difficult for you to go back to working
with kids, which is where I think your heart lies, but if
you ever need a reference you know you can always come
to yours truly for a dazzler!*

*OK, guess I've gone on long enough now. Just wanted
to be in touch and let you know you're not forgotten. Your
old mates often ask about you, but don't worry I still
haven't told anyone you've gone for good. I won't do that
until you give me the green light.*

*Say hi to your mum for us and a great big hug to you.
Do send some photos if you have time, would love to see
where you are.*

Tommy and Jackie xxx

Closing the message down as if that might in
some way quell the emotions that were tightening
her chest, Charlotte sat back in her chair and took
a breath. She couldn't allow herself to long for
Kesterly, or Mulgrove, or her old job, much less
Tommy's broad shoulders and words of wisdom. It
was all in the past now, gone, over and soon to be
forgotten. Anyway, even if she were able to go back,
her home had been sold and Tommy was returning
to his roots. Everything was changing, life was
moving on and so must she. This ache of loneliness
that seemed to be growing and growing wasn't real;
it was part of the shame, the guilt and fear that was
making her want to go back to a time before it had
all gone so horribly wrong.

Before her mother had come to find her.

Oh God, she was trying to blame her mother
again. She had to stop, because what had happened
was no more Anna's fault than it was Chloe's.

It was hers, all hers.

She was about to get up and make a fresh cup of

tea when her eye was caught by another message that had arrived three days ago from . . . Her heart gave a jolt of shock. Anthony Goodman?

Surely it wasn't the same Anthony Goodman. The one she knew had no reason to be in touch with her. They'd said their goodbyes on the phone the day of her departure and though, secretly, she'd wondered about him many times since, she'd never been under any illusion that anything could ever have happened between them. He was a lawyer, a QC in fact, with chambers in London and a lifestyle she could barely even imagine, never mind aspire to. She'd met him through his older sister, Maggie, less than six months ago, and she hadn't forgotten how intimidated she'd felt by him at first with his stern, dark features and imposing air. It was only when he'd smiled that she'd realised there was a man with normal amounts of friendliness and humour behind the lawyerly mien. A man who'd caused her heart to flutter with dreams that didn't belong there.

She couldn't say he'd ever become a friend, exactly, because their worlds had been too far apart for that, both socially and geographically. Nevertheless, he hadn't hesitated to help her when she'd been fighting for her job and reputation. Not that he'd represented her himself, as a criminal barrister that wasn't his role, but he'd put her on to the best firm he knew, and had stayed in touch throughout the whole horrible affair.

Then, at the last, he'd called to wish her well in New Zealand – he'd even suggested coming to the airport to say goodbye. She'd told him not to, they were already running late and she hadn't wanted to waste his time. It hadn't been easy to tell the lie, but she'd forced the words out, because she'd had no choice. Had she hurt his feelings? Not nearly as much as she'd hurt her own.

Why was he emailing now, if it really was him?

Feeling an uneasy beat stalling her heart, she clicked to open the message and held her breath.

Dear Alex, I'm not sure if you're still using this email address, but as it's all I have for you I'm taking a chance. I hope you're well and enjoying life Down Under and have gone some way towards recovering from the difficult time you had before leaving.

Maggie and I often talk of you and wonder if you'll ever come back to England. Speaking personally I'd quite understand if you didn't – it certainly isn't the most inspiring place to be these days, and with the way things are going it's difficult to generate much hope for the immediate future. Sorry for the pessimism, but this little island of ours really isn't in a happy state.

It's largely for this reason that I have decided to take a sabbatical with a view to making some changes in my life and career. I won't bore you with details of that, I'll simply say that I find myself needing to broaden my horizons in a way that might enrich my mind (and my soul) rather more fully than criminal law. I'm sure I won't give up the law completely, but I'm going to take some time to explore other areas of it that might allow me to sleep a little easier at night.

Before embarking on this new phase I am intending to visit friends and family in Australia and New Zealand (Maggie and I have a cousin in Christchurch and a great-uncle in Melbourne), and I was rather hoping you might be up for a visit too.

Charlotte swallowed drily as the possibility of it started her head spinning.

I don't have any flights booked yet, or any particular

dates in mind, I simply thought I would be in touch now to say how very much I'd like to see you again.

I leave you in the hope that this reaches you, and that you will welcome an opportunity for us to meet at some point in the not too distant future,

Yours

Anthony

Feeling slightly unsteady, Charlotte put her tea mug down and dragged her hands over her face. What was she going to do? What should she say? The truth, that she wanted him to come more than anything? If only she could, but she knew already that she never would.

Feeling the need for some air, she took herself outside and inhaled deeply, once, twice, three or more times. Before she could stop it she found herself imagining how wonderful it would be to show him this bay, to introduce him to her family, to show him around Kerikeri and take him to Kauri Cliffs or right up to Cape Reinga to where the Pacific Ocean swirled and roared into the Tasman Sea. They could light a fire on the beach here in the cove and poach scallops or mussels; or dine in restaurants belonging to vineyards, or explore galleries exhibiting local art. Chloe could teach him some Maori – dancing and words – and show him how brave she was now in the way she rode Diesel with Danni, or allowed Bob to tow her and Craig around the bay on a tyre.

That was where the dream had to end, because of course Chloe would never teach him or show him anything.

'Mummy? I'm behind you.'

Turning round, Charlotte broke into a smile as she saw Chloe's tousled hair and sleepy face. 'I was wondering,' she answered, going to kneel in front of her, 'when you, little sleepyhead, were ever going to wake up.'

Chloe yawned and rubbed a fist into one eye.

'Breakfast?' Charlotte suggested.

'Eskimo pie,' Chloe replied, wobbling on her bare feet as Charlotte turned her around to propel her back inside.

'You can't have ice cream for breakfast,' Charlotte laughed.

Chloe grinned and gave a little jump. 'Weet-bix,' she cried. 'And you can have Berry, Berry Nice.'

'Actually, I'm not feeling all that hungry this morning . . .'

'I can't have Berry, Berry Nice, because I'm not old enough, am I?'

'That's right, muesli's for grown-ups, now if you sit yourself up at the table . . .'

'No, no, no,' Chloe suddenly exclaimed, backing away.

Realising too late that she shouldn't have left her laptop out, Charlotte stepped in quickly to move it out of the way. 'It's OK,' she told Chloe firmly, 'it's Mummy's computer and there's . . . Chloe, come back, sweetheart. There's nothing to be afraid of, I promise.'

'Don't like it,' Chloe shouted from the bedroom.

'I know you don't,' Charlotte said, going to her, 'but lots of people have computers, including me . . .'

'Don't like it,' Chloe insisted, climbing into Charlotte's lap.

'Ssh, there now, it was silly of me to have left it there. I'm sorry. I promise not to do it again.'

'Not again,' Chloe agreed, shaking her head. 'Don't like it.'

Kissing her gently, Charlotte pulled her into a

more comforting embrace and carried her back to the table. Though Chloe didn't always react this way to a computer, the fact that she was reacting at all was a timely reminder for Charlotte to take more care. 'There you are, all gone now,' she declared, putting Chloe down on a chair. 'So are you ready for some Weet-bix?'

Chloe sniffed as she nodded. 'And Boots,' she reminded her.

'Of course,' and after tilting her sweet little face up to make sure she was smiling, Charlotte began preparing breakfast.

Anthony wasn't sure she'd pick up his message, so probably the best thing to do now was delete it and let him think it hadn't reached her.

Rick Reeves was a slight, wiry man who, until recently, had sported an unruly shock of dark, wavy hair. Now, it was closely cropped to his head in a way that made his arresting blue eyes and infectious smile seem all the more striking.

Though his success in the advertising world meant a great deal to him, Charlotte suspected that his family and Te Puna would always mean more. Not that there was a contest – his father had always been fully supportive of his career choice, and Hamish, Rick's partner, completely understood why Rick would want to take off to the Bay of Islands any chance he got. Who wouldn't when there was such a fabulous home to go to, and since Rick never let a client down, or failed to roll up his sleeves and burn the midnight oil along with the rest of the team when the pressure was on, Hamish never questioned his partner's commitment.

However, Hamish did have other issues where

Rick was concerned, and a fairly major one was threatening to come to a head, but since Rick still wasn't ready to deal with it he'd done his usual trick of hopping on a plane to Kerikeri, which this weekend had been a bit like jumping out of the frying pan straight into the fire.

Katie was not happy with him, not happy at all. Nor was his father going to be when he found out that his commitment-phobe of a son had rejected the house on Opito Bay. Commitment-phobe. That was what Katie had called him and he'd had no defence, because in this instance she was right, he couldn't make the kind of commitment that was wanted of him.

Now, as he wandered through the evening sunshine down the incline towards the beach in front of the bach and saw the way Charlotte's face lit up when she spotted him, he felt his own spirits take a much-needed lift.

'Hey, crazy lady,' he smiled affectionately, as she came to the footbridge to greet him. 'How's tricks?'

Hugging him, she said, 'I wasn't expecting to see you today. How did the viewing go?'

He pulled a face, and since she'd been prepared for that sort of response, she took his hand and led him to the bach. 'Chloe's up at Shelley's for the night,' she told him, taking a cold Steinie from the fridge. 'Here, you look as though you need it.'

His eyes twinkled. 'Did I ever tell you you're my favourite person in the universe?'

She scowled. 'Don't you try and work that famous Reeves charm on me,' she warned. 'I'm immune.'

Laughing, he touched his bottle to hers and went back outside to slump down at the table and stretch out his legs. 'Look at this,' he sighed, sweeping a hand towards the glistening blue bay, where the evening sky was turning a smoky orange and terns and shags were skimming the waves. 'I mean, just look at it. I've grown up with it, I know every inch of it, yet I still don't ever grow tired of it.'

'Why would you when it's paradise?' she asked, pulling up a chair for herself.

He frowned thoughtfully. 'It would be, if it weren't for *people*, but then without them I guess it would be hell.'

'Very philosophical. So are you going to tell me what happened this afternoon?'

'No, you're going to tell me about your day, starting with why you were looking so sad when I arrived.'

Her eyebrows went up. 'Sad?'

'It was coming off you in waves.'

Sighing, she said, 'Not sad, exactly, more nostalgic. I checked my emails this morning and . . . Well, I guess I'm finding it harder to let go of the past than I expected.'

'And you're surprised by that?'

'No, I suppose not, just disappointed. I thought it would get easier, but then I had a message from someone I . . .' Her eyes went briefly to his. 'It doesn't matter,' she said, shaking her head.

'Well, it clearly does, so come on, out with it.'

'No, honestly, it's nothing.'

'OK, so tell me, would you go back to Blighty, if you could?'

She didn't need any time to think about it. 'No, I'm certain I wouldn't. It's just that there's all this . . . I don't know, unfinished business, I guess.'

'Can you find a way to finish it?'

'That's what I'm trying to do.'

'And in the process it's making you sad. So I'm guessing it's either about your sister, Gabby, or maybe it's a . . . man?'

She smiled wryly. 'I'm not sure I'm comfortable with the way you read me so easily,' she chided.

He looked amazed. 'Believe me, there's nothing easy about it. In fact, I'm putting you down as the *Finnegans Wake* of the female world.'

'Is that another way of saying I'm dense?'

His eyes lit with mirth. 'No, it's a way of saying you're completely impenetrable and there's a very good chance you've lost the plot.'

She gave a cry of laughter. 'Oh, I definitely have,' she agreed, 'and if you've got any ideas for how to get it back on track, I'm listening.'

'I'll work on it,' he promised. 'Meanwhile, I'll need to know more about this bloke. Was it serious between you?'

Her smile faded as she shook her head. 'No, not at all. In fact, there wasn't anything really. We just met and I guess there was some sort of chemistry . . . At least there was for me . . .'

'And now you've heard from him and you think there might have been for him too?'

'Alex heard from him,' she corrected. 'He doesn't know I'm Charlotte now and I don't want to tell him. So that's it. All over before it even began.'

'Mm,' he grunted, apparently unimpressed.

'Another?' she offered as he stared at his near-empty bottle.

His eyes narrowed as they came to hers. 'Are you trying to get me drunk – again?' he challenged.

'*Me* get *you* drunk,' she protested. 'I'll have you know it was the other way round last weekend . . .'

'Guilty as charged, and and do you know what, I feel just like getting blasted again, so if Chloe's with Shelley for the night . . . Is this her first sleepover, by the way?'

'It is, so I'm fully expecting to have to go and fetch her at some point.'

'Shelley'll bring her back, if you're about to use that as an excuse not to get blasted with me.'

'I know she will, but . . .' Did she want to get into how much she'd been drinking lately, or did she just want to go for it? Catching his roguish grin and feeling her own need blossom she decided the hell with it, and said, 'I've only got a couple more Steinies, but I can do you a bottle of the house Pinot Gris.'

'My dad's evil brew?' he scoffed. Then, laughing as she tossed a bottle top at him, 'It's actually not bad, but don't tell him I said that. So, bring it on, oh you of iron will, you.'

Giving him a quick throttle on the way into the kitchen, she fetched a freshly chilled bottle, two glasses, a dish of aioli and a white crusty loaf which she carried out to the table. 'It's all I have to eat,' she told him, 'and I guess we should have something.'

'Did you make it?' he asked, peering suspiciously at the aioli.

'No, my mother brought it over last night. I made the bread though, and Chloe saved me two of her prized cupcakes from a baking session at Aroha yesterday. I know she'd be thrilled if you had one, or even both.'

Since Chloe wasn't showing any early signs of becoming a master baker, Rick's eyes gleamed with irony as he twisted the top off the wine. 'The thrill will be all mine,' he said drily. After filling the glasses he passed one over saying, 'OK, you're not off the hook yet. I want to know this chap's name.'

'It's Anthony, but honestly, there's nothing to tell and you're making me wish I'd never brought it up.'

'But you did, and as it's what was on your mind when I arrived, you need to let it out to someone, and who better than me?'

She eyed him defiantly. 'You don't *know* it was on my mind.'

'OK, I confess, I thought at first you were pissed at not doing so well with the waterskiing earlier.'

Her eyes flew open. 'How do you know about that?' she protested. 'You weren't even there, and I bet Bob didn't tell you.'

'Craig,' he confessed. 'Can't keep a thing to himself. Said you were bloody awful . . . Well, he didn't say bloody or awful, come to think of it. I forget what he did say, apart from the fact that you kept falling in.'

'I'm not a natural,' she stated defensively.

'Rubbish, it's just your focus wasn't there. It happens. I can't stay up myself when my mind's on other stuff, and I'm already wishing I'd phrased that another way.'

Laughing, she said, 'So tell me how it went at the house on Opito Bay. I'm guessing not brilliantly, or you wouldn't be here.'

His eyes lost some of their lustre. 'It was great. Perfect, in fact, if it's the kind of place you're looking for.'

'And Katie is, but you're not? Where is she now?'

Looking glummer than ever, he said, 'She stormed off on me, and who can blame her? I'd have stormed off on me too in her shoes.' He sighed heavily. 'She so doesn't deserve this.'

Charlotte was regarding him closely. 'You have to tell her, you know that, don't you?' she said softly.

His eyes flicked to hers and away again. 'Kiwis,' he stated, spotting the family of daft birds pecking about under the puka.

'They've been there on and off for the past week, so stop trying to change the subject.'

'And what, pray tell, would the subject actually be?'

'You know what I'm saying.'

'I do, and it would seem you can't put it into words either.'

'Of course I can, but it's you who needs to, not me.'

He sighed again as he reached out to try and grab a moth.

'I don't understand why you're having such a problem with it,' she said, genuinely puzzled.

He shrugged. 'I guess you wouldn't, as it's not happening to you.'

'Sorry, that was insensitive of me, but you can't go on living a lie . . .' She broke off, flushing as he cocked an eyebrow. 'My situation's different,' she protested.

'But you're still not completely out there.'

'For good reasons. Anyway we're not talking about me.'

'I'd prefer it if we were.'

Sitting forward, she said, 'Look, everyone has secrets, things they'd rather others didn't know about them, but in your case . . . Well, it's not as if you've got anything to be ashamed of. For God's sake, it's hardly unusual these days, and I'm sure, when you're in Auckland . . .'

'It's different when I'm there,' he interrupted. 'It's

a big city, people lead different lives. Out here . . .
This is a small town. And I'm Bob Reeves's son.'

Shaking her head in bewilderment, she said, 'You
can't seriously think your dad would cut you off, or
do something drastic, just because you're . . .' She
stopped short of saying the word, determined he
should be the one to utter it first.

'Frankly, I don't know what he'd do, and it's not
like I really care about being cut off . . . Well, I do,
because we're a close family and I know how much
it would hurt him if he felt he had to do that.'

'But he wouldn't,' Charlotte insisted. 'In fact, it
wouldn't surprise me one bit if, in his heart, he
already knows.'

'Right, so that would be why he arranged for me
and Katie to go and see this house today? Actually,
yeah, it could be. That'd set me on the right track
if he could get me married off.'

'He's not as devious as that and you know it. In
fact, it sounds to me as though you're telling yourself
all sorts of things about your father that just aren't
true. And the only reason you'd do that is because
you're the one having difficulty facing up to who
you really are.'

His eyes came to hers with a wry, though sad
respect.

'You're using your father as an excuse,' she said
more bluntly, 'and what about Katie? This isn't fair
on her, you've got to see that, and . . .'

'I know, I know. Don't you think I hate myself
for what I'm doing to her? She really doesn't deserve
it, but if I break it off I'll have to give a reason, and
once I start getting into it . . .' He picked up his
glass and drained it. 'Actually, I've got an idea,' he
said, reaching for the bottle. 'Why don't you marry

me? We could be really happy, you, me and Chloe, and . . .'

'Rick, get real. I might be into a lot of things, but human sacrifice isn't one of them.'

He gave a splutter of laughter. 'Nicely put, if a touch cruel. I mean, look at me, why wouldn't you want to marry me?'

She pinned him with her eyes. 'Do you really want me to answer that?'

'Actually, yes I do,' he challenged.

'Only because you're trying to get me to say the word that for some bizarre reason you can't bring yourself . . .'

'Gay, OK?' he broke in. 'I'm gay. Gay, gay, gay, gay. Is that enough for you? Are you happy now? Have I given you what you wanted?'

'It's not about me. It's about you and those you need to tell, and you have to face up to it at some point, you know that. You can't go on lying to them. In fact I'm amazed you've got away with it for this long, except I guess people only see what they want to see.'

Having finished his second glass of wine, he got up from the table and wandered down to the foot-bridge. A moment later, he was splashing through the stream and climbing on to the swing.

Taking a glass down to him, she stood on the shingle watching him, the only sounds coming from the creak of the ropes, the buzz of cicadas and gentle swish of the waves.

'Tell me, how come I can talk to you when I've never been able to talk to anyone else?' he demanded.

She shrugged. 'I guess you feel you can trust me.'

'Can I?'

'I'll try not to be offended by that.'

He laughed. 'Maybe it's because you've got secrets too,' he said. 'I mean, I know what they are and I think we should . . .'

'Stop trying to switch this round to me,' she scolded. 'We're discussing something serious here, something that's going to affect the rest of your life, so stop trying to avoid it.'

'But it's OK for you to avoid talking about you?' Without waiting for her to answer, he jumped off the swing and came to take the glass she'd brought him.

'How have you left things with Katie?' she asked as they wandered down to the water's edge.

He shook his head. 'I'm not sure. She called me a few names, richly deserved, I might add, then got in her car and drove off. I had to hitch a lift to Shelley and Phil's.'

'Do either of them know? I mean about you being gay.'

He shrugged. 'They've never mentioned it if they do. Unless . . .' He turned to her. 'How did *you* know?' he asked. 'I mean, when we spoke last weekend . . . I didn't tell you straight out, you just seemed to get it. Did Shelley say something to you? Maybe she does know.'

'It wasn't Shelley, it was instinct. I could tell right from the off and if I can see it . . . Well, perhaps she can too.'

'We have to assume Katie can't.'

'Mm, yes we probably have to assume that, which is why you have to tell her.'

'I know. I just don't want to hurt her, because actually I do love her, just not in the way she wants me to.' He looked down to where their bare feet were sinking into the sand as the waves swirled

71

around them. 'When I saw the look in her eyes earlier, when she realised I was going to turn the house down . . . God, I wanted to go out and shoot myself. She loved the place, she was so excited . . . She was all ready to call Dad to tell him it was perfect and then I go and crush her. What kind of a bastard does that make me?'

Not holding back, Charlotte said, 'One that has to start being honest, not only with her, but with your dad too. You know, in your heart, that he loves you far too much to turn his back on you. He's just not that judgemental, or unfeeling, so you have to stop hiding behind the prejudices that are entirely yours.'

He was gazing out at the changing colours of the sky, his face taut with concern, his eyes focused on only he knew where. 'I know you're right,' he replied, 'but I can't get past the feeling that I'll be letting him down. I know he sees me taking over this place one day, running it the way he does, producing a stream of grandkids, carrying on his legacy . . . OK, it's all dead corny stuff, but it matters to him, and because of that it matters to me. I don't want him to be ashamed of me, or feel he has to make excuses for me . . .'

Putting a hand on his arm, she said, 'You know that's not how he's going to feel, but why don't you talk to him and let him speak for himself?'

His smile was ironic as he looked down at her. 'You're a lot like your mother, do you know that? Don't worry, I mean it in a good way. I know how you women always hate being compared to your mothers, but Anna's in a class of her own.'

Charlotte's laugh was empty. 'You know, she's actually more your mother than she is mine. I mean, she brought you up . . .'

'Since I was eight and Shell was ten. I don't think we gave her an easy time of it at first, but it didn't take us long to realise that you just *have* to love her.'

'When did she tell you about me?'

He frowned as he thought. 'I don't remember an actual time. It's like we always knew you were out there, with this family that had adopted you, and that one day we might get to know you.'

'So,' she said playfully, 'here I am, and getting to know me's turning out to be a lot of fun?'

'You're a bit of a nag,' he told her, 'but otherwise you're kind of cool.'

'Mm,' she nodded pensively, 'that sounds like me. In fact, what you see is what you get.'

He gave a shout of laughter. 'Yeah, right,' he retorted.

'What's that supposed to mean?'

'It means that if you're forcing me out of the closet, then I'm . . . Well, no I guess I'm not forcing you, because in your case I have to concede it's different.'

'Just a bit, and anyway, there isn't a closet big enough for all my baggage. Or the skeletons.'

He gave that some thought. 'Mm, you could be right.'

'You're making it sound as though you know everything about me, but I can tell you this much, you don't.'

Taking her chin in his hand, he tilted her face to look at him. 'What I know,' he said, 'is that Anna's first husband wasn't your real father, and I also know why you decided to come here when you did.'

Feeling certain he couldn't know that, she started to take a step back, needing to create a distance.

'Don't,' he said, catching her wrist, 'it's all right. I swear no one else knows . . .'

'But how do you? My mother would never have told you . . .'

'She didn't. It was Dad who told me.'

Would Bob really have broken the confidence? 'And Shelley? Does she know?'

'We've never spoken about it, so I can't say for sure. Even if she does, she'd never tell. You have to know that.'

A cold chill was running down her spine. 'Please tell me Katie doesn't know. I couldn't bear it . . .'

'No, absolutely not,' he broke in firmly. 'She doesn't have the first idea, I swear it, and as far as I'm concerned, she never will have.'

Turning back towards the bach she put her hands to her head, hardly able to think.

'It's going to be all right,' he said gently, coming to put an arm around her. 'I know it's a scary time right now, but you'll get through it.'

Touched by the sincerity in his tone she looked up at him, and felt the simplicity of his words start to buoy her.

'I'll always be there for you,' he promised. 'No matter what.'

She smiled shakily. 'I'll be there for you too,' she said, meaning it.

'I know that,' and drawing her into an embrace he held her close until they both started to laugh as the ducks, on their evening constitutional, came waddling out of the sea.

'Time for their dinner,' she declared.

'And for another drink,' he added. 'Come on, I'll race you back to the bach, last one in gets to eat the cupcakes.'

*   *   *

At the top of the incline, where she was watching through the puka trees, Katie's face was as pale as the rays filtering down to the bay. She was afraid he'd come here after she'd driven off and left him, and being proved right was tearing her apart.

She hated herself for sneaking around after him, behaving like a pathetic stalker with no courage to speak up, but she'd had to find out if she was right. Now she wished she hadn't, because she knew what she should do next was go down there and confront him.

'Just look at them,' she whispered brokenly to her friend Josie, as Charlotte and Rick fought to get across the footbridge first.

'Are you going to do anything?' Josie asked, transfixed by the scene.

'Well I can't just let them get away with it,' Katie replied miserably. Though rage was trying to break through the cracks of her despair, it wasn't doing a very good job of it.

Batting away a mozzie, Josie said, 'I told you we shouldn't have come.'

Feeling wretched right to her core, Katie turned to start climbing back through the vineyard to where they'd left the car.

Following her, Josie said, 'At least you know now.'

'Yeah, that makes me feel so much better.'

'Sorry, but you're the one who wanted to come, the one who had all the suspicions.'

'And I've been proved right. Obviously there is something going on, and frankly it's sick. She's his stepsister, for God's sake . . .'

'Which doesn't make them blood-related.'

'It's still sick. And I keep wondering if it's why

Anna brought her here. Maybe they all wanted this to happen.'

Since she had no idea if that was true, Josie stayed silent as she got into the car. 'Where now?' she asked, starting the engine as Katie slumped into the passenger seat.

Katie lowered her head, struggling with the urge to cry or run back down there and beg him to stop. They'd been together for almost two years, were engaged to be married, and everything had been perfect until Charlotte Nicholls had turned up. 'What does he see in her?' she growled desperately. 'She's not exactly a raving beauty, is she? And as far as I can tell she doesn't have anything going for her, apart from that strange little retard kid who he seems to be completely besotted with.'

Wincing at the cruelty, Josie decided now wouldn't be the time to admit that she considered Charlotte to be über-attractive. However, she couldn't let it go by about the child. 'She's not retarded,' she protested. 'I don't even know what makes you say that.'

Katie didn't either, really, and she felt terrible now for saying it.

'Where do you want to go?' Josie asked again. 'Shall I take you home?'

Katie turned to stare out of the window. She couldn't see the roof of the bach from where they were, but that didn't stop her imagining what was going on inside it. 'I should confront them,' she declared through a scalding rush of tears. 'I should go down there now and make them stop.'

When she didn't move, Josie said, 'I don't reckon it'd do any good. Not if you want to hang on to him, and I take it you do.'

Katie turned to her. 'Of course I do,' she responded

76

shakily, 'but if he's fallen for her, there's not going to be very much I can do about that, is there?'

'Maybe not, but if it's just a passing fling . . .'

'It's more than that, I just know it. He's been different since she came here . . .' Taking a breath, she put her head back and dragged her hands over her face. 'We have to get rid of her, Josie. Somehow we have to make her go back to where she came from.'

Starting to turn the car around, Josie said, 'You're the one who keeps saying she's hiding something, so maybe, if you find out what it is . . .'

Katie's eyes were so blurred by tears she barely knew what she was seeing. 'There is something,' she muttered distractedly. 'I just know it.'

'So take a little trawl around the Internet, see what you can find out. I'd come and do it with you, if I didn't have to get back for Curt.'

Katie's heartbreak swept over her again. She couldn't bear to think of going home alone, of spending the evening trying to dig up something damaging about Charlotte Nicholls instead of being with Rick. But what choice did she have? He'd turned down the house, had gone straight to Charlotte, and she couldn't imagine anything she said or did now was ever going to help her to win him back.

Chapter Five

Bob was speaking on the phone, looking worried and slightly upset, as Anna came into the kitchen. 'I see,' he said. 'Well, I'm really sorry to hear that. I only wish I understood what was going on with him.' To Anna he mouthed, 'Sarah.'

With a sigh, Anna went to wind in the awnings as a batch of storm clouds began forming over the far islands. Adolescents, as Bob would call them, since they didn't appear especially threatening, but if there were some big guys muscling up behind them it would be best to have everything secure.

'OK, I hear you,' Bob was saying as he went to pour himself a coffee. 'I'll call you once I've spoken to him,' and ringing off he gave a groan of frustration. 'Apparently Rick's rejected the place on Opito Bay,' he declared irritably. 'Have you spoken to him since yesterday? Have you seen him, even?'

'Not since he dropped by to pick up his mail,' Anna replied, 'which was before they went to see the house.'

'Mm,' he grunted, taking a sip of his coffee. 'Sarah's saying Katie's pretty upset, and I can't say I blame her, messing her around like this. For God's sake, what's wrong with the boy? It's a fantastic house, right on the bay, all the space they could wish for . . .'

'If it didn't work for him, it didn't work for him,' Anna interrupted calmly. 'And it's been a while since he was a boy.'

'Then he should stop behaving like one and start manning up to his responsibilities. He's engaged to be married, for God's sake, and not before time. He's going to be thirty-five next month; by the time I was his age I already had him and his sister.'

Unable not to laugh, Anna came to give him a hug. 'There's no rush,' she reminded him. 'Katie's not pregnant, or not as far as we know, and when the right house comes along . . .'

'I'm telling you that was the right house. If you'd seen it you'd know it too.'

'Maybe, but he's a grown man, he gets to make his own decisions, and it's high time you, my darling, came to terms with the fact that you can't rule his life.'

'I'm not trying to *rule* it, I'm just trying to . . .' He stopped and went very still. 'What are you doing?' he demanded, his troubled eyes starting to simmer with pleasure.

'Just trying to take your mind off things,' she smiled flirtatiously.

'But it's half past ten on a Sunday morning,' he protested. 'And we're in the kitchen with all the doors open and half our neighbours out there on the bay . . .'

'Oh, silly me, I get everything wrong,' she sighed, turning away.

'You come back here right now,' he growled, and putting down his cup he swept her into a crushing embrace.

79

'Mm, think I might have to be finishing what I started,' she murmured as he raised his head to look down at her.

'I think you'd better,' he agreed sternly.

'Here or upstairs?'

Before he could answer the sound of urgent footsteps running through the house caused their heads to fall together in despair. A moment later Anna was laughing and opening her arms as Chloe burst into the room shouting, 'Nanna, Nanna, we're here.'

'Hello, my darling,' Anna murmured, sweeping her up and pressing a kiss to her cheek. 'I wasn't expecting to see you this morning.'

'Boo!' Craig suddenly shouted from behind them. 'I came round the back. Grandpa, can we go fishing?'

'Hey you two,' Shelley called breezily as she followed Chloe in from the front door.

'We did a jump-off,' Chloe told Anna.

Anna's eyes rounded to show she was impressed.

'Yeah, last night,' Craig broke in. 'We were practising for when Chloe does it.'

'And who did you jump off to?' Anna asked Chloe.

'Me and Danni,' Craig answered for her, 'because it was just a practice. Grandpa, please can we go fishing?'

'We've got flowers,' Chloe whispered to Anna. 'We picked them in the bush.'

'How lovely,' Anna smiled. 'So where are they?'

Chloe spun round in search of them, and spotting Danni on the veranda waving to a friend on a boat in the bay, she wriggled to get down and charged outside. Moments later she was back with a ragged bunch of stitchwort, pimpernels, toadflax and several dandelions. 'I got them for Mummy,' she explained, 'but Mummy's sleeping.'

Anna's eyebrows rose. 'Is she now?' she responded, glancing with interest at Shelley.

Shelley merely shrugged and carried on loading food into the fridge.

'Who's for lemonade?' Bob offered.

'Yay!' Craig cheered. 'And then can we go fishing?'

'I'd like some lemonade,' Danni shouted.

'Then you can come in and get it,' Shelley told her.

Taking out a jar for the flowers, Anna popped them in some water and had to hide a smile as she carried the little arrangement to the table. Chloe was watching her in fascination, her curly head tilted to one side, her eager eyes not missing a move.

'They're beautiful,' Anna told her.

Chloe broke into an ecstatic smile.

Why, Anna wondered, was Chloe always so anxious about the flowers she brought? The only answer was that something must have happened while she was with her father to make her doubt how well her gifts might be received.

It made Anna's heart ache merely to think of it.

After handing out beakers of lemonade, Bob cried, 'So who wants to go fishing?'

'Me!' Craig and Danni chorused, punching their hands in the air.

'Me!' Chloe echoed, doing the same, and catching her knuckles hard on the edge of a chair.

As her face creased with pain, Anna stooped down to kiss it better. Chloe almost never cried; if she did, it was always silently. 'There, there, it's all right,' she soothed. 'Naughty chair, it got in the way, didn't it?'

Chloe's bottom lip was trembling as she nodded. 'Naughty chair,' she whispered.

'We won't let it go fishing with you.'

'No. It can't come.'

'But you're going with Grandpa and Craig and Danni.'

Chloe turned to look at Bob, her eyes going no higher than his knees. 'Want you to come too,' she said, bringing her worried gaze back to Anna.

Glancing at Bob and feeling for how sad and frustrating he found this divide, Anna said, 'But I have to go into Kerikeri to the market this . . .'

'You don't have to be afraid of Grandpa,' Craig piped up, 'he's just a great big pouffty,' and throwing himself at Bob he began landing punches anywhere he could.

'Ooh, ow, ow, ow,' Bob cried, trying to fend him off. 'I'm getting beaten by the champ.'

'He's not the champ, I am,' Danni shouted, launching herself into the fray.

'Why don't you go and get him too?' Anna said softly to Chloe.

Chloe took a quick peek over her shoulder, but then pushed in more closely to Anna. 'Can we do pipi dancing?' she asked in a whisper.

Smiling, Anna stroked her hair. 'I'm sure we can, later, but Grandpa's taking you fishing now.'

Chloe kept her head down.

'You don't want to go fishing?'

'Want Mummy to wake up,' she mumbled.

Looking at Shelley, Anna said, 'I guess it's time she did.'

'And Uncle Wick,' Chloe added.

Anna looked down at her curiously.

'Rick's over there,' Shelley explained. 'They were

both out for the count, which is why Chloe's still with us.'

Her expression sharpening slightly, Anna turned to Bob.

As though picking up her concern, he reached for the phone and pressed to connect to the bach.

Charlotte's groggy voice eventually came down the line. 'Hello?' she said. 'Is that you, Mum? Sorry, I was in the bathroom. Is Chloe with you?'

'Yes, she's with us,' Bob confirmed. 'And I believe Rick's with you. If you can put him on . . .'

'Actually, he's just left,' Charlotte told him. 'I think he's on his way up to the lodge.'

'Good. Then I'll talk to him when he gets here. I think Anna would like to have a word with you now.'

Taking the phone, Anna put a hand over the mouthpiece as she said to Shelley, 'Would you mind keeping Chloe for a while longer?'

'I'm doing a shift at the Stone Store this morning,' Shelley reminded her.

Remembering it was why Shelley had brought the children here while Phil did a shift at the Observatory, Anna said into the phone to Charlotte, 'I'm bringing Chloe down to you in a few minutes. I hope you don't have anything planned . . .'

'It's OK, I'll come and get her.'

'You don't need to do that. I'll see you there,' and putting the phone down she looked across the kitchen at Bob.

After meeting her gaze with a similar expression he began rubbing his hands together as he said to Craig and Danni, 'Right you guys, off you go and get the rods. I'll meet you down at the boat.' Then, careful not to address Chloe directly, 'Are we sure no one else wants to come with us?'

Apparently realising he meant her, Chloe turned away, keeping her head bowed.

'Is Uncle Rick coming?' Danni asked, clearly having listened to the phone call.

Bob glanced at Shelley. 'I don't know what he's doing, sweetheart,' he replied gravely. 'I'm hoping he might enlighten us as to that when he gets here.'

Immediately after ringing off at her end, Charlotte rang Rick's mobile. 'I've just spoken to your dad and my mum,' she told him when he answered. 'I'm not sure what's happened, but neither of them sounded happy.'

Sighing, he said, 'Why doesn't that surprise me?'

'I didn't think it would, but if you start getting into some kind of fight with your dad now, while you're this hung-over, you might end up saying things you'll later regret. So I don't think you should go to the lodge.'

'How did I ever manage my life without you?'

'I often wonder. Have you spoken to Katie this morning?'

'I tried a couple of minutes ago, but she hung up on me. I probably ought to wait until I've properly sobered up before I go over there.'

'Not a bad idea. Is it your intention to tell your dad anything today?'

'I'm not sure. Of course I could always tell no one at all.'

'Sorry, not an option. We agreed somewhere between the second and third bottle last night that even if you aren't going to fess up for yourself, you're going to do it for Hamish.'

'Did I say that?'

'You did, and if you love him as much as you say you do . . .'

'Oh God, did I tell you that too? What did you put in that wine?'

She smiled fondly. 'You told me a lot more than that, and he sounds wonderful, but you can't expect him to carry on . . .'

'All right, all right, I hear you. God, you're bossy.'

'Believe me, I haven't even started. When are you flying back to Auckland?'

'First thing tomorrow.'

'OK, I'll call you after Mum's been over. Meantime, why don't you ring Hamish and let him know that you're halfway out?'

'You think you're so funny.'

'You're right, I do,' she laughed. 'Speak later,' and as she put the phone down she waited for an alcohol-induced dizzy spell to pass before putting on the kettle to make more coffee.

A few minutes later she was standing outside, holding her face up to a refreshing mizzle of rain and inhaling the acrid-sweet smell rising from the hillsides as the parched earth drank in the moisture. It was badly needed, but wasn't going to be nearly enough to slake the real thirst of the land, or to save Bob from having to order more water for the household tanks.

Hearing the sound of a car door slamming she waited for Chloe to come flying down the slope, already perking up at the prospect of her sunny little smile and the pleasing weight of her in her arms. It was good that she'd spent the night away, but at the same time, Charlotte couldn't help hoping it wouldn't happen too often. She'd missed her, in spite of having Rick for company.

When only her mother appeared she experienced a bolt of alarm. 'Where is she?' she cried, already on the brink of panic. Her mother had sounded serious on the phone; Shelley hadn't brought Chloe back here; something must have happened to her.

Waiting until she was crossing the footbridge, Anna said, 'Shelley's taken her to the Stone Store so I can speak to you alone. I'll go and pick her up after, unless you want to go yourself.'

Feeling herself bristle at her mother's tone, Charlotte turned back into the kitchen and quickly pushed last night's empty bottles out of sight. 'Would you like some coffee?' she offered, as Anna came in. 'Or tea?'

'Thanks, I'll have tea.'

As she busied herself with making it Charlotte waited for her mother to speak, but it wasn't until she put the cup on the table that Anna finally said, 'Exactly what's going on between you and Rick?'

Charlotte's eyes flashed. 'What do you mean, *going on*?' she snapped.

'He stayed here last night . . .'

'Yes! Is there some kind of law against it? Are you saying I need to check with you first if I have guests?'

Anna sighed, as though stepping away from the belligerence. 'He's engaged to be married,' she said.

Charlotte watched her, feeling nauseous and guilty and irrationally angry.

'You're not making this easy,' Anna told her.

Charlotte's demons were still raging. 'Making what easy?' she demanded. 'Exactly what are you trying to say? You think I'm having an affair with him, is that it?'

'I'm just trying to . . .'

'Well, what if I am? There's nothing to say . . .'

'He's your stepbrother, for God's sake, and at risk of repeating myself, he's engaged to Katie.'

Putting her hands on the table, Charlotte said, 'Are you really that blind? Are you telling me that you honestly can't see what's staring you right in the face?'

Anna met her challenge unflinchingly, but in the end she was the first to look away.

'You do know, don't you?' Charlotte said bluntly.

Anna swallowed. 'I think so,' she replied.

Feeling a surprising sense of relief, as though it was her own secret that was finally out, Charlotte pulled back a chair and sat down facing her mother. 'There's nothing wrong with it,' she stated. 'He's still the same person we all know and love. It doesn't change anything about him . . .'

'I know that, but Bob . . . It'll be hard for him . . .'

'Says who? Why won't anyone let him speak for himself?'

'Because Bob's a man's man, a traditionalist, and finding out that his son's . . . That he's . . .'

'The word is gay.'

Anna's eyes sharpened. 'You think you have it all sorted out, don't you,' she said tartly, 'that all you have to do is decide it's time the truth was out and that everything will be just fine. Well it doesn't work like that, Charlotte. There are people's feelings to consider . . .'

'Of course there are, but why should Rick have to hide who he is? Can't you see that the longer he goes on pretending, the more hurt everyone's going to be . . .'

'Listen,' Anna cut in angrily, 'you've hardly been here five minutes, and if it's your plan to turn this family inside out . . .'

'What are you talking about, turn the family inside out? I deeply resent that comment, when I've done everything I can to try and fit in, to build a home here for me and Chloe, to create a new life for us . . .'

'I know, I know, I'm sorry. I should have chosen my words more carefully. I just don't want you involved in any upset that might come about because of this. In fact, given the position you're in, don't you think it would be wiser to keep your head down and mind your own business? At least until you've been here for a year or two. It might also be a good idea to cut down on the drinking. I understand why you feel you need it, but it's not the answer. If anything you're going to end up making things a hundred times worse . . .'

'Please tell me exactly how they could be any worse,' Charlotte broke in hotly. 'Here I am in your little piece of paradise, loving it just like you said I would, but it doesn't mean everything else has just gone away.'

'Of course it doesn't, but if the past is going to come to find us we'll deal with it then. Meantime, there's no reason to think it will, and if you carry on like this you're going to end up having some sort of breakdown. And where would Chloe be then?'

Charlotte was already starting to snap a reply before realising she didn't have one.

'You owe it to her to pull yourself together and give her the life she deserves,' Anna pressed on. 'You can't change what went before, none of us can, but you only have to look at her now to see how she's come on during these last few months. She's a different child to the one she was when she first arrived. OK, she still has problems, but we'll work on them when the time is right and I'm sure we'll get past them. The question is, when are we going to face what's going on with you?'

'Nothing's going on with me. I'm fine . . .'

'Oh, Charlotte . . .'

'Just stop, will you?' Charlotte cried, throwing out her hands. 'I know Chloe's doing great. I spend virtually every minute of every day making sure of it, and I'll continue to do it, because she's mine and I love her and nothing matters to me more than her. I'd never let anything bad happen to her. God knows, I'd never go off and leave her the way you left me when I was her age.'

As the words fell between them like stones a horrible, echoing silence followed.

'So here we have it,' Anna said quietly in the end.

Charlotte turned her face away.

'You know the reasons why I had to leave you,' Anna continued, 'and you know very well how deeply I regret it . . .'

'Do you?' Charlotte snapped. 'What were you doing all those years I was growing up with a mother who didn't really want me? Don't worry, I can answer that for you. You were bringing up somebody else's children; that's what you were doing. You let Rick and Shelley take the place of me and my brother, because it was easier to do that than to face up to what had happened to us.'

Anna's face had turned deathly pale. 'If that's what you're telling yourself . . .'

'Tell me I'm wrong.'

Anna simply stared down at her hands.

'You can't, can you, because I'm right. You blocked us out of your mind like we didn't exist.'

'Charlotte, stop, please.'

'The truth is hard, isn't it?'

'Yes it is, but the way you're telling it . . .'

'What other way is there?'

Anna met her gaze. 'We've been through it, but if you need to go through it again . . .'

Charlotte shook her head. 'No, no I don't,' she said bleakly. *Why do I keep feeling the need to punish her?* she was asking herself desperately. *Hasn't she suffered enough? Haven't we both? She loves me, I know she does, but every time I feel her coming close I just want to push her away.*

'I've known Rick and Shelley since they were ten and eight,' Anna said softly, 'so I won't apologise for loving them, but they've never taken the place of you and Hugo. You're a mother yourself now, so surely you understand that no one will ever be able to do that.'

Inexplicably angry that she'd brought Chloe into this, Charlotte was about to respond with words she knew would hurt when the phone started to ring. Avoiding her mother's eyes she went to it, and kept her back turned as she said, 'Hello?'

'Hi babe, it's me,' Shelley told her. 'I think it's all proving a bit much for our little angel with all these tourists and strangers about. She wants her mummy . . .'

'Tell her I'm on my way,' Charlotte interrupted, already reaching for her keys. 'I have to go,' she said to her mother as she rang off.

Anna nodded and got to her feet. 'Please will you consider coming to talk to someone with me?' she asked as she stepped outside and waited for Charlotte to close the door.

Charlotte put up her hood and started towards

90

the footbridge. Since the awful turmoil of emotions where her mother was concerned was impossible to fathom on her own, maybe she should agree to some counselling. Provided all they discussed was what had happened in the past, and didn't venture forward to today, where would be the harm? For her there was probably nothing to fear and everything to gain; for her mother, who'd been hospitalised for almost a year following the brutal attack that had robbed her of the rest of her family, it would be an excruciating experience. And yet she was prepared to go through it in order to make things right between them.

Charlotte simply couldn't let her. It would be cruel and selfish of her even to consider it. So no, somehow she was going to make herself let go of the resentment, or whatever was driving this wedge between them, and ensure her mother never had to live through the sheer hell of that time again.

The Stone Store, along with the mission house, was Kerikeri's main tourist attraction, sitting in small grandeur on the edge of town between the river basin and Hongi Hika Recreation Reserve. To Charlotte it looked rather like a child's drawing of a house with two windows either side of a central front door, three windows upstairs, a red tiled roof and tall brick chimney. It was held to be the region's oldest building, constructed in the early eighteen hundreds by a Maori workforce to hold mission supplies and wheat for the settlers. Today it was a thriving gift shop selling everything from T-shirts, to jewellery, to Kiwiana-inspired homewares on the ground floor, while the upper level was reserved for offices, storerooms and the occasional guided tour of old artefacts.

Leaving her car next to the river Charlotte splashed across the road through the rain, waited impatiently for a group of Chinese to spill out of the door, and ran inside.

Spotting her from behind the counter, Shelley pointed her in the right direction and carried on serving her customer while Charlotte moved swiftly across the shop to the stairs. Chloe was halfway up, hunched in close to the wall with her face buried in her knees and her arms around her head. Boots sat next to her.

'Hey you,' Charlotte called gently.

Chloe looked up and choking on a sob of relief she grabbed Boots and flew into Charlotte's arms. 'Mummy,' she gasped, wrapping herself so tightly around Charlotte it was as though she was trying to get inside her skin.

'It's all right, I'm here,' Charlotte soothed, squeezing her back. 'Shall we take you home now?'

Feeling Chloe's head nodding, Charlotte turned back down the stairs and carried her over to Shelley.

'Thanks for taking care of her,' she said, as soon as Shelley was alone. 'And I'm sorry it fell to you.'

'Don't be,' Shelley responded, waving a dismissive hand. 'How're you feeling? It looked like you two tied one on pretty good last night when I stopped by earlier.'

Charlotte pulled a face. 'Let's just say I've felt better,' she confessed. 'Was Chloe OK? Did she sleep through?'

'She did brilliantly, didn't you, my darling?' Shelley replied, running a hand over Chloe's head. 'She wasn't any trouble at all, but that Boots, well he's a right chatterbox, isn't he?'

Chloe folded the bear more closely to her, and kept her face pressed into Charlotte's shoulder.

'I'm sorry,' Shelley whispered, 'I know I shouldn't have brought her here with all these people around, but Anna was really keen to talk to you . . .'

'It's OK. She'll be fine,' Charlotte assured her. 'Have you seen or heard anything from Rick this morning?'

Shelley's eyes sparkled with irony. 'You mean he's alive and capable of speaking? Well that's good to hear. No, he hasn't been in touch, but I'm told he rejected the house on Opito Bay, so I take it he was down at yours hiding from Katie, or Dad – possibly both.'

'Something like that,' Charlotte replied with a smile. 'Is your dad furious?'

Shelley pondered. 'I think exasperated would be a better way of putting it,' she decided, 'and baffled. He really thought Rick would go for it, and from what I hear there's nothing about it not to love. But hey, that's my brother for you, he's never been easy to please.'

Realising someone was hovering behind her, hoping to pay, Charlotte said, 'I'd better leave you to it. I'll see you later and thanks again,' and keeping her own head down as a rowdy bunch of English tourists entered the store, she ran back through the drizzle to the car. Though it wasn't likely anyone would recognise her and Chloe as the young woman and child whose faces had been splashed over their TV screens and papers a few months ago, it wasn't impossible either, and the last thing Charlotte wanted was any more unwelcome brushes with fame. This was why she so rarely came to the Stone Store with its constant flow of tourists, because if anyone were to tip the British press off to where she was, then someone would be sure to want to make an issue of it. And if they did it would be an end to everything she was trying to build here.

Actually, it would be an end to everything, full stop, she thought, as her mobile rang.

'Hi,' she said, tucking the phone under her chin as she buckled a sleepy Chloe into her car seat. 'Where are you?'

'At a mate's,' Rick answered, 'Gavin Hume, I don't think you know him. Are you still with Anna?'

'No, I've had to come into town to get Chloe.'

'Into *town*? What's she doing there?'

'Long story. I think I should tell you that Mum knows about you.'

'Oh my God, you told her?'

'No! Or not exactly. I just got her to admit what she already knew. You don't need to worry about her telling Bob, though, I think she sees that as your job. Have you seen Katie yet?'

'No. She left a message on my mobile saying she needs some space. I went round there anyway, but she wasn't in. Christ, it's a mess, and it's all my fault, which makes me feel so much better.'

'You can't exactly help the way you are,' she reminded him.

'No, but I should never have let things get this far. It was just that everyone seemed so happy when Katie and I got together, like it was all meant to be, and obviously I had feelings for her. I still do . . .' He broke off with an agitated sigh. 'I was an idiot then, and I'm no better now, because I can't for the hell of me think how to put things right without hurting her.'

'I'm afraid that won't be possible if she's in love with you, and I don't think there's much doubt that she is. Still, better you sort things out before you marry her than after.'

'Of course, but I'm afraid it's not going to happen this weekend. I've just booked myself on the seven thirty back to Auckland tonight. No, I'm not running away, I swear it. A meeting scheduled to start at eleven in the morning has been brought forward to nine and I can't miss it.'

'OK, I believe you. Now I need to go, I'm afraid. I have to get Chloe home and it looks like my mother's trying to get through. Let's speak later,' and clicking to the next call she said, 'Hi, Mum, I'm about to start driving . . .'

'Actually, it's me,' Bob interrupted, 'and I won't keep you a moment.'

Bracing herself, since she was sure this was going to be about the scene she'd had with her mother, Charlotte said, 'Is everything all right?'

'I think so,' he replied. 'It's simply that I've had an idea for Chloe's birthday that I'd like to run past you.'

Touched that he was already making plans, Charlotte averted her head as the English tourists wandered by, saying, 'I'm all ears.'

'Well, actually, I'm hoping you might be free to discuss it over a coffee in the morning. I have to be in town first thing, and I expect you're taking Chloe to Aroha, so would ten at the Pear Tree work for you? My treat.'

Glancing at the restaurant in her rear-view mirror, gleaming like a colonial jewel on the banks of the basin, Charlotte was about to remind him that it was a bit close to the Stone Store when she remembered that Chloe wouldn't be with her. It was seeing them together that would be most likely to jog a memory, whereas a thirty-year-old woman seated at a table with an older man, quite possibly her father, wasn't likely to draw much attention at all.

And Mondays were generally quiet.

'OK, see you there,' she said with a smile, 'you get the coffees, I'll get the cake.'

Chapter Six

The following morning Charlotte was up at seven, keen to use her laptop before Chloe woke. Seeing the computer at the table could sometimes scare her into thinking she was going to be shown the images of herself that her father had shot and uploaded for the sick edification of his paedophile chums. Since this had been Chloe's first experience of computers, it was no wonder she was so nervous of them. However, Celia at Aroha was gradually coaxing her to watch videos on the computer there, and since she was having some success with that Charlotte felt it was probably time to start trying it at home.

After dealing with the few emails she found for Charlotte@TepunaLodge, she quickly called up her old address and without reading Anthony Goodman's message again she deleted it. Though it had taken a couple of days, she'd finally persuaded herself that this really was the only way to deal with it. It might also prevent her from constantly thinking about him and imagining what she'd really like to say if she emailed back. She wasn't going to, so she needed to remove the temptation in the only way she knew how and stay focused on reality.

Once the computer was tucked out of sight she bundled a pile of washing into the machine, ironed

Chloe's clothes for the day, then went to take a shower. By the time she was ready to wake Chloe she realised that all she'd been thinking about this past hour was Anthony Goodman and how wonderful it would be if she were able to see him when he came to NZ.

Of course, she hadn't really believed that erasing his message would obliterate him from her thoughts entirely; after all, there wasn't any way of unknowing someone, but she had hoped it might at least help put an end to all the nonsense going round in her head.

So much for that, she was thinking wryly, as she rolled Chloe on to her back and smiled down into her sleepy face. 'Hello you,' she whispered fondly. 'The Good Fairy's just been by to remind me it's a painting day at Aroha and you love painting, don't you?'

Chloe nodded and rubbed her eyes. 'Going to do a picture for Nanna today,' she said huskily.

Moving past the pang of awkwardness as she thought of her mother, Charlotte said, 'She'll love that. She'll be able to put it on her fridge along with all the others.'

'Yes, because I've done lots.'

'Indeed you have.'

'For you too, and they're on our fridge.'

'They're all over our little bach making it a very lovely and colourful place to live in. Are you ready for some Weet-bix now?'

'Yes please.' She yawned loudly and stretched out her little limbs, managing to crush the trusty Boots in the process. 'Is Uncle Wick gone in the plane now?' she asked, padding into the kitchen after Charlotte.

'You know he has because we went to wave him off, didn't we?'

'Yes, and he waved back because we could see him in the window. I'm going to paint a picture for him too. And for Auntie Katie to cheer her up.'

Surprised at that, until she realised Chloe must have been listening to her conversation with Rick at the airport last night, Charlotte dropped a kiss on her head just for being so sweet-natured.

'I can't do a jump-off today,' Chloe sighed, as Charlotte popped a Weet-bix in her bowl. 'I have to wait till I'm five, but when I'm five I'm going to jump off to Uncle Wick.'

Smiling at the image, Charlotte said, 'That will make him so proud, but before that you have to decide what we're going to do for your fourth birthday in a couple of weeks.' She wouldn't tell her she was going to meet Grandpa later to talk about his idea just in case the plan, whatever it was, didn't work out. Besides, mentioning Grandpa often rendered her silent, and since there were nightmares in that silence it was best avoided.

'I'm going to bake a cake and take it to O-a,' Chloe stated, unable to pronounce Aroha. 'Then I'm going to blow out the candles and make a wish.'

'Ah yes, have you decided yet what to wish for? Don't make it a jump-off because you know that's for when you're five.'

Kicking her legs back and forth, Chloe pretended to give Boots a mouthful of cereal, which she then ate herself. 'Want to do wees,' she suddenly announced, and sliding off her chair at speed she darted into the bathroom.

An hour later, with Boots tucked loyally under one arm and her pink backpack dangling over the other, Chloe led the way over the bridge up to the car, calling out 'Good morning,' to Mr Kingfisher and a crowd of noisy parrots on the way. There was also a stop to wonder if there were any pipis at the water's edge, and another to gasp as a dolphin leapt out of the bay. At the car Charlotte had to run back for her mobile, and when she returned it was to find Chloe at the edge of the pond telling the ducks she would see them later.

The drive along the peninsula into town was one Charlotte always enjoyed, even on lacklustre mornings such as this one, for the breathtaking vistas of rich green meadows rolling down to the ocean, in some places both sides of the road, could make her feel as though they were on top of the world. As usual they sang nursery rhymes and named things they passed – oyster racks, black cows, fluffy sheep, orange and lemon trees, children waiting for the school bus, the Little Dippers swim school, a possum squished in the road.

'A dead possum is the best possum,' Chloe shouted, echoing what she regularly heard at Bob and Anna's get-togethers.

'And why is that?' Charlotte asked her.

'Because they eat the trees and make them sick.'

'That's right,' and spotting their postman driving towards them, Charlotte flashed her headlights to say hello.

'Need any extras today?' he asked, as they slowed up alongside one another.

'Thanks, but I'm going to the supermarket later,' she told him, still entranced by the fact that the postman was a willing runner of errands.

'OK, well don't forget to call if you forget anything. I can always pick it up and bring it tomorrow,' and with a jolly little wave to Chloe, he drove on his way.

'That was Greg,' Chloe announced. 'And Maya's his mummy. I can count in Maori, *tahi, rua, tora* . . . '

Loving what a chatterbox she was turning into, Charlotte checked her phone as it rang, and seeing it was her mother a surge of guilt made her hesitate. They hadn't spoken since their showdown yesterday so things still weren't right between them, and no doubt Anna wanted to try and remedy that.

'Hi,' Charlotte said as she answered, sounding stiffer than she'd intended. 'Are you OK?'

'Yes, thank you, I hope you are too.'

'I'm fine. Just taking Chloe to Aroha.'

'I thought you would be. There are a couple of things I want to ask, if you have a minute. First, are you still helping me with the shoot at Kauri Cliffs on Thursday and Friday? I only ask, because if you've changed your mind . . .'

'I haven't changed my mind,' Charlotte cut in quickly. 'Actually, I'm looking forward to it.'

There was relief in Anna's voice as she said, 'Me too. I think we worked very well together the last time, don't you, and this one's a bit special, given the location. Anyway, the second thing is . . . Well, I know you're having coffee with Bob this morning, so I need to ask if you're intending to tell him about Rick.'

With a flash of disbelief Charlotte retorted, 'What do you take me for? Of course I'm not going to tell him. First of all it's hardly my place to, and even if it were, I certainly wouldn't do it in public.'

'I'm sorry, of course you wouldn't. It was wrong of me . . . I'm sorry, let's change the subject. How's Chloe this morning?'

Glancing in the rear-view mirror to where Chloe was still counting in Maori, Charlotte said, 'Chatty.' Then, because she felt she ought to, 'I'm sorry for snapping, and I'm sorry I ran out on you yesterday . . .'

'It's OK. It was my fault and . . . Well, you had to go and fetch Chloe . . . Anyway, I'm seeing Sarah later, and I'm feeling in a slightly awkward position since our conversation yesterday. So I wondered if you knew whether Rick is intending to tell Katie that he's, you know?'

'Gay?' Charlotte provided helpfully. 'As far as I know he is. In fact, I'm sure he is, but why does it affect you seeing Sarah? You don't have to tell her anything, you can let *her* tell *you* when the time comes, because I'm sure Katie'll confide in her.'

'Sarah is my closest friend of many years' standing. We don't normally have secrets from one another and, well, frankly we have discussed this . . . possibility about Rick in the past.'

More surprised than she ought to have been, Charlotte said, 'And she's never mentioned anything to Katie?'

'It was hardly her place to, when we didn't know for sure if we were right.'

Conceding the point, Charlotte said, 'Well, in my opinion I think Rick should tell Katie himself, but if you're thinking Sarah might want to . . .'

'No, I'm sure she doesn't, but if I can tell her that our suspicions are correct at least then she'll be ready and prepared to do what she can for Katie when Katie finds out.'

After agreeing it would be a good idea, Charlotte dropped her phone back on the passenger seat and turned into the garage on the corner of Waipapa Road.

'Gay, gay, gay, gay,' Chloe was singing happily in the back.

Barely suppressing a smile, Charlotte got out to fill up with petrol before driving on to Aroha. Though she'd have liked to stay at the Centre for a while watching Chloe interacting with the other kids, it was important that she didn't create a scenario where Chloe might want her to stay every morning. So after making sure she was settled and Boots was safely tucked in her locker, Charlotte drove on to Kerikeri to pick up some new socks and vests for Chloe and maybe a pair of jandals, as the locals called flip-flops, for herself, before meeting Bob.

With it being a Monday Katie's salon would be closed so there wasn't much chance of running into her, which Charlotte could only feel grateful for, since she really wouldn't want to be facing her right now, knowing what she did. However, after Rick had told Katie, Charlotte would want to be there for her in any way she could, since heartbreak was something Charlotte knew all about. When it had happened to her she'd truly believed she'd never get over it, yet here she was, six months on, and she hardly thought about Jason Carmichael at all. When she did, she had to admit that a part of her longed to go back to the happier days they had shared, or at least to a time before her world had turned inside out. And yet she wouldn't really have things any other way than they were now, because painful as it had been to lose Jason back then, he'd left her to return to his wife and children, which was where he belonged, and now she was here with Chloe, where they belonged.

It would all come right for Katie in the end too,

Charlotte felt sure of it, because sooner or later it did for everyone. She just hoped, for Katie's sake, that the process of letting go of her dreams and moving on to new horizons wasn't going to prove anywhere near as difficult as Katie might fear.

Katie was sitting at the table beside the window in her flat, staring down at the comings and goings of the street below. She was barely taking anything in, not even the roar and wail of a fire engine as it lumbered out of the station, or the wave of a friend who'd spotted her sitting there.

She was usually to be found here when working at her computer, often with a coffee and very occasionally a cigarette if she was in the mood. The table was only cleared when someone came round for a bite to eat, or on Mondays when she had a general tidy up. Neither was on the agenda this morning. In fact housework and socialising couldn't have been further from her mind. She'd even forgotten she was supposed to be going surfing with Josie and a few others at Matauri Bay. She'd cried off with menstrual cramps when Josie had rung to find out where she was, so now she was simply sitting here trying to compose an email to Rick, but nothing was coming out right.

She didn't want to lose him, she felt panicked, terrified, desperate at the mere thought of it. She'd do anything, literally *anything* to keep him, but what was it going to take? The images of him embracing Charlotte Nicholls on the beach on Saturday night were brutal and tormenting. Every time she tried to blot them out they seemed to grow larger and sharper and more intimate than ever. They'd been so easy and natural with each other . . .

She swallowed hard on the tears drowning her throat. The memory hurt so much, made her feel broken and worthless and vengeful inside. She'd loved him for so long, far longer than even he knew. He was the reason she'd given up her degree course at Durham and moved out here. Of course they hadn't been an item then, in fact he'd been seeing someone called Ursula, from Perth, at the time. They'd been at uni together, apparently, but the relationship hadn't lasted. Katie had gone out of her way after the break-up to get him to notice her as more than the niece of his stepmother's friend. It hadn't worked, but at least he hadn't brought anyone else home in the years that had followed. It would have been truly insufferable to be forced to watch him with someone else, to pretend that she was happy for him, and willing to befriend a girl who was threatening to waltz off with every last part of her dreams.

When they'd finally got together she'd truly believed the time had come for them. They'd been so crazy for each other at first that they'd been unable to keep their hands off one another. She couldn't really remember now when that had changed, probably because it had happened so slowly.

'But you can't keep up that level of passion for ever,' she used to tell herself, sure it was what would be said if she confided in her Aunt Sarah or one of her friends. She hadn't told anyone, because she was afraid of injecting life into her insecurities by spreading them around. The only time she'd ever mentioned it to Rick was on the phone one night after he'd failed to come home from Auckland three weekends in a row. She hadn't made a big deal of it, simply remarked, almost casually, that she hoped he wasn't going off her, and when he finally showed up, on the fourth weekend, he'd brought a diamond ring with him and had asked her to marry him.

Of course she'd said yes, it was what she'd been waiting and praying for virtually since the day they'd met.

Both their families had been ecstatic. Her divorced parents had flown over from their separate parts of England to attend the beach party Bob and Anna had thrown to celebrate the engagement. And during the months that followed she, Katie, had actually paid for several old friends to visit. They'd been as blown away by Te Puna as she'd hoped, and of course by Rick: how could they not be when he was so welcoming and charming and his parents were such generous hosts? She'd read her friends' gossip on Facebook afterwards and had felt so proud of how well they said she'd done for herself, and was so thrilled by how pleased they all were for her, that she'd only wished she could fly *everyone she'd ever known* to Te Puna, so they could see it all for themselves.

Sighing shakily as she checked her mobile in spite of knowing it hadn't rung, she got up from the table and wandered across the spacious sitting room with its tan leather sofas and animal-skin rugs to the open-plan kitchen. Rick's dad had found this place for her, the salon with a two-bedroom apartment above, back when she'd first decided to follow her heart and take up hair-styling for a living. Her parents had always been against it, saying she needed a proper career, but when she'd chucked in uni and come here to live, her Aunt Sarah had encouraged her to exploit what appeared to be a natural skill. So, using most of her savings, she'd trained at the Northland Hairdressing Centre in Whangarei, and within days of qualifying she'd landed a job with one of Auckland's most prestigious salons. Two years later, just after she'd got together with Rick, Bob had told her about the shop in Kerikeri and before she knew it a team of workmen was redesigning the place to her and an architect's specifications. This meant that Bob, who'd put up most of the funding, was her partner now – though not sleeping, he was always uncomfortable with that title, even in jest. His role, he said, was to let her run her business the way she deemed best while he kept an eye on the books.

So far the arrangement had worked perfectly, and since her client list was constantly increasing – she now employed four stylists and two juniors – there was no reason for anything to change. And nor would it, as long as she kept her head and did nothing rash. She needed to tread very carefully now, so carefully that she barely knew what the first step should be, though she guessed she'd taken it by leaving a message for Rick to call as soon as his meeting was over. What was she going to say to him then, how was she going to put what she'd discovered into words he would even believe, never mind be ready to hear?

Unless he already knew.

No, he couldn't, it just wasn't possible.

She was still so stunned by what she'd learned, and how easy the information had been to find once she'd started looking, that she'd returned to the computer several times just to make sure she wasn't dreaming. In some ways she almost wished she was, until she remembered that her and Rick's physical relationship had slumped into another decline around the time Charlotte Nicholls had arrived at Te Puna. And recalling the scene on the beach on Saturday evening, she was ready to believe anything of Charlotte Nicholls, or Alexandra Lake as she'd been known before.

It was ten fifteen now, and Rick's assistant had said the meeting was due to finish at ten. He was usually quite prompt at ringing back, but maybe the meeting had dragged on longer than expected. For all she knew there hadn't been a meeting at all and he was deliberately avoiding her. If that were the case then maybe it would be good for him to know that she only had to make one phone call now, just one, and within a matter of days, maybe even hours, Charlotte Nicholls would be right back where she belonged.

Glancing at the clock she decided to wait until eleven and if she hadn't heard from him by then . . .

She took a deep, shuddering breath.

Did she actually have the courage to make that call?

She guessed she wouldn't know until the time came.

Chapter Seven

Charlotte had learned early on that being anywhere in town with her stepfather was a bit like being with a celebrity – everyone knew him and everyone wanted to say hello, or get stuck into a chinwag if they possibly could. Though she'd arrived at the Pear Tree, on the outskirts of town, over ten minutes ago they hadn't managed much more than a greeting yet, in spite of Bob having deliberately placed himself on the river-view terrace with his back to the door. His friends and neighbours were still somehow finding him, and the obvious touristic couple at the far end of the terrace were clearly dying to know who he might be.

'Sorry about this,' Bob apologised with an endearing blush as yet another backslapping, loud-laughing townsman took himself off to wherever he'd appeared from. 'I should have come to the bach, it would have been easier.'

'It's OK,' Charlotte assured him, as entertained by all the comings and goings as were the audience of two still glancing their way. 'But I can't help wondering what you're doing here. Aren't you Mr Dentist at the Maori Health Trust on Mondays and Tuesdays?'

'I am indeed, and I shall be heading over there as soon as we've had our coffee,' he told her, checking who was ringing his mobile and letting the call go to voicemail. 'Not many on the list today, or there weren't when I rang in earlier. Funny how no one ever likes going to the dentist, when I thought I was such an amiable chap.'

Knowing that the government paid him handsomely for his surgeries at the settlement these days, and that he used most of the money to bribe his reluctant patients to come for treatment (the rest went to various other Maori causes), Charlotte was about to respond when a waiter appeared with their coffees, followed by Grant Romney in full police uniform and the usual playful gleam in his eyes.

'Hey you guys,' he mouthed with a thumbs up as he listened to someone at the end of his mobile. 'Yeah, right Jack, got it. I'll be there in about ten. OK mate, see you,' and tucking the phone in his shirt pocket, he came to shake Bob's hand. 'Sorry to interrupt,' he said, stooping to kiss Charlotte's cheek, 'but I saw your car outside and thought I'd come and invite you for a sleepover.'

Startled, and no less so when she realised he was speaking to her, Charlotte said, 'Well, that's very kind of you, Grant. How could I possibly refuse? Let me see . . .'

Laughing, he told her, 'I mean Chloe, of course. Bev's staying with me and Polly the weekend after next, so we said he could have a few friends over on the Saturday night and he wants Chloe to be one of them.'

Surprised, and touched by the offer, especially since Bevan was at the big school now, Charlotte replied, 'To be honest I'm not sure if she will, but I'll put it to her . . . Who else is going to be there?'

'He's got a few on his list, a couple more girls if that's what you're thinking.'

It was. 'OK, I'll see what she says. It'll only be her second sleepover, and you know how shy she can be . . .'

'You're welcome to join in,' Grant assured her. 'We'll do a barbie and get the kids to put up tents. If the weather's good they might sleep out, but that's not a given and I guess that could be a big ask for a delicate little thing like Chloe, sleeping rough.'

'Oh, she's camped on the beach with Danni and Craig before now,' Charlotte assured him, 'and actually lasted right up until the tide came in, which was about three hours, so she's not such a lightweight.'

Grinning, he said, 'Give Polly a ring and let her know what you decide. Of course, there's room for you too, mate,' he told Bob, 'don't want you feeling left out now, do we?'

'I was just getting there,' Bob informed him, 'but darn it, I'm sure Anna and I are going to a wedding in Paihia on that day.'

'And if you're not, you are now,' Grant retorted with a laugh. 'Well, seems like I've got myself a villain to take to the courts in Kaikohe, so I'll be on my way. You have yourselves a great day now,' and fishing out his phone as it rang he gave them a salute as he disappeared back inside.

'We're going to get to the point of why we're here in a minute,' Bob commented wryly as he picked up his coffee. 'In fact, you know what I'm going to do . . .' And getting to his feet, he called over one

111

of the waiters, spoke quietly in his ear and by the time he sat down again Charlotte realised they were now going to have the terrace entirely to themselves, apart from the couple already there, with no more interruptions.

'Best coffee in town,' he declared, after downing his double espresso in one go.

Unable to argue with that, Charlotte sipped her cappuccino and glanced away from the couple who were still watching them with interest.

'So, our little sweetheart's birthday,' Bob announced, switching his mobile to vibrate only.

Though Charlotte was smiling, she couldn't help feeling nervous too, since the last thing she wanted was to find herself pouring cold water on his suggestion, especially when he was finding it difficult enough to forge a relationship with Chloe.

'I was thinking,' he stated, looking up at her with his clear, frank eyes, 'with your permission, of course, that she might like a puppy.'

Charlotte almost gasped with surprise as all her tension vanished. 'That's a fantastic idea,' she gushed. 'She'll love it, I know she will. Oh Bob, it's so lovely of you to think of it. You'll have to give it to her yourself, of course . . .'

'Oh now, I don't know about that,' he interrupted. 'We don't want to frighten her off the poor little beast before she gets a chance to know him – or her. Which do you think? Male or female?'

Already caught up with the idea, Charlotte pondered. 'I guess we should decide on a breed first,' she replied. 'Or maybe we should rescue a mutt. I think that would appeal to her quite a lot, if she thought the puppy wouldn't have a home without her.'

Bob's eyes twinkled. 'I was hoping you'd say something like that,' he told her, 'because there's a dear, gentle dog at the settlement whose puppies are about ready to leave her, and the owner's saying if he doesn't find homes for them all he'll just drown them.'

'Oh God, no, we can't let him do that,' Charlotte protested. 'I mean, I don't suppose we can take them all . . . How many are there?'

'Five, and don't worry, I'll rustle up enough takers, but I thought we could keep one for Chloe. The mother's part-Lab part-springer, I'm told, and the father is probably a neighbour's Border collie. Last time I saw them the pups were mostly black, apart from one which is a kind of caramel colour. She's very sweet, not at all manic like the rest, in fact she seemed quite timid, which was what made me think of Chloe.'

'She sounds perfect,' Charlotte swooned. 'Can you take a photo of her when you're over there and bring it for us to see?'

'Sure I can. What, you're thinking we should let Chloe decide for herself? That's not a bad idea.'

'No, I think it should be a surprise, from you, it's just that I'd like to see her myself. How are we going to stop the owner from doing anything drastic between now and the birthday?'

'Oh, don't worry. I'm intending to bring them back to town with me later and leave them over at Jessie Green's kennels until their new owners are ready for them.'

Charlotte couldn't have felt more excited. 'Which means I can go and have a peek before we take her home,' she smiled. Having been desperate for a puppy when she was small, she could hardly believe now that she hadn't come up with this idea for Chloe herself.

Clearly thrilled with how well his suggestion had gone down, Bob held out a hand to shake, then laughed delightedly when Charlotte got up to give him a hug. 'You're a genius,' she told him, 'and you really must be the one to give her the dog. She won't reject it, I promise you, she's too mad about animals for that, and it could prove exactly what's needed to help her stop associating you with her father. She'll associate you with the puppy instead.'

As some of the light faded from Bob's smile, Charlotte immediately regretted the mention of Chloe's father. 'I'm sorry this has been so difficult,' she said, hardly able to imagine how ghastly it must be to be mistaken for a paedophile.

'You think I'm thinking about myself?' he objected. 'No, no. I'm thinking about her and everything she's been through. I'd give anything, everything I own, to be able to make it all go away, to erase it completely from her memory so she'd never be affected by it again.'

Moved by his passion, Charlotte said softly, 'I know you would. I would too, if I could, but all we can do is love her and make her feel as safe as we can – I guess without trying to smother her, which I know I'm guilty of at times.'

'That's understandable,' he assured her. 'Anyone would do the same in your shoes, so you've nothing to chastise yourself for, or to feel guilty about.'

There was such meaning in his final words that Charlotte felt herself colouring, and looked down at her cup. She and Bob had never actually discussed what had happened during the weeks before she'd brought Chloe here. He knew all about it, of course, so he couldn't be in any doubt that guilt was a constant presence in her mind, but what he actually thought of what she'd done her mother had never told her, nor had Charlotte asked.

'I know you're finding it hard to settle,' he said gently, 'but it's going to take time, not only to get used to your new environment, which you're already doing very well at, but to put the past behind you.'

Charlotte's eyes came up to his. 'Do you think it's ever possible to do that?' she asked, genuinely wanting to know.

'What I think,' he said, wrapping her hand in both of his, 'is that we find a place for it under all the other rubbish we carry about in our heads and then we leave it there and try never to bring it up again. I know that's much easier said than done, especially while it's all still fresh in our minds, but over time you'll find that things can take on new perspectives and meanings that we're simply not capable of seeing when we're in the thick of it all.'

Charlotte's gaze drifted past the tourists, out across the terrace to the garden as she allowed herself to recall, albeit briefly, the night that had changed her and Chloe's lives for ever. The panic, the fear, the blood . . . Dear God, the blood! What had happened during those terrifying minutes seemed so disjointed and unreal now that it might have belonged to another lifetime. And yet the stark, unrelenting horror of it remained as clear in her mind as the feel of Chloe's limbs around her body as she'd run from the house. 'Do you think what I did was wrong?' she asked hoarsely.

Waiting for her to look at him again, he said, 'You did what you had to do at the time. If you hadn't

. . . Well, there's no point going into that because it's history and you're here now and this is where you're going to stay. Both of you, for as long as you want to, or perhaps I should say for as long as you can put up with us.'

The wryness of his tone made Charlotte smile, but she felt sure he was referring to how impatient, even difficult she could sometimes be with her mother. Never with him, of course, but she didn't have the same kind of issues with him. 'I don't ever want you to think that I'm not grateful for . . .' Her voice faded as he raised a hand.

'I don't need your gratitude,' he told her frankly. 'I'm doing it for Anna, because I love her, and for you and Chloe, because you're members of my family who I happen to be growing to love too. However, I don't mind admitting that it saddens me to see how hard you're finding it to be with your mother. She won't thank me for telling you this, but I'm going to anyway; she's been very hurt by some of the things you've said, and she's constantly struggling to find a way to reach you. It would please me a lot, Charlotte, if you tried to help her to do that, instead of always rebuffing her.'

Embarrassed by the reprimand, but in a way glad of it too, Charlotte said, 'I hope you understand that I don't mean to hurt her, it's just that . . . well, the words seem to come out of their own accord and sometimes it's like I want to hug her, but then I end up saying things that just push her away.'

He smiled, as though appreciating her honesty. 'Can I tell you what I think?' he asked.

She nodded. 'Please do.'

'What I think is that you're afraid to trust her, which isn't surprising given your history. That's not to say you don't want to, because I'm sure you do, but something inside just won't let you. There are those who'd say – Shelley would be one – that it's the small child inside you that's taking control. What I'll say is that Anna was your mother for the first three years of your life, always there, loving you, caring for you, being the centre of your world, but then she left you and though you know and understand why she did it, you're afraid now that she's going to let you down again.'

Though Charlotte didn't deny it, she wasn't sure that was the extent of it either. In fact she knew it wasn't. 'Would it shock you,' she said, 'if I told you I want to keep punishing her?' Embarrassed by the admission, she gave a scornful laugh. 'Listen to me. I'm a grown woman, with a child of my own, and a degree that should help me understand the workings of my own mind. You'd think by now I'd be over what happened all those years ago, but clearly something in me isn't, because even sitting here talking to you like this, I feel so angry with her, so wretched, so resentful even. I find myself thinking of all the time she's spent with you and your children . . . I didn't even realise that was an issue until the other day. It just came out of me. I even accused her of using Rick and Shelley to replace me and Hugo. Did she tell you that?'

He nodded silently, still holding her gaze.

'It's not as if I don't care for Rick and Shelley because I do, a lot,' she continued. 'I want to be a part of your family, more than anything, and most of the time I can feel it happening. Then suddenly, out of nowhere, all these horrible, negative feelings come over me and I just want to lash out . . .'

'And who better to lash out at than your mother?'

Charlotte looked at him helplessly.

'We've all done it,' he told her, 'and not many of us are proud of it after. Luckily, because they're our mothers they generally forgive us, and believe me, Anna's no different. She'll forgive you anything, but that's not really the point here, is it? What we have to do is persuade you, or that small person inside you, to forgive her for the past, and you know there's only one way of achieving that.'

With a groan Charlotte said, 'Counselling. Of course, but you have to understand why it's not a good idea, at least not yet.'

'I do, but I'd like you to think about it some more before you rule it out completely, for both your sakes. Anna's not going to be able to forgive herself until you lead the way, and frankly, she's suffered enough for a crime that wasn't hers. You both have. OK, I know you're going to say she could have come to find you long before she did, but as far as she knew you were happy with your adoptive parents. She didn't want to do anything to spoil that, and I daresay a part of her was afraid that if she tried to find a place in your life you'd reject her. You were with good people who'd provided you with a home and protected you at no small risk to themselves, given that the man who'd massacred your family, your mother's first husband, was still on the loose. As you know, he remained on the loose for many years and so remained a threat to you until he was finally shot and killed in Africa by men of his own type. When we received that news it was one of the most joyous and yet difficult days for Anna. His death freed her to come and find you, there were no obstacles now, but what if you didn't want her? She wasn't even sure if you knew about her. She had no idea what the rector and his wife had told you, and if you didn't know about Gavril Albescu and what he'd done to your real family, would it be fair to tell you?

'Believe me, she'd always agonised over these questions, but once he'd gone the agony got strangely worse. She truly didn't know what to do for the best, yet she couldn't do nothing, which was why, in the end, she contacted the old lady, her father's stepsister . . .'

'Helen,' Charlotte provided.

He nodded. 'Your mother had no idea if your great-aunt was in touch with you, at that point her call was no more than a first step towards finding out anything she could, whatever it might be. When she heard that you'd once written to the old lady asking if she had any news of her . . .' He broke into a smile. 'I don't believe I've ever seen anyone sob so hard with joy, and hope, and I guess still quite a lot of trepidation. But the important thing was you did know about her, and had even asked your great-aunt to let you know if she was ever in touch.'

Tilting his silvery head to one side, he looked intently into her eyes. 'I'm telling you all this to try and help you understand that you were never forgotten, and certainly never unwanted. Nor abandoned, at least not in her heart. At the time of the massacre she was too badly injured to be able to protect you herself, and by the time she was released from hospital almost a year had gone by. You, of all people, know how a small child can develop in that time, forming new attachments and even accepting a new name, which by then you had.'

Charlotte's eyes went down as she thought of Chloe and how different she was now to the little girl of a few months ago.

'You called yourself, *thought* of yourself as Alex,' he told her. 'You had an older sister who you'd become very attached to, and you were being taken care of by a woman you called Mummy.'

Almost flinching as she thought of how hard that must have been for her mother, Charlotte looked away.

'In spite of everything,' he continued, 'your mother would never have left you there if it hadn't been for Gavril Albescu's threats. The trouble was, he'd shown her in the most brutal of ways what he was capable of doing and she couldn't take the risk of him striking again, particularly as you were his main target.'

Charlotte's eyes returned briefly to his before she looked down at her hands again.

'You know all this, of course,' he said. 'You've been over it with your mother several times, and no doubt many more times in your own mind. And now, here we are, discussing it again. There's no harm in that, in fact it's a good thing, because contrary to what I said just now about burying the past, this is something that needs to come out, be understood and accepted so that you can put it back again and move on. What happened to Chloe is completely different. Nothing good could ever come of her seeing her father again, or of being made to relive what he put her through. Later, perhaps, she will need help, indeed we can be sure of it, but not right now. Now is about you and your mother and how you can properly find your way back to each other, so that you can feel able to trust her again, and she can believe that she is truly forgiven.'

Taking a deep breath, Charlotte sat back in her chair and blew it out slowly. In spite of having expected something like this when she came here today, she apparently hadn't been at all prepared for it. In fact, she felt so shaken that she had no idea what to say now, apart from offering a promise to try harder.

'And here she is, right on cue,' he smiled as his mobile vibrated. 'Your mother, but I'll let it go to messages.'

'You don't have to,' she told him.

'I know that, but as I'm sure she's calling to find out how you took the suggestion of a puppy, it can wait.'

Remembering the puppy, Charlotte started to smile. 'I wonder what she'll call it,' she said, glad of the change of subject. 'I think we should let her name it, don't you?'

He gave a playful wince as he said, 'I made that mistake with Rick many moons ago. He wanted to call his new dog Gordon after Speed Gordon, as the character was known here – you'd know him better as Flash Gordon. I guess one of the movies had just come out, or perhaps it was on TV, I only remember that it was all the rage at the time. Fortunately we persuaded him to choose Rosie in the end. It seemed to work better than Gordon for a female golden retriever.'

Charlotte gave a splutter of laughter. 'In Chloe's case I can see her going either for Diesel to honour Danni's horse, or maybe she'll choose Wick, after her Uncle Wick. It'll probably depend who's around when she first sees the dog. If you give it to her she might end up wanting to call it Bob.'

'Let's hope not,' he murmured as he checked who

was calling him now. Letting it go through to messages again, he said, 'Speaking of my son, have you been in touch with him this morning? I texted him earlier to ask him to ring, but I haven't heard back from him yet.'

'I believe he had an early meeting today, so maybe he's still in it.'

He nodded thoughtfully. Then, bringing his eyes back to hers, 'I'm going to be blunt again, if you don't mind,' he told her.

'Carry on,' she smiled, glancing at the tourists as they wandered past on their way out. They were still staring, and as she caught the look the woman was blazing her way her heart gave a thump of alarm. She felt convinced they were English and had recognised her.

Thank goodness Chloe wasn't there.

'I've noticed that you and Rick are becoming quite close,' Bob was saying. 'Not that I have any objection in principle, but if it's anything . . . I mean, if you think it might develop into something serious between you . . .'

Letting go of the unease the woman had left her with and almost wanting to smile at Bob's remark, Charlotte said, 'I promise you, ours is totally a brother–sister thing – friends too, because he kind of feels like the best friend I never had.'

Bob's colour deepened slightly as he took out his wallet. 'That's good,' he mumbled, 'because I wouldn't want you getting hurt, and I'm very much afraid it's about to happen to poor Katie.'

Charlotte swallowed her reply, deciding it would be wiser not to venture an opinion on that.

'Has he said anything to you about it?' he asked.

'Not really,' she lied.

He sighed gloomily and shook his head. 'I swear I don't know what goes on with him,' he said. 'I felt sure he'd put an offer on the house in Opito Bay. Still, what is it they say about taking horses to water?'

Feeling for him as they got up and walked back into the restaurant, Charlotte linked his arm as she said, 'We were supposed to be having cake.'

He looked at her in amazement. 'So we were,' he cried, 'and now here we are, all out of time. Can I take a rain check?'

'Of course. Whenever suits you. You know where to find me.'

Smiling, he gave her a hug, paid the bill and walked her to her car. 'Are you still doing the shoot with your mother at the end of the week?' he asked, as he held open the door for her to get in.

'Absolutely,' she confirmed.

'Good. It turned out well the last time, and it's great that you have something you can work on together, I mean that's apart from all the issues.'

In total agreement with that, Charlotte went up on tiptoe to kiss both his cheeks. 'Have a good time drilling and tugging,' she teased.

Smiling, he said, 'I will. And if you happen to hear from that son of mine before I do, tell him I'm getting tired of waiting for his call.'

It was just after eleven when Katie's mobile rang, and seeing it was Rick her insides gave a twisting lurch of relief, quickly followed by dread. She still wasn't entirely sure what she was going to say to him, but guessed that would largely depend on what he said to her.

'Hi,' she said quietly into the phone. If she was

nice to him, friendly and calm, the worst might not happen. 'Gemma said you were in a meeting when I rang . . .'

'It's finished now,' he said, 'but I'm afraid I can't stay long. I'm on my way downtown to an edit. Are you OK?'

Would he be rushing if he was speaking to Charlotte? 'Actually, I'm not sure,' she replied. 'I mean, well, I need you to tell me what's going on, and please don't say nothing, because I know you were with Charlotte on Saturday night.'

The line crackled, snatching parts of his reply. '. . . not a good time . . . this conversation. I'll be home at the weekend . . .'

'Did you spend the night with her?' she asked, closing her eyes and fists as though to fend off the reply.

'. . . at the bach, but . . . not what you're thinking.'

'So what should I be thinking?'

When he didn't answer right away she felt her world collapsing around her. Then she realised they might have been cut off.

'Are you still there?' she said.

'. . . I swear the last thing I want is to hurt you . . .'

'So you get it on with your own sister . . .'

'She's not my sister and . . . Katie . . . everything wrong. There's nothing going on . . .'

'Then tell me you're not about to finish with me. Tell me we're still getting married and that you want to find a house with me.'

There was no reply again, and unable to stand it she cried, 'You don't even have the courage to admit you don't love me any more. Maybe you never did. Maybe you're someone who just plays with people, who doesn't care about their feelings . . .'

'Of course I care . . . Listen, Katie, I need to see you. I'll be able to explain everything then . . .'

'I don't want to hear your explanations. I just want you to tell me we're still getting married.'

Agonising seconds passed.

'Rick, please,' she begged. 'Everything was all right between us until she came along . . .'

'No, Katie, it wasn't. She's just . . . to see that I can't go on lying to you, or to myself. I'm sorry, I really am . . .'

Panicked and desperate, she leapt to her feet. She couldn't let him do this, she just couldn't. 'I take it you know the truth about her,' she cried frantically, 'who she really is and what she's done?'

'Katie, calm down . . .'

'You might think you want to be with her, but I'm telling you she's not who she says she is. Neither of them are . . .'

'Katie, listen to me,' he broke in forcefully. 'You don't know what you're saying . . .'

'I know exactly what I'm saying. Her name isn't Charlotte Nicholls, it's Alexandra Lake. She was a social worker in England and . . .'

'Katie . . .'

'You have to listen to what I'm telling you, Rick. She stole that child. Do you hear me? Chloe isn't hers. She stole her and brought her here. Your parents are harbouring a criminal . . .' She stopped, having no idea what she thought he might say to that, but all that came from the other end was silence. *She shouldn't have said it. She'd gone too far.* But how could she pretend not to know now that she did? 'Are you still there?' she asked huskily.

'Yes, I'm here,' he replied. His tone was flat, hardly like him at all.

125

In the end, he said, 'I don't know how you've come to the conclusions you have, but they're wrong, Katie. OK? They're completely wrong.'

'What, like I was wrong about you wanting to end our relationship?'

'That's another matter altogether.'

'To you it might be, but to me it's all that matters, and if you think I'm just going to stand back and let you run off with someone who's not even who she says she is, who's actually *stolen a child*, then you need to think again,' and before he could say any more she ended the call.

Seconds later she was at the computer, shaking badly as she returned to the websites she'd found earlier. Her mobile rang, followed by her landline, but she ignored them both. She hated herself now for the way she'd begged him, and for how worthless he'd made her feel, but how much more was she going to hate herself if she called the number she was staring at on the screen?

It would be the early hours of the morning in England, but she was barely registering that. All she could make herself think about was whether she had the courage to go through with this. It was no way to get him back, but it was a way to make Charlotte Nicholls go.

What was the point of that if she, Katie, was going to be left with nothing anyway?

It took only moments for the familiar double ring of a British phone to come down the line, followed by a voice at the other end saying, 'Dean Valley Police, how can I help you?'

Reading from the screen in front of her Katie said hoarsely, 'Can I speak to Detective Chief Inspector

Terence Gould please. I have some information I need to pass on to him.' She could always hang up before she was connected and no one would ever have any idea she'd rung.

Chapter Eight

Bob was driving along Kapiro Road on his way back from the settlement when his mobile reconnected with the server and immediately rang. Seeing it was Rick he clicked on the hands-free ready to lay into him, but before he could utter a word Rick was saying, 'Dad! Where the hell have you been? I've been trying to get hold of you . . .'

'I should think so,' Bob retorted. 'It's hours since I left a message . . .'

'And I've been trying you all afternoon. But listen, are you driving? If you are, pull over now.'

Experiencing a beat of alarm, Bob swerved to the roadside, saying, 'Is it Anna? Please tell me . . .'

'No, it's not Anna. She's fine, as far as I know. It's Katie and the conversation I had with her earlier. Dad, she knows about Charlotte and Chloe.'

Bob went very still. His brain leapt into over-drive. 'How?' he asked grimly. 'And please don't tell me you told her.'

'Of course I didn't. What the hell do you take me for?'

'I guess we'll get on to that another time. For now, I need you to tell me exactly what she knows.'

'I'm afraid I have to say everything, because she accused Charlotte of stealing Chloe.'

128

'Oh Christ,' Bob muttered, feeling a horrible darkness coming over him.

'She also knows Charlotte's real name.'

'Charlotte *is* her real name,' Bob snapped.

'Not legally.'

'Yes, legally. Anyway, it's not the name that has to worry us. Has Katie told anyone else, do you know?'

'I've no idea. After she told me she put the phone down and I haven't been able to get her to answer it since.'

'Great,' Bob muttered. 'Have you spoken to Charlotte about this? And the answer to that better be no.'

'Of course it's a no. I knew I had to speak to you first, but you weren't answering your bloody phone.'

'I'm a dentist on Mondays,' Bob reminded him sharply. 'How long ago did you have this conversation with Katie?'

'Late morning, around eleven.'

Bob glanced at the time and groaned in dismay. It was after five now – Katie could have told anyone in the past six hours. 'OK, I want to hear everything that was said,' he barked, 'starting with how it even came up.'

After running through it, as accurately as he could remember, Rick said, 'I tried her again, only minutes ago, and she's still not answering. I've got no idea where she is, whether she's at home, or if she's gone to a friend's, but I think someone should go round to her flat to check if she's there.'

'You're right,' Bob retorted. 'First though, have you tried Sarah? There's a chance she could be there.'

'She isn't and Sarah hasn't heard from her all day.'

Still thinking fast, Bob said, 'Well at least we know

she hasn't told her. If she had Sarah would have been on the phone to Anna by now. So now the question is whether it should be me or Anna who goes round to the salon. Actually, not Anna. She doesn't need to know about this until she has to, and we're going to hope it never comes to that.'

'Then get Shelley to go. She knows everything, and she's always had a good relationship with Katie.'

'Mm,' Bob responded thoughtfully. 'You could be right. Do you know where your sister is today?'

'Not a clue, but at this time I'd say she's overseeing the kids' homework.'

'Of course. I'm about to pass the house, so I'll call in and get back to you when I have some news.'

'OK, I'll keep my mobile with me.'

'Before you go, we'll talk another time about why you've decided to break up with Katie, because it's obviously played a big part in this.'

After cutting the call off, he made a quick connection to the lodge.

'Hi darling,' Anna said, as she answered. 'Are you on your way back now?'

'Almost there,' he told her, 'but I'm popping into Shelley's for a few minutes.' Realising he'd probably have to stay with the kids while Shelley went into town, he added, 'Actually, it could be longer than that, there's some business to do with her trust we need to go over and I'm not sure how long it'll take.'

'OK, no problem. Call me when you're on your way and I'll make sure there's a beer waiting. Incidentally, Charlotte was very nice to me on the phone when I spoke to her earlier.'

Thankful Charlotte had no idea what was going on – yet – he said, 'Why the surprise? She doesn't always bite your head off.'

'No, but she doesn't always have coffee with you in the mornings either, so I'm guessing you had a little chat with her?'

'Well, we definitely didn't sit there in silence,' he admitted. 'What the . . . ?' he spluttered as Danni and her friend leapt their horses over a fence into the road.

'What is it?' Anna asked.

'My granddaughter's novel way of getting a horse out of a paddock,' he responded irritably. 'Anyway, I'll see you as soon as I get there, and don't forget that beer.'

Ten minutes later, after reading Danni the riot act for her reckless behaviour, then watching her and Melly gallop off in the direction of only they knew where, but at least it was his land, he was standing in Shelley's kitchen listening as she spoke to Katie on the phone.

Since Katie seemed to be doing most of the talking, he paced impatiently, still not sure how the hell he was going to troubleshoot this. In the end, Shelley said, 'OK, well I'd like to see you anyway. I can come round now . . . Of course. I understand how upset you are, I would be too . . .'

'*Shelley*,' Bob hissed fiercely.

Shelley held up a hand. 'I'm sure we can sort things out. I'll be speaking to Rick later, but I really need to talk to you about what you . . .' Her eyes went to her father as she listened to Katie trying to speak through her sobs. 'Listen, I'm going to get into the car now and come to you,' she said in her gently forceful way. 'I don't think you should be on your own and . . . OK, that's fine. I'll be there in about twenty minutes.'

'So has she told anyone?' Bob demanded as Shelley hung up.

131

'I'm not sure. She's not making much sense at the moment. I think she's probably been drinking, and she's just asked me to bring some wine.'

Bob groaned. 'If she's drunk you need to sober her up, not give her any more.'

'Of course. Will you watch Craig? He's upstairs doing his homework. Danni's finished hers and has gone down to the bach with Melly, so you don't need to worry about her.'

Bob's expression told Shelley he disagreed. 'She's a danger to herself, the way she rides that horse.'

'She knows what she's doing, and I trust Diesel. Now, Phil's not due home for at least an hour, so if you want to take Craig to the lodge with you don't forget to leave a note or send a text so Phil will know where he is.'

'OK. Call me when you're on your way back, and whatever you do, don't say anything to inflame the situation.'

'Dad, this is me you're talking to. The hotheads belong to you and Rick, remember?'

With a grudging smile, Bob pulled her into an embrace. 'Thanks for doing this,' he said, as she took her keys from a hook. 'I don't know how we're going to sort it out, I really don't, but there must be a way.'

Shelley looked at him in amazement. 'Well, I think we should start by persuading her she's wrong, don't you?' she replied.

Bob frowned.

'Charlotte didn't steal Chloe,' she reminded him, 'she rescued her,' and grabbing her handbag she left him standing in the kitchen, feeling slightly foolish for not having remembered that himself.

* * *

132

Charlotte was laughing and waving from the beach as Chloe shrieked with the delight of being swum around the bay on Diesel's back. Danni was sitting behind her, holding her tightly, while Melly with her own horse, Maybelle, watched from the shore. Maybelle wasn't keen on water, but Diesel loved it – almost as much as he seemed to love rearing and spilling his riders into the waves.

As Chloe and Danni plunged in for the second time and Chloe, in her rubber ring and armbands, bobbed about on the surface, spluttering and gasping and clearly loving every minute, Charlotte could feel her heart overflowing with pride. She was so brave, so ready for adventure, and the way Danni included her in the fun, and Melly fussed over her too, made Charlotte want to lavish them with every last one of their heart's desires. There weren't many girls their age who'd take so much trouble with a small child, but it seemed they got as much pleasure out of Chloe's excitement as Chloe got out of being with them.

'They're getting back on,' Melly shouted, her sunny face flushed with laughter.

Charlotte waved to Chloe again and shouted, 'Bravo!' as Chloe turned to make sure she was watching. 'Are you staying for the cook-up?' she asked Melly.

'You bet,' Melly replied. 'We made some harpoons, did you see them?'

'I did,' Charlotte responded wryly as she glanced at the roughly sharpened sticks propped up against the rowing boat. 'So, mullet for supper, if our fishing skills are up to it, and let me see . . . French fries or potato salad?'

'Definitely fries,' Melly twinkled. 'Oh look, he's tossed them again.'

As Charlotte laughed and Chloe screeched with joy, the landline started ringing inside the bach. Leaving them to it, Charlotte ran back over the bridge to find out who it was. 'Hello?' she panted breathlessly into the receiver, certain it would be her mother or Shelley at this time of day.

'Hi you, it's me,' Rick told her. 'You sound rushed.'

'Had to run in from the beach,' she explained, going to the freezer to take out some fries. 'Diesel keeps giving Danni and Chloe a dunking, so a bit of hilarity going on in our part of the bay. How are you? Have you spoken to your dad? He was trying to get hold of you earlier.'

'Yeah, I spoke to him on his way back from the settlement.'

'So I guess he gave you a bit of a roasting about the house on Opito Bay?'

'Actually, he still hasn't quite got there yet, but I'm sure he will. Meantime, I managed to distract him with a couple of other issues I needed to discuss with him. Have you seen him today?'

'Not since we had coffee this morning. Are you OK? You sound a bit . . . I'm not sure, worried, down, not your usual self anyway.'

'No, I'm great. Just been a busy day.'

'Have you seen Hamish?'

'Sure. He's here, well, in his own office actually, but we've been at a couple of meetings together today.'

'And is he over the moon that you're on your way out?'

To her surprise there wasn't much of a smile in his voice as he said, 'He will be when I've completed the route. I'm not sure when that's going to be, exactly, but hopefully soon.'

Sensing that he didn't want to be pushed any further, she set the oven to warm and went back to the door to check on progress in the bay. 'We're having a cook-up tonight,' she told him, enjoying the spectacle of Diesel and his riders emerging from the waves dripping and glistening in the evening sun, while the promenading ducks scurried to get out of the way. 'Red mullet with French fries, and no doubt a few pipis will find their way into the mix. I'm getting quite good at filleting fish now, by the way. Not so hot on catching them with spears, but as you know, Danni's a natural so I'm sure we won't go hungry.'

'That's good to hear,' he commented, 'because we definitely wouldn't want that.'

Puzzled by how unlike himself he sounded, and wondering if in fact he did want to talk, she said, 'Are you sure you're all right? You know you can tell me anything.'

This time there was a note of humour in his voice as he replied, 'I thought I'd already done that.'

She smiled. 'So no more secrets?'

Before he could answer she gasped as Chloe crept up behind her and wrapped her wet body round her legs. 'You little minx,' she laughed, as Chloe giggled and shivered. 'Come on, into the bath with you. Danni too, wherever she is.'

'You sound busy,' Rick told her, 'so I'd best let you go.'

'Hang on, just a minute, you must have called for a reason. Danni, sweetheart, could you go and run the bath,' she added, as a very wet and sandy Danni appeared on Diesel's back in the doorway.

'I just wanted to check in with you,' he said, 'make sure life was good and you're both OK.'

135

Charlotte wrinkled her nose, then out of nowhere an image of the staring woman at the Pear Tree flashed in her mind and her heart skipped a beat. 'Is there something you're not telling me?' she asked, feeling her throat turning dry.

Sounding surprised he said, 'I don't think so. No, everything's good here, just a bit tired as I said, and probably in need of a drink. Give that little minx a hug from me, won't you, and tell her I'll be expecting her to catch a mullet for me when I'm back at the weekend.'

'So you're coming this weekend?'

'That's the intention.'

'To speak to Katie?'

'Probably. Yes, almost certainly.'

'But not until you've told your dad? Chloe, Chloe, no,' she gasped, dashing forward as Chloe tried to clamber into the bath on her own.

Chloe immediately shrank back, shielding her head with her hands.

'It's OK, I've got her,' Danni said, embracing her.

'Not pull my hair, not pull my hair,' Chloe cried in a panic.

'It's OK, it's OK,' Charlotte soothed. To Rick she said, 'Sorry, I have to go,' and dropping the phone on the floor she scooped Chloe into her arms. 'Ssh, ssh, there, there,' she whispered, as Chloe shook and sobbed and continued to clutch her head. 'I'm sorry, sweetheart, I didn't mean to make you jump. I was just afraid you were going to fall.'

'Not pull my hair,' Chloe whimpered.

'No, of course not, my darling. I'd never pull your hair, you know that.'

'Why does she think you're going to pull her hair?' Danni asked in a whisper.

Charlotte shook her head briefly, and holding Chloe's face to her own she said, 'I think Chloe Nicholls is a big brave girl who can catch fish with a stick that Mummy can cook. What do you think, Danni?'

'I know she can,' Danni loyally chimed in, 'because Chloe's really good at fishing and I think we should do a pipi dance too, don't you, Melly?'

Charlotte and Chloe both looked round to find Melly standing in the doorway.

'Definitely we should,' Melly confirmed. 'I've collected some twigs and things to build a fire, but I'm going to need some help finding more.'

Chloe's eyes were suddenly rounding with zeal. 'I can find sticks,' she said, struggling to get down.

'You need to have a bath and get dry first,' Charlotte reminded her.

'I have to bath first,' Chloe told Melly.

'Come on, I'll get in with you,' Danni said, starting to strip off her swimsuit.

All of a sudden Chloe dashed out of the bathroom, and returned a moment later clutching Boots. After setting him down on a chair, she looked up at Charlotte and for one ludicrous moment Charlotte thought she herself was going to cry. She knew Boots was intended to look over Chloe and keep her safe, though of course Chloe would never be able to articulate that. It was just something she did when she felt insecure, as though Boots could help her feel brave, and Charlotte couldn't be in any doubt that he did.

'There you go,' Charlotte said, lifting her gently into the water. 'Is it warm enough?'

Chloe nodded and broke into a happy grin as Danni climbed in after her.

Relieved by how quickly her little angel could bounce back after a frightening brush with her past, Charlotte decided to leave them to it for now and returned to the kitchen. 'Do you want to give me a hand?' she asked Melly who followed her out. 'Actually, we need to feed the ducks. Listen to them out there. Chloe! Is it all right if Melly feeds the ducks for us tonight?'

'Yes,' Chloe called back, 'but make sure they're not too greedy.'

Exchanging a smile with Melly, Charlotte handed her the canister of pellets and started to pile up a tray ready to take down to the beach. Then deciding she could do with a drink, she went to the fridge and took out a bottle of wine. She was still baffled by the oddness of Rick's call, which hadn't seemed to have any point to it, and seeing Chloe cowering in fear the way she had was upsetting her a lot. She had no idea what had happened at bathtime when Chloe had been with her father, but whatever it was, it must have been awful for her to have reacted the way she had when Charlotte had shouted.

'Not pull my hair, not pull my hair.'

It wasn't the first time it had happened. Charlotte had seen it once before when she'd spoken sharply to Chloe about something else – she couldn't even remember what it was now – but they'd been in the bathroom at the time and Chloe had cowered away from her then, clutching her head and begging her not to pull her hair.

Taking a generous sip of Pinot Gris, Charlotte went to stand in the doorway to stare out at the bay. She needed to breathe in the air, to reassure herself that they were as far from that world now as it was possible to get and that everything really was working out well. She didn't want to believe that Chloe's demons had followed them here, but of course they had, because there was never any escaping what went on in the mind.

The image of the woman at the Pear Tree flashed in front of her again, the repeated glances, the accusing look as she'd left. It made Charlotte's heart lurch to recall it. People were so quick to judge. They read things in papers or saw them on TV and without any knowledge of the person concerned, or of the circumstances leading up to what had happened, they were ready to condemn.

She used to be the same before the press and public had turned on her. Now she knew better than to take anything at face value; there were almost always more sides to a story than most got to see, and even her own perceptions of what had happened to her and Chloe could change by the day.

'Mummy!' Chloe shouted.

Going to the bathroom and finding Chloe's impish face almost disappearing under a pink-and-blue spotted shower cap and an outsize pair of swimming goggles, Charlotte burst out laughing. 'What a picture,' she declared.

'I'm being you,' Chloe giggled.

'I can see that,' and going to sit on Boots's chair, careful to put the bear on her lap, she said, 'And look at all those bubbles. Are there any left in the bottle?'

'Some,' Danni replied, 'but I kind of dropped it in the water.'

'We can put my goggles on Boots,' Chloe told her.

'I think we probably could,' Charlotte agreed, 'if we knew where they were. We've searched high and low, but I don't know where we put them, so I guess we'll have to buy some more next time we're at the store.'

'I expect I've got some you can have,' Danni told her. 'I've got lots at home.'

Seeming to like the idea, Chloe began asking her what colours they were while Charlotte listened to her chatter, loving how easily and fluently she spoke now, when it wasn't so very long ago that she would hardly speak at all. What conversations had she ever had with her real mother, Charlotte often wondered. None that Charlotte had ever witnessed. In fact, the poor woman had been so strange – schizophrenic, it had turned out – that it was doubtful she'd ever had a coherent conversation with anyone at all until she, Charlotte, had come along.

Bob was getting out of his car as Shelley came out of the house to greet him.

'Bye Grandpa, see you tomorrow,' Craig shouted, as he ran inside.

'Bye Champ,' Bob called after him. He used to call him Tiger, but not since Charlotte and Chloe had arrived. '*No, no, not Tiger,*' Chloe had sobbed the first time he'd said it, and he knew now that this one innocent mistake was what had caused her to associate him with her father. 'So? What did she say?' he asked Shelley, referring to Katie.

Shelley looked vaguely glassy-eyed in the twilight and unusually pale. 'She's adamant she hasn't told anyone,' she replied.

'Do you believe her?'

She sighed. 'I'm not sure. Part of me does, but then another part . . .' She shook her head helplessly. 'She's really cut up over Rick, I can tell you that much. What's more, she's convinced he's involved with Charlotte. She says she saw them together on Saturday night.'

Bob's jaw tightened. 'Do *you* think he's involved with Charlotte?' he demanded, almost angrily.

Shelley shrugged. 'I've no idea, but the fact that she thinks he is is what's got us to where we are now.'

His face remained taut. 'So how did she come up with her amazing conclusion?'

'About Charlotte and Chloe? How do you think? She went online and eventually found her way to the right websites.'

'But what made her look in the first place? OK, she thinks Charlotte's involved with Rick, but to go from that to launching a major Internet search . . .'

'According to her she always knew "something wasn't right", as far as Charlotte's concerned, so she Googled what she knew about her which I think only amounted to where she comes from. But apparently it was enough to get her on to the local paper's website and from there she didn't really need to take the short step to the nationals, though apparently she did.'

His eyes were glinting fiercely. 'So what did you tell her?'

'Obviously that she was wrong in her assumptions, but I'm afraid she wasn't buying it. She kept saying, "It's right there on the screen in front of you, look for yourself and tell me if you can read it any other way?"'

'And you said what?'

'That I didn't need to look, because I know everything I need to know and that I'm sorry I can't tell her any more at this stage.'

'That was it?'

'More or less, apart from promising to speak to Rick to find out what's really going on with him.'

Bob grunted his annoyance. 'Good luck with that,' he muttered. 'For the record, I spoke to Charlotte today and she says there's nothing between them – why are you looking at me like that?'

'What made you bring it up with Charlotte?' she cried, amazed at his presumption.

'Well, Katie's got a point, Rick and Charlotte do seem very close, and the way he just dismissed the house on Opito Bay then apparently went straight to the bach . . . In Katie's shoes I might be thinking the same way.'

'But you're not now?'

'Not really. I didn't have any reason to doubt Charlotte.'

'And Katie says Rick's denying it too, but obviously she doesn't believe him, because she can't see why else he would be ending their relationship.'

Bob's expression turned flinty. 'Why else indeed?' he growled. 'Maybe you can throw some light on it.'

'Not until I've spoken to him, and even then, he doesn't have to tell me if he doesn't want to. He's a grown man, Dad, with every right to start and end relationships whenever he pleases . . .'

'What's going on between them isn't really the main issue, is it?' Bob cut in snappishly. 'How did you leave it with her?'

'That I'd call round again after I've spoken to Rick.'

'And meantime she's going to do what, exactly?'

'About Charlotte, you mean? I'm hoping nothing, but I didn't press for a promise to keep things to herself. I thought if I did that I'd end up making it seem as though she was right and we really did have something to hide.'

Turning away, Bob stared down through the trees to where the lights of the lodge were twinkling in the distance. In his mind's eye he could see Anna getting the supper ready, probably glancing at the TV or singing along with some music, completely oblivious to the disaster heading their way – a disaster he absolutely had to find a way to avert. 'OK,' he said in the end, 'you did your best and it sounds, for the moment, as though it's paid off. What'll happen if Rick really does end the relationship . . . Well, I guess we'll have to cross that bridge when we come to it.'

'And in the meantime we'll hope that Katie was being truthful when she told me that she hasn't spoken to anyone else about it.'

Bob eyed her meaningfully. 'Indeed,' he responded shortly, and after kissing her goodbye, he got into his car to drive back down to the lodge.

Katie had turned the computer off now and was lying on the bed, exhausted, still half-drunk and heavy with despair. She'd hoped to hear from Rick after Shelley had left, but he hadn't rung, or emailed, or even sent a text. Maybe Shelley hadn't spoken to him yet. She wondered if he'd rung Charlotte today, and the burn of jealousy was so intense she could hardly bear it.

Turning her face into the pillow, she sobbed and begged Rick to ring. 'Please God, please, please, please, don't let this be happening.' It hurt so much, more than anything she'd ever felt before. It seared and twisted through her, tore at her heart and wrenched her insides so viciously it made her want to throw up. It couldn't be over between them, it just couldn't. They were getting married. She'd chosen the invitations, the dress, the venue for the reception. He didn't know any of that, but maybe if she told him he'd understand just how much he meant to her. He wasn't a cruel man, he wouldn't want her to be suffering like this, so maybe she should call him now and tell him she was sorry for everything she'd said, that she loved him more than anything and that if he said he wasn't involved with Charlotte then she believed him.

That was what he'd said, that he'd spent the night at the bach, but 'it's not what you're thinking.' It could have been innocent. What she'd seen on the beach . . . They hadn't actually kissed, or lain down together, or even touched in a particularly intimate way. All of that was in her mind. She'd imagined it, tormented herself with it, over and over, but for all she knew none of it was real. 'She's not my sister,' he'd reminded her. 'There's nothing going on.' But later he'd said, 'She got me to see that I can't go on lying to you, or to myself.' What else could that mean but that Charlotte Nicholls had convinced him he was living a lie, that he shouldn't be with her, Katie, and why would Charlotte do that if she didn't want him herself?

She hadn't told Shelley about her call to Detective Chief Inspector Gould of the Dean Valley Police, mainly because there wasn't really anything to tell. At four in the morning, British time, the detective hadn't been at his desk, and because it was still Sunday over there she didn't suppose he was going into work today. She'd left a message with her name and number and why she was calling, but whether or not she'd ever hear back she had no idea.

If she did and they took her seriously, it would

be the end of Charlotte Nicholls, and though Katie realised that it would be the end for her too, at least if she couldn't have Rick then Charlotte couldn't either.

How much better would that make her feel?

It wouldn't, not at all, but on the other hand could she really sit here knowing the truth of what Charlotte had done and do nothing about it?

Chapter Nine

It was turning into a strange sort of a week. The weather wasn't helping much, with sudden violent downpours pelting the landscape followed by an atmosphere that felt even more belligerently stifling than before. Rick was behaving oddly too, calling randomly with nothing particular to say other than to tell her about an amusing incident at the office, or what he thought of something in the news. He'd never done that before, so Charlotte couldn't think why he was doing it now.

'Anything exciting going down your end?' he'd asked a couple of times, tossing it in like an afterthought, while managing to land her with the feeling that he was expecting more of an answer than she could give.

'Not especially,' she'd tell him, since she couldn't imagine he'd be interested to hear that she'd covered for the receptionist at Dr Polly's surgery, as the children called it, on Tuesday. She didn't mention anything about Polly chasing her up for Chloe's medical records either, because why would he want to know about that? Thankfully, Polly understood that Chloe's old GP had been involved in the same paedophile ring as Chloe's father and consequently his surgery had been shut down, which was the reason for the delay and confusion.

'Heaven only knows what's happened to the files,' Charlotte had grumbled. 'Obviously they must be somewhere so I'm sure we'll track them down eventually.'

Luckily Chloe didn't have any pre-existing conditions, and enjoyed good health, so Polly wasn't unduly worried. However the vaccination records were important, as was the Personal Child Health Record, aka the NHS Red Book, charting Chloe's development. Charlotte really ought to have had that, but she'd never been able to get it from Chloe's father.

There was no chance at all of that now, which Polly understood, so she no longer pressed for it, only the official GP records.

Like Rick, Shelley didn't seem quite herself this week either, Charlotte had noticed when they'd met for a coffee after yoga on Wednesday. She was unusually distracted, as though worried about something, but when Charlotte voiced her concern Shelley insisted she was fine.

'Just didn't sleep all that well last night,' she smiled. 'It happens to me sometimes. I go through periods of insomnia that drive poor Phil mad, especially when he has to be up early.'

Since it was a reasonable explanation, Charlotte had changed the subject, saying, 'Have you seen anything of Katie lately?'

Shelley looked surprised. 'Not for a couple of days. Why? Have you?'

'No, not at all, but that's not unusual, we don't often meet up.'

Trying to sound casual and not quite pulling it off, Shelley asked, 'Has Rick mentioned anything to you about her?'

Since Charlotte didn't want to break Rick's confidence, but nor did she want to lie to his sister, she hedged by saying, 'I think they might be having a few issues at the moment.'

Shelley's expression turned wry as she replied, 'Well, that's definitely one way of putting it. Poor Katie's beside herself, or she was when I saw her on Monday. I promised to try and talk to Rick, to see if I can make some sense of what's going on with him, but when I rang last night all he'd say to me was that he's coming back at the weekend and he'll speak to Katie then. The big question is, what, or who is he going to speak to her about?'

Realising Shelley was trying to probe into her own relationship with Rick, Charlotte said, 'I'm incredibly fond of your brother, and I like to think he feels the same about me, but as far as anything of a romantic nature goes that's definitely not us.'

Shelley blushed slightly as she smiled. 'I was that transparent?'

Charlotte's eyes twinkled as she considered it. 'Well, there's subtle and there's not, and you were kind of . . . not.'

Shelley laughed. 'Well, that's me told,' she retorted, clearly enjoying the bluntness. Then, after sipping her coffee, 'So he isn't going to break up with her for you?'

'Absolutely not. Apart from being related to one another, sort of, which would make it a bit weird, we're definitely not each other's types.'

'Mm,' Shelley murmured thoughtfully, 'I'm afraid he's decided that Katie isn't his type either. The problem is she's really set on marrying him, and I'm not sure what she'll do if he lets her down.'

'Do? In what way?'

Shelley sighed. 'I guess the only one who can answer that is Katie,' she replied, 'but at least when I pop into the salon later I can assure her there's nothing going on between you and Rick.'

Startled, Charlotte said, 'Why, did she think there was? My God, that's terrible if she did.'

Shelley smiled reassuringly. 'Whatever she may have thought, there's no reason for her to fear it now, is there, which is very good news.'

Afterwards Charlotte had spent the rest of the day organising her mother's samples, portfolios and collection of weird and wonderful accessories she kept for shoots into the large estate car Anna used for business, while Anna herself spent the afternoon at the Kauri Cliffs hotel on a final recce with the client. Though Anna called often there was no opportunity to discuss any personal or family issues; this was a time for Anna's work to come first, and Charlotte could tell from her mother's voice that her excitement – and tension – was building. She absolutely loved being at the heart of a shoot, getting right into the demands of framing and styling the shots as she worked with designers and decorators to create visual masterpieces from the client's sumptuously expensive furniture and homewares. From the two previous occasions when Charlotte had assisted her she'd been left in no doubt that her mother was really very good at what she did. She was also extremely popular with her clients, as well as the crews, who seemed to appreciate her as much for the air of fun she brought to proceedings as for her readiness to consider and often act upon other people's ideas. She wasn't someone who was in any way troubled by the petty or querulous scrabblings of an ego; she was, in her words, just an ordinary woman who still felt surprised and a bit baffled by being involved in such a rewardingly creative process.

It was going to be an enjoyable, though hectic couple of days, Charlotte was thinking as she collected Chloe from Aroha just after four on Wednesday afternoon and went on to Countdown to pick up a few things for dinner. Chloe was full of a new Maori song she'd learned that day, singing it over and over to Boots and Charlotte and even, shyly, to the woman at the checkout.

Laughing, the woman said, 'She's adorable.'

'Thank you,' Charlotte smiled, and steering the trundler out to the car park she settled Chloe and Boots in the back seat before loading the groceries into the boot.

As they turned on to the peninsula heading for home, she decided to drop in on Grant and Polly to check whether the weekend's sleepover was still on.

'It sure is,' Grant assured her, wiping his oily hands on his overalls as he came out from under the trailer he was repairing. 'The weather might have settled down by then, but if it doesn't we'll find plenty of other stuff to do. Thrilled to bits Chloe's coming,' he added, directing his words to Charlotte in a way Chloe could hear.

'She's really looking forward to it, aren't you darling?' Charlotte asked, turning to make sure Chloe was listening.

With a giant yawn Chloe nodded, up and down, up and down, but she didn't look at Grant.

'We're going to try to catch some snapper for the barbie,' Charlotte told him, 'and we'll have our chilly bin full of drinks. I'm thinking of bringing a salad of some sort and I expect Chloe will make some cupcakes.'

'Wow. I've heard Chloe's cupcakes are the business,' Grant responded heartily, 'so I'll look forward to a couple of those.'

Longing for the day Chloe would feel brave enough to look at him, Charlotte said softly, 'Sorry, I promise it'll get better.'

Waving a dismissive hand he said, 'I was going to call you later anyway. Did you see the notice in *The Bay Chronicle* about the Kerikeri Players looking for new talent? I'm sure I remember you telling me once that you used to do some theatre back in England.'

'I did,' Charlotte agreed, feeling the eagerness for it lighting her up, 'only amateur productions, but I loved it and I've been meaning to get in touch with the Players.'

'Go for it,' he told her, slapping the side of her car. 'I might even have to join up myself. Now, you watch how you go, you girls, give me a call if there's anything you need, and watch out for those pesky caterpillars. You've heard about them, I take it.'

'You mean the ones with poisonous spines?' Charlotte replied with a shiver. 'Have they turned up in Kerikeri now?'

'Old Willard's farm. The biosecurity guys have just confirmed it. Probably won't be any down your way, but better make sure little Chloe doesn't go hunting for one to put it in a jar.'

Charlotte and Chloe were back on the road heading

for home before Chloe said, 'Mustn't pick up cater-pillars. They're poison.'

'That's right, but we don't like caterpillars very much anyway, do we?'

'No. Only butterflies. They come after caterpillars. Mummy?'

'Yes?'

'Can we watch *Tiki Tour* when we get home, please?'

'Of course we can.'

'I like *Tiki Tour*, it's one of my favourites.'

'I know you do.'

'They jumped in muddy puddles the last time. I wish I could jump in a muddy puddle.'

Smiling, Charlotte said, 'So is that going to be your birthday wish?'

'No!' Chloe shouted with a grin. 'For my birthday I'm going to wish . . . Um . . . I'm going to wish that I could go swimming every day with Diesel and Danni.'

'Even in the rain?'

'Yes, even in the rain.' She took a rapid breath. 'Are you going to work with Nanna tomorrow?'

'Well remembered, yes I am, so Auntie Shelley will be coming to pick you up from Aroha in the afternoon to take you to her house for tea. I expect you'll like that, won't you?'

'Yes,' Chloe answered obediently. However, she fell silent until finally saying, 'Will you come to pick me up after?'

'Of course I will,' Charlotte assured her warmly. 'I'm just going to be a bit late back with Nanna to make it in time for Aroha, that's all. But I'll definitely come to Auntie Shelley's for you. You don't mind Auntie Shelley picking you up, do you?'

Chloe lifted Boots to her face. 'I like it when you come,' she murmured.

Feeling terrible and torn, Charlotte said, 'I know you do, sweetheart, but it's only this once and you'll be able to show Auntie Shelley all the things you've made during the day. Hang on, let me answer this,' and clicking on her mobile she said, 'Hi, Charlotte speaking.'

'Charlotte, it's Polly,' the voice at the other end announced. 'I've just been talking to Grant and he tells me you might be interested in joining the Kerikeri Players.'

Amused by how quickly news got round, Charlotte said, 'I am. In fact, I was thinking about giving them a call as soon as I get home.'

'Great, because I've been thinking about joining too, so I was wondering if you felt like going to see them together.'

'I'd love that,' Charlotte cried happily. 'Shall I set it up? I'm driving at the moment . . .'

'Don't worry, I'm still at the surgery so I'll do it. Any day next week you can't make?'

'Not that I can think of. Just let me know when it works for everyone else and I'll be there.'

As she rang off Charlotte glanced in the rear-view mirror to check on Chloe, and finding her gazing drowsily out of the window she allowed herself a moment to revisit the memories of the theatre days that had come swimming to the front of her mind. She really had loved running the Mulgrove group, it had provided such a stimulating, energising contrast to the challenges she'd dealt with in her everyday life. They'd been a tight-knit bunch, always rooting for each other and ready to try out new things. She still received the odd email from some of the cast and crew who were old friends and neighbours, though there hadn't been any word the last time she'd checked. Or maybe there had and she hadn't noticed it amongst all the junk – and the shock of hearing from Anthony. It was at the opening night of one of her shows that she'd first met him. He'd come with his sister and brother-in-law, and she could only wish now that she'd taken more notice when they'd been introduced after the performance. She guessed she'd been distracted by several ovations, and given that she'd still been pretty mad about Jason at the time, she hadn't been likely to either notice or feel a romantic interest in anyone else.

She wondered where Anthony was now, what he was doing. Had he given up on hearing back from her yet, or was he still hoping? Just over two weeks had gone by since he'd sent his email – only days since she'd read it – so he might still be hoping. More likely he'd written her off and was getting on with his travel plans.

Distracted by Chloe yawning behind her, she glanced in the mirror again and said, 'So it's *Tiki Tour* when we get home?'

Chloe nodded, and Charlotte smiled as she heard her whispering, '*Pak dakeha, pak dakeha.*'

'Can you remember what that means?' she asked.

Chloe giggled. 'Hairy faces,' she answered.

'Very good. And why do we say hairy faces?'

'Um. I forget.'

'It's what Maori people called English people, isn't it, because English people were the settlers and they row backwards and the Maoris row forwards. So when the settlers came to New Zealand they had their backs to the land, so the Maoris thought they had hairy faces.'

'You have a hairy face,' Chloe cried wickedly.

Realising it was because she had her back to her, Charlotte said, 'I'll give you what for when we get home.'

Chloe gave a noisy, cheesy sort of chuckle then suddenly shouted, 'Blueberries,' as they passed a fresh-fruit stall on the roadside. 'And kiwis and pom'granate.'

'I think they had some peaches too.'

'I like peaches.'

'I know you do, so shall we turn around and get some?'

'Yes!' Chloe cheered. 'And one for Boots too.'

As they drove back to the stall with its large blue canopy and open-top honesty box, Charlotte could feel the pleasure of being in their new world spreading even deeper roots. She just needed to remember, when she was feeling fretful or home-sick for England, that four months really wasn't very long to become established in a new place. She needed to give it more time and maybe make more of an effort. Joining the Kerikeri Players was going to be a good start, and it shouldn't be too long now before it became possible for her to begin looking for a full-time job, and maybe a small house close to town for her and Chloe. They'd miss the bay, of course, especially their magical little cove, but they'd be visiting Bob and Anna at Te Puna all the time, and there would be lots of other adventures waiting for them in their new surroundings as well as all kinds of other people to meet.

All that really mattered, though, was that they were together.

* * *

'Have you seen or spoken to Katie today?' Bob asked Shelley as she stopped her car next to the Shiraz vineyard on Te Puna where he was testing the grapes.

'Yes and no,' she replied. 'I dropped by the salon, but she wasn't there, and when I rang her flat to ask if it was OK to go up she told me she was on her way out and didn't have time to stop.'

Bob's eyes were narrowed against a dazzling breakthrough of sunlight. Out in the bay a family of dolphins were putting on a playful display, while an attending retinue of terns and shags provided a restless aerial audience. 'Did you get the impression she's avoiding you?' he said.

'Just a bit,' she replied drily. 'She hesitated when I told her I'd spoken to Rick, but then said she was sorry but it was too late.'

Bob's expression darkened. 'I don't like the sound of that.'

'I can't say I did either, but it was all I could get out of her. I was wondering if she might have confided anything in Sarah. I think she was over there last night . . .'

'If she had, Sarah would have been on the phone to Anna by now.'

'It might be worth asking though.'

He shot her a look. 'Exactly how do you propose I phrase it' he enquired, 'without actually telling Sarah, or Anna, that we're afraid Katie might have contacted someone, i.e. the police, about Charlotte?'

At a loss, Shelley could only shrug. 'I rang Rick a few minutes ago to ask him to call Katie, but he said he doesn't want to get into anything with her until he comes home at the weekend. I couldn't argue because he was on his way into a meeting so he had to ring off.'

Bob's expression was turning grimmer than ever. 'I just hope he doesn't find an excuse not to come,' he growled. 'If he does I'll be flying to Auckland to get him myself.'

'I'm sure he won't put it off,' Shelley responded loyally. 'I think he's genuinely busy and it's not as though he doesn't care about Katie, even if their relationship isn't in a good place. And Katie's obviously playing games of some sort . . .'

Bob's eyes flashed sharply to hers. 'With other people's lives,' he stated angrily.

Unable to argue with that, Shelley said, 'I'm sorry, I have to go now. If she calls me, or if I hear from Rick I'll get in touch right away,' and putting the car back in gear she continued on down the drive.

Grant was still working on his trailer when his mobile rang again. Grumbling irritably to himself, he used a rag to wipe his hands as he returned to the phone. 'So what did you forget?' he asked, assuming it was Polly ringing back about something or other.

'Grant, it's Wex here,' his sergeant told him.

'Oh, mate, sorry, I was thinking you were the wife. What can I do for you?'

Wexley Harris's voice was unusually sombre as he said, 'You know the Reeves family pretty well, don't you?'

Surprised and puzzled, Grant said, 'I guess so. Why are you asking?'

'It's about Anna Reeves's daughter, Charlotte. Do you know her too?'

'Sure I do. She was just here, as a matter of fact. What's going on, Wex?' His blood turned suddenly cold. 'Jesus Christ, don't tell me there's been an accident.'

'No, no, nothing like that,' his boss assured him. 'I've had a call from CIB in Auckland . . .'

More baffled than ever, Grant said incredulously, 'Criminal Investigation Branch?'

'That's who they were last time I checked.'

'What do they want?'

Taking a breath, Wexley said, 'I'm going right out on a limb here, mate, I want you to know that, but we've known each other a lot of years. I guess I can trust you to keep what I'm about to tell you to yourself, at least until we've had a chance to discuss it here, at the station, in the morning.'

As Grant listened he found himself needing to sit down. Then he stood up, walked inside the house and took a beer from the fridge. He couldn't believe what he was hearing. 'No, no, no,' he broke in finally, 'you've got this wrong, Wex.'

'I'm just repeating what the guys in Auckland told me,' Wex informed him. 'If it's wrong, no one'll be happier than me, but if it's not . . . Listen, I know you're not due in till two tomorrow, but I'd like you here for ten if you can make it. We're going to have a lot to talk about, and by then we might have some more news in that'll throw a different light on things.'

The instant Charlotte saw the Kauri Cliffs hotel she was completely blown away by it. It surely had to be one of the most stunningly romantic places in the world. With its elegant pale grey roofs, white walls, airy loggias and succulent tropical vegetation, it sat in such exotic splendour overlooking the crystal blue sweep of Matauri Bay that it just kept on taking her breath away. As far as luxury went it had every last word. Everything, from the paintings inside the plantation-style mansion, to the rugs, to the hand-picked antique furniture was of a quality that even her inexpert eye could see was the very best. And the billowing flow of the landscape with its immaculate fairways and greens, enormous infinity pool and private surf beaches glinting on the shoreline of this glittering swathe of the South Pacific had to be the very definition of paradise.

She wasn't going to imagine how impressed Anthony would be by it, because she would never know, but it was very definitely the kind of place she could see him in.

With her?

What a dreamer.

Cinderella comes to Kauri Cliffs.

'How much does it cost to stay here?' she whispered to her mother, as they transported themselves and Anna's paraphernalia in a golf cart over to the pool.

The Cinderella analogy had to end there, before someone turned into a pumpkin.

'I think around twelve hundred dollars a night,' Anna replied, waving out to the crew who were already setting up for the shoot. 'Or eight thousand if you go for the owner's cottage.'

'Eight thousand *a night*,' Charlotte almost shrieked.

Laughing as she switched off the cart and hopped out, Anna embraced the scruffy individual who came to greet her, introducing him as Wolf, the photographer with more awards to his name than she had dollars in the bank.

With a droll grin, he turned a salute to Charlotte

into a wave towards an enormous four-poster bed perched like a grand old duchess in scant robes at the far end of the pool. 'As you can see, the star prop's in place,' he drawled.

'Perfect,' Anna declared, planting her hands on her hips and inhaling the pungent sea air as though taking in an energy shot. 'We need the damson quilt, white linen sheets and four round cushions to start,' she reminded Charlotte. 'The cushions should be black or mink, we'll try both, and the white voile should be in that hamper there.'

Turning back to the cart, Charlotte immediately began unpacking the voile, while her mother headed over to the bed to start organising its morph into a lady of tantalising elegance and style. At least a dozen people were milling around the area, photographer's assistants, models, dressers, make-up artists and numerous executives from Owens Lifestyle, the client. Anna's regular team of two was already at work inside a nearby guest cottage, pressing, folding, stitching and pinning; while Hemi Bennet with his muscles of rock and heart of marshmallow was limbering up ready to move the heavy stuff. Charlotte wouldn't have been at all surprised to learn that he'd carried the bed into position on his own, since he worked most of the time as a house-removal man (literally, because in NZ people often moved their entire property, not just the contents), and his Herculean strength was legendary.

'Hi, I'm Lucianne,' announced an attractive middle-aged woman with a rumpus of curly blonde hair and arresting blue eyes. 'And you must be Charlotte, Anna's daughter.'

'That's right,' Charlotte smiled, managing to tuck the voile under one arm as she took the hand being offered. Lucianne was the owner and founder of Owens Lifestyle and ex-wife of a world-champion American golfer. 'It's lovely to meet you,' she told her, meaning it. 'You've chosen the most incredible setting. The colours are so rich it's like they've been freshly painted on the landscape.'

Lucianne's eyes twinkled. 'In the case of the golfing greens they have, but you didn't hear it from me.' She turned to drink in the spectacular vista and gave a luxurious sigh. Up here at the top of the cliffs they could see for miles, with nothing interrupting the tranquil perfection of the sea but a handful of rocky islands and the occasional break of the surf. 'I think it's ideal for the new collection, don't you?' she said. 'And your mother is full of such good ideas. I mean, who'd have thought of putting the bed next to the pool?'

'Anna's middle name is quirky,' a willowy brunette declared, wandering up to join them. 'It's what sets her apart.'

Guessing she was one of the models, Charlotte quickly introduced herself, and was just reaching back into the cart for her clipboard when her mother shouted for her.

'Thankfully there's hardly any wind,' Anna stated, as Charlotte hurriedly joined her at the bed, 'so we can drape the voile round the posts without fear of it taking off. Actually, we might try a shot with a swathe of it airborne, it could be fun. I'll mention it to Wolf.'

'Are you using any models for this sequence?' a make-up artist wanted to know.

Anna shook her head. 'Not until we get to the sea-green linens,' she replied. 'Do you have an order of shoot? I'm sure Lucianne's office emailed them . . .'

'It's OK, I've got duplicates,' Charlotte assured her, fishing one from the back of her clipboard. 'You should have the model ready for eleven, we should get to her by then.'

'I've brought a bag of jewellery,' Anna added, 'which is probably all she should wear for the sea greens. We'll cover the vital bits with sparklers and a carefully draped sheet.'

'Are we using the bedside lamps for these first shots?' Wolf demanded.

Anna considered it.

'It could be one of your trademark quirky touches,' Charlotte whispered, 'especially if a model's holding one.'

Anna looked amused. 'Yes, let's do it,' she declared.

Happy to oblige, Wolf trundled back to where his assistants were sorting out gels and screens and lenses, while Lucianne barked instructions into a phone to only she knew who.

It wasn't long before they were ready to take the first shots, with the bed now fully dressed in artfully rumpled velvets and cottons, and cascades of voiles tumbling around the posts like bridal veils. Charlotte and Anna were constantly checking the viewfinder and jumping in to adjust a pillow or a fold or the carefully spilled crystal bowl of marbles that were glinting like jewels, or even raindrops, in the sunlight. This last had been Charlotte's idea, for which she'd received much praise from Lucianne.

By lunchtime they'd completed the pool shots and were ready to move on to the ocean-view loggia, where Charlotte and the Owens Lifestyle designers were already sorting through the required throws and quilts. As the crew started to arrive trays of sandwiches and cold drinks were brought through from the kitchens, so Charlotte seized the brief break for lunch to call Aroha. Chloe had been close to tears when Charlotte had left her at the start of the day, so she was anxious to find out how she was now.

'She seems fine,' Celia insisted when Charlotte got through. 'She was a little quiet after you'd gone, but as we speak she's outside in the shady areas playing Farmer in the Dell. Would you like me to go and get her?'

'If you wouldn't mind,' Charlotte replied, and wandering out to the front of the hotel as she waited, she called Hemi over to ask him to fetch the rotary washing line from the golf cart and take it down to the eighteenth green. This was the location for the next set-up and it was her job to be thinking ahead.

'Hello?' Chloe said softly into the phone.

'Hello sweetheart,' Charlotte replied, her heart tripping with love. 'I hope I haven't spoiled your game.'

'No,' came the breathy reply, 'because we finished anyway. We're doing some baking this afternoon for Melody's birthday, and soon we're doing some for mine.'

Feeling her throat knot with pride, Charlotte said, 'We still haven't finished making a list of who you'd like to invite to your party, so we'd better do that tonight.'

'Yes. Please can I invite everyone?'

Loving her kind heart, Charlotte said, 'Well, if the weather's good and we can hold it on the beach, I don't see why not.' And if the weather wasn't good she knew her mother and Bob would happily host it at the lodge.

Taking breaths in all the wrong places, Chloe said, 'I think we should do it on the beach and then everyone can do the pipi dance and go for a row in our boat and a swing on our swing.'

'I'm sure they'll love every minute of it.'

'And we can eat the cakes that we make.'

'Absolutely, and lots of jelly and ice cream. I've got a nice little surprise for you now, Auntie Shelley sent me a text earlier to say that Danni's coming with her to pick you up today.'

Chloe fell silent.

'I thought you'd be happy about that,' Charlotte pressed, feeling bad now for even bringing it up.

'I want you to come,' Chloe whispered.

'I know, darling, but it's just this once and I'll be home right after you've had your tea. Knowing you, you'll be up in the pasture with Danni and Diesel by then. Think how happy Diesel's going to be to see you, because he really loves you and Danni, doesn't he?'

'Yes, and we love him.'

'There you are then. You'll have a lovely time, just don't forget to put on a hat if you ride him, OK?'

'I've got my own hat now.'

'I know you have, so remember to take it with you. Or is it already at the stables?'

'It's in the tack room next to Danni's.'

Touched by how proud she sounded of that, Charlotte told her, 'I have to go now, sweetheart. So you have a happy bake this afternoon and if there's anything left I'll look forward to a cupcake with my tea.'

'I'm going to make one for you with chocolate buttons on.'

'Oh, lovely, that's my favourite. My mouth is watering already.'

There was a small silence before Chloe said, 'I want you to come.'

Almost wishing she hadn't rung now, Charlotte said, 'Tell you what, if you go home nicely with Auntie Shelley and Danni today, we'll go to town for a fluffy on Saturday, and a look round the dollar store. How does that sound?' Chloe loved the dollar store with all its little bits and pieces at her eye level.

Realising she was going to repeat, 'I want you to come,' Charlotte went on quickly. 'I'm going to ring off now, OK? So you be a good girl. I love you.'

'Love you,' Chloe whispered.

After ringing off and reassuring herself again that Chloe would be fine as soon as she saw Danni and Shelley, Charlotte went in search of her mother, grabbing a sandwich and glass of lemonade on the way.

'Ah, there you are,' Anna smiled, as Charlotte joined her and Lucianne at a quiet end of the loggia. They were viewing the morning's shots on Lucianne's laptop, discussing why some worked while others didn't. 'We were just saying what a good start we're off to,' Anna commented, as Charlotte leaned against the balustrade next to her.

'I especially loved what you did with the marbles,' Lucianne told her. 'Wolf's picked up the sunlight perfectly, and we'll probably add more in the edit. I wouldn't mind having them as a kind of theme running through this catalogue. No colours to them, just plain glass marbles; we can always use Photoshop to tint them if we feel the need to.'

'I was thinking they'd work well mingled with red or pink rose petals when we come to do the vintage lace collection,' Charlotte suggested.

Lucianne's eyes widened with interest. 'Where, when are we doing that?' she asked.

'It's scheduled for tomorrow in one of the guest cottages,' Charlotte replied. 'I'll try to set something up this afternoon if there's time, so we can get an idea of how it might look.'

Clearly thrilled by her creative input, Anna said to Lucianne, 'I'm hoping she'll come into a full partnership with me eventually.'

'Well, she's certainly showing signs of having inherited her mother's talent,' Lucianne commented. 'What were you doing before you came here, Charlotte?'

Feeling her cheeks starting to burn, Charlotte avoided her mother's eyes as she said, 'I just worked in local government, nothing particularly interesting, and definitely not arty.'

'But she has a passion for theatre,' Anna chipped in, 'which I believe can be termed arty.'

'Amateur theatre,' Charlotte was quick to add, 'and it was really only a hobby, not a *passion*.' She needn't have emphasised that last word, making it sound condescending, especially when her mother had only been trying to show support, and pride. Now she was clearly embarrassed and hurt.

Sensing Lucianne's surprise at her attitude, Charlotte said, 'I should go and make sure there are no problems for the next set-up,' and grabbing her empty glass and clipboard she took herself back into the fray.

An hour later the loggia sequence was complete and they were ready to move down to the eighteenth green, where Charlotte had already organised the dressing of the rotary washing line. Hemi was carrying in a wind machine, taking care not to tangle up with the cables Wolf's assistants were running from the hotel, while in the shade of a frangipani tree a make-up artist was applying finishing touches to a male model wrapped in an Owens Lifestyle bathrobe.

Spotting Anna assessing the rotary line, Charlotte went to join her, hoping to apologise for earlier, but before she could speak Anna was saying, 'I can't make up my mind whether the damson sheet should be tangled with the white cotton bedspread or remain as it is, hanging separately. Of course it'll all look much livelier when the wind's blowing through it . . .'

'Is it difficult to shoot it both ways?' Charlotte asked.

Anna glanced at her and realising she'd sounded critical and snappy, rather than helpful, Charlotte said, 'I'm sorry, I was just saying . . .'

'Yes, I heard you,' Anna cut in, 'and you're right, we could do it both ways.' Moving past her, she went to clip arum lilies to the clothes pegs and turned to Wolf to discuss the direction of the wind. Her back made it clear that she had no more time to talk to Charlotte.

Deciding she'd have to try apologising again later, preferably when she was feeling less annoyed with herself for never seeming to get it right with her mother, Charlotte set off for the nearest guest cottage. The vintage lace collection should have been delivered by now, so she could start arranging it over the bed and go to find some petals and marbles when she got a chance later.

'Charlotte, where are you going?' Anna called after her.

Coming to a stop, Charlotte was about to turn

round when she noticed a police car pulling up outside the hotel. Since there was no good reason for her to experience a bolt of unease, or even to pay the arrival any further attention, she should have turned back to her mother. However, a sixth sense – or maybe a rogue streak of paranoia – was making it impossible for her to stop watching it. Then Grant and another officer got out and she felt herself relaxing. They must have decided to take a drive up the coast for a look at what was going on here, and they'd chosen a good time because refreshments were still being served.

As they came towards her she wanted to go and greet them, but found she couldn't. Her heartbeat was slowing and her mouth was suddenly dry. Something wasn't right; she could feel it even before Grant was close enough for her to see that there was no hint of the usual playful gleam in his eye.

Realising her mother was standing next to her, she felt herself turning dizzy. Why was her mother here? She hadn't been a moment ago. What was unnerving Anna? Nothing had happened, nothing was wrong, so why were they both behaving as though it was?

'Grant,' Anna said, going to greet him in her usual friendly manner. 'What a lovely surprise. You too, Wex. You've chosen a great day to visit.'

As Charlotte watched them she could feel fear closing in on her like ravens starting to swoop.

Grant was close enough now for her to see how haggard he looked.

Anna turned around and Charlotte noticed her colour had gone.

It was like a dream, a nightmare, everything was happening in slow motion and she could neither move nor scream.

Wex was speaking, and as the crowding fear suddenly rushed at her it was turning to panic.

'No,' Charlotte begged, 'please, please no.'

'It's all right, it's all right,' Anna cried, putting her arm round Charlotte. 'Grant, stop this, you have to . . .'

'I'm sorry, Anna,' he said roughly, 'there's nothing I can do.'

Wex started again. 'I'm detaining you, Charlotte Nicholls, for the abduction of a child. You have the right to remain silent. You do not have to make any statement. Anything you say will be recorded and may be given in evidence in court. You have the right to speak with a lawyer without delay and in private before deciding whether to answer any questions.'

'Chloe,' Charlotte whispered desperately.

'Do you understand your rights?' Wex asked.

'I can't leave Chloe,' Charlotte sobbed. 'Please Grant, you know her . . . *Grant, please,*' she cried as he turned his head away.

Wex repeated the question. 'Do you understand your rights?'

Wave after wave of panic was crashing through her. She couldn't let them do this. She had to get to Chloe. Breaking free of her mother, she started to run.

Wex grabbed her, so did Grant. 'I have to get to Chloe,' she choked. 'I promised her. Grant, I can't leave her . . . Don't make me, please, please don't make me.'

Unable to take her distress, Grant turned away again. 'I'm sorry,' he mumbled. 'If it was up to me . . .'

'You have to do something,' Anna implored. 'You know the situation. Chloe's been through enough. If you do this . . .'

'Anna,' Wex interrupted gently, 'it's not up to us. The Brits are already on their way here.'

Anna turned her stricken eyes to Charlotte.

'Charlotte, I have to ask if you understand your rights?' Wex insisted.

Charlotte could hardly think or speak. She could only see Chloe waiting for her to come home, waiting and waiting . . . 'She's just a baby,' she gasped, 'she needs me . . .'

Putting an arm round her shoulders Grant said, 'Come on, let's get you to the car.'

Every muscle, every instinct Charlotte possessed wanted to lash out, to scream, to run and run and never stop until she reached Chloe, but there was nothing she could do. Her worst nightmare was happening and she had no way of stopping it. They were arresting her, taking her into custody. Today, tomorrow, she would be flown back to England and . . . and what?

'Oh God, Mum, get Chloe,' she cried. 'Please, just go and get Chloe.'

Chapter Ten

'Shelley, where the heck are you?' Bob barked into his phone.

'At the farmer's market in Paihia. Why?'

'Charlotte's been arrested. I'm . . .'

'What! How . . .'

'. . . on my way to Aroha to get Chloe. You know I can't do it alone, so I need you to get back as fast as you can.'

'Oh my God!' Shelley murmured in a panic. 'I thought Charlotte was at Kauri Cliffs today . . .'

'That's where they picked her up. Anna's on her way back . . .'

'What about the shoot?'

'She had to abandon it. I've been trying to get hold of Grant Romney, but he's not answering his phone. Apparently he arrested her. And Wex Harris.'

'Jesus Christ. Oh Dad, I don't know what to do, I feel so scared . . .'

'Shelley, get a grip.'

'OK, sorry. I'll be there as fast as I can. Call me if there's any more news.'

After ringing off Bob swerved to the edge of the road to bring up Grant Romney's number again. This time, when he tried to get through, to his great relief Grant answered.

'Bob, I'm sorry, mate,' Grant said, before Bob could speak. 'This is right out of my hands. CIB, immigration, CYFS, they're all over it . . .'

'But how did it happen?'

'Wex got a call from Auckland last night asking him to check out information they'd received from Britain. When he realised who they were talking about he rang me. I couldn't tell you anything, he shouldn't even have involved me, being a friend of the family, but he broke the rules to try and make it easier on Charlotte.'

Suspecting he should be grateful for that, Bob said, 'Where is she now?'

'Here in the car with us. We're bringing her back to Kerikeri.'

'Can I speak to her?'

'Sure, but . . .'

'Hang on, before I do, what happens next?'

'We're still waiting to hear. Our instructions are just to bring her in and hold her, I guess until they've decided whether we have to take her to Auckland, or if they'll come here . . .'

'OK, put her on.'

A moment later, Charlotte said, 'Bob, I'm really sorry. I . . .'

'You stop that now,' he told her, finding himself choked with emotion. 'You've got nothing to be sorry for. You did what was right and we're going to get this sorted.'

'What about Chloe? She's all that matters . . .'

'I'm on my way to get her now. Your mother's going to meet me there, so's Shelley. I'm waiting for a call back from one of Auckland's top lawyers, Don Thackeray. He'll know what do . . .'

'I can't go back,' she said brokenly.

Wanting to hold it together for her, he said, 'We'll get through this, I promise . . .'

'But what's going to happen to Chloe? You can't let them take her, Bob.'

'We won't. She'll be fine. I'll stay with her until your mother or Shelley arrives, then I'll come to see you at the station. OK?'

'OK.'

'Put Grant on again.'

'I'm here,' Grant told him.

'Keep me as informed as you can,' Bob said. 'I don't want to cause any trouble for you, but I need to stay on top of this.'

'Sure, I'll do my best.'

'How long before you're back in town?'

'Twenty minutes.'

'She's not talking to you, is she? You can't let her talk to you,' Bob insisted.

'Don't worry, she understands that. Does she have a lawyer yet?'

'I've got a call in to Don Thackeray and someone's trying to get through, so I'm going to ring off in case it's him.'

It turned out to be Anna. 'Are you at Aroha yet?' she demanded, not sounding much calmer than when she'd rung to deliver the shock.

'Two minutes away,' Bob told her. 'I've just spoken to Charlotte. She's holding up, but this isn't going to be easy for her. What's happening with the shoot?'

'Lucianne's got my notes. She was very good about it, but obviously she doesn't know the whole story. She thinks it's just a mix-up. Do we know yet how they found out?'

Though he had a fairly good idea, all he said was,

'Not yet. The point is, the Brits have taken it seriously enough to fly out here.'

'In that case I'm terrified of what's going to happen . . .'

'One step at a time,' he cautioned. 'I'm at Aroha now. Get here as soon as you can, but don't go running yourself off the road.'

Leaving his car across two spaces, he ran to the side gate of the Centre and up the ramp to the main veranda. To his alarm there was no sign of any children, but when he put his head in the door he saw them hunched in a group around two of the carers.

Celia was already coming towards him, her face drawn with confusion.

'Where's Chloe?' he asked.

Gently ushering him outside, she said, 'She's not here.'

A thump of real fear hit Bob's chest.

'Someone came from CYFS,' she continued, referring to the government agency, Child, Youth and Family Services. 'They had an emergency order so there was nothing I could do. They said,' her eyes flicked anxiously to his, 'they said Chloe's not her real name and that she . . . she . . . She was abducted from her home in the UK. Is that true, Bob? Did Charlotte . . . ? Isn't Charlotte her real mother?'

'You've seen them together,' he replied, almost viciously. 'So what do you think?'

Apparently at a loss, Celia gestured indoors. 'It was very upsetting for the other children . . .'

Not caring about them right now, he said, 'Was Chloe scared? Did she fight them?'

Celia's eyes were tormented. 'She didn't really

understand what was going on,' she replied, 'but yes, I have to say she was scared.'

Bob was already punching a number into his phone. 'Did you get any names?' he asked. 'Do you know where they were taking her?'

'One of them left a card. I'll go and get it.'

Connecting to the most senior social worker he knew, Bob said, 'Mary, Bob Reeves here. I need your help.' After explaining the situation without going into the real crux of it, he took the card from Celia as he asked, 'Can you find out where they've taken her? I've got the name of someone here, Angie Jeffries. She's from the Whangarei site office . . . You've heard of her? Great. Call me back as soon as you have some news.'

After ringing off and apologising to Celia for the upset, he returned to his car, connecting to Rick as he went. 'All hell's breaking loose up here,' he growled into the voicemail. 'Call me back as soon as you get this.' As he ended the call he clicked on to take another.

'Bob, Don Thackeray. Secretary said it was urgent so what can I do for you?'

Knowing there was nothing to be gained from hedging around the issue, Bob launched into the full details of what had happened, holding back on nothing, not even his own compliance in it all.

'Well, this is a very interesting scenario you've got on your hands,' Thackeray responded in a dry, lawyerly way when Bob had finished. 'I wouldn't worry too much about your own position . . .'

'Believe me, I'm not,' Bob assured him. 'It's Charlotte and Chloe . . .'

'Where are they now?'

'Social services have got Chloe, I'm trying to find

out where, and Charlotte's being taken into custody here in Kerikeri.'

'I see. And you say the Brits are already on their way. That makes it doubly interesting. Have they applied for extradition yet?'

'No idea, but I think we have to assume it'll happen if it hasn't already.'

'Indeed, but it's not a foregone conclusion, and from what you've told me, I think we have some good grounds for fighting it.'

Shocked into relief, Bob said, 'That's what I wanted to hear. So what do we do next?'

'Let me make some calls this end to try and find out how far this has gone. It could be I need to come there to speak to her, but obviously not if they're going to bring her here.'

'OK. Meantime, is there anything we can do to get Chloe back into our care?'

'Frankly, I'm doubtful about that. When it comes to kids . . . Well, as an ex-social worker your stepdaughter will know better than most how powerful the authorities can be. That's not to say you shouldn't try, because you never know. After all, the child's interests are supposed to be paramount and she's obviously come to no harm while she's been with your family.'

'To the contrary,' Bob assured him, and after thanking him with a promise that he'd receive top dollar for his help he rang off in time to take a call from Shelley.

'I'm about ten minutes away,' she told him. 'Rick just rang me because he couldn't get through to you. I told him what's happened. Like me, he's pretty sure Katie's behind it, but obviously we don't know that for certain.'

Putting a hand to his throbbing head, Bob said, 'I'll let him deal with that, because frankly I'm just not up to fathoming what's going on there. On the other hand, if it does have something to do with this . . .'

'Are you at Aroha yet?' Shelley broke in.

'Yes. Anna's just turned up, so I'll talk to you when you get here.'

As he clicked off the line and watched Anna pull up next to him, he felt as helpless as he ever had in his life.

'Where's Chloe?' she asked hoarsely as she got out of her car.

He shook his head.

Panic shot through her eyes. 'Do you know where they've taken her?'

'Not yet. At least we know they won't harm her,' he said, by way of comfort.

'Do we?' she demanded. 'How do we know that? We've no idea who they might put her with. Oh my God, this is the very thing Charlotte feared, it's why she did what she did . . .'

'I know that, but things are different here . . .'

'Not so very different that we can rule out the possibility of her going to a bad family.'

'We won't let it happen. I promise.'

She looked away and back again. 'I don't know how we're going to break this to Charlotte,' she said shakily. 'And what's going to happen to *her*? I'm so scared, Bob, if they take her back to England . . .'

'I've spoken to Don Thackeray and he's saying we stand a good chance of blocking an extradition.'

A flicker of hope showed in her eyes, but quickly died. 'It's all my fault,' she mumbled. 'I should never have . . .'

'Stop that. You're not to blame. No one is, apart from Chloe's father and he's already serving his time.'

Anna nodded absently. 'Do you know where Charlotte is? Can we see her?'

'She should be at the station by now, so we should head over there.'

'There you go,' Grant said, putting a cup of tea down on the table in front of Charlotte and sinking into the small sofa opposite hers. They were in what he'd called a soft interview room at the Kerikeri police station, where non-violent offenders were taken before being questioned. It was small, not much more than ten feet by six, had no windows, nothing on the walls and no locks on the doors that she could see. At least it was clean. 'Would you like some biscuits?' he offered.

She shook her head. Her face was ashen, her eyes blurred and sore, her whole body rigid with the horror of what was happening. 'I have to see Chloe,' she told him hoarsely.

'Wex is on the phone to Aroha now,' he replied, not quite meeting her eyes.

She looked down at the tea, but found herself unable to pick it up. 'I don't know what to say to you,' she told him. 'I feel so ashamed, you trusted me, you were kind to Chloe, and now . . . but even if I had the time over . . .'

'I have to remind you you're under caution,' he said gently.

Nodding abstractedly, she turned to stare at the wall. All she could think about was Chloe and how terrified she'd be if social services took her.

'I'll get some Kleenex,' Grant said, as she put a hand to her head.

Closing her eyes as the door clicked shut behind him, she struggled to hold back the panic that was trying to crush her. The thought of what lay ahead was so terrifying it was making her dizzy. Nothing was ever going to be the same again. She'd committed a terrible crime and the time had now come for her to pay. Never mind that she'd done it for the best of motives: loving a child who had no family, apart from a paedophile father who would soon be sent to prison, was no excuse for stealing her.

She could bear the consequences of what she'd done, just, but knowing what it was going to mean for Chloe was devastating her over and over and would never stop, not ever, until she could make it right again.

What chance was there of that?

None.

How could there be when she was blatantly guilty of the crime? She'd stolen a child and kept her hidden from the police until she'd felt it safe to take her out of the country and bring her here. Then she'd given her a new name, a better life and all the love any child could ever need. For the first time in her tragic little life Chloe had felt happy and safe, had found the confidence to speak and play, to make new friends and become part of a loving family.

How could that be a crime?

Whatever they do to me, please, please God don't let anyone hurt Chloe ever again.

Knowing how lost Chloe was going to be without her, how much she had come to trust and depend on her, was increasing her fear to a degree she could hardly bear. She thought of Charlotte as her mother now, and it was how Charlotte felt. It simply wouldn't be possible for her to love Chloe more if she was her own. She'd even decided that if it turned out to be in Chloe's best interests to be her only child she'd be happy to have no others. Something special had happened between them right from the day they'd first met in a park, in Kesterly. That was when she'd found Chloe, who'd been Ottilie then, sitting alone on a swing with Boots squashed in next to her and her feet unable to reach the ground. 'Hello, and who are you?' Charlotte had asked, and her heart contracted now to recall the way those deep brown eyes had gazed unblinkingly into hers. She'd seemed almost ethereal, Charlotte remembered thinking, as though she'd stepped out of an Impressionist painting.

Her father had turned up then and led his child away, leaving Charlotte feeling a strange sort of wrench at the parting, as though she was trying to hold on to something of the little girl, or maybe the child was trying to hold on to her. She'd had a bad vibe about the father, but it wasn't until several weeks later that their paths had crossed again. An anonymous caller had rung social services to express concern about a child who lived at number forty-two North Hill. So Charlotte had gone round there and as soon as she'd set eyes on the little girl, she'd recognised her from the swing in the park.

It had felt as though some greater force was at work, drawing them together in a way that was as powerful as it was irresistible and inexplicable.

In spite of knowing instinctively that things were wrong in the house, it had turned out to be almost impossible to prove. Chloe's – Ottilie's – father was an intelligent man, the deputy headmaster of a primary school and well respected in the community. Her mother, it turned out, was suffering with paranoid schizophrenia, and so was completely unable to form a natural and loving relationship with her child. However, in the end, it was the mother who'd sent Charlotte the email with links to the websites that showed what Ottilie's father was doing to his three-year-old daughter.

Ride the tiger, Ottilie. Come on, ride the tiger.

It made Charlotte sick to her very soul even to think of it. If hatred could execute a person, that man, that *perverted monster* would be dead a thousand times over. But it was his wife who was dead, stabbed through the heart with a kitchen knife. It was how Charlotte had found her the night she'd taken Ottilie from the house, lying in a pool of blood while her husband worked frantically at the computer in his studio/shed, trying to erase the evidence of his crimes.

Charlotte hadn't allowed herself a moment to think of what was right or wrong. She'd dashed upstairs, desperate to get to Ottilie, terrified that she might already be too late, but she'd found her, locked away in a cupboard, trembling and so traumatised that Charlotte had simply grabbed her and run.

She'd known then, and she knew now that she shouldn't have kept her. She should have gone straight to the police and put her into emergency care, but after everything that sweet little soul had been through Charlotte simply hadn't had it in her to turn her over to strangers. Maybe, if Kesterly had had a stronger list of foster carers, or if she'd been able to make sure Ottilie was homed with Maggie Fenn, Anthony's sister and the most naturally maternal woman Charlotte had ever met, she'd have found it easier to give her up, but in truth she doubted it. The bond between them was wrapping itself around her by then, and she'd known that Ottilie was feeling it too. They were together and no matter what the law or anyone else might say, it was where they needed to be.

So Charlotte had kept her, and because Ottilie always did as she was told she'd stayed quietly upstairs every time the police came to the house to discuss the little girl they feared had been murdered by her father. Not that anyone suspected Charlotte of taking the child, they came because she was Ottilie's social worker. She should have known everything about Ottilie and what had gone on in the house on North Hill. Yet Ottilie was missing, and she, as the person responsible for Ottilie's care, had somehow failed her. The police had never actually said that, it was the press who'd made her their target for scorn, so she knew already just how cruel – and wrong – they could be. Over time it had been assumed that Ottilie's father, Brian Wade, had killed her and hidden the body, or passed her on to one of his paedophile ring, and Charlotte had never spoken up to contradict it. She'd simply kept Ottilie with her, waiting for her mother to arrive from New Zealand . . . much as she was waiting for her mother to arrive now.

'You didn't drink your tea,' Grant said kindly as he came in with some tissues. 'Can I get you a fresh one?'

She shook her head and dabbed a tissue to her swollen eyes. 'Do you have any news of Chloe yet?' she asked.

He was propping the door open with his foot,

and glanced over his shoulder at the sound of voices along the corridor in reception. 'Your mother's here,' he told her.

Charlotte's heart jolted with relief. 'Can I see her?' she asked. 'Is it allowed?'

Grant didn't say, only told her to hang on, he'd be right back.

Moments later the door opened again and as Anna came in, ashen and trembling, Charlotte went straight into her arms.

'Where's Chloe?' she gasped as Bob came in too. 'Please tell me you have her.'

'I'm sorry,' he said gruffly, 'they got there before us.'

'No! *No*,' Charlotte cried in a panic. 'Where have they taken her? Oh God, you have to get her back. She'll be so scared. She won't understand what's happening. She'll think we don't want her . . .'

'We're doing our best,' Anna promised. 'Bob's already made some calls . . .'

'Does she have Boots with her?' Charlotte demanded. 'Please tell me they let her take him. You know what he means to her . . .'

Bob was already connecting to Aroha. After speaking to Celia he rang off and looked at Charlotte with an expression that confirmed the worst.

'You have to get him to her,' Charlotte urged. 'Whatever else happens, she has to have Boots. Please can you do that?'

'Of course,' he assured her, and opening his phone again he went out of the room.

Charlotte's reddened eyes moved to Anna. They stared at each other, barely knowing what to say as the fear, the guilt that was racking their hearts, seemed to suck the air from the room.

'It'll be all right,' Anna said shakily. 'Bob's already got a top lawyer on it, and he's optimistic he can make a case for keeping you here.'

Keeping you here.

So there really was a chance she'd be taken back. How was she even doubting it?

'What about Chloe?' she asked hoarsely.

'All I can tell you is that we're going to do everything humanly possible to keep her here, with us.'

Knowing the power of the authorities as well as she did, Charlotte felt herself collapsing inside.

'They'll put Chloe's interests first,' Anna told her, 'and no one can argue that she wouldn't be better off with us . . .'

'Of course she'd be better off with you, but that's not how the system works.'

'Maybe not in England, here they take a different view.'

'How do you know that when you've never been in this position before? Do you think they care any less about their children here?'

'Of course not. What I'm saying is we could find they care more . . . Charlotte, we have to stay positive . . .'

'I know that. I know, *I know*, but as long as I've got no idea where she is, or who she's with . . .' An image of Chloe's father flashed in her mind and she reeled with the fear of Chloe ever ending up in a place like that again. 'She's already been through too much. She can't take any more,' she sobbed.

'She won't have to, I promise . . .'

'It's her birthday soon. I've ordered her a bike, and Bob's getting a puppy . . .'

'Charlotte, listen to me,' Anna urged, gripping

her shoulders. 'I understand what you're going through, I know how hard it is . . .'

'How do you know? What . . .'

'Because I've been there, remember? I lost you when you were Chloe's age . . .'

'And it took you twenty-five years to find me,' Charlotte choked. 'Thanks for the comfort. And you didn't *lose* me, you gave me away . . .'

'No!'

'Yes! So don't tell me you know what it's like, because it was totally different for you and I could never turn my back on Chloe the way you turned yours on me.'

Anna's eyes were harsh as she said, 'I can't keep apologising to you, Charlotte. You know what happened back then. Gavril Albescu would have killed you . . .'

'Stop, just stop,' Charlotte gasped, turning away. 'This isn't about him, or me, it's about Chloe . . .'

'It's about you too. For God's sake, look at where we are . . .' She broke off as Bob came back, looking alarmed at the raised voices.

'It's OK,' Anna told him quietly. 'What's happening?'

'I've just spoken to the social worker who collected Chloe from Aroha,' he answered. 'She wants us to know that Chloe's safe and with a good family, and she'll go back to the Centre now to collect Boots.'

Though relieved to hear that the importance of the bear was understood, Charlotte was less convinced by the 'good family', since the social worker was hardly going to say anything to the contrary. 'Can't Mum take the bear to her?' she asked desperately. 'At least then we'll know where Chloe is and the kind of people she's with.'

Bob's expression was helpless as he said, 'I asked that, but apparently we're not allowed to have any contact with her . . .'

'*We have to*,' Charlotte shouted. 'We're the people who love her, who know what's best for her. They can't do this, they just can't.' But they could, as she knew only too well.

'What's happening with the police?' Anna asked Bob.

With a glance at Charlotte he said, 'They're still waiting to hear from CIB in Auckland.'

'What's CIB?' Charlotte asked.

'Criminal Investigation Branch. The same as your CID. Grant's just suggested we go and pack a bag for you in case they have to take you to Auckland.' He didn't add that he'd also been advised to bring the passports. Not that Chloe had one, but he wasn't going to worry about that now.

Fear was burning in Charlotte's eyes as she turned to her mother.

'It might not come to that,' Anna told her hastily. 'It'll just be a precaution. Is there anything in particular . . .' She stopped as Bob's phone rang.

'Shelley,' he told them, clicking on.

As he went outside again Charlotte said, 'If I ask you to bring me some photos of Chloe it'll be like . . .' Her voice started to break. 'Giving up,' she finished in a ragged whisper.

Going to wrap her in her arms, Anna held her close as dread threatened to overwhelm them both. 'It's all my fault,' she murmured. 'If I'd had more courage when you were young, if I'd brought you here with me . . .'

'If you had then I wouldn't have been around to rescue Chloe,' Charlotte said huskily.

'It was good that you did, no one's ever going to doubt that, but my mistake was not encouraging you to give her up when I came back to England and found you had her.'

'Don't say that! I was never going to give her up and besides, I'd already had her for a week by then.'

Sighing, Anna said, 'Yes you had, and because I'd only just found you I wasn't prepared to give you up either. So between us, we found a way for us all to be together.'

It was as simple, and as complicated as that.

Suddenly realising how much bigger this was than just her and Chloe, Charlotte cried, 'Oh my God, I hadn't thought about what this is going to mean for you and Bob. Will they press charges against you? Oh Mum, I'm sorry, I'm sorry . . .'

'Stop,' Anna insisted, grabbing her hands. 'We'll be fine. You and Chloe are the only ones who matter now.'

Charlotte buried her face in her hands as the door opened and Bob came back. 'Rick's taking the evening flight home,' he told them.

Anna looked puzzled. 'But we . . .'

Putting up a hand, Bob said, 'Shelley's gone to Aroha to try and speak to the social worker when she gets there.'

'Oh God, I'm dragging your whole family into this,' Charlotte wailed. 'I don't want you getting into trouble . . .'

'We can handle whatever they throw at us,' Bob assured her. Then to Anna, 'I can go to the bach if you want to stay here.'

Anna looked at Charlotte. 'I guess I'll have a better idea of what you might need,' she said. 'Will you be all right?'

'Yes, yes I'll be fine,' Charlotte lied. 'Don't worry about me, just find out what you can about Chloe, and if it's at all possible for Shelley to see her please ask Shelley to tell her that I love her and I'll . . . I'll . . . Oh God, what do I tell her when she won't understand why I'm not there, or why she's wherever the hell she is.'

Chloe was inside a cage with lots of toys and crayoning books. A TV was on across the room and a lady was sitting on a sofa watching it. Earlier the lady had brought her some squash and a biscuit, but it was still on the floor where she'd left it. Chloe didn't want it. She just wanted her mummy and Boots.

Mummy, Mummy, Mummy.

She didn't understand what she'd done wrong. Why hadn't Auntie Shelley and Danni come for her like Mummy had said they would? Maybe Mummy was cross with her for saying she wanted her to come and now she didn't want Chloe at all.

The lady kept telling her not to cry, that everything would be all right, but Chloe was scared of her and wanted to go home.

'Are you doing OK over there?' the lady called out.

Chloe didn't answer. She kept her head down waiting for Mummy to come and wishing she had Boots, because he made her feel brave.

When it was her birthday she was going to blow out all the candles and wish that Boots was always with her. And Mummy and Nanna and Auntie Shelley and Danni.

She didn't understand why she was here.

Mummy, Mummy, Mummy.

The lady went to answer a knock on the door.

Chloe got to her feet. It would be Mummy coming to get her.

She could hear voices, but the TV was loud so she didn't know who it was. She'd been told not to get out of the playpen but she had to go to Mummy so she climbed over the bars and ran towards the door of the room. Before she got there it opened and the lady came in.

'Here she is,' the lady smiled, and she stood aside for another lady to come in. It was the lady who'd picked her up from Aroha. She was going to take her back now and Auntie Shelley would be there with Danni.

Or Mummy would be there.

'Hello pretty girl,' the lady said, stooping down to her height. 'Look what I've got for you.'

Chloe watched her hand going into her bag and when it came out it was holding Boots.

Chloe went to snatch him, but then wasn't sure if it was allowed. This lady might be like her other mummy who'd teased and tormented her, pulled her hair, and banged her head on the floor and hissed at her like she was a snake.

She lowered her eyes and waited to be told what to do.

'Here you are,' the lady said, and she put Boots into Chloe's arms.

Chloe hugged him hard. He must have been very lonely without her. She'd never shut him up in her locker again. He was going to stay with her all the time for ever and ever.

'There you are,' the lady who watched the TV said, 'has that made you a bit happier?'

Chloe kept her head down. She didn't want to

look at anyone. She was going to close her eyes and pretend she was at the bach with Mummy.

Maybe Mummy had sent Boots because she didn't want them at the bach any more. She must have been very naughty, but she didn't know what she'd done wrong.

Chapter Eleven

Anna was at the bach sorting out clothes and toiletries for Charlotte, her mind spinning with the fear of what might happen next. She hoped to God Don Thackeray was as brilliant a lawyer as everyone said he was, because they were going to need nothing short of a spectacular miracle to make even a small part of this go away.

And she was to blame for it all.

Her life was littered with mistakes for which those she loved had paid the harshest, cruellest price, starting with her impulsive marriage to Gavril Albescu. That disastrous union had ended with the slaughter of her entire family including their five-year-old son.

Hugo, Hugo, she gasped inwardly. The image of the way his father had killed him would haunt her until the day she died.

Only she and Charlotte had survived the massacre, which was the strangest, and possibly the cruellest twist of all, since it was learning that Charlotte wasn't his that had tipped Albescu over the edge. He'd come that night with the intention of killing them both, but Charlotte had been hidden away and, thank God, he'd never found her. The rest of the family, and Charlotte's real father, Nigel Carrington, hadn't managed to escape the attack, and the injuries he'd inflicted on her, Anna, had been so vicious that she should have died too, but somehow she'd been saved. By the time they'd released her from hospital almost a year later she no longer had a womb, or a right breast, and the scars all over her body were so severe that even now they seemed to ache along with her heart. By then Charlotte had acquired another name; another life; another family. So in order to keep her safe Anna had taken the heartbreaking decision to leave her only remaining child with the rector who'd rescued Charlotte the day after the killings.

Never, in her worst nightmares, had she imagined that twenty-five years would go by before she would see her again.

Now, here they were, she and Charlotte, back in each other's lives, trying to heal what had gone before and find their way through to each other . . .

'For God's sake,' Bob gasped as he came into the bach to find her sobbing. 'It's going to be all right, Anna. We'll get through this . . .'

'What is it about me that brings such tragedy to my family?' she choked. 'If I hadn't told Charlotte to bring Chloe here neither of them would be where they are now, and we don't even know where Chloe is.'

'Wherever that might be at least we know she's safe . . .'

'And terrified and confused and desperate for her mummy.'

'Anna, you have to pull yourself together.'

'I'm trying, but I'm so afraid of what's going to happen to them . . .' She broke off at the sound of a car arriving at the top of the slope.

'I'll go and see who it is,' Bob said, and after a fierce gaze into her eyes meant to bolster her, he went outside, expecting to see his daughter coming down to the bach. To his alarm it turned out to be two police officers, and more were arriving behind them.

'Sherman, what's going on?' he demanded of Rick's old schoolfriend, who was already coming over the footbridge. 'What are you doing here?'

'We've been told to search the bach,' Sherman explained awkwardly. 'They need her computer and stuff.'

Realising he should have been prepared for this, Bob spun round to check if Anna had heard, but for the moment there was no sign of her. 'We're just collecting a few things to take to the station,' he said. 'I guess you'll need to see what's in the bag?'

Sherman nodded and looked past him to where Anna was now standing in the doorway of the bach. 'I'm sorry about this,' he called to her.

Anna didn't answer. She was watching the forensic team milling and drifting down the slope like ghosts in their baggy white overalls. *This wasn't a murder scene, no one was dead.*

'I packed a bag for Chloe too,' she told Bob as he came back to her.

Hugging her, Bob said, 'They'll need to have a quick look through what's inside before we go.'

Standing aside as Sherman and the others began swarming around the bach, she gazed out at the bay, wondering what on earth hell was doing in their little spot of paradise.

A few minutes later they were in Bob's car on their way back into town. Anna knew she should call Lucianne to apologise again and find out how the shoot was going, but Lucianne would want to know if she'd be there tomorrow and Anna didn't know what to tell her. As things stood she couldn't imagine being able to get away, but who could say what tomorrow might bring?

Picking up Bob's mobile as it rang, her heart skipped a beat when she saw who it was. 'Eddie Leeman,' she told him, and passed the phone over. Apart from being a long-standing golfing partner of Bob's, Eddie was the Commander of Northland District Police.

'Eddie,' Bob barked. 'Thanks for getting back to me.'

'I'd have been in touch sooner,' Leeman responded, 'but I wanted to find out as much as I could before I spoke to you. Where are you now?'

'On our way back to Kerikeri station.'

'Then you need to get a move on. The order's come down to move her to Auckland.'

'Oh Christ,' Bob groaned.

'What?' Anna cried, putting a hand on his arm.

'They're taking her to Auckland,' Bob told her. 'What else do you know?' he asked Leeman.

'A couple of British detectives are due to arrive in the next couple of hours, but there's the extradition process to go through before they can take her anywhere. I hear you've got Don Thackeray on the case.'

'You bet. I'll pass this on to him now.'

After calling Thackeray, who assured him he'd be waiting when Charlotte got to Auckland, Bob said to Anna, 'We need to find out if we can go down there with her.'

'They can't stop us if we go under our own steam,' she pointed out. 'But maybe we need to be here for Chloe. Or I do. You can go to Auckland.'

'Is that Shelley?' he said, squinting as an oncoming driver flashed their lights. 'Yes it is,' and slowing up he put his window down as she drew alongside him.

'I'm just taking Craig home,' Shelley informed them as Craig waved out from behind her. 'Phil's on his way back from the labs and Rick's plane should be here in half an hour. I'll pick him up when I go for Danni.'

'We've just heard they're taking Charlotte to Auckland,' Anna told her, 'so Rick might be more use there. Can you get hold of him?'

Taking out her phone Shelley pressed the quick-dial, but was pushed through to voicemail. After leaving a message in case Rick hadn't already boarded the plane, she said, 'Any news on Chloe?'

With a catch in her heart Anna shook her head. 'How did you get on with the social worker?'

'She was very nice, but no way was she going to tell me where Chloe is. She promised to take Boots straight to her, though, and I'm sure she meant it.'

'Well, at least we can tell Charlotte that,' Anna said to Bob as they drove on. 'I wonder if she knows she's going to Auckland yet.'

Charlotte was with Grant beside a marked car outside the police station when her mother and Bob pulled into the parking lot. There was no trace of colour in her face and her eyes felt as raw and heavy as the dread in her heart. 'Have you seen Chloe?' she asked, as soon as Anna got to her.

'I'm afraid not,' Anna replied, glancing at Bob as he went to give Charlotte's bag to Grant, 'but Shelley just told us the social worker's taken Boots to her.'

As a whisper of relief brushed through her fear,

Charlotte said, 'Do you know they're taking me to Auckland?'

'Yes,' Anna replied. 'Bob's going to try and go with you. I'll stay here in case something changes with Chloe.'

Charlotte nodded distractedly. 'I'm sure they'll be making plans to take her back to England by now,' she said, stiff with the fear of it. 'Maybe if we could find out which flight she's on . . . If I could go with her . . .' Her eyes moved to Grant. 'They won't let me of course.'

He shook his head forlornly. There was nothing he could add.

Wishing she knew how to comfort her daughter, Anna said, 'We'll find out what we can and as soon as we do we'll make sure it's passed on to you.'

Coming to join them, Bob said to Charlotte, 'Apparently I can't go in the car with you, so I'm going to try and get a seat on the next plane down. Don Thackeray, your lawyer, will be waiting when you reach the station in Auckland and the first thing he'll do is try to get you out of custody.'

Charlotte's smile was weak. Didn't anyone understand? She'd stolen a child, some might even say kidnapped, and no jurisdiction in the world was going to look on her leniently for that.

Looking round as Wex, the sergeant, came to talk to Grant, she felt her insides turning to liquid. They must be ready to go. 'I keep wondering,' she said to Bob, 'how they found out, and all I can think of is a woman who was at the Pear Tree when we were having coffee. She kept staring at me and I know she recognised me, but Chloe wasn't there so how did she . . . I guess . . . Maybe she followed me . . .'

Bob's eyes were grave as he took her hands in his. 'I don't think it matters how they found out right now,' he said, 'what does is making sure we get you and Chloe all the legal and moral support we can.'

'I'm afraid we need to go,' Wex told them, opening a rear passenger door for Charlotte to get in.

As a fresh wave of fear broke through her, the urge to run was so intense she felt it might break through her skin. Her arms, her legs, every muscle in her body needed to get away from here, to go to Chloe and take her somewhere no one would ever be able to find them again. She had never felt so powerless, so wretched or afraid. Seeing her mother's stricken face, she said, 'I'll be fine,' while feeling that she never would be again. 'Just be there for Chloe, if you can.'

'Of course, of course,' Anna assured her, giving her a hug, 'and Bob'll try to be there when you get to Auckland.'

'There's a six o'clock flight,' he told her as he hugged her too. 'If I can get on it, it should get me in before you, so I'll be waiting with Don.'

Feeling that she didn't deserve such loyalty when she'd brought so much chaos to his life, she said, 'You don't need to . . .'

'I'll be there,' he replied firmly. 'You just hold on during the drive. It could be, because of how late you'll arrive, that you'll end up having to spend tonight in custody, but we'll be straight on the case in the morning. OK? Do you hear me?'

Charlotte nodded and tried to smile. *She was going to spend the night in a cell. The first of how many? Oh dear God, what was going to happen, how could she have done this to herself, to Chloe?*

'Thanks,' she whispered. 'I hope nothing . . . I mean, if anything happens to you because of what I've done . . .'

'Let me worry about that, but anyway, it won't.'

'Charlotte,' Wex said gently.

As she got into the car Anna stooped down beside her. 'We've put a bag in the back for you,' she told her, speaking through her tears. 'Let me know if there's anything else you need . . .'

'Don't,' Charlotte said abruptly. 'Please, don't break down now or I won't . . . I won't be able to hold it together.'

Standing up, Anna took a step back and swallowed hard. 'It'll be all right,' she said hoarsely. 'We'll get through it.'

Knowing it was what she had to say, Charlotte simply nodded and turned away.

Minutes later Bob and Anna were watching the back of the car as Grant drove out of the car park. They waited for Charlotte to turn around and wave, but she didn't.

'Come on,' Bob said, and pulling Anna to him he led her to where she'd left her car. 'I need you to go and pack me an overnight bag,' he told her, opening the driver's door for her to get in.

'What are you going to do?' she asked.

His expression was grim as he looked off towards the airport. 'Make sure I can get on that flight,' he replied, 'and if Rick's on his way in from Auckland, I'll be there to meet him off the plane.'

Chloe was in the corner of an armchair with Boots, keeping her head down and pretending she was invisible.

The lady was back on the sofa, watching TV. Every

now and again she sucked on a little white stick and blew out smoke like a dragon. Chloe was scared of her even though she spoke in a kind voice like Auntie Shelley's and kept asking her if she was all right. She didn't know if it was a trick so she kept her face buried in Boots.

'Won't you eat something, petal?' the lady asked, crushing her little stick in a saucer. 'You haven't eaten all day.'

Chloe didn't look up.

'What about your bear? Isn't he hungry?'

Boots didn't want to eat either.

They just wanted to go home to Mummy.

The lady sighed and used a remote control to change the channel.

A few minutes later she was saying, 'Oh my God,' in a way that made Chloe tense even tighter.

'So that's who you are,' she said. 'Wow, no wonder I've only got you for a couple of days.'

Chloe peeped up and her heart gave a leap. A big picture of Mummy was on the TV.

'Mummy,' she whispered, starting to cry. Why was Mummy on the TV? Could she see her and Boots? Was she going to come to get them now?

'Oh, there, there,' the lady said, coming to comfort her.

Chloe buried herself back in Boots. She didn't like the way the lady smelled. Why didn't she take her back to Mummy?

'Poor little thing,' the lady murmured, stroking her back. 'It's all right, no one can get to you here. You're nice and safe with me.'

Spotting his father's car as he came out of Kerikeri airport, Rick went straight to it. 'What's happening?'

he demanded as Bob started the engine. 'Where's Charlotte?'

'They're taking her to Auckland,' Bob informed him, driving out to the main road.

'And Chloe? Shelley said . . .'

'We still don't know where she is, but we're working on it.'

'Poor thing,' Rick murmured, 'she must wonder what the heck's going on.'

Pulling up outside the Marsden Winery where a tractor was turning in with a trailer full of bottles, Bob killed the engine and turned to his son. 'She's not the only one who's wondering that,' he said bluntly.

Rick bristled. 'And what's that supposed to mean?'

'It means why the hell would Katie go digging around the way she did if it weren't for *you* and whatever the . . .'

'Just a minute,' Rick cut in angrily, 'I'm not taking responsibility for what's happened . . .'

'Oh yes you are. You're engaged to be married to that girl, then Charlotte comes on the scene . . .'

'There's nothing between me and Charlotte.'

'Well Katie obviously thinks there is and now look where we are. And please don't tell me you're not taking responsibility again, or I swear to God I'll swing for you.'

Stunned, Rick said, 'If I'd had any idea what Katie was going to do, don't you think I'd have stopped her? And we don't even know if it was her yet. It's what I'm here to find out . . .'

'And then what? What are you going to do with her after that? She's got plans for the wedding, we all have . . .'

'I know that, and I'm sorry, but right now Charlotte has to be our main concern.'

'Don't tell me where my concerns lie. I'm perfectly clear about that, I just wish you were. But I'm telling you this, if you've got some idea in your head that . . .'

'Dad, will you get off my case?'

'No, I won't. It's time you heard a few home truths about what an embarrassment you are to me.'

'You want embarrassing,' Rick cried savagely, 'then how about you start dealing with the fact that I'm gay!'

Bob blanched as his next words turned to air.

'Yeah, that's right, Dad, *gay*. I like men, not women, that's why I can't get married, or hold down a relationship with a girl, but I keep trying. Oh yeah, I keep trying all right, not for me, for *you*, because I've always been afraid of what it would do to you if you knew the truth. Well, you know it now. I'm gay and whether you like it or not it's not going away. It's who I am and I'm not going to feel ashamed of it any longer.'

Bob was looking as though he'd been punched. His eyes were glassy, his breathing laboured as he tried to take this in. He started to speak, but hardly knew what he wanted to say.

Letting his head fall back against the seat, Rick closed his eyes in dismay. 'I'm sorry,' he said quietly. 'I never meant to tell you like that . . . I . . . Oh Christ, Dad, I'm sorry, OK? I get how hard this is for you . . .'

Bob started the engine. 'Does Katie know?' he asked stiffly as he started to drive on.

'I haven't told her yet. I was going to tell you both, at the weekend.'

'So why did she go digging around about Charlotte?'

'Because like you said, she thinks there's something between us. I can see now, if I'd told her straight away why we were splitting up she might not have done that . . .'

'No, she might not have.'

Rick turned his head away.

'Why the hell did you allow her to think you were going to marry her if . . .'

'Because I did intend to marry her, I swear it, until I realised I couldn't go through with it. But it wasn't her I was finding it so hard to be honest with, it was *you*. What you think of me matters more than just about anything, and I was afraid you'd cut me out of your life . . .'

'What the hell are you talking about? Cut you out because you're *gay*? What kind of father do you think I am? All I've ever wanted is for you to be happy. Don't you think if you'd come to me I'd have understood? I thought you knew me.'

'What I know is how important it is to you to pass Te Puna on to your son and heir, who'll pass it on to his son and heir . . .'

'Christ, Rick, what do you think we've got going here, some sort of dynasty? We're not the bloody Rockefellers, or the royal family . . .'

'I know that. I was just afraid . . . God, I don't know what I was afraid of. I guess Charlotte was right when she said I was the one who couldn't really accept it, so I made out like it was you who had the problem.'

Casting him a look, Bob said, 'I suggest we talk about this later. Am I taking you to Katie's now?'

Rick nodded.

'Does she know you're coming? She's been avoiding Shelley.'

'I know, but I'll catch up with her. What are you doing after you've dropped me?'

'Getting a flight down to Auckland. They're taking Charlotte by road.'

Closing his eyes tightly, Rick muttered, 'I've screwed up so badly. I've caused a major bloody catastrophe through being a coward . . .'

Unable to offer much comfort right now, Bob let the silence run until they were pulling up outside the salon. 'If you want to fly back to Auckland with me tonight,' he said, 'I'm on the six o'clock. Please, just don't walk out on Katie if you think she's in danger of arranging any more payback for being dumped.'

Failing to see what worse she could do, Rick got out of the car and turned back to his father. Before he could speak, Bob said, 'Later. Call me when you're done.'

In the end Rick found Katie at her Aunt Sarah's, huddled into a relaxer with a blanket around her legs and a bunch of ragged Kleenex clutched in one hand.

'We've seen the news,' Sarah told him, her normally sunny demeanour looking disturbingly bleak as she gestured for him to sit down, 'and I've just spoken to Anna. It's terrible, awful. I can hardly bear to think of what's happening to them.'

'Did you know?' Rick asked. 'I mean before today.'

Sarah nodded. 'Of course. Anna could never keep anything from me.'

Rick looked at Katie, but she couldn't meet his eyes.

'It's started up on the news now,' Sarah told him. 'I expect you've already seen it.'

'Not really,' he replied, inwardly cringing at how much worse the inevitable media storm was going to make everything.

Looking from one to the other, Sarah said, 'Right, I'll leave you two to talk. I'll be down with the chickens if you need me.'

After the door closed behind her Rick said to Katie, 'You know why I'm here.'

Still she couldn't look at him as she struggled not to cry.

'Was it you who told the police?' he asked, feeling for how wretched she looked, and aching for how much he was hurting her.

'If it was, then you only have yourself to blame,' she mumbled.

Letting her words weight his conscience along with his father's, he said, 'Exactly what did you think you were going to achieve?'

Her eyes flashed as her head came up. 'She's stolen a child, for Christ's sake. It was my duty to report it.'

'Except we both know that's not why you did it.'

'How can you stand there trying to make me feel guilty when she's the one who's committed a crime . . .'

'Do you really not understand what you've done?' he demanded incredulously. 'Didn't you once spare a thought for Chloe and what you might be doing to her? You know what she went through before she came here, so you surely understand why Charlotte took her . . .'

'Stop trying to make out like I'm the one who's in the wrong,' she retorted. 'I did what anyone in my position would have done if they'd . . . What are you doing? Where are you going?' she cried as he started for the door.

'There's no point in continuing this right now,' he replied. 'What's done is done, we can't change it, but I have to try . . .'

'Please don't tell me you still want her after what she's done . . .'

'She's my *sister*,' he shouted, throwing out his hands, 'and Chloe's my niece . . .'

'She's not your niece. She doesn't belong to . . .'

'She belongs here, with her family, and if you can't see . . .'

'All I can see is how pathetic you are. Charlotte Nicholls is a criminal, a kidnapper. She *stole a child* and now she's going to find out what happens to people who *steal children*.'

Going back to her, he said, 'It's not your fault you've got everything so wrong, Katie, it's mine. I know that, and I accept it, I only wish there was a way to change it, but there isn't. We can't be together, Katie, not because I don't love you, because actually in a way I do, it's because I'm gay. So you see it has nothing to do with Charlotte, or Chloe, or anyone else. We would never have been right for each other and now I'm only sorry I didn't tell you the truth sooner – God knows how sorry I am about that.'

Feeling the lightness of relief, while struggling with the millstone of guilt, he continued to look down at her, waiting to hear what she would say. In the end, leaving her still stunned by his admission he returned to the door.

'Rick?' she said tremulously.

He stopped but didn't turn round.

'Is that really true? You're actually gay?'

Turning to her, his heart aching with regret and pity, he said, 'Yes, it's true.'

Her eyes came to his, large and flooded with tears. 'Is it Hamish?'

He nodded.

She nodded too, as if she should have known, and looked away.

He went on standing where he was, not sure whether to go to her or not.

'I wish I hadn't made that call about Charlotte,' she said brokenly. 'I swear, if I could take it back I would.'

Knowing she meant it, he told her, 'I should go now, but we can talk again later if you like.'

When she didn't answer he simply left the room, and after waving to Sarah in the chicken coop he returned to the main road to hitch a lift back into town. 'Hi Dad,' he said, answering his phone as it rang.

'Where are you?' Bob asked.

'Just leaving Sarah's. It *was* Katie.'

Bob sighed. 'OK, well we knew it anyway, and we've got bigger problems than that now. I've just had some news.'

As he listened, Rick felt the breath leaving his body. 'Can they do that?' he demanded.

'It's not a question of whether they can or not, they *are*.'

'Jesus Christ,' Rick murmured. 'Does Charlotte know yet?'

'I've no idea, it's what I'm trying to find out.'

Charlotte was staring absently into the darkness as Grant steered the car through a U-turn and continued back down the busy highway they'd just come along. She presumed they were close to

Auckland's police headquarters by now, but she wasn't taking in much of her surroundings, nor was she going to ask. She didn't want to know. All she wanted was for this to turn into a nightmare she could wake up from, so she could find Chloe and get on with her life.

Where was Chloe now? Were the carers being kind to her? How much of what was happening did she understand? Imagining her sweet little face pale with fear, her eyes clouded with confusion, was tearing her apart. *Please God let them understand how important it is for her at least to speak to Anna.*

During the journey Wex or Grant had kept asking if she was all right and she'd said yes, because what else could she say? None of this was their fault; they were simply doing their jobs, and even if she could persuade them to let her go, what would she do? No one was going to let her see or speak to Chloe even if she could find out where she was, and she knew she couldn't.

Chloe, Chloe, Chloe. The silent cries were like sobs shuddering all the way through her.

As the car came to a stop she looked out of the window and frowned in confusion. 'What's happening?' she asked. 'I thought we were going to the police station.'

'There's been a change of plan,' Wex told her awkwardly. 'The call I got, back when we stopped at the gas station . . .'

'What kind of a change?' she blurted. 'I don't understand.'

Opening the door for her to get out, Grant said, 'I'm sorry, we were given instructions . . .'

As she tried to interrupt again a voice behind her said, 'Charlotte Nicholls?'

She spun round to find two men in suits and raincoats coming towards her.

'DC Donahoe,' the taller one told her, holding up his badge. His face was waxen and pockmarked, his eyes were grey. 'This is DC Felix,' he added, gesturing to the other officer.

'What's – what's happening?' she cried, stepping back towards Grant. 'Who are you?'

'We're from Dean Valley Police,' Donahoe explained. 'We'll be escorting you back to the UK.'

As horror leapt through her the roar of a jumbo jet all but drowned her words. 'But what about . . . ? Can't I . . . ? I *have the right to a lawyer*.'

'Of course,' Donahoe agreed, checking his phone. 'As soon as we get back to England.'

'But what about extradition?' she protested. 'I thought . . .'

'It's all been signed off,' Felix assured her as Donahoe turned away to take a call.

'But how? I don't understand.' She was looking at Grant, imploring him to explain.

Grant glared at Felix, challenging him to be more specific.

With an expression that was kinder than his words, Felix said, 'I guess the simplest way to put this is that our government has spoken to the New Zealand government, and everything's been cleared.' He glanced briefly at Grant.

Charlotte couldn't fight down the panic. 'You have to speak to Bob,' she told Grant urgently. 'Please will you call and tell him what's happening.'

'Sure.' He was already taking out his phone.

'Oh my God,' she gasped, as Wex handed her bag to Felix. They really were taking her. 'Do you know where Chloe is? Will she be on the same flight?'

'No, she won't,' Donahoe replied, coming back to them. Then, 'We need to go get ourselves checked in now, flight leaves . . .'

'Can I make a call?' she asked desperately. 'Please can I just ring my mother? She needs to make sure no one calls Chloe Ottilie. It's really important . . .'

'I'm sorry, but the little girl's not your concern any more,' Donahoe informed her, and taking her arm he steered her into the terminal building.

'Gone! What do you mean, gone?' Anna demanded when Bob broke the news.

'It seems some deal went down between Whitehall and Wellington . . .'

'But they can't do that. She has rights . . . Where's Don Thackeray? I thought he was meeting her.'

'He would have if we'd received the information in time, but he didn't stand a chance of getting to the airport before the flight left.'

Anna's eyes were wild. 'So they just took her? Bundled her on to a plane without allowing her to make a single phone call, or to see a lawyer . . . You can't let them get away with that, Bob.'

His face was bleak as he said, 'I'm afraid they already have, because no matter what arguments Don puts up now there's no way in the world the Brits are going to turn around and bring her back.'

Anna looked to Rick and Shelley, whose expressions reflected the helplessness in her own. 'I have to go over there,' she suddenly declared. 'I can't leave her to face this on her own.'

'I'll go online and sort out some flights,' Bob said, opening up the kitchen laptop.

'But what about Chloe?' Anna cried. 'It'll be like we're abandoning her . . .'

Rick said, 'If they've already flown Charlotte back, you can be sure they're going to do the same with Chloe. And Dad, before you go booking any flights you ought to consider the position you might put yourselves in if you go over to England. Anna helped Charlotte to bring Chloe here, and you've given them shelter since. The authorities here might turn a blind eye to that, but I don't think it'll be the same over there.'

Bob was staring at him in stunned realisation.

'Oh my God, what are we going to do?' Anna gulped.

'For now, I'd say the best thing,' Rick replied, 'is to get in touch with someone who can help her when she gets there.'

'Of course,' Anna agreed. 'Actually, there's a lawyer . . . Oh God, what's his name? He's a barrister, a QC even, he's kind of a friend of Charlotte's . . .'

'He won't be able to help at this stage,' Bob interrupted. 'It's not what barristers do. She needs a solicitor. I can get Don Thackeray to recommend someone.'

'Or I could speak to her sister, Gabby,' Anna suggested. 'I'm sure she'll help. I wonder if she knows yet. I guess she must now it's hit the news.'

Shelley said awkwardly, 'They haven't been in touch since Charlotte came here, and this is something . . . Well, she might not want to get involved.'

Anna nodded uncertainly. 'I know who I can speak to,' she declared. 'Tommy Burgess. He used to be her boss. I *know* he'll want to help, and as he's with social services he might be able to help us with Chloe too.'

'Good idea. Try to find a number for him. Rick, could you get the phone?'

As Rick went to pick up the landline Bob took out his mobile to call Don Thackeray while Anna Googled Dean Valley Social Services.

'No thanks, not now,' Rick said sharply and hung up.

'Who was that?' Bob asked, cutting his connection.

With an uneasy glance at Anna, Rick said, 'I think we're going to need some security around here, at least for the next few days.'

Bob frowned.

'It was someone from Sky News,' Rick explained, 'asking if this was where the missing child, Ottilie Wade, has been living.'

As Shelley gasped, Anna said, 'They can't call her Ottilie. She'll think she's going back to where she was before.'

'I'll speak to the social worker,' Shelley said, reaching for her phone. 'I don't suppose we can stop it in the press, but at least we can try to do something about it with her carers.'

'Who are you calling?' Anna asked Bob.

'The elders at the settlement,' he replied. 'They'll take care of the security.'

The landline rang again.

'And so,' Bob murmured as the voicemail picked up, 'the media circus begins.'

Chapter Twelve

Charlotte was going through motions that felt utterly surreal. It was as though she'd been caught up in some Kafkaesque movie, or someone else's nightmare, for surely to God it couldn't be her own. Throughout the flight, and the change at a Middle Eastern airport, she'd remained locked inside herself, barely eating, or sleeping, or speaking, while attempting to find distraction in movies and magazines. She kept telling herself that her mother had somehow managed to take custody of Chloe – if she could believe that she could get through this.

If only she'd tried harder with her mother while she'd had the chance. That last day – only yesterday, or was it the day before, she'd lost track of time now – at Kauri Cliffs, she'd been unforgivably hostile towards Anna without even meaning to be. Now she'd very likely lost her a major client as well as causing her the hideous embarrassment of having her daughter arrested and removed by the police.

Their relationship didn't have the kind of roots most mothers and daughters shared; it wasn't strong enough, or stable enough for her to expect anything of her mother now, so she must try not to. Anna and Bob had given her everything they could to help her and Chloe build a new life, and she would always be grateful for it, but it had to end there. She wasn't their responsibility, and nor was Chloe, though please God they'd continue to do all they could for the little girl. For her, there would be nothing they could do apart from stay as far away from the British legal system as possible. The crime that had been committed was hers, and hers alone, and though they might have been a party to it, were either of them to find themselves under arrest, possibly even on trial for what *she* had done, she would never be able to forgive herself, or face any sort of relationship with them again.

Perhaps they wouldn't want one after this. They might feel the price of knowing her, including her in their lives, was too high.

She was somewhere in the depths of Heathrow airport now, in an airless, grey-painted area with a section of empty desks and computer terminals sprawled across the back of it, a large glassed-in room to one side where a uniformed officer was speaking on the phone, and an unlit corridor leading off to what could be cells. Detectives Donahoe and Felix had disappeared a while ago, leaving her with two fellow officers from Dean Valley Police who'd been there to meet them. DS Karen Potter and DC Darren Wild. No sign of Detective Chief Inspector Terence Gould yet, the officer who'd led the hunt for Chloe, or Ottilie as he'd known her then. He wasn't someone Charlotte was looking forward to meeting again.

Karen Potter was rearresting her. The words were making her feel nauseous and dizzy.

'. . . you do not have to say anything,' Potter was reciting, 'however, it may harm your defence if you do not mention when questioned something which you later rely on in court. Anything you do say may be given in evidence. Do you understand your rights?'

Charlotte nodded, and swallowed dryly. 'Yes,' she managed, the word seeming to echo from somewhere far inside her. *Would those be the same rights I was supposed to have before leaving New Zealand?* she wanted to ask.

She was tired to the point of exhaustion and felt in sore need of a shower, but didn't imagine one would be on offer here.

When might she get one again?

'Do you have a lawyer?' Potter asked.

Charlotte's grainy eyes drew focus. Potter was probably around forty, she thought, with a flaky complexion and dyed blonde hair. She didn't look like a happy woman.

'Can I have an answer please?' Potter prompted.

'No, I don't have a lawyer,' Charlotte replied. Her mind filled with thoughts of Anthony, but nothing in the world would persuade her to call him for help.

Did he know yet? He must do; the police had taken some pleasure in telling her she was all over the news. She wasn't going to torment herself with what he might be thinking of her now, it wouldn't help in any way, unless she wanted to make herself feel even worse than she already did.

No one had offered her anything to drink, or to eat. It didn't matter, she didn't want anything anyway. All she really wanted was to use a phone so she could find out what was happening to Chloe.

As a fresh wave of fear came over her, DC Wild appeared, announcing that the car was outside.

Twenty minutes later, wrapped in a shawl her

mother had thought to pack for her, she was huddled in the back of a saloon car with Wild at the wheel and Potter sitting in a preoccupied silence beside him.

Charlotte was silent too, gazing out at the passing countryside through weary eyes and seeing only New Zealand, as she wondered if Chloe was still there. She felt sure she must be, but where exactly, and for how long? Who would bring her back when the time came, unless by some miracle it was decided she should remain with the family she knew and loved? It might be hard for her at first without Charlotte, but she'd have Nanna and Auntie Shelley and Danni. She could carry on going to Aroha where she'd settled in so well. She'd be able to bake cakes for her birthday and ride her new bike and play with her puppy. She could make wishes and practise her jump-off and dance on the beach for pipis.

Oh God, oh God, oh God. Why, for the sake of one tiny innocent girl, couldn't it just happen?

Would Dean Valley send a social worker to collect her, or would someone from New Zealand escort her back? Just please God don't let it be a man, especially if he was going to call her Ottilie. The dread of it lurched sickeningly inside her. Chloe wouldn't be able to handle that. It would send her spiralling back into a place of anguish and terror.

She had to stop tormenting herself like this, somehow shut down her mind or at least force it to go elsewhere. Yet how could she, when not to worry about Chloe would be like abandoning her all over again?

You have to try, Charlotte, she told herself firmly. *For the sake of your own sanity you have to rein in your fear and take one step at a time.* How often had she given that advice to parents of children in her caseload? More often than she could remember; never had she imagined giving it to herself. Now she knew how easy it was to say, and how very hard to follow.

She hadn't expected it to be so sunny here in England, so eagerly springlike, as though the whole landscape was pausing before an exuberant burst into bloom. She used to love days like this when she'd lived here; they'd filled her with such hope and anticipation, a feeling that it was nothing but good to be alive. Today the sunshine seemed to mock her, and knowing what she was facing in the hours, weeks, months to come it was impossible to generate even the merest flicker of cheer, no matter how beautiful her surroundings.

As they turned into the Leigh Delamere services she remembered the time she'd stopped here once with her ex-boyfriend, Jason. She wondered what he was doing now, if he'd seen the news and what he was thinking of her if he had.

It didn't matter. Nothing did apart from Chloe – and how she, Charlotte, was going to survive being sent to prison.

It might not come to that, she told herself forcefully. There was still a long way to go, and in that time anything could happen.

Like what? You stole a child, lied to the police, deceived your friends and colleagues . . . There was no escaping what she'd done; the guilt, the shame of it was all over her, and yet she only had to think of Chloe's laughter and spirited little dances, her big eyes gazing up at her full of love and an eagerness to learn, or to please, to know that she'd do it all over again.

'Do you need the toilet?' Karen Potter asked over her shoulder.

'No,' Charlotte answered. 'I'm fine.'

Seeming satisfied with that, Potter returned to whatever she was doing on her phone while Darren Wild got out of the car to fill up with petrol.

Charlotte wondered what Karen Potter's home life was like. Was she married, a mother, a carer for an elderly father? She couldn't imagine ever getting into conversation with the woman, or certainly not in a friendly way, but that was hardly surprising. She, Charlotte, wouldn't be the Dean Valley force's favourite person right now, given what fools she'd made of them over Chloe's disappearance. No doubt they were getting a rough ride of it in the press and none of them would be enjoying that, DCI Gould least of all.

On the other hand, Karen Potter's reasons for seeming hostile could simply be that a life in law enforcement had taken its toll on her in ways that brought out the worst in her. It happened to social workers too, making them hard and cold and judgemental of the people they were supposed to be helping. She'd known a few like that, but with a couple of exceptions, her colleagues at the North Kesterly hub hadn't been amongst them.

What were they making of all this now?

As she thought of Tommy and his unquestioning friendship she felt more guilt and shame tearing at her. She'd love to be able to turn to him now, to seek his advice, but he didn't deserve to be embroiled in a scandal that was entirely hers. As her team leader, though, he could hardly avoid it. She wondered if he'd already left to start his new life up north. *Please, please, please let him still be there.* Not for her sake, for Chloe's, because Charlotte trusted him more than anyone to make sure Chloe was placed with the right people. He might even be able to swing it for her to go to Maggie Fenn. Thinking of Maggie caused another catch in Charlotte's heart, not only because of Maggie being Anthony's sister, though probably that most of all, but because of how Maggie must be viewing her now.

Maggie was so decent and kind, so ready to see the best in people, that finding out how gravely Charlotte had deceived her would have come as a horrible blow. How was she going to explain it to Sophie, the feisty teenager who'd come into her care through Charlotte, or Alex as they'd known her then? If Sophie was still with her, which she might not be. How were any of Charlotte's charges going to respond to what she'd done? She wasn't afraid of their scorn so much as of them feeling angry and rejected that she hadn't chosen to take one of them.

There were so many people to consider, people she'd hardly allowed herself to think about after she'd gone. It was as though she'd simply shut them out of her life, pretended they no longer existed, but they were all still there, and seemed to be crowding in on her now, wanting her to know how she'd hurt or offended them, disappointed or betrayed them. There would be those like her old boss, Wendy, or the reporter, Heather Hancock, who'd feel nothing but pleasure at her disgrace, and would probably want to make sure it was utterly complete.

Where, she wondered, did her sister, Gabby, fit into it all? How was she feeling now? What was she telling her five-year-old twins, Phoebe and Jackson, about their favourite aunt and what she'd done? Charlotte could hardly bear to think of her niece and nephew's confusion. She'd adored them since their birth and yet she'd ended all contact with them in order to protect Chloe. What would that mean to them? What did it say about her? How could she not have considered them before this? Two more innocent victims of a crime she had committed and Gabby had known about, though please God Gabby had never told anyone that.

'Go safely,' Gabby had said on that last day, outside the vicarage, '. . . and don't forget to send Phoebe's passport back when you're ready,' she'd added in a whisper.

So she'd known that Charlotte had taken Phoebe's passport and had obviously guessed why. She hadn't condemned Charlotte, or tried to stop her. She'd simply blown a kiss, got back into her car and driven away.

How was that going to reflect on her now?

Not at all if Charlotte could help it, though of course she'd be asked how she'd managed to get Chloe out of the country. She'd have to say she'd 'acquired' a passport and refuse to give details of how or where. With the kinds of families she'd been involved with as a social worker, it wouldn't be hard for anyone to imagine her knowing the 'right' people. Anyway, the issue wasn't *how* she'd got Chloe out of Britain, but the fact that she'd taken her at all.

It was gone four thirty by the time DC Darren Wild drove them into Kesterly-on-Sea, and as they turned along the seafront where the amusement arcades and fish and chip shops, surfers' sheds, beach huts and tired old stucco hotels were glittering in the late afternoon sunlight, Charlotte found herself overwhelmed by nostalgia. It was as though no more than a day had gone by since she was last here. It hadn't changed a bit; the Punch and Judy tent was in its usual place on the beach, presumably brought out early to take advantage of the lovely weather; same with the donkeys lined up ready to trot their young riders along the sand; the hands on the clock tower were still stuck at a quarter past eight; and banners announcing a half-marathon were strung along the railings of the promenade.

And there was the sweet old-fashioned carousel that she and Chloe had ridden so many times together. She felt a surge of emotion, remembering how Chloe had loved that carousel. It was such a simple treat that had made her eyes glow with awe.

Just along from the carousel, next to the station, was the Pumpkin playgroup, where she'd taken Chloe to nursery when Chloe's real mother had failed to do so. She'd made a friend there, the first she'd ever had, and she'd learned how to play the kind of games that had never happened at home.

Memories were waiting on every corner, tucked inside the narrow streets and all along the beach. It was true Charlotte's actual home had been in Mulgrove, a village about half an hour inland, but this was where she'd gone to school, taken part in sports, done her shopping, spread her young wings. She'd only left to go to uni, and for a crazy two weeks with fellow graduates in Ibiza. Her first and only job had been here – and her real family, her mother's family, had owned a home over on the upper reaches of Temple Fields. That house had long since gone, but the tragedy that had played out there, that had become known as the Temple Fields Massacre, lived on in the local psyche.

'Thought you might enjoy a little sightseeing,' Potter declared with a sneer in her voice.

Realising they were turning on to North Hill, Charlotte found herself fighting to resist it. This was where Chloe had lived with her schizophrenic mother and abusive father, in a forlorn Victorian house on the wrong side of the hill where there were no views of the sea, or neighbours to speak of. Every other old property or purpose-built block had been turned into a hotel or bed and breakfast, so the family at number forty-two had gone all but unnoticed. Obviously, the house and its position had been carefully chosen by Chloe's father, Brian Wade, possibly with some help from his paedophile chum and Chloe's GP, Timothy Aiden.

Both men were in prison now and in Wade's case, since he'd also pleaded guilty to murdering his wife, it was unlikely he'd ever come out.

How bitterly, tragically ironic that Charlotte was going to end up in prison too.

Though she said nothing as Wild pulled into the Wades' old driveway, inside she was struggling to block out images of the horrors that had happened here. The garden was covered in weeds now and ivy had laid claim to the house, even smothering the boarded-up windows and stringing across the entrance to the porch. Someone had visited with a paintbrush to scrawl words including 'pervert' and 'nonce' over the garage doors.

'See that there?' Potter said, pointing. 'The one that says "child killer"? That's what everyone thought, that he'd done away with her. You wouldn't know this, but we were getting ready to charge him, because we thought he'd killed her too. What would you have done if we had? Would you have let him take the rap for a murder he didn't commit, that hadn't actually taken place? Or would you have come forward?'

It was a question Charlotte couldn't answer, though it had been one of her biggest fears. Would she really have allowed Brian Wade to be convicted of a crime she knew he hadn't committed?

It didn't matter now because they knew Chloe was safe and alive, and the only one being charged for her disappearance was already under arrest.

'OK, time to face the music,' Potter announced chirpily as Wild turned the car around. 'I'm afraid we're too late to put you in front of a magistrate today, but we're happy to have you as our guest for the night.'

Charlotte's stomach churned. It wasn't that she hadn't expected to find herself in a cell, but the prospect was about to become a reality and today was Friday, so maybe it would be more than just a night. Already it was starting to feel as though the walls were pressing in on her. 'What about my lawyer?' she asked in a parched voice.

'We'll get on to it as soon as we're at the station,' Potter informed her, taking a call on her mobile. After listening for a few moments, she rang off. 'We'll go in the front way,' she told Wild.

Wild glanced at her in apparent surprise.

Even Charlotte knew that offenders were usually escorted in through the back.

It didn't take her long to realise the reason for the change in procedure. She was going to be paraded in front of the press.

As the car entered the Quadrant, where the town's police headquarters occupied two old mansions and a sixties block on the north side, she saw with a wrenching dismay that the green at the centre of the square had been taken over by TV crews, reporters, photographers and their endless paraphernalia. She'd never seen such a large gathering of reporters, and as they began closing in around the car, banging on the windows and grabbing whatever shots they could snatch, she felt herself drowning in helpless humiliation.

'Seems you're quite popular,' Potter commented drily. 'Look at that, they're here from America, Japan, Australia, New Zealand, well of course New Zealand. I expect they'll be asking for your autograph in a minute.'

Charlotte kept her head down, knowing how unethical this was, yet unable to do anything about it. The disgrace, the sense of persecution, the fear was exactly what the police meant her to feel, and why Wild was driving so slowly.

Had DCI Terence Gould instructed this to happen? She felt sure the call Potter had taken as they were leaving North Hill had been from him.

The car was rocking from side to side, photographers were throwing themselves on to the bonnet, microphones were crashing against the windows, faces were yelling words she could barely hear. Then the cacophony swamped her as Wild brought them to a stop and came round to open her door. As she got out her ankle suddenly twisted and she winced with pain.

She didn't know it then but it was the shot that would make the next day's front pages: her face in close-up, her eyes tightly closed and her lips pressed harshly together.

'Alex, where's Ottilie?'

'Is she coming back?'

'Where were you hiding her?'

'Are you in touch with her father?'

'Did he know where you were keeping her?'

Charlotte felt sick. How could anyone think she'd stayed in touch with that monster?

'Come on, move aside,' Wild urged dispassionately as he led the way through to the station doors.

'Has she been charged yet?'

'Is it kidnap or abduction?'

'Will you plead guilty, Alex?'

There were so many voices shouting the same questions, it was as though she was trapped in a monstrous echo. She couldn't walk upright, or straight, or without a limp as she struggled to get through the teeming mass of humanity. More police were surrounding her now, and as someone threw a blanket over her head she felt smothered in fear. They'd done this to humiliate her further, she knew that, but the shame was compounded by the terror of being shrouded in sudden darkness with so much swirling around her. Her arms scrabbled forward to find the way; as she stumbled and grasped the crowd surged all around her.

'It's all right, you're OK,' she heard someone say, and as a strong arm took hold of her she was all but carried forward into the station.

She had no idea who her rescuer was, she only knew that once inside she still seemed surrounded by people. The blanket was stripped away, catching in her hair and making her stagger.

'Was that absolutely necessary?' an angry female voice demanded.

Charlotte swept the hair from her face. A striking young woman with a neat blonde bob and hazel eyes was standing in front of her, glaring at the officer who'd removed the blanket.

'Get over yourself,' he sneered, and shuffled off to where his fellow officers were beginning to file through a side door.

'Are you OK?' the blonde woman asked Charlotte.

'Yes, I think so,' Charlotte answered, actually feeling faintly dizzy.

'When your ladyships are quite ready,' Potter called out.

Ignoring her, the blonde woman said, 'My name's Kim Giles. Your stepfather has asked my firm to act for you. Are you sure you're OK? Is there anything I can get you?' Before Charlotte could answer, Kim Giles was saying to Potter, 'I've been reliably informed that my client brought a bag with her from New Zealand, but I don't see it anywhere.'

'The bag is safe,' Potter pronounced. 'Now, if you'd like to come this way.'

Taking Charlotte by the arm, Kim Giles steered her towards the door, let her go through first then held back as she passed Potter. 'Can I ask why it was necessary to bring my client in through the front door?' she demanded.

Potter's surprise at being challenged turned to such hostility that Charlotte half expected the lawyer to take a step back, or at least to flush. She did neither, merely blazed her own stare at the detective before moving on. 'We're going through to the custody area now,' she explained to Charlotte as they followed Potter along a scuffed, narrow corridor with offices each side and a locker room at the end. 'I know they formally arrested you when you got to Heathrow, have you spoken to either of them since?'

'No.'

'Good, that's what I want to hear. From now on you speak only to me – or to them if I'm there. They have to give us some time together now, as much as we need, so we can start the process of getting you out of here.'

Latching on to the lawyer's confidence, Charlotte attempted to push her numbing tiredness aside so she could stay focused. How long had it been since she'd last slept? Given the time difference, and her exhaustion, she couldn't even begin to work it out.

It felt like a week.

'Is this your first time in a custody suite?' Kim Giles asked, as Potter released a heavy door and directed them through.

Charlotte shook her head. She'd collected plenty of children from this very reception in her time, so she was almost as familiar with the cold grey-painted walls, glassed-in custody desk and scratched wooden doors as she was with the offenders' homes.

Spotting a tall figure at the desk with his back to them, Charlotte felt herself shrinking inside. She knew exactly who it was, even before he turned round to regard her with his piercing blue eyes. Detective Chief Inspector Terence Gould, the officer who'd visited her home on numerous occasions to talk about the missing child who had all the time been upstairs in a bedroom.

'I have to say,' he told her in a drawl, 'that I never imagined we'd meet again this way.'

Since there wasn't a question, Charlotte didn't answer, though she felt sure her expression showed how unnerved and ashamed she was.

'Good evening, Detective Chief Inspector,' Kim Giles said affably.

After a brief nod in her direction, Gould turned

to the custody sergeant. 'Charge her,' he said, and without another glance in Charlotte's direction he left the suite.

Ten minutes later Charlotte was in a cramped, foul-smelling interview room with Kim Giles.

'Well, we know now,' Kim was saying as she unpacked her briefcase, 'that they're going for child abduction. I guessed they would, but I was afraid they might throw in perverting the course of justice, which can carry a seriously stiff sentence.'

'And child abduction can't?' Charlotte cried, still reeling from the shock of finding herself charged so abruptly.

'Believe me, perverting the course could be worse,' Kim responded.

'The fact that they've charged me already must mean they're pretty sure of their case,' Charlotte stated. 'And why wouldn't they be when they've just brought me back from New Zealand? As far as they're concerned this is all in the bag, and it is, isn't it?'

'They probably think so,' Kim conceded, 'and I'm not going to lie to you, it's serious, but try to think of being charged in a positive light. It not only tells us what they're convinced they can make stick, it means the press are no longer able to vent their own opinions on what's happened.' Her eyes came to Charlotte, and the crispness of her tone vanished. 'Oh God, I hope you don't mind me saying, but you look all in. Did you manage to get any sleep on the plane?'

'Not really,' Charlotte replied, still struggling to catch up with the last few minutes. 'I guess I was too worried.'

'Of course,' Kim murmured sympathetically. 'We'll just go through some basics for now, then you need to rest. I'm sorry it has to be here, but there's no way of getting you in front of a magistrate until tomorrow, at which point I'm hopeful you'll get bail.'

'We can go into court tomorrow?' Charlotte asked.

Kim nodded. 'In the morning.'

'Can you actually get bail for someone who's absconded from the country with a child that's not her own? A child she allowed the police to think was dead, even murdered by her own father?'

Kim raised an ironic eyebrow. 'I probably won't phrase it quite like that,' she responded, and sitting down at the table she opened her laptop ready to make some notes. 'OK, first up, you probably want to know how I arrived in your life, so I should tell you that your stepfather's lawyer in Auckland, Don Thackeray, has had previous dealings with my boss, Jolyon Crane. Obviously Mr Thackeray wanted Jolyon himself to take you on, but unfortunately he's tied up on a fraud case over in Kent that looks set to go on a while. So he asked me to step in, but don't worry, I've had a lot of experience, and I'll be keeping him up to speed with everything that's happening. If you have any worries about me, you just have to say.' She smiled briefly in a way that almost made Charlotte smile too.

'I expect you know this,' Charlotte said, 'but it was someone from your office who represented me when I was fired from my job.' She didn't add that it was the barrister Anthony Goodman who'd recommended Jolyon Crane on that occasion – there was no reason to. However, hearing Jolyon's name had caused a flutter in her heart.

'Eliza Flack repped you for that,' Kim Giles stated. 'She's just gone off on maternity leave or she'd be here now, given that she already knows some of the background. Don't worry, it's all on file, and as soon as I get back to the office I'll be familiarising myself with every last word. If there had been time I'd have done it before coming, but we only got the call this morning while I was in court, then I had to hotfoot it down from Bristol in order to try and get here before you. Luckily I managed it; it was just unfortunate that I couldn't stop them bringing you in the front. Gould knows he was well out of order with that, and I'll be letting him know that I know it too.'

Impressed by how unfazed she seemed by powerful alpha males, Charlotte said, 'I should thank you for rescuing me from under that blanket. I don't suppose they'd have let anything happen to me, but I can't say it was one of the best experiences I've ever had.'

'Pathetic,' Kim scoffed. 'Any more tricks like that and I'll be contacting the top brass. They won't want to mess with someone from Jolyon's office . . . Listen, before you start keeling over on me I expect you'd like to know that I spoke to your mother earlier.'

Charlotte wanted to grab the words and hold them to her as though they were Anna herself. 'Is she all right?' she asked.

'She's fine, but worried about you, obviously. In fact, she's very keen to get over here, but for the moment we're advising her to stay put, at least until we can be sure the British police aren't after making any more arrests.'

Charlotte's eyes went down as the shame of what she'd done to her mother swept through her. 'I don't suppose there's any chance I can speak to her,' she said hoarsely.

'As soon as we get you out of here, absolutely, so I think we should start that ball rolling. First up, I need to know if you have an address here in the UK, somewhere you can go while you're on bail?'

'You really think I'll get bail?' Charlotte said, still not able to believe it.

'I can't guarantee it, I'm afraid, but it's certainly what we're aiming for. So, address? Doesn't have to be yours, it can be a friend's or a relative's.'

Charlotte's first thought was of Gabby and then some of her old friends in Mulgrove. Eventually, though, she shook her head. It simply wouldn't be fair to inflict her problems on any of them, even if they agreed to take her, which they might not.

Would Gabby come to the court tomorrow? Did she even know Charlotte was due to appear? She would know once the press reported it, and that was no doubt happening even as she sat here.

Since she'd made no suggestions, Kim said, 'Not to worry, we'll get something sorted. Now, obviously, the prosecutor's going to paint you as a flight risk, so I'd like to be able to counter that with something impressive enough to make the magistrate believe in you.'

Charlotte pulled a face. It would be hard to feel less impressive than she did right now.

'I'm proposing we offer to post bail,' Kim told her. 'So, do you have any cash, assets, rich mates who might stand you . . .'

'I have two hundred and fifty thousand pounds,' Charlotte came in hopefully. 'It's the proceeds from the sale of my adoptive parents' house.'

Kim's eyes widened. 'That could do it, especially if it's every last penny you have.'

'It is.'

'And is it in an account here, or overseas?'

'In New Zealand, but I can always transfer it back.'

'Indeed. It would just be more helpful if it was immediately accessible, we don't want them banging you up until the banks have got their transfers together. Still, let's not worry about that now, I'm sure your stepfather will work something out with Jolyon if necessary. You know, you're looking so shattered I think we ought to call it a day for . . .'

'I have to know about Chloe,' Charlotte interrupted. 'Do you know where she is, what might be happening to her?'

Kim's eyes reflected her understanding. 'I realise worrying about her must be the hardest part of all this for you,' she said, 'so I'll try to find out what I can. It's not going to be easy, obviously, but if there's anyone in social services you can put me in touch with . . .'

Though Charlotte knew exactly who she wanted to choose, she wasn't sure she could bring herself to put him in such an impossible position.

'Whoever it is,' Kim said gently, 'they can always say no, but without some inside help it's unlikely we'll get very far. You know that better than I do.'

Charlotte's eyes came back to hers, and reminding herself she was doing this for Chloe, she said, 'Tommy Burgess. He was my team leader. I'm not sure if he's still there, in his last email he said he was moving back up north, but if he is, I think he'll tell us what he can.'

Kim wrote down the name, along with the mobile number Charlotte added. 'Anyone else?' she asked. 'Just in case.'

Hoping it wouldn't come to it, Charlotte said, 'Lizzie Walsh. She's a part-timer, and has enormous problems with her family, so I'd really rather not drag her into it if . . .'

'It's OK, I promise not to contact her unless I have to.'

Feeling her nails digging into her palms, Charlotte said, 'They will bring Chloe back here, won't they? I mean, there's no chance of her being returned to my mother?'

With a regretful smile, Kim replied, 'All I can tell you is that she's a British subject, so as far as the authorities are concerned this is where she belongs and . . .'

'Surely she belongs with people who love her,' Charlotte broke in desperately.

'Of course,' Kim agreed, 'and maybe now is a good time to tell you that I, personally, believe you acted in Ottilie's – Chloe's – best interests when you took her, and while the law isn't exactly on our side, I'm going to do everything in my power to stop it from working against us.'

Touched by the sincerity of her tone, even as more fear welled inside her, Charlotte tried to reply, but found she couldn't.

'OK, that's enough for tonight,' Kim decided, closing down her laptop. 'We'll have time to talk in the morning before we go in front of the magistrate.'

Getting to her feet, Charlotte said, 'Whoever you speak to at social services, could you ask if it's possible to get Chloe placed with Maggie Fenn?

She's a foster carer, here in Kesterly, who I know would be wonderful with her.'

After writing the name down, Kim began packing away her files. 'I'm hoping,' she said, as she opened the door, 'that you're so tired now you won't even know where you are once your head hits the pillow.'

Somehow Charlotte managed a smile. 'They have pillows here?' she asked drolly.

Kim cast her a glance. 'I use the term loosely,' she responded. 'Just try to get some sleep, OK? And please, no matter how awful the food looks when they bring it, eat it.'

Knowing the sense of this advice, Charlotte said, 'Will I be allowed to change into fresh clothes before we go to court tomorrow?'

'Don't worry, I'll track down that bag and make sure of it.' As they came to a stop in front of the custody desk Kim turned to face Charlotte, her frank brown eyes full of concern. 'Your mother and step-father will be waiting for my call,' she said, 'so if you have any messages . . .'

Putting a hand to her mouth as more emotion tried to overwhelm her, Charlotte said, 'Tell my mother . . . Please tell her not to come. She mustn't run the risk of being arrested. I just couldn't bear it if that happened.'

Kim nodded her understanding.

'And could you tell Bob,' Charlotte added, 'that he's found me a great lawyer.'

Kim smiled. 'We've a long way to go,' she replied, 'but I'm going to stay hopeful that you're still saying that at the end of it.'

Chapter Thirteen

It was just after five in the morning when the phone shocked Anna out of an unsteady sleep. Grabbing it as Bob came awake too, she said, 'Hello? Anna Reeves speaking.' *Please let it be Charlotte, or at least the lawyer. Or someone with news of Chloe.*

'Mrs Reeves, it's Kim Giles,' the voice at the other end told her.

The lawyer. Anna's heart was already thudding hard. 'Have you seen her?' she asked, swinging her feet to the floor. 'Is she all right?'

'She's fine,' Kim Giles replied firmly. 'Pretty tired, but that's to be expected, and a bit emotional, but all in all she's holding together. I left her about twenty minutes ago just about ready to drop. I'm afraid she'll have to spend the night at the police station, but I'll be trying to get her bailed tomorrow, and I'm hoping you can help me with that.'

'Of course. Anything you need, just tell me . . . If it's money, you know that's not a problem.'

'Thank you. We'll come on to that. First though, she's going to need an address in the UK, preferably Kesterly, and at the moment she doesn't seem to have one. Nor is she seeming inclined to ask any of her friends, so is there anyone you can think of who might be willing to let her stay for a while?'

Frowning, Anna said, 'She has a sister. Didn't she mention her?'

'No, she didn't. Is she in the area?'

'Not exactly, but she's not far away. I can't think why Charlotte . . . Oh God, I know what's going through her mind. Gabby hasn't been in touch since we left, plus she has children and Charlotte'll be concerned about how this might affect them. But why hasn't Gabby come forward anyway? I'd have thought she'd want to help Charlotte . . .'

'Maybe you could try speaking to Gabby,' Kim suggested. 'It would make a huge difference tomorrow if Charlotte does have somewhere to go.'

'Of course, but what if Gabby . . . I mean, we have to accept that she might not want to be involved. Have you tried her old boss, Tommy Burgess? They were very good friends.'

'I've left a message for him to call me back, but given his position in social services he might not feel it's the wisest thing to do.'

Feeling for how devastated Charlotte would be to hear that, Anna said, 'What about if we rent a flat for her? She'd have her own address then, somewhere she could stay while this is all going on.'

'It's a great idea for the long term, but . . .'

'What time is it there?' Anna cut in, suddenly having had an idea.

'Ten past six – in the evening.'

'OK, I'm going to pass you to my husband so he can talk money with you while I try to sort something out,' and pushing the phone into Bob's hand she began scrabbling about in her bag for her mobile. Finding it, she searched frantically for the number of the person who might answer her prayers, and pressed to connect.

Busy.

She tried again.

'Don't worry,' Bob was saying to Kim, 'the Kiwibank's open on Saturdays so I'll organise an urgent transfer as soon as it opens. With any luck it'll be with you first thing tomorrow, your time. You just have to tell me where to send it.'

'I think our company account will be safest,' she replied, 'unless Charlotte still has a bank here.'

'I don't think she has, but I'll check with her mother.'

'Mr Lang,' Anna was saying into her mobile, 'I'm not sure if you remember me. My daughter and I signed a lease on one of your seafront apartments a few months ago, which we had to cancel . . . Yes, that's right, we decided to return to New Zealand. No, no, I'm not trying to get our deposit back, please don't think that. I'm ringing to ask if you might have another apartment available . . . I realise it's . . . OK, yes, thank you, I'll hold on.' Putting a hand over the receiver she asked Bob, 'Is Kim still on the line?'

'Yes, she wants to know if Charlotte still has a bank account in the UK.'

'No, she hasn't. Is that going to be a problem? Yes, of course it is. We must open one for her . . .' Anna's mind was racing.

'We can't, she has to do it herself, and she'll need an address for that too.'

'I'm trying to fix that now. How are we going to get money to her in the meantime?'

'Through the lawyer. I'm arranging . . .'

'Hello, Mr Lang, yes I'm still here,' Anna said urgently. 'Do you have . . . Yes, that's the . . . You do!' Her eyes lit up as she turned to Bob. 'No, the first floor is perfect,' she assured Mr Lang. 'Of

236

course the rent will be more than we were going to pay for the second floor . . . I understand. The balcony sounds lovely. It has two bedrooms. No, part-furnished is fine. When will it be available?' Her jubilation faded as she said, 'Not for another month? Oh dear, I was hoping . . . Is there any chance . . . ? No, we really don't need it to be freshly painted . . . We're happy to clean the carpets . . . When are the current tenants moving out?' She glanced at Bob again and crossed her fingers. 'So would it be possible for us to take it the following day? No, I promise we really don't mind . . . That would be perfect. A week from Saturday, thank you so much. Can I give your details to our lawyer? She'll get the deposit to you. I just need to write down the details . . .' Grabbing the pen Bob was passing her she noted everything quickly, read it back and after thanking Mr Lang again she rang off almost dizzied by adrenalin. 'That's a good sign,' she told Bob. 'I know it doesn't give her an address for when she appears in court, but if we can show we're arranging one . . .'

'Here, talk to Kim,' he said, handing her the phone. 'We might need to give her power of attorney so she can sign the lease on our behalf, unless Charlotte's able to do it herself, of course.'

'Kim,' Anna said into the receiver, 'I think I've got somewhere in Kesterly.'

A few minutes later, having checked and double-checked that all names, bank accounts and addresses were correct, Anna asked, 'Before you go, has there been any news on Chloe?'

Sounding regretful, Kim replied, 'Not from this end. How about you?'

'We heard yesterday that she was about to be

flown back to England, but it's still early in the morning here, so we don't know yet if it's happened.'

'OK, well anything you do hear please let me know so I can pass it on to Charlotte. Same goes this end.'

'Thank you. Please send Charlotte our love when you see her and tell her I'll be there as soon as I possibly can. We both will.'

'I know she'll appreciate that, but she's keen you don't run the risk of being arrested.'

'I understand that, but please tell her not to worry about us. We're doing everything we can, and we'll look forward to speaking to her as soon as she's allowed to use a phone.'

After ringing off Anna took a deep, steadying breath as Bob went to pull open the curtains. Though it was still barely light it was already showing signs of turning into a drab, misty morning, with little promise of sunlight breaking through the clouds. Autumn had arrived in the bay while in England, from what she'd seen on the news, they'd skipped spring and gone straight into summer.

What was it like for Charlotte being back there – and in a cell! How lonely she must be, and afraid.

'We need to speak to Don Thackeray again,' she declared. 'I have to go over there. She shouldn't be going through this on her own.'

'I'll call him in a couple of hours,' Bob promised, glancing at the time. 'Where are you going?' he asked, as she suddenly headed for the door.

'To try and find a number for Gabby,' she replied. 'I can't believe she hasn't contacted us yet, and it could be she doesn't know how to.'

Once in the kitchen she turned on the computer and a few minutes later she was pressing Gabby's number into the phone. After the fourth ring a machine picked up, asking her to leave a message.

'Gabby, it's Anna Reeves, Charlotte's – Alex's – mother,' she said, as Bob began filling the kettle. 'I was wondering if you might be trying to get hold of me. If you are, here are my numbers . . .' After repeating them, she went on, 'I'm sure you're as worried about what's happening as I am, so please call when you can. I mean, I understand if you're finding it difficult, but I know it would mean a lot to Charlotte if you were in touch.'

As she put the phone down Bob came to put his hands on her shoulders. 'They could be screening their calls,' he told her, voicing her thoughts. 'The press are bound to have found out where they are by now.'

Leaning back against him she said, 'It's awful to think they might have been listening to me, and didn't pick up.' She decided not to deal with how dreadful Charlotte would feel if Gabby did turn her back on her until she knew this had happened. 'You know what's really hard, and sad? It's that we can find ways to try and help Charlotte, but there's nothing we can do for Chloe.'

'I know,' he said softly, 'but hopefully that'll change once we know where she is.'

Chloe was fast asleep in the window seat of an aeroplane that was like the one she'd flown in with Mummy and Nanna. Her head was resting on Boots as if he was a pillow, and in the seat next to her a lady called Tracy was sleeping too. She was a small lady with brown skin and a nice smile, and she was taking Chloe home. That was what she'd said when she'd come to the house where there were toys and a lady who blew out smoke like a dragon, that she was going to take Chloe home. Chloe had thought that meant the bach, but now they were on a plane, and she hadn't seen Mummy or Nanna yet. She wanted to see Mummy more than anything else in the world, and so did Boots. Maybe she'd be waiting when they got off the plane.

Charlotte was sitting on the edge of the bunk in her cell with her arms clutched tightly around her as she rocked back and forth, imagining Chloe was in them. She was missing her so much, the feel, the sound, the smell of her; the flouncy little wisps of her hair, the lustrous curl of her lashes and her wide, soulful eyes. She could almost hear the infectious music of her laughter; the joyous whoops of her delight, her careful pronunciation of words as she learned to read. She could see her dancing in the waves for pipis, sailing back and forth on her swing; pouring flour into a bowl to help Nanna bake; tilting her head all the way back to look up at Diesel. She was in the bath, shiny and wet; bouncing on her bed; charging about Aroha; watering flowers on Nanna's veranda.

And wherever she was, Boots was always there too.

Please, please let him be with her now.

As a sob wrenched itself from the depths of her she pressed a hand to her mouth to try and stifle the wretched keening she could feel building inside her. She knew exhaustion was making this worse, and yet she couldn't imagine how it was possible to feel any better. She loved Chloe more than she loved her own life. She'd never felt the same kind of bond with anyone, and knowing it was the same for Chloe was tearing her apart.

What was Chloe making of all this? What were they telling her?

They should be together, no matter what the law, or social services, or even Chloe's father might say. She had to get her back. Somehow she had to make everyone understand that they belonged together. It was the reason fate, or God, call it what you will, had brought them into each other's lives, so that she, Charlotte, could give the dearest, sweetest little creature on earth all the love she'd never had. She could put her back together after the terrible things that had been done to her, and the short time they'd lived as mother and daughter had already proved that. Chloe had been happy; she'd felt safe and loved, and was so ready to love in return that merely thinking about it now was breaking Charlotte's heart.

How was she going to get her back? *Someone, anyone, please tell me what I have to do to get her back.*

Having decided to stay in Kesterly for the night, Kim Giles had just checked into the Starfish hotel on Abbots Road, two back from the seafront, when her mobile started to ring. Dropping her bag next to the lift, she let the doors close without her as she quickly clicked on.

'It's Tommy Burgess here,' the voice at the other end told her in an accent she recognised as Geordie. 'I got your message and I want you to know I'll do whatever I can to help Alex through this.'

'That's marvellous,' Kim replied. 'Wonderful. Thank you. She'll be so relieved.'

'Where is she now? They said on the news she's in custody?'

'I'm afraid that's true, but we're hoping to

change things in the morning. She wasn't sure if you were still in Kesterly . . .'

'I'm working out my notice – three weeks to go. I'm guessing the reason you're in touch with me is she'd like some news on Ottilie.'

'That's certainly one of the reasons. Obviously, I understand you can't tell us exactly where she is . . .'

'Right now she's on a flight back to England. One of the social workers from our office flew out to get her. Tell Alex it was Tracy Barrall. She'll know the name, she might even have met her once or twice. She was part of the South Kesterly hub before we merged and became one. Anyway, it should put her mind at rest a bit to know it was Tracy. I'm afraid I'm not being allowed anywhere near the case myself, the powers that be are feeling very sensitive about all this, given how much criticism they're coming under for not having tighter controls on their staff. Idiots, the lot of them. Anyway, they want to avoid me passing on any information that Alex probably ought not to have. Probably the way I just did.'

In spite of understanding what a tricky position he was in, Kim kept her client's interests at the forefront and pressed on regardless. 'Tell me, have the police interviewed you or any of your colleagues yet?' she asked.

'No. I'm told they're coming to the office some-time next week.'

'OK, and *your* general feeling about what happened would be . . . ?'

'That she broke the law, fair and square, but do I condemn her for it? No, I don't, because I know how attached she'd become to the child, and I also know how much good she did for her . . . Obviously it's a lot more complicated than that, but that's my basic feeling about it.'

'That she did wrong, but for the right reasons?'

'Precisely. She should have entered her into the system, of course, but having first-hand knowledge of what the system can do to a child it doesn't surprise me that she chose not to.'

Mentally filing that away, Kim said, 'Speaking of the system, Charlotte, which is now her legal name by the way, so is how she'll be referred to in court, wanted me to ask you if you can fix it for Chloe – or Ottilie as you know her – to go to a foster carer by the name of Maggie Fenn. Would that be possible?'

'I wish I could tell you it was, because Maggie Fenn would be my first choice too, but as I said, I'm not being allowed any influence on the case. Besides which, they're not likely to keep her in the immediate area.'

'So do you have any idea where she might go?'

'All I can tell you is that a placement has already been set-up, probably with a neighbouring authority, and that the files containing all the information on Ottilie are now password-protected. Needless to say I don't have the password.'

Unsurprised by that, Kim said, 'OK. There's one other thing that you might be able to help with. Charlotte's very concerned about anyone using the name Ottilie. Given what happened to her when she had that name, well, I expect you can guess where I'm going with this . . .'

'Of course I can, and Alex – Charlotte's – right, the new carers should be told to avoid using it. I'll try calling Tracy once the plane's landed. Meantime, you should probably contact our department manager and speak to her about it yourself, or she'll

243

know we've been in touch and I don't think you want that.'

'No, I'm sure I don't. Thanks. What's her name?'

'Wendy Fraser. I ought to warn you that Alex was never her favourite person, and Alex had no fondness for her either. However, I'm hopeful Wendy will be professional enough to set aside her prejudices over something as important as this.'

'I hope so too. Anyone else I should be concerned about?'

'Not really. Alex had a good working relationship with most of her colleagues. The only one she didn't get on with especially well lost his job during a recent merger of the Kesterly hubs.'

'OK. We can go into all of this further when we meet, which I hope will be tomorrow, at the magistrates' court? Charlotte's applying for bail, and this is where you could come in again. She needs to have an address and . . .'

'She can stay with us, I know my wife would insist, and when you speak to her, please tell her Jackie and I are going to be there for her every step of the way.'

Impressed by his warmth, Kim said, 'I'll be happy to tell her. Do you happen to know her sister?'

'Gabby? Not really. We only met a couple of times, but they were pretty close, in spite of Charlotte being adopted.'

Kim's eyebrows rose. 'You mean Anna's not her real mother?'

'No, Anna is her real mother. She came back into Charlotte's life about six months ago, which was wonderful for Charlotte. For Anna too. I don't know if you're aware of their history . . .'

'No, I'm not.'

'Well, it's for them to tell you, not me, but it's quite a story. Going back to Gabby, have you spoken to her yet? I'm sure she'd offer Charlotte an address just in case you think it might jeopardise things if Charlotte comes to us.'

'You know, for some reason Charlotte didn't tell me about her,' Kim confided, 'so I've left it to Anna to contact her. Let's hope we get some good news from her soon, because you're right, it probably would be better if Charlotte could go to her sister.'

'How is Charlotte in herself?'

'I guess the first word that springs to mind is shattered, both emotionally and physically, but hopefully things should improve once she's had some sleep. Anyway, I must go now, I've a lot to do before tomorrow's hearing. It's been good talking to you, I'll look forward to when we meet, and should you happen to receive any news on Chloe that you feel able to share, please give me a call, any time day or night.'

'OK, I'm off now,' DCI Gould declared, coming out of his office into the main CID area. 'Match starts in fifteen, so plenty of time to get to the pub. Are you up for it, Darren?'

'Right with you,' Wild responded, signing off his computer as he got to his feet.

'How about you, Karen? Or football not your thing?'

'More of a rugby man myself,' Potter replied, barely glancing up from her screen.

'What are you up to there?' he asked, coming to look over her shoulder. 'Catching up on Facebook, or Internet dating?'

'Actually, sir, I was just doing a bit of digging around about Charlotte Nicholls.'

Gould's expression darkened. 'And?'

'And nothing so far, but I have discovered that Ottilie Wade's father was moved to HMP Long Lartin a couple of weeks ago.'

Gould's eyebrows rose. 'And that would be of significance because?'

She looked at him askance. 'Because he's her father, sir.'

'And?'

'And as such I don't think we should forget his existence. I know, after what he did, there's no way he'd get a say in what happens to her, but unlike the mother, he's not dead.'

'That piece of scum will never be going near his daughter again in his lifetime. Chances are he'll never set foot this side of his prison walls again either, so I'm not getting what your issue is.'

'I don't have one. I'm just making sure we know where and who everyone is, so we're not made to look . . .' She stopped, flushing deeply.

'Fools again?' he finished for her. 'Well, that's not a bad idea, so stay with it. Just don't bother wasting any more time on that nonce, cos I promise you, he's being well taken care of where he is. It's Alex Lake who concerns me. We know from experience how sly she can be, and the last thing we want is her walking out of that magistrates' court tomorrow making us look a right bunch of tossers again. And now she's got Jolyon Crane's team on her case it could seriously happen.'

'Don't worry, sir,' Potter responded. 'Andy Phipps is the prosecutor and he's with us all the way on this, so our friend *Charlotte* doesn't stand a chance of getting bail, especially when she's already fled the country once.'

Gould's eyes were narrowing. 'You'd better be right about that,' he muttered darkly. 'You'd just better be right,' and leaving her to it he started towards the lift.

Chapter Fourteen

Charlotte knew that if the police were feeling friendlier towards her, one of them might be driving her to the magistrates' court this morning. As it was, after being allowed to shower and change into the clean clothes Kim had delivered to the station late last night, she'd found herself being escorted to the Reliance security van, where the usual Saturday morning rabble of Friday night drunks were already waiting to be transported.

Now they were riding alongside her in their own cramped cubicle, snorting and coughing and generally telling the world to 'shut the fuck up.'

For Charlotte, far worse than travelling in a steel box with barely enough room to stand, never mind sit, was knowing that the press were following its brief journey from the station to the old town hall where the court was held. Though she couldn't see them, she could hear the commotion, and as soon as the van turned on to Victoria Square progress became even slower, telling her that there were as many reporters and camera crews here today as there had been outside the police station yesterday. Most likely there were more.

After the security shutters rolled down behind the van, sealing it into the cavernous basement of the court, Charlotte waited tensely for someone to come and release her. It seemed she was going to be the last out, which was both awful and a relief, since she had no desire to go into court, but nor did she want to remain trapped in this coffin of a cell.

Eventually, a guard snapped open the lock on her door, and giving her a mocking bow as she came out, he said, 'Didn't realise we had a celebrity on board this morning.'

Keeping her eyes down, Charlotte made her way along the van's narrow corridor to step out of the back door to where her fellow unfortunates were being frisked and signed in before being delivered into one of the two holding cells. As she was the only female she was allotted the second cell, whose bleak stone walls didn't appear to have seen much in the way of a paintbrush in at least fifty years.

Just as the horror of it started settling around her again, trying to lock her into its claustrophobic grip, the iron gate suddenly clanged open and she was being told to follow a guard.

At the far end of the holding area she was shown through a door into a large, sparsely furnished room with harsh strobe lighting and dismal grey walls. She almost swayed with relief when she saw Kim Giles waiting.

'Are you OK?' Kim asked worriedly as Charlotte started to shake.

'Yes, yes, I'm fine,' Charlotte lied. 'I didn't know . . . I thought I was being taken up . . . Sorry, I'll have myself together in a moment.'

Sitting her down at the table, Kim said, 'Here, I brought us some coffee and pastries. I thought we could have breakfast together.'

Smiling through the tumult of her nerves, Charlotte said, 'That's lovely. Thank you.'

'I expect it'll be a bit more edifying than whatever you were offered first thing,' Kim commented wryly. 'Have you eaten at all since I left last night?'

Charlotte grimaced. 'Half a pot noodle and a ham sandwich,' she confessed. 'Not the tastiest meal I've ever had, but the room service wasn't bad.'

Kim smiled and passed her a steaming carton of coffee. 'How about sleep? Did you manage any?'

'Actually, I did, on and off.' Her eyes closed as the taste of a hot cappuccino began spreading its magic through her system. God, she'd needed that.

'You're looking a lot better than you did yesterday,' Kim told her frankly. 'Are you feeling it?'

'Definitely now,' Charlotte confirmed, sipping the cappuccino again. 'Did you know this was my coffee of choice, or did you guess?'

'I texted your mother.'

The mention of her mother led her straight to Chloe's love of fluffies, or babyccinos, and suddenly she wanted no more coffee. If Chloe couldn't have her favourite drink it didn't seem right that she should have hers.

Kim was opening up her laptop as she tucked into a pastry. 'Your mother and stepfather have been pretty busy over there while we've all been in bed,' she was saying. 'They've sorted out bank transfers, rented an apartment, contacted your friends . . .'

'Which friends?' Charlotte interrupted, managing to sound as though she didn't have any.

Unfazed, Kim said, 'Apparently your mother contacted Tommy Burgess after I did last night, to try and send him money to cover your expenses while you're with him over . . .'

'Hang on, hang on, what do you mean while I'm with him?'

Kim smiled. 'If we get bail today, and I'm very hopeful we will, he and his wife are keen for you to go and stay there. As it's the only address we can offer the court at the moment, I strongly advise you to accept.'

Charlotte was feeling slightly dazed. 'But I lied to him, the way I did to everyone else . . .'

'Please put that out of your mind now. What you did, how your conscience is behaving, isn't relevant to anything we're trying to achieve here today. We just have to go in front of the magistrate – actually it's a district judge sitting this morning, Charles Edmore, do you know him?'

Charlotte shook her head. 'The family courts were more my territory. What's he like?'

'I haven't come across him before, but Jolyon says he's OK. Bit humourless, but generally tends more towards the lenient than the severe, which is great for us. We're last up, apparently, so that gives us the chance to prepare you. Would you like another?' she offered, as Charlotte finished a pastry.

Surprised to realise she'd eaten it, Charlotte replied, 'No, that was plenty, thanks.' Then, unable to go any further without asking about Chloe, she said, 'Do you have any news on where she is?'

Clearly knowing straight away who they were talking about, Kim met her eyes and Charlotte felt her heart turn over.

'What – what is it?' she stumbled. 'Is she all right?'

'I heard just before coming here that she's back in England now.'

Charlotte wanted to get up. She needed to go to her, to make sure she understood that she was still loved and that she didn't have to be afraid . . .

'Tommy thought you'd want to know that Tracy Barrall went to bring her back,' Kim said softly.

'Tracy?' Charlotte echoed.

'I believe she was at the South Kesterly hub while you . . .'

'Yes, yes of course,' Charlotte said, remembering. 'That's good. Tracy'll be kind to her. Oh God, she must be so scared, so confused . . .'

'Charlotte, you can't let yourself get into a panic over it,' Kim cautioned gravely. 'Somehow you're going to have to accept that for the time being at least, she's in the custody of social services and there's nothing any of us can do about it. I'm sorry if that sounds brutal, but you need to be worrying about yourself now, and how we're going to get you through this.'

Charlotte swallowed dryly as she nodded. 'I'm sorry,' she said hoarsely, 'it's just to think of her being shunted about the world by strangers, brought back to this area and not being able to see her . . . Will she be staying here? She must be if they sent Tracy for her.'

'I don't know what the long-term plans are, and Tommy's not being allowed any involvement so he can't tell us either. For the moment, though, we can probably safely assume that she's heading this way, given that the plane touched down about eight this morning.'

Imagining her sitting in the back of a strange car, not tall enough to see out of the window, having no idea of where she was going or what to expect when she got there, Charlotte barely knew how to stifle the anguish. Please God she wasn't thinking Mummy would be waiting at the end of her journey, because if she was the disappointment was going to be so crushing when she got there. 'Do you think I'll be allowed to write her a note?' she asked, already knowing the answer.

Looking at her steadily, Kim said, 'I'm sure you realise that if you get bail there'll be conditions and one of them . . .'

'. . . will be that I can't go anywhere near her,' Charlotte interrupted in a strangled voice. 'I know, I just . . . It's . . .' She pressed her fingers to her lips as her eyes burned with tears. 'I'm sorry,' she said, 'I don't seem to be handling this very well at all.'

'You're still jet-lagged,' Kim reminded her, 'as well as shell-shocked, traumatised and probably half-starved. So don't be too hard on yourself, and do your best to try another pastry while I tell you what your family in New Zealand have been doing.'

Though she had no appetite, Charlotte obediently picked up another mini-Danish and took a bite. What she wouldn't give to be back in New Zealand, to be the person she'd been there, instead of the wreck she was here, but thinking that way wasn't going to help her at all, so she made an effort to push it to the back of her mind.

Glancing at her watch, Kim said, 'I'm waiting for a call to tell me if the transfer your stepfather made yesterday has arrived in our bank yet. This will be the money for bail, just in case it's needed.'

Both embarrassed and grateful for Bob's generosity, Charlotte said, 'I hope he realises that as soon as I can access my own account . . .'

'Of course, and you can deal with that then. For now, it's important that we're able to demonstrate how serious you are about remaining in the country. If you stand to lose everything, financially, you should be seen as less of a flight risk.' She scrolled through her notes and continued, 'In addition to Tommy's offer for you to stay with him your mother has arranged to rent an apartment for you, here in Kesterly, through a Mr Lang. Apparently you've rented from him before, but had to cancel the lease when you decided to go to New Zealand?'

'That's right,' Charlotte confirmed. 'He has flats all over the place, I believe.'

'He does, but this one is in the same building as you were going to rent in before, on the Promenade. We're due to meet with him on Monday to sign a lease and pay the deposit. The flat itself should be ready for you to move into the week after.'

Feeling faintly dizzied by the speed at which her life was changing, and anxious about how out of control she felt, Charlotte put the pastry down again, unable to eat any more. 'It's good,' she said, 'that I won't have to put on Tommy and Jackie for too long, but taking a flat . . . I mean, I realise I have to, it just makes it seem so . . . permanent here.'

Kim regarded her carefully, and Charlotte flushed as she thought of another, and worse, form of permanence.

'What about going to stay with your sister?' Kim suggested.

Charlotte tensed. Then her eyes lit with hope. 'Have you spoken to Gabby?' she asked. 'Has she been in touch?'

Kim shook her head. 'I'm afraid not. Your mother's tried contacting her, but so far she hasn't been able to get through. It could be that the press have already tracked her down so she and her family have gone to stay elsewhere.'

Hating the thought of the press hounding her sister almost as much as she hated them hounding her, Charlotte said, 'If they have gone away, there's a good chance they'll be with our Aunt Sheila who lives quite close to them. Of course, they might be with Martin's parents . . .'

Kim picked up her mobile. 'Would you like me to try your aunt?' she offered.

Charlotte wasn't sure. If Gabby and Sheila wanted to be in touch they'd surely have found a way by now, so maybe she should accept the silence as their way of telling her that they didn't want to be involved.

'Do you know the number?' Kim prompted.

Charlotte nodded, but the fear of being rejected made her say, 'I don't think we should call. It's not fair to drag them into this when it's really got nothing to do with them.'

'Tommy said you and your sister were close.'

Charlotte's eyes drifted as the gulf of missing Gabby opened wider in her heart. She loved her sister, had always had a far deeper bond with her than she'd ever had with anyone else, and there was no one she wanted to see more right now.

Apart from Chloe, of course.

'No, we can't call,' she told Kim. 'As I said, it wouldn't be fair. Gabby has to put her children first and they don't need to become embroiled in my affairs.'

'OK, it's your decision,' Kim said, 'but if you change your mind . . . Well, if you do, you'll be able to make the call yourself because hopefully you'll have your phone back by then.'

The ghost of a smile passed over Charlotte's lips. She appreciated Kim's optimism, it was the single positive force in all of this that kept hauling her back from the brink.

It was just after eleven when a knock came on the door to inform them that it was time for Charlotte to go up to the court.

'You'll be fine,' Kim told her as they rose to their feet. 'Just focus on the judge and speak your name clearly when you're asked. That's all you'll be required to say.'

Charlotte nodded. She was so tense it was difficult to move.

As Kim turned to leave, Charlotte said, 'Are the press being really awful about me? They were before, when they thought Chloe was missing and I was to blame for not getting her away from her father sooner . . .'

'To be honest, they seemed split down the middle when the news first broke,' Kim replied. 'But remember they can't print anything detrimental about you now, or they'll be in contempt of court.'

Charlotte was still clinging to those words as a guard took her up the stark, stone staircase a few minutes later. She could already hear the buzz of the courtroom, a deep, mainly masculine drone that seemed to seep into the stairwell and mingle with the stench of unwashed bodies still lingering from those who'd gone before her. She was hardly breathing, and her hands were so tightly clenched her fingers felt close to breaking. She wished her mother was there, and Bob, or Rick, someone to make her feel less alone.

Or Gabby.

Don't start feeling sorry for yourself now. Think of Chloe and be strong for her.

She wished she'd asked Kim if Tommy was going to be there. It might have helped to know there was a friendly face in the room, even if she couldn't look around to find it. Had any of her old neighbours made the journey in from Mulgrove? The cast and crew of her theatre company; her adoptive father's parishioners; the locals from the village pub? She thought of dear old Millie who'd lived next door to the vicarage and whom she'd known for most of her life. She'd have been a friendly face today if she were able to come, but Alzheimer's had made it necessary for her to go into care. She'd always remembered Charlotte, though. Every time she'd visited the home Millie's crinkled old face had lit up to see her, and even when she'd talked nonsense she'd still seemed to know who she was talking to. She'd been moved now to a place in York to be closer to her niece and nephew. Charlotte hoped they went to see her.

She was almost at the top of the steps by now, and the urge to turn and flee was like a physical force. What if Jason, her ex, was there with his wife and their good friend Heather Hancock? As a reporter for the local paper Heather Hancock must be relishing the fact that Alex Lake, the social worker who'd refused to be intimidated by Heather's position in the community, was now handing her the story of her career. Then there was Ben, her ex-colleague who'd taken two calls alerting him to the problem at Ottilie's home before she, Charlotte, had got hold of the case. Would he be there? Had it been left to him, Chloe might still be in that dreadful house on North Hill suffering the physical and mental abuse of her schizoid mother and repulsive father.

Where was she now?

Oh God, where was Chloe?

If only she could be with Maggie Fenn, but Charlotte knew, in spite of asking Kim to talk to Tommy, that they wouldn't put Chloe with someone Charlotte knew. Would Maggie come today? Would Anthony, Maggie's brother? There was no way he'd put in an appearance, and feeling as wretched and ashamed as she did Charlotte could only be glad of it.

As she arrived in the main body of the court the noise seemed to wrap itself around her like a fog. The place was packed and she already felt hunted, trapped, condemned. The babble drained to silence, and she felt everyone's eyes on her as she followed the guard to the dock. It was on a level with the bench, above the rest of the court, and looked old and worn, ready to buckle under the weight of past troubles and tragedies.

Keeping her head down she mounted the three steps into it, and following the guard's instruction sat on one of the chairs. She was aware of the sunlight blazing in through tall arched windows, set too high in the walls for anyone to see in or out, and pooling dustily around the dark wooden seats for the lawyers. Kim was already there, appearing unruffled by the austere-looking figure beside her. He was short and wiry, with a narrow face and eagle eyes. As far as he was concerned she'd fled the country with the child she'd abducted, so why on earth should she be trusted not to flee again?

She wouldn't run away again, but no amount of promises given by her, or by Kim on her behalf, could convey the absolute truth of that. It would be down to the judge to decide whether or not he believed she was honourable enough to stay and face up to what she'd done. And since she'd already demonstrated to the police just how capable she was of deception, she couldn't think of a single good reason why anyone would grant her bail.

'All rise.'

Feeling the weight of scrutiny bearing down on her, Charlotte got to her feet and fixed her eyes on the door beside the bench. When the judge came in, wearing a dark suit and red bow tie, he seemed impatient, she thought, or cross, or maybe that was his normal expression and it would change when he smiled. Except there wasn't much to smile about today.

Once everyone was seated again the clerk spoke quietly to the judge before turning to the dock and asking her to identify herself.

'My name is Charlotte Nicholls,' she replied, and a murmur of confusion erupted from the press and public gallery. They probably thought she was lying, or playing some sort of game. They'd know soon enough that Alex Lake was no longer her name.

Ignoring the noise, the judge returned to the paperwork in front of him as the charge was read out and the lawyers identified themselves. Then the prosecutor, Andy Phipps, began to explain why the bail application was nothing short of outrageous.

'The defendant has already shown her complete disregard of the law by taking a child out of the country to New Zealand,' he stated. 'Once there she sought to change both her own and the child's names . . .'

'Sir,' Kim stepped in, 'this is a bail hearing . . .'

'My point is,' Phipps continued, 'the very fact

that the defendant's already absconded once to a country where she has family should make the court wary of granting any freedom of movement at this time.'

The judge frowned in Kim's direction.

'Sir,' she said, 'my client didn't put up any resistance to arrest, she returned willingly to this . . .'

'Presumably not willingly if she was under arrest,' the judge pointed out.

Charlotte's stomach churned as Kim said, 'Once she was in police custody she complied with the law every step of the way, and will continue to do so . . .'

'How can we be sure of that, Ms . . .' he checked his notes, 'Giles? Does she have a home to go to in this country, in the event the court grants her bail?'

'Yes, sir. You'll find the address in the papers.'

Locating it, he said, 'Who is Tommy Burgess?'

'He was her team leader when she worked for social services. He and his wife are good friends of my client's and trustworthy members of the community.'

'Mm,' he grunted, not seeming entirely impressed. 'Do we know if Mr Burgess aided her initial flight from the country?'

'He didn't, sir.'

'We only have your word for that,' Phipps piped up.

'I can assure you he didn't,' she retorted, 'and may I add that Mr Burgess's actions and integrity are not the subject of this hearing.'

'No, but they're relevant if the court is going to release her to his custody,' the judge commented, almost to himself.

'Can I also say, sir, that my client is willing to post

bail in the sum of two hundred and fifty thousand pounds?'

Another murmur spread through the room and Charlotte could almost hear them saying, *A social worker has a quarter of a million pounds?*

The judge's eyebrows were arched.

'This sum is the entirety of my client's savings,' Kim explained, 'and was come by as the result of the sale of her adoptive parents' house, both parents now being deceased.'

'I see, and these funds are where, exactly?'

'In the process of being transferred from a bank in New Zealand. I'd hoped to be able to assure the court that they'd arrived by now, but with it being a weekend . . . However, I do have details of the transaction from the originating Kiwibank in Auckland.' Leaning forward, she handed a copy to the clerk, who looked it over and passed it on to the judge. 'This confirms the amount of the transfer and the fact that it's already left New Zealand. It could very well be in my firm's client account by the end of the morning and therefore ready to transfer to the court on Monday.'

'By which time the defendant could already have left the country,' Phipps declared. 'Let's not forget her family is still in New Zealand, so she has every reason to want to go back.'

The judge inhaled deeply as he looked the transfer document over, seeming to take a very long time to read a mere few lines. 'I presume the defendant's passport has been surrendered?' he asked, glancing towards the seats behind the lawyers where Karen Potter was sitting with another detective.

'Yes it has,' Phipps confirmed.

'Mm,' the judge grunted again. 'And the child is where?'

Phipps consulted with Karen Potter. 'I'm told she's now back in this country, sir, and is in the care of the state.'

Charlotte's insides were in knots. She'd always hated that phrase; it sounded so cold, so devoid of anything remotely to do with care, and now to think that Chloe was its latest victim . . .

She couldn't let her mind go there, not yet. She needed to stay focused on what was happening here.

'. . . we understand that if the court is willing to grant bail,' Kim was saying, 'it'll also wish to impose certain conditions which my client will strictly adhere to . . .'

'Yes, yes, yes,' the judge interrupted impatiently, 'I'm sure she would if the court were to do as you ask, Ms Giles, but I'm afraid your client's past actions make it necessary for me to remand her in custody until . . .'

He was still speaking, but Charlotte could no longer hear. The buzz in the room was deafening her; the horror of what was going to happen now was making her shake uncontrollably.

'No! You can't!' someone was suddenly shouting. 'You can't, do you hear me?'

Registering the words, Charlotte turned in a stunned daze to see Gabby on her feet, her face ravaged with shock and tears.

Gabby was here.

Someone was calling for order, but the judge had gone and the press were pushing towards the doors and Charlotte was being escorted from the dock.

'Let me see her,' Gabby cried, trying to elbow her way through the crush. 'Please, please let me see her.'

'Gabby,' Charlotte choked, turning to look back over her shoulder, as she was forced down the stairs.

Minutes later she was being locked into a cell and the guard was saying, 'Van's not due back for another hour, so you'll have to wait here.'

'Can I see my sister?' Charlotte begged. 'Please, just for a few minutes.'

'Only your lawyer's allowed down here,' he told her, and pocketing the keys he walked away.

Charlotte watched his back. She'd never felt so helpless in her life. She was being treated like a caged animal and there was nothing she could do. Her heart was pounding so fiercely it was hard to breathe. She couldn't deal with what was about to happen. She had to wipe it from her mind or she'd start to scream. 'Please,' she shouted, 'will you contact my lawyer? I have to speak to her.'

Ignoring her, the guard pressed a button and the basement flooded with sunlight as the security shutters rolled up. Another guard came through, and the shutters went down again.

'Please,' Charlotte called desperately. 'I need to speak to my lawyer.'

'Will you shut the fuck up, keeping on,' a voice grumbled from the next cell. 'Some of us are trying to get some kip in here.'

In increasing panic, Charlotte shouted to the guard again. He still didn't bother to look round, merely answered the phone when it rang, while the second guard settled down in front of a computer. She might as well not have been there for all the notice they were taking of her.

Realising they must deal with frantic prisoners every day of the week and would see her as no different to the rest, she forced herself to let go of the bars and turned to the stone bunk behind her. She was still shaking badly and her head was spinning, but what mattered most in that moment was the fact that Gabby had come. She'd been in court. She wasn't turning her back . . .

'OK, Miss Popular, your lawyer's waiting,' the guard announced, coming to unlock her door.

Unsteadied by relief, Charlotte swayed as she rose to her feet.

'Are you all right?' he asked roughly.

'Yes, yes I'm fine,' she assured him, and quickly followed him back to the room she'd been in earlier.

Kim was there – and so was Gabby.

'Alex!' Gabby cried, running to her. 'Are you all right? This is terrible, awful, I don't think I can bear it.'

Hugging her hard, Charlotte said, 'It'll be OK. I promise. Oh God, I'm so glad you're here.'

Pulling back to look at her, Gabby searched her face with teary red eyes. She was taller than Charlotte, with lustrous raven hair and a beautiful smile, though right now her lips were trembling with emotion. 'I wanted to come before,' she said brokenly. 'As soon as I heard you were back, but I was so afraid they'd arrest me too. Do you think they will? I couldn't bear it if they did. I'm not like you, I can't stand up for myself, and what about the children?'

Taking her by the shoulders Charlotte said, 'There's no reason for anyone to arrest you. You haven't done anything . . .'

'But I knew you were taking her . . .'

'No you didn't,' Charlotte cried.

'Yes I did. As soon as I noticed Phoebe's passport had gone I realised . . .'

'Gabby, listen to me,' Charlotte urged. 'You had no idea about anything, OK? You didn't notice Phoebe's passport was missing until I sent it back. And the day you came to say goodbye you only gave me a cheque. Nothing else was said. You had no idea Chloe was in the car . . .'

'Chloe?'

'Ottilie. You didn't know she was there. Did you?'

Gabby shook her head uncertainly.

'Of course you didn't. Now please tell me you haven't told anyone else you guessed what was happening.'

'Only Martin and Aunt Sheila,' Gabby confessed warily. 'They said I could be in trouble for being an accomplice and that I shouldn't come here today, but I had to. I kept thinking of you being all on your own, and I couldn't let that happen. You're my sister and I love you, and I know you'd never have done anything to hurt that little girl.'

'Of course I wouldn't. Why? Is someone saying I did?' She turned to Kim. 'Is that what the press . . . ?'

'One or two insinuated,' Kim told her, 'you know what they're like, but they don't have any proof . . .'

'How could they when it didn't happen?' Charlotte demanded, horrified to think she was being accused of harming Chloe, when it couldn't have been further from the truth.

'I told them you're a good person,' Gabby assured her.

'You've spoken to them?' Charlotte cried, appalled.

Gabby almost shrank back. 'Only when I was on my way in here,' she insisted. 'That was all I said, that you're a good person, because you are and if they knew you they'd know it too.'

Realising how hard this was for Gabby who, in spite of her beauty, had never been brimming with self-confidence, Charlotte said, 'I need you to promise me two things, first that you won't give any interviews to the press . . .'

'I swear I won't. Martin wouldn't let me anyway. He thinks they'll just twist everything I say to suit what they want . . .'

'They'll stop hounding you now, anyway,' Kim told her.

'And the second promise I need from you,' Charlotte continued, 'is that you'll *never* under any circumstances tell anyone that you guessed I was taking Chloe and didn't report it.'

Gabby glanced uneasily at Kim.

'You don't need to worry about my lawyer,' Charlotte assured her. 'She's on our side.'

Gabby's anxious eyes came back to Charlotte. 'I feel so terrible about this,' she wailed. 'If I'd spoken up at the time you might not be where you are now.'

'Yes I would, because I'd already had her for over a month by the time you realised. Anyway, we can't turn back the clock. We can only deal with what's happening now, and I need to know that you aren't going to implicate yourself, because none of it's your fault. Do you hear me? I'm the only one to blame, so I'm the only one who should take responsibility.'

Gabby swallowed hard and looked down at the torn tissue in her hands. 'Are they taking you to prison?' she asked miserably. 'I can't bear to think of you being locked up. I won't be able to sleep or eat or do anything.'

Used to Gabby making everything about herself, and actually loving her for it, Charlotte said, 'Please don't worry about me. All you have to do is take care of yourself and the children and maybe come to see me if I do end up . . .' She turned to Kim. 'Will I be allowed visitors before the trial?' she asked.

Kim nodded. 'Of course, but we'll put in another bail application when we go to the Crown Court next Wednesday. It looked like you were going to get it today. I don't know what made him suddenly rush his decision at the end. Even the prosecutor was shocked when he ruled.'

Fighting back the fear that was building again, Charlotte said to Gabby, 'What really matters about today is that you came. I was so afraid you wouldn't . . .'

'I told you.' Gabby was trying not to cry. 'I couldn't let you be here on your own.'

'Thank you,' Charlotte said, hugging her. 'You don't know what a difference it's made.'

'Tommy was here too,' Gabby told her, 'and lots of our old friends from the village. They're all rooting for you.'

'Please thank them for me,' Charlotte said shakily. 'I'm not sure I deserve their support . . .'

'Of course you do. Even Jason came today, which is really saying something when you're no longer together. I think he regrets going back to his wife . . .'

'If he does then I'm sorry,' Charlotte came in gently. 'He did it for the children and it would be awful if he ended up leaving them again.'

'Yes, it would, but if you two . . .'

'We won't,' Charlotte assured her. 'Our relationship is in the past and that's where it has to stay.'

Gabby's lips started to tremble as she nodded. 'I wish you had someone,' she said. 'It would be . . .'

'I've got you,' Charlotte reminded her, 'and my mother and Bob.'

'But they're not here.'

'Because they can't be, and anyway, there's nothing anyone can do with the way things are. I have to get myself through this, with Kim's help, obviously, and knowing that I have some friends out there, especially you, is already helping a lot.'

Grasping her hands, Gabby said, 'I'll always be there for you, you know that, and I'm sure your mother will be too. She rang me, but I haven't rung her back yet. I will now I've seen you.'

'I'm sure she'll appreciate that, but maybe you should leave it till tomorrow morning, it'll be the middle of the night there now.'

'Of course.' Gabby glanced at Kim as someone knocked on the far door.

'It's time for us to go,' Kim told her. To Charlotte she said, 'I'm so sorry about today. I truly thought it was going our way . . .'

'It's OK,' Charlotte replied, even though it wasn't. 'We always knew I was an obvious flight risk.'

'Don't give up. I'll be talking to Jolyon as soon as I leave here and . . .' She broke off as the door swung open.

'Van's here,' the guard announced brusquely.

Charlotte's limbs turned weak. She felt nauseous, gripped by fear and panic, weighted by dread.

'Oh my God,' Gabby sobbed.

As she went towards Charlotte Kim took her by the arm, but she shook herself free. 'I know you're scared,' she whispered as she hugged Charlotte hard, 'but you'll get through this, I know you will.'

'Of course I will,' Charlotte responded, trying to smile. 'We all will,' and to Kim, 'I know there's a lot for you to do now, but if you can, please try to get me some news of Chloe.'

'I'll do my best,' Kim promised, and taking Gabby's arm again she held it firmly as Charlotte turned to follow the guard out to the waiting prison van.

'Now, to bring us up to date on the Ottilie Wade case over there in England,' the New Zealand news anchor was saying, 'we're going to our Foreign Affairs correspondent Hamilton Terry who's outside the women's prison in Dean Valley. Ham? What have you got for us?'

'Well, Marc, Charlotte Nicholls arrived here a few minutes ago, having been remanded in custody following the bail hearing earlier. I have to say, it was a bit of a surprise to those of us who were in court, because for a while there it was looking as though she might be going home today. Anyway, it didn't happen, and now we're being told that she's likely to seek the protection of Rule Forty-Three when she checks into the prison, which is when a prisoner chooses to be segregated for their own safety. In general it's those who've committed crimes against children who opt to go on the rule, as it's known here . . .'

'So are you saying she fears for her own safety?'

'If she does choose to go on the rule, then yes, we can assume she's worried about how other prisoners will respond to her. You have to remember that before the alleged abduction she was a social worker in this area, so she'll have been involved in the removal of children from their homes – official removal, that is. It could be that the mothers of some of those children are in this prison serving time for various offences and could be holding a grudge . . .'

'Oh God, oh God, oh God,' Anna murmured,

bunching a hand to her mouth. 'I never thought of that. She'll be a sitting target for those women . . .'

'Not if she seeks the protection they're talking about,' Bob reminded her. He was looking almost as strained and tired as she did, and was no more ready to go to bed. 'And Kim's assured us they'll apply for another bail hearing at the Crown Court, so she could be out by Wednesday.'

'But in the meantime she's going to be cooped up in a cell . . .'

'If that's where it's safest for her to be, then maybe we should be thankful that there are these systems in place.'

'Ssh, ssh,' Rick broke in, 'they're talking about Chloe.'

'. . . there hasn't been any official confirmation that the child is back in Dean Valley,' Hamilton Terry was saying, 'and I don't expect we'll get one, but it's widely assumed that she must be by now. Unless, of course, she's been transferred to the protection of another authority, which is always possible. Whatever, we know she has no family, or none that she can be returned to, so . . .'

'She has us,' Anna cried. 'We're her family.'

'. . . she will almost certainly be placed into foster care and no doubt kept under very close supervision.'

Grabbing the remote control, Anna turned the TV off and stormed out of the room.

There was a moment of solemn quiet before Bob said to Rick, 'Have you checked the end of the drive this evening? Are the press still there?'

'No sign of them,' Rick replied. 'Like Don Thackeray said, it should start to go quiet now she's been charged.'

'Thank God for that. Not that I wanted her to be charged, but the last thing she needs is the whole thing playing itself out in the court of public opinion.'

'With the Internet that's going to be difficult to avoid,' Rick pointed out, 'but we don't have to involve ourselves in it. Probably best that we don't.'

'Do either of you want one?' Anna asked, coming back into the sitting room with a decanter of brandy and three glasses.

Bob stood up to do the honours, then sat thinking. 'I'm worried that we don't have the best lawyer on the case. I thought we were going to get the top man. I'm sure that's what Don Thackeray expected too. I'll have a chat with him tomorrow. Everything all right?' he asked as Rick checked his mobile phone.

Rick glanced up. 'Yes, it's fine. Just Hamish replying to a text I sent earlier.'

Bob nodded. Then after an awkward moment, 'I guess Hamish . . . is the one?'

'Yes, he is,' Rick replied.

Barely noticing the exchange, Anna said, 'When you talk to Don will you ask if there's any way I can go over there yet?'

'Of course,' Bob replied. 'Rick, you don't have to be here, son. We can cope with this.'

'I want to be here,' Rick told him. 'As the person who's responsible for what's happening, I need to try . . .'

Frowning, Anna said, 'What are you talking about? How on earth can you be responsible?'

Glancing at his father, Rick said, 'It's because I wasn't honest with Katie that she started digging around about Charlotte.'

'Yes, you've told me all that, but it doesn't make it your fault. You didn't set out to make it happen, no one did, with the possible exception of Katie, and God knows she's suffering for it now. No, if anyone's to blame it's me. Why I ever thought we could get away with this I'll never know. I must have been out of my mind.' Anna sighed deeply.

'Perhaps we all were,' Bob said grimly, 'but I'm afraid it's too late for regrets now, and let's not forget the fact that none of us had a single bad intention towards Chloe. All we ever wanted was to bring her into our family and make her feel one of us, and there's no doubt we succeeded in that. At least you did, you too, Rick. She was happy here, and all we really want now is to see her back again.'

Rick's face was taut. 'Do you think we ever will?' he asked, sounding as though he didn't.

Bob looked at Anna, but she turned away. 'It's still very early days,' he said in the end, 'so there's no telling what might happen yet, to either of them.'

Chapter Fifteen

Tracy Barrall knew what it was like to grow up in foster care. From the age of five, when social services had come to collect her from school to take her to her dying mother's bedside, she'd been a ward of the state. Her mother had been beaten to death by her current boyfriend, who wasn't Tracy's father; Tracy hadn't even known, and had never been able to find out who her real father was. It seemed nobody knew, but she'd had a few substitutes along the way, a couple of whom she'd actually liked, before the time had come to move on. There had been some good temporary mothers too, and brothers and sisters, aunts, uncles, grandparents, you name it, she'd had them all. What she'd never had while growing up was a family to call her own.

She had one now, but that had only happened since she'd met Nelson Barrall and managed to turn her life around. Until then, she'd spent most of her teens and all of her twenties knocking about with gangs, living on the streets, or banged up in jail. She'd had few real friends, no money and zero prospects. No one could have hated her more than she'd hated herself, until Nelson had been assigned her probation officer and gradually, patiently shown her what it was to be loved.

They'd been together for almost ten years now, four of them as a married couple and six as the parents of Tyler and Marie. It still dazzled Tracy at times to think of her luck in coming from such wretched beginnings to be the wife of a clever and good-looking bloke like Nelson – and the mother of their two fantastic kids. What was more, thanks to Nelson's encouragement she'd managed to get herself a degree, and now she had a damned good job.

If you called social work a good job, and she most definitely did.

It meant the world to her to be in a position where she could help make a difference to a child's life. Knowing what it was to be neglected and abused, moved from one family to the next to the next, she was determined to do her very best by every child that came on to her caseload. Being pretty, jolly and generous to a fault made her popular with her charges. Just about everyone seemed to like Tracy, including her boss, Wendy Fraser, who'd chosen her, above anyone else, to go to New Zealand to bring back Ottilie Wade.

'Try to call her Chloe from now on,' Tommy Burgess had said when they'd spoken on the phone early this morning. 'She has very bad memories of being Ottilie.'

Tracy had no problems understanding that, since she knew all about Ottilie's history, so she'd immediately stopped using the name, pretty though it was. She'd make a note of the change when she came to write her report, but not that it had come as Tommy's suggestion. She'd have to say that Chloe had insisted, or maybe that she'd been told by one of the New Zealand social workers, since she was very well aware that Tommy wasn't supposed to be involving himself in this case at all. However, Tracy wasn't much of a stickler for the rules when it came to the best interests of a child. She wasn't sure she'd ever go as far as Charlotte Nicholls had, but probably only because she didn't have the courage, since she'd certainly felt tempted at times.

Even though she knew very well that there were foster families out there who were kind and loving and gave the most wonderful support to a child, she also knew that there were far too few of them. And even they couldn't always offer a child a home for life, or repair the damage that might already have been done.

In Chloe's case it was hard to gauge the extent of the damage, as she wouldn't speak. Not that Tracy thought, for a single minute, that Charlotte Nicholls had harmed the child. To the contrary, she imagined the dear little soul had been better cared for in New Zealand than she had at any other time in her tragic young life. It was the damage the father had caused that needed to be assessed and sorted, but there would be plenty of time for that in the coming days and weeks. For now, all that really mattered was getting the child and her funny, tatty old bear settled into their new home on the Devonshire border with Maxine and Steve Kosey. Since the Koseys had an excellent track record as carers, Tracy felt sure it wouldn't take them long to coax a few words out of Chloe. They were so good at drawing people out that here she was probably doing far too much of the talking, as she sat in their elegant new conservatory, drinking Earl Grey tea and soaking up the lovely afternoon sun.

'Yes, New Zealand certainly looked like the kind of place where you'd want to live,' she sighed wistfully, while fighting the jet lag, 'at least what little I saw of it. Aren't you going to drink your apple juice?' she asked Chloe, who was sitting next to Maxine Kosey on the wicker-framed sofa that creaked and rocked when Maxine pushed her foot to the ground.

As all eyes went to Chloe she kept her own lowered and clung on to her bear.

'It doesn't matter,' Maxine said gently. 'If you're not thirsty you can always have some later.'

Maxine Kosey was the kind of woman, Tracy realised, that she used to want to be, plump, blonde, with large blue eyes, quite a posh voice and a trendy sort of look that seemed to suggest horses and cocktail parties. Not that there was any sign of a horse in the fields that sloped away from the backs of the semis on Swingley Walk, though there were several donkeys. Beach troopers, every one of them, Tracy suspected, though they were at least forty miles from the coast here. Maybe it was some sort of refuge.

'This chocolate cake is very good,' Steve Kosey was telling Chloe, offering her a slice. 'If you don't have some soon I'm going to eat it all up.'

Chloe didn't even look.

Lifting a hand to stroke Chloe's hair, Maxine said, 'I expect she's tired after that long journey, aren't you, sweetie?'

Chloe seemed to sink closer to her bear.

'Do we know the bear's name?' Steve asked Tracy.

'Not yet,' Tracy confessed, 'it's still a secret, but I expect we'll find out soon. He might even talk so he can tell us himself. Does he talk, Chloe?'

Chloe didn't answer.

Maxine smiled fondly and smoothed Chloe's hair

again. 'I hope you're going to like it here,' she said, 'because I think we're going to like having you, aren't we, Steve?'

'We certainly are,' he agreed. 'You're going to be our special little angel.'

Sorry that Chloe wasn't being more responsive, Tracy put her dainty cup back on its saucer and got to her feet. 'I guess I should be going, time's . . .' She stopped as Chloe got up too. 'Oh, honey, you're staying here,' she said, as Chloe came to take her hand.

Chloe shook her head.

'But you have to, sweetheart. Maxine and Steve are going to take care of you . . .'

'Go to Mummy now,' Chloe whispered.

Relieved that she'd spoken at last, even though it wasn't what she wanted to hear, Tracy went down to Chloe's height as she said, 'You're going to have your very own bedroom with lots of toys to play with, and you'll be able to make new friends.'

A tear dropped on to Chloe's cheek.

'Oh dear,' Tracy groaned, wiping it away. 'You don't have to be upset. You're a very lucky girl, you know. Maxine and Steve are lovely people.'

'Want Mummy,' Chloe said brokenly.

'I know,' Maxine said, lifting her up, 'why don't we go upstairs to see your room? I expect your little bear is very sleepy after that long flight, so you can both have a nap.'

'Want Mummy,' Chloe sobbed as Maxine started to carry her into the house. '*Want Mummy*,' she cried, straining to get back to Tracy.

Feeling utterly wretched as they disappeared inside, Tracy turned to Steve. 'I guess you knew this might not be easy?' she said.

'They almost never are,' he reminded her, and his deep brown eyes seemed to smile sadly as they went to the small bag that belonged to Chloe. 'She'll be fine,' he added confidently.

Though Tracy was accustomed to leaving a child in distress she'd never found it easy, and today was no exception. In fact, it was proving a lot harder to make herself walk out of the Koseys' front door than she'd expected, though she couldn't exactly say why. After all, it wasn't as though she'd developed any sort of rapport with Chloe; that hadn't been possible, with Chloe not speaking. Nor was she in the least bit anxious about the Koseys, though in truth she'd have felt better if she were leaving Chloe with a single woman. It wasn't as though Family Placements hadn't gone all out to find someone, because they had, even Wendy had got involved in the search, but there simply hadn't been anyone suitable who was available to take her in at this short notice. Still, the Koseys had a good track record, and it wasn't as if Tracy was fearful that anything bad would happen to Chloe while she was here. Maybe it was because Chloe was seeming like the child of a friend that Tracy was finding it so difficult, though she hadn't known Charlotte all that well. More likely it was because, instead of having just rescued a child from a dangerous or abusive home, she'd removed her from the heart of a family that loved her.

It didn't feel right.

It didn't feel right at all.

Still, she must remember that the law was the law, and no one, no matter who they were, could be allowed to steal a child and get away with it. Especially not a social worker who people trusted to do the right thing for the kids in their care.

'Obviously, I completely understand why she did it,' Tracy said to Tommy Burgess, who rang while she was on her way home, 'but she surely had to know it would end like this.'

'I expect she did, at least on one level,' he replied, 'but on another I guess she became so attached to the child that she wasn't thinking rationally. It happens, as we know, in many different ways, and this definitely isn't the worst. Far from it, in fact. Anyway, I expect you've heard that she's been remanded in custody.'

'No, I hadn't heard. I didn't want to put the news on while Ottilie – Chloe – was in the car. Poor Charlotte. I don't suppose they were ever really going to give her bail though, were they?'

'Maybe not, but I think her lawyer was optimistic.'

'So what happens now?'

'She's in Crown Court on Wednesday and there's talk of another bail application, but I'm not sure whether or not it'll happen.'

'Do you know what she's going to plead when the time comes? I guess it'll be hard to try saying she's not guilty when they've just brought her back from New Zealand.'

'You could be right, but I haven't seen her, or spoken to her yet. It's all happening through the lawyer.'

'And I'm guessing you're calling now so you can pass on some news about Chloe?'

'Only to reassure her the child's all right.'

'Well, you can do that. Tell her she's fine, because even if she weren't there's nothing she can do about it, so why worry her?'

'You're worrying me now.'

279

'She's gone silent,' Tracy confided, 'which according to the file is how she was when Charlotte first took her on. The only words I've managed to get out of her so far happened just now when she asked to go to Mummy, and I don't think there's much doubt that Charlotte is Mummy.'

'Oh God,' Tommy groaned. 'No, I'm not going to tell her that. Like you said, there's nothing she can do about it, so there's no point in upsetting her when she's already got enough to be dealing with.'

Feeling suddenly very weary, Tracy promised to continue passing on what little information she could, and rang off. She guessed it was all in the lap of the gods now, or the hands of good lawyers, though Charlotte surely had to know that even if she managed to get off the charge of abduction, which seemed to Tracy most unlikely, the chances of her ever being allowed to see Chloe again had to be even less than nil.

Charlotte was sitting on the brutal iron-framed bed in her cell, arms wrapped around her knees, her face hidden from the drab green walls holding her captive. The letter box of a window set close to the ceiling was allowing through a vivid band of sunlight, while on the chipped and broken chest of drawers where she'd stored her few belongings a TV was showing a programme she had no interest in. All she cared about right now was dealing with the fear that she might never get out of here.

She would, of course, at some point, but the maximum sentence for child abduction was seven years, and the mere thought of losing so much of her life, of not seeing Chloe in all that time, or her mother, or the rest of her family in New Zealand, was filling her with so much dread it was virtually impossible to move. She was so tense, so bound up in the horror of what was happening to her that every muscle in her body seemed to ache with it. She was still shuddering from the indignity of the strip search she'd been forced to endure on arrival, while the sweaty stench of her cell was invading her lungs and making her nauseous.

The TV was helping to block the noise from outside her cell: the screeching and banging, clanging of doors and sudden blasts of music. Occasionally footsteps seemed to pause outside her door before moving on. Had she made a mistake in choosing to go on the rule? Was she labelling herself a harmer of children by using this system of protection? The trouble was, at least two women whose children she'd taken into care had been sent to this prison. If they were still here she didn't even want to think about what kind of revenge they might seek, given the chance. Both were in for violent crimes, one for attempted murder, the other for aggravated assault, so the very idea of attempting to explain to them that her actions hadn't been personal was so delusional it could almost be laughable.

Dragging her hands over her face, she tried to clear her mind of fear and focus on how she was going to get through this. It wasn't easy to come up with positives when there seemed so few, but at least Kim had promised another shot at bail, and if they got it this time she could be out of here on Wednesday. That would mean five nights in this small form of hell.

Springing from the bed as though to escape an attack of paranoia, she paced over to the stainless steel lavatory and back again. She couldn't concentrate on the film which was now beginning, and knew it would be no different if she picked up one of the tatty magazines someone had left in a drawer. Fear was like a hornet in her mind, buzzing around all her anxieties, stirring up mischief and stripping her of reason. Uppermost of all was the dread that she and Chloe might never see one another again. Knowing there was a chance they might not was a reality she had somehow to make herself face, but even as she tried she could feel herself swerving away from it.

What had she done to that dear little girl? Why hadn't she handed her over to the proper authorities after rescuing her? What on earth had made her hang on to her the way she had?

Love was the answer, of course. But loving a child was no defence for abduction, nor would it ever be. If she was found guilty when she went to trial, Chloe could be eleven by the time she came out. She wouldn't know her any more; she'd have moved on, become a very different person to the one she might have grown into in New Zealand. Far worse was the fear that the system would have added its own forms of damage to those inflicted by her father – and by the woman who'd stolen her when she was three, loved her, made her all sorts of promises, shown her what it was to be happy, and then abandoned her.

How could she save Chloe from that? What on earth could she do to make sure she didn't turn into an angry, frightened, even vicious adolescent who wanted to make the world pay for what it had done to her?

The answer was nothing. She was as powerless to affect the future now as she was to change the past. She couldn't make sure Chloe went to the right home, because nothing *she* wanted or advised would be taken into account any more. However, luckily, she couldn't imagine Wendy, her old boss, allowing petty grudges to affect the well-being or safety of a child. She probably wouldn't mind too much about throwing Charlotte to the wolves though, she'd done it before, when everyone had thought Chloe was missing and social services had come under fire for not removing her from the family home sooner. Wendy had never actually uttered the words 'the caseholding social worker is to blame', but still, in her usual inimitable way, she had managed to offload all her own responsibility as a manager on to the shoulders of a subordinate.

At least she hadn't gone for Tommy, no doubt because she was astute enough to know that this would have caused a revolt, given how popular he was as a team leader.

Dear Tommy, he'd fought hard during the disciplinary hearings to help the disgraced Alex Lake to keep her job; and he'd been the first to offer her a roof if she'd managed to get bail. She felt awful for the angst and disruption she was causing him. If anyone could deal with it though, he could. He'd already sent a message, via Kim, telling her not to worry, he'd be doing his best for her and Chloe.

It was wonderful to have his support, and Kim's, and Gabby's, but what good was it going to do in the end?

Realising there was no point even in trying to answer that, she attempted to push it from her mind. Perhaps she should turn over to the news to find out what was being said about her, but she wasn't sure she was any more willing to do that than she was to go to the showers.

* * *

283

Maggie Fenn switched off the news and turned to look at her brother. She was a large woman with gentle grey eyes, smudges of bright colour in her cheeks and a smile that seemed etched into every line on her face. At fifty-three she was twelve years older than Anthony, whose dark looks were striking, almost fierce, until he smiled. Then, like his sister's, his entire face seemed to light up with friendliness.

Neither of them was smiling now.

'She needs your help,' Maggie told him bluntly.

He didn't deny it.

'Being on sabbatical doesn't mean you aren't still a lawyer,' Maggie reminded him.

His eyebrows rose, showing a spark of irony.

'So what are you going to do?' Maggie pressed.

Taking an apple from the bowl he bit into it, and kept his eyes on hers as he chewed.

She watched him, knowing much more was going on in his mind than he was choosing to let on. No doubt he was remembering how he'd helped Charlotte once before, when Chloe was presumed missing and Charlotte was about to lose her job. He hadn't known her well, but Maggie had watched with interest as a certain closeness had begun developing between them, and being so fond of them both she'd harboured some hopes for it. Then Charlotte had disappeared off to New Zealand and to Maggie's dismay she hadn't remained in touch.

Now they knew why.

'Well?' she prompted.

Taking another bite of his apple, he came to plant a kiss on her cheek. Then, without uttering a word, he took himself off to the garden.

*　　*　　*

284

Kim was at her desk in the Bristol offices of Crane Jessop, going through all the case law she could find on child abduction. It didn't matter that it was Sunday morning, and she'd promised her partner, Curt, that she'd join him and his daft dog, Burt, for a walk in Ashton Court. Luckily, being a lawyer himself, Curt understood when a case had to come first, and since he wasn't living in a cave, or ten thousand feet up a mountain, he was perfectly aware of how big the Charlotte Nicholls case was. And how much it mattered to Kim, especially since she'd failed to get Charlotte bail.

She'd felt so convinced it would happen. Even now she was still mystified as to why the judge had suddenly ruled the way he had, when at that very point he'd seemed to be leaning their way.

In truth, it hardly mattered now why he'd seemed in such a hurry to end the hearing, because it wasn't going to change the fact that Charlotte Nicholls was banged up in Walworth Prison, no doubt going half out of her mind with worry, not least about whether Kim was the right lawyer for her.

Fortunately Jolyon was on his way here now to discuss the next bail hearing. Not that he felt she'd done anything wrong at the last one, but she was going to feel a whole lot better if she could call on his input for the next time around. The application would go in first thing tomorrow, which meant it would be heard with the Section Fifty-One on Wednesday. This was when the timetable would be set for the filing of papers, plea and case management, and ultimately the trial itself.

All of that was a long way off, sixteen weeks at least, and it would be an absolute travesty, not to mention tragedy, if Charlotte was kept in custody for the whole of that time. She wasn't going to bolt, Kim felt certain of it, and no way would she abuse the conditions of her bail. Actually, Kim didn't feel quite so certain about the second part of that, but as long as Charlotte didn't know where Chloe was, there was no risk of her trying to see her.

Glancing at her BlackBerry as it bleeped with an incoming email, she clicked on to read a message from Curt. *You'll be interested in this. It's about your girl. Cx*

Abandoning the task at hand, Kim turned to her computer, and after opening the email again she went through to the link he'd sent, glancing up as Jolyon came into the room. He was a large, imposing man with intense eyes, silvering hair and, when crossed, a bark that could be as lethal as his bite. 'Hi, coffee's made,' she told him, as he went to hang up his jacket.

Moments later she was staring at the screen in amazement. 'Oh my God,' she murmured. 'Did you know this?'

'Know what?' Jolyon asked.

'It says here that our client is the child that disappeared after the Temple Fields Massacre back in the eighties.'

Jolyon blinked in surprise. 'What are you reading?' he asked, coming to look over her shoulder.

'It's a Scandinavian website,' she replied, 'or maybe it's German, I can't tell. Anyway, listen to this: *before being adopted at the age of four by the Reverend Douglas Lake and his wife, Myra, of Mulgrove village, Alexandra Lake was the youngest child of Gavril Albescu, the mass murderer who slaughtered his family, including his own son, Hugo, in what was to become known as the Temple Fields Massacre. The only survivors of the crazed attacks were his wife, Angela Albescu, who sustained horrific injuries on that fateful night, and three-year-old Charlotte. Apparently Charlotte was hiding in an attic cupboard of the house when her father broke in and went berserk. Among those who lost their lives were Charlotte's grandparents, Andy and Peggy Nicholls, their daughter, Yvonne, Yvonne's fiancé, Nigel Carrington, and Charlotte's five-year-old brother, Hugo.'*

Looking up again, Kim said, 'Do you remember any of this?'

Jolyon nodded. 'Indeed I do. Albescu was Albanian, I believe, or Romanian. It turned out he was part of a human-trafficking gang, one of the first to come into this country. It was said at the time that he only married Angela to facilitate his border crossings, and that when she found out what he was doing she contacted the police. As a result he wiped out her entire family, with the exception of the little girl who was rescued from the attic the following day.'

'What a sad story,' Kim commented, turning back to the screen. 'And how vile of whoever wrote this to be trying to use it against Charlotte the way they are now.'

'Elucidate,' Jolyon prompted.

'Well, it's insinuating that Charlotte might have inherited her father's genes so it's . . . I quote, "lucky someone contacted the police about Ottilie Wade when they did."'

Jolyon's expression darkened. 'This is the trouble with the bloody Internet,' he snarled. 'Whoever's done this has deliberately put it on a foreign site to avoid contempt of court.'

'Shall I try to find out who's behind it?'

'Get the police to do it. They have the resources and this could be as prejudicial to their case as it could to ours. Before you do that though, send an

287

email to Charlotte's parents in New Zealand with a link to the piece. I think they ought to see it. Charlotte should too, so print out what's there and send it over to the prison. We need confirmation that she is the child being referred to. Jolyon Crane,' he said, answering his mobile.

His eyes widened in pleasant surprise. 'How are you, my friend?' he asked warmly. 'It's good to hear from you. Yes, yes, I'm fine, if you discount the bloody fraud case I'm up to my eyes in. That's right, the sharpest judge on the bench provided the bench is in a park and he's sitting alone.' He gave a shout of laughter at the response to his witticism. 'So what can I do for you on this sunny Sunday morning, I thought you'd be fishing or sailing . . .' He started to frown as he listened to the reply, then with a roguish sort of twinkle he said, 'Actually, she's right here. I'll put you on.'

Glancing up from the computer, Kim regarded him expectantly as she took the phone.

Grinning, he told her who it was and gave a chuckle as her jaw actually dropped.

'Blimey,' she murmured. 'Why does he want to speak to me?'

'I think you'll find it's your client he'd like to speak to,' Jolyon replied sardonically, and leaving her to it he went to his office to turn on his own computer.

Chapter Sixteen

'Sweetie, you have to eat,' Maxine Kosey was saying to Chloe. 'You're going to be ill if you don't.'

Chloe kept her worried brown eyes focused on the middle of the table, saying nothing, barely even moving. Boots was in her lap, trying to make her brave, but he wanted Mummy too so he wasn't doing a very good job.

'Mm, these chips are delicious,' Maxine told her, spearing one with a fork and eating it up. 'Steve's enjoying them too, aren't you, Steve?'

Stifling a sigh, he said, 'They're lovely,' and reaching for his wine he knocked back the rest of it before going to the fridge to fetch the bottle. 'Top-up?' he offered his wife.

'No, I'm fine, thanks,' she replied, her eyes moving anxiously between him and Chloe.

'She doesn't want it,' he told her.

'But she hasn't eaten since she got here and that's more than twenty-four hours now. I don't want you to starve, sweetie, so come on, have a chip for me.'

Chloe still didn't look at her. She was trying not to cry, because the man had got cross the last time she cried and she was really scared when men got cross. Daddy used to get cross.

Were they going to give her back to Daddy?

She didn't want to play ride the tiger again; she wanted to go home to Mummy.

'I know what, why don't we have some ice cream?' Maxine suggested brightly. 'I bet you like ice cream, don't you?'

Chloe's bottom lip started to tremble.

'Oh, sweetie, you don't have to have ice cream if you don't want to. Just tell me what you do want.'

'Want Mummy,' Chloe whispered brokenly.

'Oh dear, I know you do, but we're going to take very good care of you, aren't we, Steve?'

Putting his glass down, Steve walked out of the kitchen.

Maxine glanced worriedly at Chloe before getting up and going to the door. 'What's the matter?' she said, as he took his jacket from a cupboard. 'Where are you going?' She tried to grab him, but he pushed her away. 'Steve, it'll be all right . . .'

'No it won't,' he growled, 'so stop kidding yourself.'

'But the doctor said . . .'

'I know what he said, and he would, because he's happy to take our money.'

'He's not like that. He's trying to help us.'

'Well, I don't want his help, thank you very much, and I don't want to go on like this either.'

Her face turned pale. 'What's that supposed to mean?'

'All this taking kids in and pretending they're ours, that we can make a difference . . .'

'But we can, we do. Steve, please don't go . . .'

'Listen,' he said, careful to keep his voice down, 'that child in there is seriously emotionally damaged.'

'You don't know that . . .'

'After what she's been through? Of course she is.

290

We haven't seen it yet, except in the way she won't speak or eat, but there are going to be other problems, you mark my words, and it's not what I want to be dealing with. What I want is for us to have a child of our own . . .'

'It's what I want too, you know it is, and we're doing everything to make it possible.'

'Except it isn't working, and every time you take a child in you get attached to it, and all broken up when you have to let it go, depressed when your period comes . . . You won't discuss adopting . . .'

'No, it's you who won't discuss that.'

He stared at her hard.

'Steve, please . . .'

'I'm sorry,' he said, and pulling open the front door he left.

Doing her best not to break down, Maxine forced herself to take some deep breaths before returning to the kitchen. She couldn't leave the child on her own, but she couldn't bear the fact that Steve had walked out on her either. She needed to ring him, to remind him that his parents were coming over later, and his sister and her kids. They'd agreed to try and make Chloe feel a part of a family, it was what she needed, the social workers had said, and theirs was a family full of love.

What was she going to do? How could she make him come back and stop minding about how awful it was that the IVF didn't seem to be working?

Did he want to adopt? Was he changing his mind about that now? They needed to talk some more; she needed to decide whether she was ready to give up on having a child of her own. Merely to think of it was making her want to cry out in despair. She shouldn't have accepted Chloe into their home while she was feeling like this. She wouldn't have agreed to it if the social worker who'd contacted her hadn't been desperate.

'Hello, sweetie,' she said to Chloe, as she went to pick up her mobile, 'are you all right? Have you eaten anything yet?'

Chloe watched her with wide, anxious eyes.

Maxine forced a smile and began tapping in a text. *We have to talk. Please come home.*

'There,' she told Chloe, putting the phone down again, 'that's done, and so now what shall we do about you? Are you ready to eat something yet?' Jumping as her phone bleeped, she snatched it up and read, *Your Vodafone bill is ready for you to read online.*

Swallowing her disappointment, and playfully rolling her eyes at Chloe, she said, 'It wasn't him, but never mind. He'll be back later and he'll be so pleased if I can tell him you've eaten your tea.'

Chloe watched her sit down.

Maxine dabbed away a tear as she sipped more wine. 'Will you eat something, or speak to me and show me how clever you are?' she asked shakily.

'Want Mummy,' Chloe whispered.

Biting her lip, Maxine brushed a hand over the little girl's hair. She presumably meant Charlotte Nicholls, so what was she supposed to say when Charlotte was in prison and as things stood, it was unlikely Chloe was ever going to see her 'mummy' again?

Reaching for her mobile as it bleeped with another text, she opened it and felt her heart jarring badly as she read, *Going to stay with Guy for a few days. Need to get my head together.*

'Oh God,' Maxine groaned helplessly. It seemed

so mean to give Chloe back now, as though she was something they'd bought at a shop that didn't quite suit when they got it home, but it wouldn't be fair to keep her here while they were going through this. She looked at Chloe and her eyes welled with more tears. Where would they take her next, she wondered. Steve would say it wasn't their problem, and she guessed it wasn't really. The trouble was, if social services felt they couldn't rely on her they might not let her have any more children to take care of, and what would she do then?

'Ah, Tracy, there you are,' Wendy Fraser announced as Tracy bumped backwards through a set of swing doors into the main offices of Kesterly's child protection department. 'Do you have a minute?'

'Sure,' Tracy lied, 'I'll be with you in two ticks.' She rarely argued with Wendy, mainly because the days when she'd pick a fight with someone just for the sake of it were long gone, thank goodness. Though her eight-year-old son, Tyler, was certainly learning how to push all the buttons. His room was a bomb site, he'd started cheeking her back and this morning, after his father had left for work, he'd thumped his sister and made her cry.

Still, that was all a part of family life and challenging as she found it at times, she was proud of the fact that she'd now learned to tell the difference between normal and aberrant. And it didn't come much more aberrant than what was going on with the eleven-year-old boy she'd stopped by to visit on her way into the office. Though he'd been a part of her caseload for a while now, she hadn't known until this morning that he was becoming addicted to the most gruesomely explicit porn websites, something he shared with his mother's unsavoury boyfriend.

'I never told you how bad it was before,' Linnie, the mother, had wailed, 'because I was afraid you'd take him away, but it can't be good for him, all that stuff, can it, not at his age?'

It certainly wasn't – and nor was all the dreadful junk food he was being fed, nor his experiments with alcohol, which was why Tracy had already taken steps to remove the boy. This morning's revelation meant it would probably happen today, which was going to be hard for poor Linnie when she genuinely loved her son and wanted the best for him. Sadly, she was too weak and unworldly to cope with her own life, much less a vulnerable young boy's. Still, at least Linnie had the sense to admit that she needed help, and the removal would only be temporary if the wretched woman could bring herself to evict the vile boyfriend.

'Hey Trace, how's tricks?' Saffy Dyer asked, as Tracy dumped her heavy bag on the desk next to Saffy's.

'Magic as ever,' Tracy quipped. 'Are you in or out today?'

'Out in about twenty minutes. Why?'

'Just wondering if you can come to the Gales with me later to pick up not-so-little Freddie.'

Saffy checked her diary. 'Should be OK,' she said, 'if it's this afternoon. Where are you taking him?'

'Still waiting to hear from placements, so I'll let you know. What's all the fuss over there?' she asked, nodding towards the break-out area, where a dozen or so of their colleagues all seemed to be talking at once.

Saffy rolled her eyes. 'The police are here, taking

statements,' she said. 'And then there's this thing on the Internet about Charlotte Nicholls's father being the bloke behind the Temple Fields Massacre. That lot reckon it's why she chose to work that area when she was one of us, though why it's such a big deal sure beats me. It's not like the house where it happened is still there, and so what if she wanted to help kids on one of the worst estates in the county? In my book that's a good thing . . . Oh Tommy! Tommy!' she shouted, as he appeared at the far end of the office and looked set to go straight in to see Wendy. 'I have to speak to you urgently. I'm due in court in half an hour and I haven't got any of the paperwork through for Brooklyn Prosser. If I don't have it, they'll end up giving his mother back her custody rights, and the woman's bloody mental.'

Coming to join them, his large physique and hippy hair making him an interesting figure, Tommy said, 'Give me a minute and I'll chase it for you. Have you been interviewed by the police yet?'

'No, still waiting, but they'd better get on with it, because I should leave soon. How did yours go?'

Looking slightly strained, he said, 'It was fairly routine sort of stuff, but apparently they're going to need to talk to me again. A treat to look forward to. Trace, have you spoken to Wendy yet today?'

'Just about to,' Tracy replied. 'Why, what's up?'

'No idea, she just told me as soon as I saw you I had to send you in, but I need to speak to her myself first. Christ, will you look at that lot, anyone would think a social worker's never been in the news before.'

'Yeah, well she's the type of social worker who gives the rest of us a bad name,' Dustin Koby grumbled from the other side of the partition. 'What was she thinking, for Christ's sake, making off with the child like that?'

'If you have to ask that question I'm not sure why you're sitting there,' Tommy said shortly, and turning away he stalked back to Wendy's office and closed the door.

Dustin's bushy eyebrows were reaching skywards. 'I guess that's me told,' he grunted, 'but you have to admit I've got a point. Why should we be the ones suffering for something *she* did?'

'You don't look as though you're suffering much to me,' Saffy told him tartly, and turning back to Tracy she kept her voice low as she said, 'How was Ottilie when you left her at the weekend?'

'We're calling her Chloe,' Tracy informed her, 'and the answer is she was sobbing her heart out for Mummy.'

Saffy sighed. 'Poor mite,' she murmured. 'Poor Charlotte. This must be really tough on them both, especially Charlotte, being banged up in Walworth. You know, it occurred to me yesterday that Molly Buck might still be in there, serving time for the assault on her husband?'

Tracy regarded her soberly. 'Let's just hope she's been moved on by now,' she said, 'because Charlotte was the social worker who took her kids into care, which was what provoked the attack on the husband. She reckoned it was him who called us in.'

'He did, and he's got custody of the kids now, which I don't suppose Molly's any too pleased about.' Her eyes went to Tracy's, as their shared experience of Molly Buck deepened their concern for Charlotte. 'Going back to Ottilie, or Chloe,' she said, 'I don't suppose you can say who she's with?'

Tracy shook her head. 'But they seem like a good couple, and they came highly recommended from their own authority.'

Seeming relieved, Saffy told her, 'There goes Tommy, so you'd better pop in to see what Wendy wants.'

Glancing over her shoulder, Tracy said, 'I'll text you as soon as I hear from placements about where we're to take Freddie Gale.'

A few minutes later she was sitting slumped against Wendy's desk with her head in her hands. 'I don't believe it,' she groaned. 'Please tell me it's not true.'

'I wish I could,' Wendy responded, pushing her horn-rimmed glasses up the bony slope of her dainty snub nose. Her hazel eyes were close-set ovals, and her wide, thin mouth was an inverted smile that managed to prettify her pale face on the occasions she turned it up the other way. The expression in her eyes showed that no matter how businesslike she had to be, she wasn't without feeling for the child they were discussing.

'So when did you get the call?' Tracy asked. 'And why didn't they contact me if there was a problem?'

'I can't answer that,' Wendy told her, 'but I spoke to Maxine Kosey about half an hour ago. She sounded very upset about having to hand Ottilie back after such a short time, but she says she has to. Actually, I got the impression she might be having problems with her husband.'

Tracy nodded sadly. 'Apparently they're trying for one of their own,' she said, 'but it's not working out. As we know, IVF can put tremendous pressure on a marriage. I just wish she'd said something before we took Chloe there – Chloe is what we're calling her now, by the way. She associates Ottilie with her father, and obviously we don't want that.'

Wendy nodded her understanding. 'I've spoken to placements,' she said, 'and they're trying to sort something out with West Somerset, but it isn't going to be easy. Finding a family that's suitable when we don't want her going somewhere that already has children, and preferably no men either, is a very tall order. However, we must do our best, because she requires careful handling and close monitoring while we carry out a full and proper assessment of her health and needs in order to make decisions for her future.'

'Of course,' Tracy mumbled; as if she didn't know that already. 'So when does Maxine want us to get her?'

'As soon as possible, today preferably.'

'You're kidding me.'

'I wish I was.'

'So what do we do if placements can't find someone? She can't go into residential care, it'll terrify the life out of her.'

Wendy glanced at the clock. 'I think we give it until two this afternoon and if placements haven't come up with somewhere by then, we'll extend the search.'

Relieved by the suggestion, Tracy said, 'OK, but what about Maggie Fenn? I know she's right on our doorstep, and we're not supposed to be . . .'

Wendy was already shaking her head. 'Apart from the point you've just made, Alex Lake is friendly with Maggie Fenn.'

'But this isn't about *Charlotte* . . .'

'I'm afraid it is, and if *Charlotte* does get bail at

298

any time it'll be our job to make sure she doesn't try to see the child.'

Tracy looked offended. 'So what if she does? Can it be such a bad thing? They've become very attached to one another. Chloe calls her Mummy . . .'

Wendy was regarding her incredulously. 'Do you want her to run off with the child again?' she demanded.

Thinking she probably did, Tracy replied, 'I was just saying that we're supposed to be putting the interests of the child first . . .'

'That's exactly what I am doing,' Wendy reminded her crisply. 'In fact I have a meeting scheduled for tomorrow morning with adoption services. Given the child's age and ethnicity I don't think we'll have any problem finding a family who can offer her a permanent home, and the sooner we get on to it the better it'll be for everyone, most of all Chloe.'

Charlotte was back in her cell now, still shivering and damp from the tepid shower she'd just been taken to by the guard, Nola. The woman had stayed with her the entire time, never taking her eyes from her as she'd soaped herself with the pebble of Palmolive while a bunch of inmates had hooted and jeered from outside. She was sport for them, for Nola too, a way of livening up the monotony of their day. Still, at least no other prisoners had been allowed in during the few minutes she was there, using the last of the hot water. The others had showered ahead of her, a communal ablution that made her shrink inside even to think of it.

Was this how it was going to be for her now, no more privacy, no friends, no power to change where she was?

She'd wondered if her solitary shower meant that she was the only one on the rule, but she hadn't asked and nor would she. She just wanted to keep herself to herself as much as she could, while she prayed and longed for the day to come when she'd be allowed out of here.

Using the towel she'd worn back from the showers to dry her hair, she then rummaged in a drawer for the comb she'd spotted in her welcome pack. She was voraciously hungry, she realised, and yet still wasn't sure she could eat. Her breakfast hadn't been taken away yet: toast and porridge, cold now and congealing, but maybe she should try it.

'Room service,' Nola had sneered when she'd brought it. 'Don't get used to it.'

Charlotte pulled on the tracksuit she'd been given and felt glad of the clean clothes, rough though they were. She wanted to ask if she could use the phone. The trouble was, she didn't have enough to make a call to New Zealand. They probably weren't allowed to make international calls anyway.

Daft to think of ringing her mother. What could Anna do, apart from try to reassure her that everything would work out? It might not, they both knew that, but she needed to hear someone say it. She wished her mother was in England, but at the same time was glad she wasn't. One of them behind bars was already more than enough.

Perhaps she could call Gabby. During the night a wild idea had come to her, a rash, crazy dream that had seen Chloe in the heart of Gabby's family. She'd looked happy there, as though she belonged with the twins, who were adorable and would do everything to make Chloe feel at home. Children were often much better at drawing each other out than adults. But

Gabby and Martin weren't registered carers, and even if they were there was no way Chloe would be allowed to go to the sister of the woman who'd abducted her.

Sitting down on the bed, she pushed her bare feet into the prison-issue flip-flops and reached for the toast. As crumbs dropped on to her tracksuit top she looked down to brush them away, then her head snapped up again as the door suddenly swung open and Nola came in.

Charlotte's appetite instantly died. There was something about the way Nola was standing there, ogling her, that was deeply unsettling. To her relief, Penny, the warder who'd at least been civil to her when she'd arrived, came in behind her.

With a glance at Nola, Penny tossed an envelope on the bed and left. To Charlotte's dismay Nola continued to stare at her. Neither of them moved. Charlotte had no idea what was happening, not knowing if she should say, or do something, or simply stay as she was.

In the end, without uttering a word, Nola turned and walked out. Charlotte stared at the open door feeling as though she'd been threatened, or maybe sized up in some way, and for the first time since she'd been there she knew the true sense of being completely, inescapably trapped.

'Tommy, can I have a quick word?' Tracy said, putting her head round the door.

'Sure, how's it going?' he asked, beckoning her in as he turned from his computer screen. 'I thought you were picking up Freddie Gale this afternoon.'

Tracy threw out her hands. 'My whole day's gone to pot,' she told him, closing the door behind her.

'I'm actually about to go and collect Chloe – please don't let on to anyone I'm telling you this,' she added quickly.

Looking concerned, he replied, 'Of course I won't. What's happened?'

Sighing, she said, 'Turns out the couple she's with are having problems, so they can't keep her any longer.'

'Couldn't they have decided that *before* you took her there?'

'You'd have thought so, but apparently they've made a mistake, so she has to go.'

'So have you got someone else lined up?'

'I think so. I've just got their details from West Somerset.'

'So why are you in here talking to me?'

Glancing at the door to make sure it was still closed, she told him, 'Wendy's talking adoption already.'

Though his eyes narrowed, he said, 'I guess we have to accept that in the long term, adoption could be the best thing for the child.'

'Of course it could, but I can't help feeling Wendy's rushing this. She wouldn't let her feelings about Charlotte affect her judgement, would she?'

Sighing, Tommy shook his head. 'No, she wouldn't, but I'm afraid Charlotte will probably take it personally if she finds out.'

'So what on earth happened between those two before Charlotte went off on her little jaunt Down Under?'

'Nothing actually happened,' he replied, 'they just always managed to rub each other up the wrong way and love Charlotte as I do, she wasn't always easy to manage. On the other hand, Wendy can be

302

tricky too, as you know very well. Then along came all the bad publicity we got as a department when everyone thought Chloe was missing and probably murdered by her own father. Charlotte took most of the hits over that, while Wendy, as her manager, somehow avoided the flak, even though a child had disappeared on her watch, and the videos showed long-term, systematic abuse. Not that they were ever made public, but everyone knew of their existence and so, according to the press, social services had fallen down on the job again. Charlotte was the obvious scapegoat, and Wendy knows, in her heart, that she should have stood by her. That was before we knew Charlotte had Chloe, obviously.'

'You didn't have a problem standing by her.'

He didn't comment on that, though he'd been hauled up in front of his bosses at the time and for a while his job had looked as though it was seriously on the line. 'It wasn't Charlotte's fault she had to go through the official channels to help prove there was a problem at the Wades' home,' he said. 'Everyone has to, you know that, unless the abuse is blindingly obvious and you can get an Emergency Order to hike the victims out of harm's way. The normal procedure takes weeks, even months for all of us, and Alex – Charlotte – was dealing with a man who was too damned clever by half. Anyway, fast forward to now, and you could be right, Wendy's still having issues over Charlotte, but that doesn't mean adoption is the wrong way to go.'

'But what if Charlotte gets off and the court says she can have Chloe back? OK, I know that's not very likely, but stranger things and all that. And if it does happen, imagine how tough it'll be for the couple that think they're going to adopt her. To have come that far only to have their hopes dashed . . . Or if it's already gone through, making it too late for Charlotte . . . I'm sorry, but it feels wrong to me, going this fast.'

Tommy didn't disagree, but since he wasn't in a position to discuss it with Wendy without breaking his promise to Tracy not to reveal what she'd told him, he said, 'Leave it with me. I'll make some calls and see what, if anything, can be done to slow it up.'

Chapter Seventeen

If Charlotte closed her eyes and her ears she could imagine herself anywhere in the world: swimming in the cove at Te Puna; flying a kite on the cliffs with Chloe; producing a show with the Mulgrove players . . . As soon as she opened them there was no mistaking where she was. In a cell, with no way out. However, this particular cell wasn't in the prison; it was beneath Dean Valley Crown Court.

It was Wednesday morning, just before midday. She'd been brought here in the Reliance van over an hour ago, though her hearing wasn't due to start until three. The van couldn't make more than one journey into town, she'd been told, so she'd have to go at its convenience, not her own.

She didn't mind, anything to get out of Walworth, even if it meant being locked up somewhere else. At least Nola wasn't here. Although Nola hadn't actually said or done anything yet, she was always hanging around, watching her, as though letting her know that anything could happen at any time.

'You will get through this,' Kim had written in the letter she'd sent to the prison on Sunday. 'I know it must seem tough right now, and hard to see a way past all the crap life's throwing at you, but I promise you things are happening out here. You have some good people on your side, lots of influence being brought to bear in ways I won't go into now, but we can discuss them as soon as I see you. I'm hoping to have some news on Chloe by then, because I know she's always uppermost in your mind. Yours, Kim.'

She was right, Chloe was always there, filling her mind and her heart in ways she could never break free from, but nor did she want to. In fact, it was only thinking about Chloe, and absorbing herself in memories of Te Puna, that allowed her to escape the brutality of where she was. Even though her heart flooded with pain and longing each time she came back to the present, but while she was imagining the sound of Chloe's laughter, the joy of her swimming on Diesel with Danni, the sheer pleasure of sharing in some new triumph, it was as though she was with her. For fleeting moments she could almost feel her sweet breath on her cheek, or the clasp of her hand, or the satisfying bulk of her weight in her arms. She could hear her chattering, singing, or simply breathing; see her little shoes next to the door, and taste the sticky kisses after a fluffy. Everything about her was so pure, so cleansing, that not even the ghastliness of the coarse and violent women around her, or the menace of predatory guards could reach her when she was with Chloe in her mind.

Kim had also enclosed a printout from a foreign website.

Is this true? Kim had asked. *If so, do you have any idea who might have posted it?*

Though Charlotte had no proof she strongly suspected it had come from her old nemesis on the

Kesterly Gazette, Heather Hancock. And the most obvious way Heather would have discovered the information was by wheedling it out of Jason, Charlotte's ex, since there wasn't anyone else Charlotte had ever trusted with the story of her early life. If she was right then she felt as baffled as she did hurt by his betrayal, since she'd never known him to be spiteful, or a gossip. However, he was a part of her past now, so maybe she had to accept that he didn't owe her any loyalty.

As for Heather, whose journalistic inaccuracies Charlotte had had the temerity to point out in the past, publicly, she must be unspeakably thrilled at having such sweet revenge in her hands. Not that she could run it in the *Gazette*, but Charlotte wondered if so much righteous indignation had ever before been uploaded from this part of the world to a foreign website, with, it had to be said, yet more inaccuracies. Heather had obviously taken Jason at his word, since she was clearly in a fine lather about the fact that a mass murderer's blood ran in Charlotte Nicholls's veins.

How crushed, how incensed, she was going to be when she found out it wasn't true.

Charlotte had no idea how public the story had become by now. Obviously the main broadcasters and newspapers weren't going to risk contempt of court by running it, but there was nothing, no one, to stop it going viral on the Net. If it had, the chances were her mother had already seen it, and Bob would be doing his best to protect her, but it wouldn't be easy for either of them having the past raked up like this, uncovering its horror, exposing such painful wounds. Since reading the piece Charlotte had spent many hours thinking of her mother and feeling for how terrible it must have been for her when, after everything she'd already lost, she'd been forced to give up her daughter too. How strange life was to now be presenting Charlotte with a similar heartbreak; maybe this was its way of getting her to understand how impossible it had been for her mother back then. Had she ever really not understood? She was certain she had, but she'd still found it hard to accept.

In the end her mother had summoned the courage to give her up for adoption, certain it was the only way of keeping her safe. For Charlotte and Chloe it wasn't the same; no one wanted to harm them, apart from the state, the police, the lawyers who were going to try and make Charlotte pay for what she'd done. There were no other threats hanging over them; they were causing offence to no one, so why should she have to let Chloe go when Chloe was happy and loved by the family that already thought of her as their own?

'Time to go up,' a guard brusquely announced, coming to unlock the cell. 'Brief said she'll see you up there.'

Surprised, and unnerved by the fact that Kim hadn't come down to the cells, Charlotte tucked her tissues into a sleeve and tried to appear collected as she walked past the guard into the main area. It was probably just that Kim was running late, leaving no time for a quick pre-hearing conference, *so don't start reading something sinister into it now*, she told herself firmly.

Following the guard to the stairs, she distracted herself with the thought of how this underground chamber was hardly any different from the one beneath the town hall. The only real difference was that this was newer and painted a sludge pea-green instead of something that probably used to be white. The steps had tiles on them, and a banister to hold on to, but the stench of those who'd gone before her – sweat, vomit, old booze and the sickly residue of cheap perfume – still managed to curdle the air.

She felt momentarily uplifted by the fact that there would be no press at this hearing. Apparently they weren't allowed into chambers and that was how this application had been scheduled, meaning it would still happen in a courtroom, but only those directly involved in the case would be present. The relief she'd felt when she'd read that in Kim's letter was washing over her in waves again now, for the prospect of the press waiting up there like ravens would have been unnerving her badly. Especially now she was no longer simply Charlotte Nicholls, the child abductor; she was Charlotte Albescu, *daughter of the notorious human-trafficker who'd slain his wife's family.*

As she neared the top of the stairs she heard someone laugh in the court and felt it hit her like a rock. She tried to remember when she'd last laughed, and decided it must have been out at Kauri Cliffs during the Owens Lifestyle shoot. How long ago and faraway that seemed now, part of another world, another life.

As she entered the court with its beechwood panelling and matching benches, windowless walls and three rain-spattered skylights, no one seemed to notice she was there. The muted chatter at the front simply continued as the lawyers discussed some sporting event and the court officials went about their affairs. Charlotte spotted Kim's blonde hair right away, but her head was down as she made notes on a file in front of her, apparently not part of the male camaraderie. She recognised DS Karen Potter, and guessed the two men with her were also detectives. No sign of Terence Gould. What was he making of her new status as the daughter of a mass killer? Would he want that out there in the public domain, or was he even now taking steps to track down the story's source in order to prosecute?

As she stepped up into the dock a fresh onslaught of fear assailed her. If this hearing wasn't successful she'd be escorted back to the Reliance van, deposited into a steel cubicle and returned to Walworth. There would be no other opportunity to seek bail before the trial, and that could be months away.

Panic began clamouring for an escape, making her want to scream and run, but she forced herself to keep breathing, keep going, trying to seal herself off from the fear.

'Charlotte, I'm here.'

The whisper only just reached her, but she recognised it instantly and felt a soaring in her heart as she turned to where Gabby was sitting alone in a side bench.

Loving her for coming, Charlotte attempted to smile back, but the guard was insisting she sit down. After he'd moved away she turned to Gabby again and mouthed a 'thank you'.

'Love you,' Gabby mouthed back and Charlotte almost cried.

When she turned round again Kim was looking her way, her expression showing affection as well as concern.

Charlotte was too tense, too bound up in the dread of returning to that van, to Walworth, to give anything more than a brief nod.

Minutes later they were being told to rise and the judge came in, stout and bald-headed. His face was grim until he regarded the lawyers with some surprise, which was strange, but at least it made him seem more human. He spoke to them but Charlotte only caught it in snatches . . . '. . . so it is you . . . such an eminent presence in our midst . . .'

Whatever the response was it made him chuckle, and Charlotte took heart from the fact that he seemed to be in a good mood. But then his thin mouth set in a stern line again, and knowing he had her fate in his hands was making her resent him. He didn't know her, had never even met her, and yet he had the power to say whether or not she was a responsible citizen.

She'd stolen a child, so how could she possibly expect someone to view her as a responsible citizen?

She willed him to meet her gaze, as though she might somehow be able to transmit how trustworthy she was, but he was busy reviewing the documents in front of him, and didn't even glance up when the charge was read.

The prosecutor, Andy Phipps, was the first to speak, sounding both apologetic and long-suffering as he repeated the reasons he'd given before as to why Charlotte shouldn't be granted bail. 'Nothing has changed since Saturday,' he informed the judge, 'the fear of failure to surrender remains, and why should the British taxpayer be forced to bear the expense of bringing her back again? In fact, Your

Honour, I'd go as far as to say that this bail hearing is a waste of the court's time when the defendant has already proved herself to be a person of few social morals by taking a child at all, never mind out of the country. So I'm asking that she be returned to custody, where she will not be able to plan any more flights to New Zealand with or without a child that's not hers.'

The judge appeared impassive.

Charlotte was trying to swallow, but couldn't. It was so degrading being referred to as a defendant, a person of few social morals, when that wasn't who she was at all. Worse was knowing that people in this room, and outside it, agreed with him, and wanted to see her shut away from society as though she were some sort of pariah.

Someone else was speaking now, though she couldn't make out who at first since no one was standing up. Why wasn't Kim laying out her case? Wasn't that how it was supposed to happen? But Kim was still sitting down, and remained in her chair as the dark-haired man next to her rose to his feet, still addressing the judge.

Charlotte's heart gave a sudden and painful lurch as she realised who it was. Anthony Goodman. Who had asked him to act on her behalf? Why hadn't anyone told her? She was so thrown, so bewildered that she could hardly register what he was saying.

Yet his quiet voice was carrying through the turmoil of her shock, authoritative and commanding as he said, 'Ms Nicholls has no previous criminal record . . . She represents no threat whatsoever to the community, or to herself, or even to the child you're trying to keep her away from.'

'Your Honour,' the prosecutor objected. 'She has already taken the child out of the country . . .'

'Where the child came to no harm,' Anthony pointed out. After waiting a moment in case Phipps had any more to say, he continued. 'Your Honour, Ms Nicholls's family have gone to some lengths over the past few days to secure the lease on a flat here in Kesterly so my client will have somewhere to live until this case comes to trial. I'm sure we're all agreed that hardly demonstrates a plan to flee the country. Nor does the transfer of two hundred and fifty thousand pounds to post as bail, the entirety of Ms Nicholls's savings, should the court require it. This money is now in a client account with Ms Nicholls's solicitor . . .' He paused as Kim handed him a paper, and after glancing over it he passed it to the clerk. 'This is a statement showing details of the account,' he told the judge. 'I'm also being reminded that the flat will be ready for occupancy this coming Saturday, and until that time Ms Nicholls will be able to stay with friends here in Kesterly, Maggie and Ron Fenn.'

Charlotte almost gasped. Maggie and Ron were offering her a place to stay? Did anyone know Maggie was Anthony's sister? Did it matter? Presumably not, or surely Anthony wouldn't be suggesting it.

'It should be noted,' he went on, 'that Mr Tommy Burgess is also offering a place for Ms Nicholls to stay, but as he was her team leader while she was with social services we've taken a view that the court would prefer it if she had as little contact with her old colleagues as possible, particularly those who might have access to the child.'

Though it was horrible to be considered a threat

313

to Chloe, Charlotte could see the reasoning behind his words, in spite of still being thrown by the fact that *he* was uttering them.

'Your Honour, can I point out,' the prosecutor was saying, 'that the defendant's family is still in New Zealand, where they've already . . .'

'Actually,' Anthony interrupted, 'my client has family here, in the UK. In fact her sister is in the court today, and is also ready to offer her home to Ms Nicholls in the event bail is granted. However, she understands that the court might be less willing to accept her kindness, given that she doesn't live locally. Nevertheless, she is family, and she and Ms Nicholls are close.'

As Charlotte turned to Gabby, her heart melted to see her sister so flustered and proud.

The judge was speaking. 'I can see no reason not to grant bail,' he was saying. 'There'll be conditions, of course . . .' As the speed and reality of his decision hit her Charlotte stopped hearing his words, could hear only the jubilant cry of relief inside her. She wasn't going back to Walworth. *She wasn't going back to Walworth.* She could hardly believe it; he'd ruled that she could go to her flat, or to stay with Maggie and Ron. She was so stunned, so overcome that she wasn't registering the conditions, but she didn't care what they were. All that mattered was the fact that she didn't have to go back to prison.

She glanced over her shoulder at Gabby and saw that Tommy was there too now, and both were clenching their fists in a *yes!*

When she turned back the judge was still speaking, but her eyes were fixed on Anthony, who was watching Kim making notes on a pad. Then he looked round at her, his eyebrows raised almost comically, and she felt her heart turn inside out. QCs almost never conducted bail hearings, and yet he was here conducting hers.

She barely knew what to make of it.

'I believe,' the judge was saying as he went through his papers, 'that we're using the court's time efficiently by dealing with the Section Fifty-one while we're here.'

'Your Honour,' Anthony said, 'before a timetable is set, can I enter a request for the service of papers to be carried out within four weeks?'

Phipps was having none of it. 'Your Honour, this doesn't allow anywhere near enough time for us to prepare . . .'

'Actually, I think it does,' the judge interrupted crossly. 'Everything always takes far too long these days, so I'm setting a date of three weeks hence for the service of papers, and four weeks after that for the Plea and Case Management.' He was looking at the clerk now, who was duly noting it.

'Your Honour, this really is unprecedented,' Phipps objected.

The judge appeared astonished. 'I don't think you'll find it is, Mr Phipps,' he retorted, and a moment later he was saying, 'The defendant will return to the cells until the bail funds are in place. Thank you ladies and gentlemen, the court is dismissed.'

An hour later, with every last penny she owned now in the court's keeping, and an appointment with Reliance to fit her electronic tag sometime in the next few hours, Charlotte was in the lobby preparing to make a dash through the reporters crowding the steps outside.

'Don't say anything,' Anthony cautioned, taking her arm, 'and try not to look at anyone either.'

'They can really only take pictures and report on the fact that you've now got bail,' Kim told her, coming to shield the other side of her, 'so it shouldn't be too gruelling. Are you ready?'

Trying not to be so aware of Anthony's grip, Charlotte said, 'I guess so,' and turned to check Gabby was behind.

With a smile Gabby gave her a thumbs up.

'Stay with us,' Charlotte told her.

'Don't worry, I will.'

'Where's Tommy?'

'Gone to get his car.'

'OK,' Anthony said, and as the door opened they were instantly assailed by flashbulbs. However, Anthony didn't even hesitate as he and Kim quickly urged Charlotte into the fray, using their free arms to fight a path through.

Eventually Charlotte was being pushed into the back of a large saloon car, while Gabby jumped in the other side and Anthony quickly sat in the driver's seat. Once Kim was in next to him he hit the locks, started the engine and they began moving off.

'Are you OK?' Kim asked, turning round to check as Anthony drove out of the square and down towards the seafront.

'Yes, I'm fine,' Charlotte replied, slightly breathlessly. She glanced at Gabby. 'Are you?'

'Yes, I'm cool,' Gabby assured them, in spite of how dazed she looked.

'We'll probably be followed,' Anthony said, 'but we have the advantage of knowing where we're going, whereas they don't. Yet.'

Turning to Charlotte, Kim broke into a smile. 'We got the right result this time,' she declared. 'I'm really sorry it didn't happen before . . .'

'It's OK,' Charlotte told her, catching Anthony's eye in the rear-view mirror. What was he thinking, she wondered, what should she be saying to him? She knew now, because Kim had told her during the hour's wait in the holding area, that he'd got in touch himself last Sunday and offered to take the case on, but she had no idea why he'd done that, because she still hadn't had a chance to speak to him.

'You obviously caught old Edmore on a bad day last Saturday,' he commented, 'because there was never a strong case for custody.'

'I hope it wasn't too awful in Walworth,' Kim grimaced.

Hating Anthony knowing she'd been in such a place, Charlotte made her tone sardonic as she said, 'Let's just say I've had better weekends away.'

As Kim laughed and Anthony cocked an eyebrow, Gabby poked Charlotte and nodded towards the front as she mouthed, 'Who is he? Where did he come from?'

'Later,' Charlotte replied in the same way.

'Dead fit,' Gabby added, her eyes glittering so expressively that Charlotte had to turn away.

'I need to check the train times,' Kim announced, taking out her iPhone.

To Charlotte, Anthony said, 'When we get to my sister's you can call New Zealand. They'll be waiting to hear from you.'

Charlotte's heart gave a jolt of pure joy. 'Thank you,' she said, managing to smile past a rush of emotion.

Giving her another prod, Gabby mouthed, 'Sister?'

Charlotte barely engaged, she was too caught up in the amazement of being here, in Anthony's car, and the relief of being free to use a phone, to speak to her mother, to Bob, Rick, Shelley . . . Her heart caught on the pain of Chloe not being with them, but she had to move past it, at least for now. Anthony had managed to get her out of that terrible prison; he was driving them to his sister's who was giving her refuge . . . For the moment it was all that mattered.

By the time they arrived at Maggie's, on the leafy southern point of Kesterly Bay, both Anthony and Kim were on their phones, and Charlotte was trying to pay attention as Gabby updated her on news of the twins. Not that she wasn't interested in her niece and nephew, on the contrary, she loved them to bits, she just had so much whirling round in her head it was hard to make herself think straight about anything at all.

Maggie Fenn's natural warmth lit her softly creased face as she came to open the rear passenger door for Charlotte to get out of the car. 'Here you are, how good it is to see you,' she declared happily. 'Come along, let's get you inside.'

'I hardly know what to say,' Charlotte confessed as she stepped out of Maggie's embrace, 'or at least where to begin, with a sorry or a thank you.'

'How about with an introduction to this lovely young lady who I presume is your sister?'

Wishing again that she'd thought to bring Chloe here on that fateful night, Charlotte turned to Gabby, who was coming to join them.

'Gabby, this is Maggie Fenn,' she said, drawing Gabby closer, 'who happens to be one of the most wonderful people in the world, and not just because she's offering me her home, just because she is.'

'It's lovely to meet you, Maggie,' Gabby said, seeming startled though pleased by Maggie's friendly hug. 'And thank you for helping my sister out. It's really kind of you.'

'She's always welcome here,' Maggie assured them, 'and I'm very glad she was able to make it, which means my brother didn't let the side down.'

Laughing at the way Anthony rolled his eyes, Charlotte watched him introduce Kim and suddenly found herself having to take a moment to fight back another rush of emotion. The past hour or so had sped by so quickly she was still struggling to take it all in, and finding herself here, at Maggie's elegant Georgian home, with such kind and decent people, was feeling a bit like a dream, especially when she considered where she'd woken up that morning.

'Come on, you lot,' Ron Fenn shouted from the door, his white beard and balding head making him look as jovial as Santa. 'The pack's bound to be on the trail and we don't want them finding us all out here.'

As Anthony led the way to the house a car swerved into the drive causing a moment's alarm, until realising it was Tommy Charlotte ran over to greet him. 'Thanks for coming,' she gasped as he wrapped her in a giant bear hug. 'And for saying I could stay with you. I'm so sorry about what's happening, the position it's put you in . . .'

'Will you stop?' he chided, squeezing her hard. 'I'm big enough and ugly enough to take care of myself. It's you I'm worried about, but you're looking pretty good – at least better than I expected.'

'I brought her some make-up,' Gabby assured him, coming to join in. 'And some lovely smelly stuff, and clothes . . . Oh no, they're in my car which is back at the multi-storey next to the court.'

'It's OK, we can go for them once all the fuss has died down,' Tommy told her. 'Right now I think we need to avail ourselves of Maggie's facilities, at least I do.'

Minutes later they were in the Fenns' large farmhouse kitchen with a kettle on the boil and a tentative offer of champagne still on the table, as yet unaccepted.

It seemed everyone was talking at once about what had happened in court, the dash through the press, the bail conditions which Charlotte realised she still hadn't fully registered. She was about to ask Anthony when he put a hand on her arm and said quietly, 'A word?'

Trying not to appear flustered, she nodded a yes, and let him steer her into the sitting room. As he closed the door behind them he fixed her with playfully narrowed eyes. 'So I guess I now have answers to one or two questions that have been bothering me lately,' he drawled. 'Such as why I never heard back from you when I emailed to say I might be passing through New Zealand.'

Colouring, Charlotte said, 'I'm sorry, it just . . . Well, as you said, you know the reason now and I'm not really sure how to begin explaining myself.'

'We'll come on to it,' he assured her, 'but the important thing is that you don't end up paying too high a price for it.'

Feeling a jarring inside, Charlotte asked, 'Do you think I'm likely to?'

'Well, it's possible, but we're going to do everything we can to make sure you don't.'

'And you can do that, even though everyone knows I took her?'

'Where the law's concerned we can do almost anything, it's just a question of finding the right way to go about it – and making a point of not telling everyone we're guilty when that's almost certainly going to contradict our plea.'

Both embarrassed and moved by his use of 'we' and 'our', she watched him walk to the bay window, presumably to check if a photographer had turned up yet. 'Thanks for what you did today,' she said softly. 'I know it's not usual for someone of your standing to take on something as trivial as a bail hearing.'

'Hardly trivial when they had you shut up in Walworth,' he protested. He scowled in a way that made her feel faintly light-headed. 'I had a feeling you weren't going to contact me yourself,' he continued, 'so I thought I ought to seize the initiative before things went too far. Not that I have any doubts about Kim's abilities, you understand, Saturday's result had more to do with old Edmore's wayward temperament than it did with the case she was making. In fact, it was no different to the one I put forward today, I was just lucky enough to have a better judge.'

'Who happens to be a friend?'

'I wouldn't go quite that far.'

Still thrown by the fact that he'd done what he had, that she was actually standing here with him, she had to make an extra effort to sound collected as she asked, 'So why did you . . . ? I mean, I thought you were taking a sabbatical.'

'So did I.' He gestured for her to sit on one of the sofas, while he took the other. 'In fact, I hung up the Gone Fishing sign at the end of last week intending to start my new adventure sometime this month, but it seems it'll have to wait a little longer now.'

'But you can't postpone, not for me,' she protested.

Appearing amused, he replied, 'The decision's already been made, so let's not argue about it. Instead, let's accept the good fortune that I'm still in the country and free to take the case on.'

Unable to make sense of his decision, though intensely relieved to be in his hands, she said, 'There's no knowing how long this might go on . . .'

'I'm not in a rush, and anyway, we're doing everything we can to make sure it doesn't drag on – and we're starting out well. The Section Fifty-one's already dealt with, and the judge surprised even me when he ruled for papers to be served in three weeks.'

'Will I have to be in court for that?'

'No, your next appearance will be at the Plea and Case Management, which is scheduled for seven weeks from now.'

'Seven weeks,' she groaned, thinking of how long that was in Chloe's little world.

'Be glad it's not four times that,' he responded. 'We did really well getting such a tight timetable out of the judge today, though he has something of a reputation for wanting to move things along. In the meantime you can work on your statement so that we know everything that happened from the day you first met Ottilie Wade – or Chloe, as I believe we're now calling her – right up to when you boarded the flight for New Zealand. I'll then want to hear details of how and where you were living in New Zealand, the kind of progress Chloe made in her development, if any, and why it would be in her best interests to be allowed to return there.'

Charlotte took a breath that broke on a sob. 'Do you think she will be?' she gasped, pressing a hand to her mouth. 'Are you saying there's a chance I'll be able to get her back?'

Anthony held her gaze. 'What I'm saying is, it's our aim. Whether or not we'll make it happen is dependent on more variables than you'd ever want to hear about, but hurdles are there to be overcome and I haven't found too many yet that have bested me. My apologies if that sounds arrogant.'

Clasping her hands over her face, Charlotte began shaking her head. 'I'm sorry,' she choked. 'I just don't know what to say. When I woke up this morning I was in a prison cell and now here I am, at your sister's house, with you and you're telling me . . . I just don't understand why you'd want to be mixed up with someone like me after what I did . . .'

Coming to pull her to her feet, he said in a voice rich with irony, 'If you'd stop to think of the kinds of people I'm used to mixing with, in a professional sense, I don't think you'd be quite so hard on yourself. In fact, you were probably mixing with them yourself only this morning, so you'll have a good idea of what I mean.'

Giving a splutter of laughter, she turned her head to one side, embarrassed to meet his eyes. 'I was on the rule,' she told him. 'There are people in there who I've come across before, in a professional sense, and I'm afraid they're not too keen on me.'

'Ah, so we have a similar sort of following?'

With another laugh, she tried to meet his gaze as she said, 'I don't get why you're doing this for me. I mean, you hardly even know me.'

The intensity of his eyes seemed to deepen as he continued to look at her. 'Maggie trusts and cares for you and I trust her judgement.'

Swallowing dryly, Charlotte glanced away.

'If you remember,' he said, 'I tried to get to know you better before you left. Now I understand why it didn't work out. You had the child there in the house with you the entire time the police were looking for her?'

She nodded awkwardly. 'I'm afraid so. She never made a sound, because she won't if you tell her not to. You see, she doesn't have the same sort of disobedient streak you find in most children her age, it was bullied and beaten out of her, but we've been trying to get her spirit back.'

'With some success?'

'With a lot of success, which is why it's so important she's with the right people. She trusts me, and my mother, or she did before all this happened . . . I can't imagine what's going through her mind now. She must be so confused, so scared. I want to ask Tommy about her, but I don't suppose I should put him in that position.'

'One of your bail conditions is that you don't attempt to make any contact with her. Do you think you can stick to it?'

Feeling the need for Chloe clashing with the dread of Walworth, she replied, 'I guess I don't have a choice, but is it so wrong to want to know if she's all right?'

'Of course not, it's just that the law isn't seeing it quite that way at the moment.'

Nodding her understanding, she said, 'I'm still not entirely sure about my conditions, apart from the fact that I'm due to be fitted with a tag sometime this evening.'

'You also have to report to the police station every day at one p.m.,' he told her, 'and you have a curfew from nine at night till eight in the morning. They've also got all your money, but I think you're well aware of that.'

She nodded soberly. 'If I thought it would bring Chloe back I'd let them keep it,' she said. 'Except I'm going to need it to pay my legal fees.'

With a disarming smile, he said, 'We'll see about that. Now, I'm afraid it's time I was leaving. I have to be in London this evening, and . . .' He broke off as the door opened and Maggie put her head in.

'Sorry to interrupt,' she said, 'but Kim has to make a move and she was wondering if she could run something past you first.'

'We're coming,' Anthony assured her, and letting Charlotte go ahead he followed her into the kitchen where Kim had her laptop open on the table, with Gabby and Tommy seated either side of her.

'We've been working on a statement for Charlotte's Facebook page,' she informed both Anthony and Charlotte. 'I felt we needed to keep it brief and to the point . . .'

'. . . but we thought it was important,' Gabby chimed in, 'to let everyone know that Gavril Albescu was *not* your father.'

Charlotte's eyes closed in dismay. What on earth was Anthony making of all that?

'If he wasn't her father,' he said, 'then yes, I think it should be made clear right away.'

Cheered by the approval, Gabby went on, 'We were just trying to make up our minds whether to say who it actually was, and Tommy quite rightly felt that you should decide.'

Feeling Anthony's eyes on her, Charlotte looked at him as she said, 'It was Nigel Carrington, one of the victims, the man everyone thought was my aunt's boyfriend. In fact he was my mother's lover, and it was because Albescu found out I wasn't his that he . . . did what he did.'

Anthony nodded gravely. 'I see,' he responded. 'So do you have other family here, in the UK, related to Nigel Carrington?'

She shook her head. 'Not that my mother and I could find. His parents passed on quite a while ago and he was an only child.'

Allowing his eyes to rest on hers for a moment, he then said to Kim, 'This is definitely something we should correct, if only to get it out of the way. Do you know if the police are trying to find out who posted the story?'

'They said they would when I contacted them,' she replied, 'but I've no idea if they're making any headway.'

'Actually, I'm pretty sure I know where it came from,' Charlotte told them. 'There's a journalist, here in Kesterly, called Heather Hancock . . .'

'Oh God, not her again,' Anthony snorted. 'Isn't she the one who tried to trash your play and gave you such a rough ride at the time Chloe was missing?'

'That's her. I've only ever told one person about my real family, and he's quite a good friend of hers.'

'Let me have her details,' Kim said, 'and I'll pass

326

them on to the police, though since it's been published on a foreign website I'm not sure how much they can do.'

To his sister Anthony said, 'I need to leave now, but I'll see you at the weekend?'

Giving him a hug, she replied, 'You will indeed if you decide to come here.'

Charlotte laughed at the droll expression in his eyes as he thanked her and turned to Tommy.

'I appreciate the chat we had earlier,' he said. 'You have my number if anything else comes up.'

Charlotte's mouth turned dry as Tommy shook Anthony's hand. They must have been talking about Chloe, so why not tell her what it was? They would if it was good news, surely, so what was happening?

After saying goodbye to Kim and Gabby, Anthony had a few quick words with his brother-in-law and then turned to Charlotte. 'Walk with me to the door?'

Following him into the hall, she kept her voice down as she said, 'What was that about with Tommy?'

'He's been a bit concerned about some of the questions the police are asking your old colleagues,' he replied. 'I don't suppose it'll come as any surprise that you won't be on the guest list for the next policemen's ball.'

'None at all. What sort of questions are they asking?'

'Nothing I wouldn't have expected at this time. Now, I'm afraid I have to go. Maggie and Ron will take good care of you. I'm just sorry I can't stay longer.'

Sorry too, Charlotte said, 'The Gavril Albescu stuff . . . I guess you must be wondering how many more skeletons are packed away in my closet.'

Amused, he smiled, 'We all have them, but I must admit they're not all as . . . colourful as yours.'

With a wry tone, Charlotte said, 'I'd much prefer it if they were drab or didn't exist at all, but thank you for putting it that way. And thank you for everything you've done today . . . For everything you're doing . . .'

He took her hand. 'Thank me when it's over and we've got the right result.'

Her breath caught on the hope, and her smile wasn't quite steady as she nodded agreement.

'Maggie has my mobile number if you need to reach me,' he told her, 'otherwise I'll hope to see you at the weekend.'

After he'd gone Charlotte returned to the kitchen and the fresh pot of tea Maggie had just made. A plate of home-made scones was now at the centre of the table, oozing cream and jam, and looked so mouth-watering that Charlotte felt an immediate sting in her taste buds. Almost a week had gone by since she'd last had decent food, and suddenly she wasn't sure whether she was more ravenous or exhausted.

'Here, sit down,' Tommy said, pulling out the chair next to him. 'You're looking like you're about to pass out on us.'

Doing as she was told, Charlotte helped herself to a scone as Maggie poured her tea. 'Thanks,' she said, wondering now if she could actually manage to eat. 'I ought to call my mother,' she suddenly remembered.

'She already knows you've been bailed,' Maggie told her. 'I rang myself as soon as I heard the news.'

Touched by her thoughtfulness, Charlotte said, 'That's so kind of you. Was she OK?'

'She certainly sounded delighted when I told her you were on your way here. The phone's over there, you can use it whenever you like.'

Glancing at the time, Charlotte said, 'It's the middle of the night for her now, so maybe I should wait for a while.'

'Eat something,' Gabby ordered. 'You're really pale, and after everything you've been through . . .'

'I'm OK,' Charlotte insisted, and biting into a scone she tried not to think of how much Chloe, with her sweet tooth, would love one. 'Can I read the Facebook statement?' she asked, as Kim started to pack away her laptop.

'Of course.' Kim immediately opened the laptop again and turned it for Charlotte to see. 'It's just a few lines setting the record straight.'

'I'm as convinced as you are that Heather Hancock's behind this,' Gabby told her sister. 'She's always had it in for you, ever since she got her facts wrong in that child custody story you were involved in, and you made the paper print an apology.'

Kim was listening attentively.

'Plus,' Gabby ran on, addressing Kim, 'she's always had the hots for Jason, Charlotte's ex, which is a bit rich when he's actually married to her own best friend. The trouble was, when his wife kicked him out to move in her new boyfriend, he ended up with Charlotte instead of Heather, and if you ask me Heather's never forgiven Charlotte for it.'

'It's all so petty,' Charlotte sighed, relieved that Anthony wasn't there to hear any of this.

'Well, she's soon going to find out that she's wrong

about Gavril Albescu too,' Kim reminded them, 'and now you, Charlotte, have to decide whether or not you want me to push the police to investigate her.'

'Will they be able to prove it was her?'

'Probably. It'll depend if she used her own computer.'

'But even if she did there's still a problem with it being on a foreign website.'

'Indeed.'

'Then let the police follow it up in their own way. The last thing I need is to start worrying myself about her when she actually couldn't be less important.'

'Well said,' Maggie piped up cheerfully.

'But she is running a negative campaign through this website,' Kim pointed out, 'so we definitely need to keep an eye on her. Anyway, I need to go or I won't make the five o'clock back to Bristol. Does it read OK to you?' she asked Charlotte.

Charlotte quickly scanned it. *In the interests of accuracy, the family of Charlotte Nicholls would like to make it clear that Ms Nicholls is not the daughter of Gavril Albescu. Nor is she related to him in any way.*

'We decided not to add anything about who your real father is,' Gabby told her, 'in case it kicks off a whole other line of interest in the story that your mother, in particular, really won't need.'

'Thanks for thinking of her,' Charlotte replied. 'I know she'll appreciate it and so do I.' Getting up to say goodbye to Kim, she asked, 'When will I see you next?'

'I'm not sure at the moment,' Kim replied. 'I'm pretty crazy for the rest of this week. Did Anthony mention anything to you about working on a statement?'

'He did, and I will.'

'OK. If you need any help, just shout. For the time being though it's probably best if you rough it out first, then we can meet up and work on it together.'

'Brace yourselves, everyone,' Ron declared, coming into the kitchen, 'I think we've been found.'

'Oh God,' Kim groaned. 'How many are there? I hope my taxi can get through or I'll miss the train.'

'It's already outside,' Ron told her, 'and so far there's only one suspicious-looking chap admiring my hedges, so shouldn't be a problem. I'll come out with you.'

'He's likely to ask if Charlotte's in here,' Kim said as they went, 'so it might be a good idea to say no. He probably won't believe you, because he's obviously found out she's been bailed to this address, but no one in here's going to speak to him so he'll soon realise he's wasting his time and go away.'

After Kim had gone, Tommy and Gabby began preparing to leave too. 'Tommy's giving me a lift back to the court for my car,' Gabby explained, coming to give Charlotte a hug. 'I wish I could stay longer, but I have to pick the kids up from Martin's mum at six. Are you going to be all right?'

Charlotte glanced at Maggie and smiled. 'I think so,' she replied.

'You know I'm at the end of the phone if you need me,' Gabby reminded her, 'and I'll be with you at the weekend to help you move into the flat.'

The flat. A new home, a place she hadn't even seen yet, didn't even want to live in, except she had no choice.

'I'll be back later with the things Gabby's brought for you,' Tommy told her. 'Maggie's very kindly invited me to join you for dinner.'

Throwing a grateful look Maggie's way, Charlotte hugged Gabby hard, but her eyes were on Tommy.

He knew what she was asking, even though she couldn't put it into words, and when he gave her a nod to convey that everything was OK, she felt an unsteadying rush of tears swamping her eyes.

Chapter Eighteen

'I didn't know what else to do,' Tommy was saying to Anthony on the phone the next day. 'I realise I shouldn't have done anything at all, but the way Charlotte was looking at me, she's desperate to know something . . .'

'It's OK, you did the right thing,' Anthony assured him. 'We have no reason to believe Chloe's not settling into her new home, so let's not assume the worst. Do you know where the new home is, by the way?'

'All I know is what I told you when we spoke before court yesterday, that Tracy had to collect her from the first place after only two days – nothing to do with Chloe, apparently, it was the couple themselves having problems.'

'OK. Do you know how Wendy Fraser's meeting went with the people from adoption services?'

Glancing through his office window to where a handful of the team were going about their day, Tommy said, 'All I can tell you is that it happened, but what was said, or decided, I've got no idea. I'm presuming no one's spoken to Tracy about it yet either, or she'd probably have come to tell me.'

'How fast can it happen?'

'In this case, probably pretty fast because Chloe's

a prime candidate. In fact, setting all personal issues aside, if I was on the case I'd probably be recommending it myself.'

'This soon?'

'She has no family, apart from the father, who's never going to get custody of her again, and being as young as she is . . . There's no shortage of people out there who'd want her.'

'OK, I'm going to be candid with you now: the chances of me getting Charlotte's case thrown out before it comes to trial aren't good. So it could mean Chloe having to remain in care for anything up to six months, by which time, from what you're telling me, she could already be living with her future parents.'

'She could, and once the process has begun there's no way we'd be able to pull her out of it, unless we find the parents aren't suitable, of course.'

'OK. This is all good to know, and obviously on some level Charlotte's going to be aware of it, because she knows the system well enough. She's probably just hoping that nothing will be done until her own fate has been decided, and we need to let her carry on thinking that, at least for now. Meantime, I've arranged to see a colleague whose speciality is family law, to find out if there's anything we can do to shelve the adoption process before it goes any further.'

Relaxing slightly, Tommy said, 'That's what I hoped you were going to say. My only concern now is that Wendy and the powers that be are going to realise that someone from this office has been in touch with you. I don't care for myself, I'm out of here anyway at the end of the fortnight, but I do care for Tracy.'

'I hear what you're saying, and I'll ask my colleague to find out if there's a way of presenting

334

this from the top down. In other words, he'll probably contact the director of social services, or even
someone at ministerial level, to try and get them to
hold up an adoption order pending Charlotte's legal
proceedings.'

After thanking Anthony again, Tommy put the
phone down and went out to the main office to check
the whiteboard for Tracy's movements. Finding a
blank for the afternoon he guessed she was either
around the building somewhere, or out visiting Chloe.
If she were visiting anyone else it would be written
on the board, as would scheduled meetings, holidays
or court appearances.

'Anyone know where Tracy is?' he called out to
the handful of those who were in.

Receiving only shakes of the head or shrugs, he
returned to his office and picked up the phone.
'Trace, where are you?' he asked when she answered
her mobile.

'Visiting a friend,' she replied.

Certain from her tone that it meant Chloe, he said,
'Have you heard any more about the adoption thing?
Do you know how the meeting went?'

'Not a word, but it was only yesterday.'

'Sure. If you do hear something you'll let me
know?'

'Well, actually, I've been thinking about it, and
you know, maybe that is the best way forward.
Anyway, I can't really talk now, I'll see you when I
get back to the office.'

'Sir,' Karen Potter called out as DCI Gould sailed
past her desk.

Barely pausing, Gould said, 'Whatever it is, make
it quick.'

'It's Charlotte Nicholls and her connection to the Temple Fields Massacre. We haven't managed to trace who posted the information yet, and I'm wondering how much time you want us to spend on it.'

Glancing at his watch, he said, 'Has anything else gone up since?'

'Not on the foreign site, but there's a message on her Facebook page saying she's not Albescu's daughter. It's here if you want to take a look.'

Coming to read over her shoulder, he checked his mobile as it rang, and barked into it that he was on his way.

'The CPS guy is not happy about any of it,' Potter told him as he read the Facebook posting again. 'He's saying it could prove highly prejudicial to the case and . . .'

'I know what he's saying,' Gould snapped, 'and if he'd like to find a way of increasing our resources we might be able to track down who's behind it. As it is, it's out of our jurisdiction anyway, and as I don't see anything there to sway a jury against us I'm not feeling too bothered about it. But keep an eye on it,' and answering another call he strode off towards the lifts.

'She's definitely not a chatterbox, are you, honey bun?' Carrie Jones was saying teasingly to Chloe. 'I think she likes it here though, don't you? Well, why wouldn't she when she has her own room with lots of toys to play with, and even a TV? Not that she's allowed to watch any old thing,' she assured Tracy. 'Only a half-hour here and there of children's programmes, and a little bit of wildlife. I find that most kids enjoy watching animals in their natural habitat, and it can be very educational, I'm sure you'll agree.'

Carrie Jones's smile was so full of teeth that Tracy could almost imagine her starring in one of her favoured programmes. In fact, according to the file, she'd hosted a popular series of animal adventures back in the nineties, as most of the photographs and paintings around her cluttered terraced home, here in Minehead, proved.

Minehead! Thanks, Wendy, for the near-seventy-mile round trip to come and visit.

Though Tracy had never seen Carrie Jones's *Animal Escapades* herself, she was aware from the notes she'd been sent that every child who came into Carrie's care was required to watch an episode a night for the time they were there. Apparently, in some cases it meant they came away able to recite whole chunks of a programme, which, depending on the child, could be extremely entertaining, more than one social worker had written.

Tracy couldn't imagine Chloe reciting anything, or even taking in much of a programme. Sitting there at the back of an armchair with her head hanging limply over her bear and her fragile limbs seeming to twitch each time she was addressed, she couldn't have appeared more lonely or forlorn. What was going through her mind, she wondered.

As if she didn't know.

'Is she eating?' she asked Carrie.

Carrie's smile came forth again. 'We had a boiled egg and soldiers this morning, didn't we?' she responded bouncily, putting Tracy in mind of a jolly kangaroo. 'And we ate two whole fingers of bread and half the egg.'

337

Receiving no response from Chloe, Tracy said, 'What about lunchtime?'

'Well, we didn't do so well with that, did we, sweet pea? But we've got some lovely chicken nuggets and chips for tea and a delicious upside-down pudding for afters. Have you ever had upside-down pudding?'

Chloe juddered and pulled Boots closer to her face.

'I think she's going to like it,' Carrie told Tracy brightly. 'All my other children have wolfed it down and come straight back for more. You can help me make it if you like,' she said to Chloe. 'That should be fun, shouldn't it? Have you ever done any baking?'

A tear dropped into Chloe's lap.

'Oh dear,' Tracy murmured, going to her. 'You mustn't be upset, Chloe. Everything's going to be all right. Carrie's going to take very good care of you and you're starting back to nursery next Monday, which'll be lovely, won't it? Lots of other children to play with and friends to make.'

Chloe began shaking her head and as tiny, whispering sobs broke from her heart Tracy pulled her into her arms.

'There, there,' she soothed, rocking her back and forth. 'I know everything's new and a bit scary right now, but there's nothing to be afraid of, I promise.'

'Certainly not me,' Carrie piped up cheerily. 'I'm the least scary person in the world.'

Unable to stop an unkind thought about the teeth, Tracy told Chloe, 'Everyone loves Carrie. She was very popular when she was on TV, and all the children who come here say what a lovely time they've had.'

Beaming at the compliment, Carrie said, 'I know it can take a bit of time to settle into a new place, but I shall do everything I can to make you happy. We can do lots of things together like going to the beach, or the park, or the zoo . . .'

Chloe was shaking her head faster than ever. 'Want Mummy,' she sobbed. 'Go to Mummy now.'

Tracy smoothed Chloe's wispy curls and kissed her head, as she said, 'Do you remember what tomorrow is? It's your birthday, isn't it, and you're going to be four. That's so grown up.'

'You've got a birthday tomorrow,' Carrie gasped in excitement. 'Well, we'll have to do something about that. Shall we make a special cake and put four candles on it?'

Chloe was fighting to catch her breath as her hysteria grew. 'Mummy!' she choked. 'Want to go to Mummy!'

'All right, all right,' Tracy murmured, holding her close. 'You need to calm down now . . . Chloe, you need to calm down, there's a good girl.'

Chloe was kicking her and writhing so wildly that Tracy had to put her down. Immediately snatching Boots from the floor, Chloe ran to the front door. She couldn't reach the handle, so she spun round to watch Tracy coming after her, her eyes so distraught and beseeching that Tracy could hardly bear to look at her.

'Go now,' Chloe said, grabbing Tracy's hand.

'Oh Chloe, you know you have to stay here,' Tracy murmured, stooping down to her height.

Chloe started shaking her head again, and afraid she might make herself sick, Tracy caught it between her hands.

'Listen to me,' she said softly, 'I know it's hard

right now, but I promise everything's going to be fine. You'll have a lovely birthday. I'll come too and bring you a surprise present, will that be nice?'

Chloe was still trying to shake her head.

'I wonder what the surprise will be,' Carrie said from behind them.

Chloe mumbled something Tracy couldn't hear.

'What was that?' she asked.

'Make a wish,' Chloe gasped.

Tracy might have smiled if she hadn't already had an idea what the wish would be. 'Of course you can make a wish,' she replied. 'But you know, don't you, that wishes don't always come true straight away?'

Chloe looked at her with such desperate eyes that Tracy would have done anything to be able to give this dear little girl what she wanted, but she couldn't, so she might as well put it out of her mind now.

Heather Hancock's insides gave a twist of unease as the restaurant door opened and Charlotte Nicholls came in, accompanied by a middle-aged couple and a bloke who looked a bit like an ageing hippy.

'Blimey, I wasn't expecting to see her out in public,' she commented to her lunch companion. 'At least not this soon, or somewhere like this.'

'What's that supposed to mean?' Jason Carmichael demanded, though he too was looking decidedly awkward as he watched Charlotte and her party being shown to a centre island table.

'Well, it's pretty high profile, for Kesterly anyway, and she never struck me as the type to do posh.'

Jason's handsome face turned sour. 'You so don't know her,' he muttered derisively.

Heather looked at him in surprise. 'I know her a

bit better now, thanks to you,' she reminded him, her eyes glinting with a malicious sort of humour.

They were in a window booth of the Crustacean Brasserie, a sprawling clifftop eatery with live lobsters and crabs in the fish tank, and impressive views down over the metal-grey sweep of the bay. As it had recently earned itself a Michelin star it wasn't easy to get a table these days, especially in the evenings. However, in the middle of the day, as it was now, there was usually less demand, which was how Heather had managed to acquire one of the premium tables. Of course, being who she was had helped; the management were understandably keen for good write-ups in the local press, and with the way things were Heather could see no reason not to oblige.

'You'll never guess who's here,' she hissed to Gina, her supposed best friend and Jason's wife, as Gina came back from the loo. 'You are going to be sooo thrilled.'

Gina, who took her style tips from *The Only Way Is Essex*, lit up with intrigue. 'Is it someone famous?' she asked, casting an eager eye around the room.

Heather laughed. 'You could say that,' she replied. 'It's only our old mate the child-snatcher.'

As Gina's expression dulled Jason said, 'For God's sake, Heather, give her a break, will you? This is serious what's going on, and the way you're treating it, like you've got some exciting new toy to play with . . .'

'Hang on, hang on,' Heather interrupted imperiously. 'First, don't make out like I'm not clued into how serious this is, because believe me, I know. And second, since when did you become her defender?'

'Good bloody question,' Gina muttered, straining

to locate her husband's ex-girlfriend amongst the crowded tables. 'Where is she?' she demanded.

'Did you ever learn to do discretion?' Heather asked tartly.

Gina's eyes flashed. 'That's rich coming from you, who posted all the stuff about her having a mass killer's blood in her veins – and got it wrong.'

Heather's nostrils flared. 'I only repeated what I was told,' she retorted, 'because I believed my source was reliable.' The look she gave Jason was as withering as the put-down itself. How she'd ever fancied him, when nothing about him seemed remotely appealing now, she'd never know. OK, he was good-looking and kind and great with his kids, but when it came right down to it he wasn't her type at all.

'I told you in confidence,' he said sharply, 'and you swore to me it wouldn't go any further, so as far as I'm concerned it serves you damned well right that Albescu turns out not to be her real father. In fact, I reckon you ought to print an apology.'

'Yeah, like I'm really going to do that,' she sneered. Why was she here having lunch with them today? Oh, that was right, they'd invited her as a thank you for driving them to the airport later. A second honeymoon in Tenerife. Lovely.

'What I'd like to know is who her real father is,' she muttered, almost to herself.

'Why don't you just leave it?' Jason advised.

Having caught sight of Charlotte now, Gina said, 'Blimey, she's not looking her best, is she. Who's that with her? Do you know?'

'Never seen them before,' Heather replied. 'Actually, what's really interesting me is whether she's got something going with that lawyer, you know, the one who showed up in court the other day. It only turns out he's the same one as got all hot under the collar about the review I gave her play back in the autumn, do you remember?'

'That was a spiteful review and completely unjustified,' Jason told her bluntly.

Gina and Heather both drew back to look at him.

'Will you listen to him,' Heather jeered.

'Well, it was,' he insisted.

'You know what,' Heather said to Gina, 'I don't reckon he's over her.'

'Oh, for God's sake,' Jason snapped. 'It's got nothing to do with that.'

'Well, you do seem a bit keen to take her side,' Gina pointed out. 'She stole a kid, for God's sake. I suppose the next thing we know, you're going to be telling us she ought to get away with it.'

Not wanting to enter into an argument that was going to end him up nowhere he'd want to be, he merely grunted and picked up his wine. If the truth were told he'd never have left Alex – or Charlotte as she now was – were it not for his kids, and seeing her walk in a few minutes ago had brought it all rushing back. He'd been happy with her; he missed her; he still wanted to be with her.

'Oh my God, she's only coming over here,' Gina suddenly hissed.

Heather's heart skipped a beat, but she quickly mounted the moral high ground. There was only one person here who had a charge of child abduction hanging over her, and Alex Lake had had the last word between them once too often for her liking. Heather's day had surely arrived.

As Charlotte came to a stop in front of the table, looking shaky and yet oddly steely, Heather and Gina regarded her with disdain while Jason kept his eyes averted. 'Hello Jason,' she said, her greeting cutting straight past the other two.

Flicking her a glance, he grunted, 'Hi, how are you?'

The challenge in her eyes didn't falter. 'I'm wondering why you felt it necessary to break my confidence over what happened to my family when I was a child,' she said, her voice as steady as the rocks outside. Only her hands, clenched tightly at her sides, betrayed how tense she was.

'The nerve of her,' Gina sneered to Heather.

Charlotte's eyes were still boring into Jason.

'And I'm wondering,' Heather piped up, 'what makes you feel you've got the right to steal a child.'

Managing to ignore her, Charlotte said to Jason, 'It was a pity you didn't know the whole story, or you could have saved your friend here from making a fool of herself with yet more lies. I can only wonder how many more she's going to publish before the police find out who's behind the contempt of court. I believe the sentence for that is anything up to two years,' and turning on her heel she walked back to her table, leaving them as dumbstruck by her thinly veiled threat as she'd intended.

Ron Fenn refilled her glass with wine as she sat down again.

'Are you OK?' Tommy asked gently.

In spite of how shaken she was, she said, 'Yes, I'm fine. I'm sorry, I just had to say something.'

'Don't be sorry,' Maggie told her. 'You were extremely brave to go over there. I'm not sure I could have done it.'

With an ironic smile, Tommy said, 'This one's always had a bit of a gift for speaking her mind.'

'And getting myself into trouble over it,' Charlotte added. 'But I just couldn't let them sit there and think I'm afraid of them, or that I don't know who posted my family history on that website.'

'Well, I hope you gave it to Heather Hancock good and proper,' Ron declared. 'Personally, I'm amazed the local paper still employs her, with all the rubbish she comes out with.'

'I don't expect there are very rich pickings around these parts,' Tommy commented, 'so they probably can't get anyone else. Anyway, pet, are you still feeling all right about being here?'

Charlotte forced a smile as she nodded. She wasn't, though not because of Heather, or Jason, but because the only place in the world she really wanted to be was Te Puna, celebrating Chloe's fourth birthday the way they'd intended.

It couldn't happen, so somehow she had to put it aside or she was going to ruin the lunch, and she really didn't want to do that when everyone was being so kind.

As they gave the waiter their orders Charlotte watched Ron and Maggie fondly, wishing she could hug them, or at least tell them how grateful she was for these past two days. They'd put no pressure on her at all, asked no questions and made no demands. They'd simply got on with their lives, while allowing her to call her mother whenever she liked, to sleep at odd times of the day, eat or not eat; they'd even driven her to the police station in the middle of the day to meet the terms of her bail.

How on earth did she deserve such support, when she couldn't even claim to have known them well before she'd left?

'I sometimes think,' her mother had said on the phone last night, 'that angels are actually people who come into our lives when we need them, then go again when the crisis has passed.'

Though Charlotte had liked the thought, she hoped Maggie and Ron would always be a part of her life. Tommy too, with his brash affection and unswerving loyalty. She was going to miss him terribly when he went to join his wife, Jackie, up north. They'd stay in touch, of course, and Tommy would undoubtedly be back for the trial, but it wasn't going to be the same as having him close by. Nor would she be able to seek the unspoken reassurances he was able to give her about Chloe.

Where was her darling, sweet little girl now? What was she doing today? Did the people she was with know it was her birthday? Were they arranging something special for her? As the questions crowded in on her, her heart ached with the thoughts of what should have been happening – the new bike Charlotte had promised; the cake bake at Aroha; the party at Nanna's; the practice jump-off; the wishes she wanted to make; the puppy she didn't know anything about.

Bob had told her last night that they'd decided to let the puppy go to another home, since they couldn't be sure when Chloe would be back. 'I don't want you to think we're giving up hope,' he'd rushed on, 'because we're never going to do that. It's just that if we bring it home now it'll get used to being with us, and it's important for it to bond with her.'

Though Charlotte could see the reasoning, it had upset her terribly at the time, and if she didn't pull herself together quickly it was going to upset her again now.

'Lovely, lovely,' Ron declared, as Tommy topped up their glasses. 'I think we ought to drink a toast to Charlotte's new flat, and a trouble-free move tomorrow.'

'We'll all be there to help her,' Maggie reminded him, 'unless Anthony's whisking you off on one of his fishing trips. Is he?'

'Haven't heard from him,' Ron replied, and clinking his glass against Charlotte's he said, 'To you and to all your wishes coming true.'

Having to swallow hard as she thought of Chloe again, Charlotte forced a smile as she thanked him and took a sip of her drink.

'Tell me, what news on your mother coming over?' Tommy asked, putting his glass down.

Sighing, Charlotte said, 'Apparently their lawyer's still trying to get information out of the police here as to whether or not she'll risk arrest if she does come. So until they get an answer she has to stay where she is.'

'I imagine she's finding it very frustrating,' Maggie commented, 'and I ask you, whose interests are going to be served if they do arrest her?'

As Charlotte started to reply a young woman, about her own age, came up to the table and said to her, 'Excuse me, I don't expect you remember me, but we went to the same school. I was in the year below you?'

Charlotte smiled politely. She didn't remember her, but she wasn't going to say so. 'Were you in Abbots House?' she asked, hazarding a guess.

'No, Manfield,' the woman replied. 'Anyway, I just wanted to say that some of us have been going on to your Facebook page to add our support for what you did. We think saving the little girl from that monster was lovely, and that you shouldn't be in the position you are now. That's all – I'm sorry for interrupting your meal.'

As she walked away Charlotte almost went after her, but realised if she did she'd end up embarrassing them both.

'How sweet of her,' Maggie commented, teary-eyed.

'Wasn't it?' Ron agreed.

'I ought to go on to Facebook to find out what everyone's saying,' Charlotte mused. 'It's OK,' she added quickly as Tommy scowled, 'I realise it won't all be like that, but I should probably keep up with what's being said.'

'I heard this morning,' he told her, 'that Dean Valley Council's launching an internal inquiry into whether any of us helped you get Chloe out of the country.'

'Oh God,' Charlotte groaned. 'Still, at least we know no one did, so there can't be any comeback on anyone.'

'Exactly.'

'I guess they have to be seen to be doing it,' Ron chipped in, 'but it all sounds a bit of a waste of money to me.'

'Particularly when it can be better spent on the department itself,' Tommy added meaningfully.

'How's everyone responding to it there?' Charlotte asked.

He shrugged. 'Those who've been at the job longer are tending to be a bit more supportive, given that they've had more experience of what can happen to children in care. It's mainly the younger ones who are being judgemental, especially those who never met you, but as we know, there are none more opinionated and less informed than the young.'

With a wry smile, Maggie said, 'I think the important thing is to look at your conscience and if you don't feel you've done anything wrong, and I personally don't believe you have, then there's nothing for you to feel guilty about.'

Charlotte's eyes went to Tommy. 'I feel bad about how much trouble this is causing for you,' she told him, 'and for you,' she added to Maggie and Ron. 'And for my parents, and the authorities, and the police . . . It all feels so huge, I guess because it is, but all it's really about is one dear little girl who's four today.'

Clasping her hands together in excitement, Carrie Jones said, 'OK, Chloe, are you ready?'

Chloe's eyes were fixed on the candles as she nodded. She was standing on a chair in front of the cake, Boots tucked securely under one arm while the other held her steady as she prepared to blow.

'Remember,' Carrie said, 'you have to blow them all out in one go for your wish to come true.'

Tracy winced. Why had Carrie said that? Hadn't she worked out for herself what the child was going to wish for?

'OK, close your eyes,' Carrie instructed.

Chloe was trembling hard as she screwed her eyes tightly shut.

'And off you go,' Carrie urged.

Tracy could hardly bear it as Chloe turned pink with the effort of wishing with all her heart. When she was done, she opened her eyes and looked expectantly at Carrie.

'Time to blow,' Carrie whispered.

Tracy smiled mistily as Chloe blew so hard she'd have doused a dozen candles if they'd been there.

'Hooray!' Carrie cheered, clapping her hands. 'You did them all. What a clever girl.'

Still trembling, Chloe got down from the table and took hold of Tracy's hand. 'Go to Mummy now,' she said, looking up at her, and Tracy could have wept.

Chapter Nineteen

'Wow! This place is totally amazing!' Gabby exclaimed as Charlotte showed her through from the hall into a large white-painted sitting room. The high ceiling and arched French windows somewhat overpowered the solitary sofa and small dining table, but the granite fireplace and buffed pine floor were homely and welcoming. 'And look at the views,' she cried, crossing straight to one of the windows to take in the panoramic vista of the bay. It was a dull day with only sporadic outbreaks of sun, but a few hardy souls were riding the waves and a good number of dedicated joggers were chugging along the beach and promenade.

'Is this where you're going to be living, Auntie Lotte?' five-year-old Jackson demanded as he and his sister burst into the room.

Charlotte glanced at Gabby, who grimaced in apology.

'Is that OK?' she asked. 'We've been practising, and it was the name they preferred.'

'It's fine,' Charlotte laughed, cupping Jackson's adorable freckly face between her hands. 'It's lovely to see you,' she told him. 'I've missed you.'

'We missed you too,' Phoebe cried, wrapping her arms around Charlotte's waist. 'Why have you

351

changed your name? Can I change mine?' she asked her mother.

'Ask Daddy,' Gabby replied, as Martin came into the room.

'The answer's no,' he informed Phoebe before she could draw breath, and opening his arms he drew Charlotte into a brotherly embrace. 'I hardly know what to say to you,' he confessed, 'so I'm going to start with it's bloody good to see you.'

'And you,' she smiled, surprised by how much she'd missed him too. Though his expression was habitually stern, he never could hide the merriment that shone from his velvety blue eyes, and although he and Charlotte didn't always hit it off, their mutual love of Gabby and the twins had created its own fondness between them. 'And I expect I ought to be apologising,' she added, 'which I do, unreservedly, if I've caused you any embarrassment or worry.'

'I can handle that better than I can the look of you,' he said bluntly. 'I'm guessing you're not sleeping too well, or eating much either . . .'

'You are so right,' Maggie informed him, coming through from the main bedroom where she'd been making up the bed. 'Hi, I'm Maggie Fenn,' she smiled, holding out a hand to shake. 'And my husband's around here somewhere . . .'

'Actually, he and Tommy have gone to B&Q,' Charlotte told her. 'Would anyone like a drink of something? We have tea or coffee, pink lemonade, diet Coke or white wine.'

'We've got all those things,' Phoebe piped up. 'We stopped in the supermarket on the way here, didn't we, Mum? We've got loads of shopping for you.'

Turning to Gabby, Charlotte said, 'You didn't have to do that . . .'

Waving it away, Gabby said, 'We'll take home anything you don't need.' She looked around. 'Did you bring it in?' she asked Martin.

'Not yet, but if you two care to come and help I'll do my duty.'

As the twins went charging after him Charlotte couldn't stop herself imagining Chloe charging out there with them, eager to keep up with the older ones, thrilled at having something important to do.

Feeling Gabby's eyes on her, she forced a quick smile as she said, 'Why don't I show you the rest of the place?'

'And I'll make some tea,' Maggie announced. 'Remind me, milk and sugar, Gabby?'

'Just milk, thanks,' Gabby called over her shoulder as Charlotte directed her back to the hall and into an adjacent room. 'Gosh, this is so gorgeous,' she gushed, taking in another high ceiling, decorative cornices and a tall sash window. Again there wasn't much furniture, only a king-size bed with no headboard, two side tables and a frameless cheval mirror in one corner.

'It just needs a bit more storage,' Charlotte declared, opening up a cupboard to show a short hanging rail with a handful of hangers and a three-drawer chest. 'Except given the few clothes I have, mainly thanks to you, I don't need much.'

'You're sure to accumulate more, and if you do you can always pick something up from Ikea. What's through the other door?'

'It's a small shower room,' Charlotte replied, gesturing for her to go and take a look. She was trying to feel more upbeat about the place, particularly as she knew how lucky she was to have it, but lovely as it was, it just didn't feel right without Chloe.

'Are you OK?' Gabby asked, looking concerned.

Charlotte forced a smile. 'I'm fine,' she assured her.

Gabby didn't seem convinced. 'Have you got the tag on yet?' she said.

Charlotte lifted the hem of a trouser leg to show the black band with its transponder clamped to her ankle. 'Attractive, isn't it?' she quipped without humour.

'Well, at least you can hide it there better than if it was on your wrist. Do you have any idea how long you have to wear it?'

'Until the trial's over, I suppose.'

'And you don't know yet when that's likely to be?'

Feeling a tightening of her nerves, Charlotte said, 'All I know is that I have to enter a plea seven weeks from now. I think that's when they set a date for the actual trial. Please God it doesn't drag on for too long, or I'll go out of my mind.'

'What are the lawyers saying? Are they giving you any idea of a time frame?'

'Not exactly, and I'm ashamed to admit I haven't found the courage to ask. But I will, on Monday when I next speak to Kim.' *Or before if Anthony comes down from London,* she was thinking, but didn't say. Neither Ron nor Maggie had mentioned him that morning, which probably meant he wasn't planning on coming to Kesterly this weekend after all. She felt foolish for minding, and angry with the hope that kept springing to life every time Maggie's mobile rang. He had a whole other life in London, a life she knew nothing about, apart from the little Maggie had told her. Actually that little was enormous, since his fiancée had been killed in an accident a couple of years ago, but Charlotte had no idea what his situation was now.

'And along here,' she said to Gabby, heading back down the hall towards the front door, 'is the second bedroom which is a little bit smaller, and doesn't have a closet or a bed, but it has a lovely high ceiling again, and the bathroom is opposite rather than en suite.'

'It's got a really nice atmosphere,' Gabby commented, on her way to the window to check the view. Some gardens and garages and the backs of the houses opposite. 'I could live here,' she declared, turning to Charlotte. 'I think you're going to like it. Don't you?' she added uncertainly.

'It would be very churlish of me not to,' Charlotte replied, 'particularly considering how much it's costing, but I'm definitely going to pay Mum and Bob back – and the only reason I can do that is because of you and what you did . . .'

'Oh stop,' Gabby interrupted, coming to give her a hug. 'We're sisters, aren't we? It was only right you got half of everything.'

Knowing it wasn't what her adoptive mother had intended, Charlotte returned the embrace. They were so different in their ways, she and Gabby, but maybe that was what made her love her sister so much.

'I know the court's holding on to all your money now,' Gabby said, 'so if you'd like a loan to tide you over . . .'

'Oh Gabby, you've done enough.'

'No, I mean it . . .'

'It's OK, honestly. Mum's already sent some; it'll keep me going for a while.'

'Well if you need any more, you just have to say.'

Charlotte hugged her again. 'Thank you,' she whispered.

Drawing back to look closely into her eyes, Gabby said, 'Have you had any news about Chloe yet?'

Loving her for asking, while crippled by the reminder, Charlotte shook her head helplessly. 'She was four yesterday,' she replied, trying to keep her voice steady.

Gabby immediately looked stricken. 'Oh my God, why didn't you say? It must have been so hard for you, especially with not knowing where she is, or even *who* she's with. This is so mean. Isn't there anything anyone can do?'

Pressing a hand to her head, Charlotte said, 'No, not right now.'

'But what about Tommy?'

'He can't, you know that.'

'Or Anthony? As a lawyer he might be able to . . .'

'The conditions of my bail,' Charlotte interrupted, 'don't allow me to go anywhere near her, even if we could find out where she is.'

'But that doesn't exclude knowing *how* she is.'

'I guess it shouldn't, but the police aren't seeing it like that. Tommy's doing his best with it, anyway.' She took a breath. 'I'm sorry, but we need to change the subject, or I'm going to start getting upset.'

Groaning with sympathy, Gabby linked her arm closely and walked her back down the hall. 'What about the kitchen?' she said, sounding excited. 'The most important room of the house!'

Charlotte had to laugh. 'It's not going to wow you,' she warned, 'but it's definitely enough for me. There you go.' Standing back so Gabby could see in, she announced, 'The ultimate galley kitchen, sink unit and cooker one side, washing machine and fridge the other, and Maggie Fenn making the tea, except she's not a permanent fixture.'

'Look out, we're here!' Phoebe shouted behind them. 'These bags are really heavy, Auntie Lotte.' She turned quickly to her mother. 'Did I get that right?' she whispered.

Laughing, Charlotte whisked away the bags and scooped her niece into an enveloping embrace. 'Yes you did,' she told her, 'and anyway, you can call me anything you like, because no matter what it is I'll still love you.'

'What, even if it's Smelly?' Jackson demanded, bringing up the rear.

Charlotte rolled her eyes. 'He's such a boy, isn't he?' she said to Phoebe.

'He's the one who's smelly,' Phoebe told her.

'I'm not, you are,' Jackson shot back.

'Enough,' their father cried, coming in behind them. 'Come on, Jackson, put those bags down and make some room.'

Grabbing the tea tray from Maggie, Gabby spirited it off to the sitting room and set it down on the table. 'Sun's coming out,' she declared, taking in a little more of the view.

Coming to stand with her, Charlotte put a plate of Maggie's home-made biscuits next to the tray and leaned in against her. 'Thanks for being here today,' she said softly.

Turning to her, Gabby smiled. 'Of course we're here. Where else would we be on such an important day?'

Not sure she'd seen the move as quite so salient, Charlotte squeezed her hand. 'It's a shame Mum can't be here too,' she said.

'Yes, I know, but I can almost feel her watching

over us.' Then, realising her mistake, 'Oh, sorry, I thought you meant . . . You're talking about Anna.'

'I was,' Charlotte admitted, 'but I'm sure you're right, your mother's looking over us from wherever she is.'

'And Dad,' Gabby sighed. 'He'd be really concerned about you now, with all that's going on. I keep asking him in my mind what I should do to help you, and I think he'd just want me to be as supportive as I can.'

Certain that would be true of her adoptive father, Charlotte smiled. 'He was a very special man.'

'Who?' Jackson demanded, coming into the room.

'Grandpa,' Charlotte replied. 'And he's not the only one, because I think you're a bit special too.'

Jackson beamed, then did a prompt about-turn as Phoebe shouted for him to come and get his lemonade.

'I'm so glad you brought them today,' Charlotte said.

Looking relieved, Gabby said, 'They wanted to see you, but I was worried it might be difficult for you.'

'It's fine. I'd much rather see them than not.'

'Maggie said we can have biscuits,' Phoebe announced, skidding across the floorboards in her socks with Jackson in speedy pursuit.

'Maggie said *a* biscuit,' Martin told her, carrying the lemonade in after them. 'And I'm ready to kill for a cuppa.'

'Right here,' Charlotte assured him, passing over the mug Gabby poured. 'Are you having one, Maggie?' she shouted.

'On my way,' Maggie called back.

'OK, well here's to you, Charlotte,' Martin declared when they were all holding a drink and a biscuit. 'Let's hope this can all be sorted out to everyone's satisfaction.'

Almost amused by how matter-of-fact he'd made it sound, Charlotte smiled her thanks as she tapped her cup against his. The fact that she was a tangle of nerves inside wasn't something she had to share, especially not with the children around.

'So what happens next?' Martin asked, going to perch on the arm of the sofa. 'How long do you have this place for?'

'Six months, with a further six-month option,' Charlotte replied, 'but I hope to God it'll all be over long before that.' Or did she, if it being over meant she'd be in prison?

And where would Chloe be by then?

She missed what Martin said next, but her heart flipped as Maggie said, 'We'll be able to ask my brother when he gets here.'

'Is he coming today?' Charlotte asked, aware of Gabby watching her.

Maggie shrugged. 'I thought he said he'd be back at the weekend, but I haven't heard from him yet, so maybe his plans have changed. I guess we'll find out soon enough. Is that my phone ringing, or yours?' she asked Gabby.

'Not mine,' Gabby replied.

'Or mine,' Martin added.

'Then I guess it's mine,' Maggie chuckled. 'You never know, it could be him,' and helping herself to another biscuit she went off to the kitchen to find out.

'We need to get you a mobile,' Gabby said to Charlotte.

'And a computer,' Charlotte added. 'I have to start working on my statement and I'm not sure I could do it by hand.'

'What happened to your old computer?' Martin asked.

Picturing the raiding of the bach, while feeling the pull of the place, Charlotte said, 'Apparently the police took it, so I guess it's been sent over here by now. I can't imagine them letting me have it back any time soon.'

'It's Ron,' Maggie announced, bringing her mobile into the room. 'Who wants fish and chips for lunch?'

'Me, me,' the twins instantly cheered.

'Heaven,' Gabby swooned.

With raised eyebrows, Martin said, 'Count me in. You too, Charlotte. You're looking way too thin for my liking, and I'd rather just be your brother-in-law than your doctor.'

'I'm up for it,' she assured him.

'We've got takers all round,' Maggie said into the phone. 'Bring a couple of sausages and fish-cakes in case the children prefer them.'

'We do,' Phoebe informed her.

As Charlotte's eyes met Gabby's they both smiled at the memory of how they'd preferred sausages and fishcakes when they were small, and coming to link her arm Gabby said, 'If I can get away tomorrow would you like me to come and help you get started on the statement?'

Touched by the offer, Charlotte replied, 'That's lovely of you, but there's no rush and the kids'll want you at home tomorrow.'

'You know, you can always come down to us. I wish you would, I'm afraid you might feel a bit lonely here on your own once we've all gone.'

Suspecting it was exactly how she'd feel, Charlotte said, 'I'm afraid my ankle bracelet won't let me go that far, but don't worry, this flat is such a step up from where I was at the beginning of the week that I'm sure I'll cope.'

Gabby seemed mystified, until remembering she gave a little gasp. 'I'm so glad you're not in that terrible place any more,' she murmured. 'I hardly got a wink of sleep worrying about you.'

'What terrible place?' Phoebe piped up.

Pretending to go all witchy on her, Charlotte said, 'It was a haunted castle with gremlins and ghosts and things that go bump in the night.'

Jackson's eyes rounded with glee. 'Cool,' he pronounced. 'Can we go there too?'

Laughing as she went to put her cup on the table, Charlotte said, 'Believe me, Jacks, you definitely wouldn't want to, but if you like, you can come shopping later to help me choose a computer.' It would have to be after she'd reported to the police station, but that was fine.

'I will, I will,' Phoebe cried, jumping up and down.

'You both can, if Mummy and Daddy will allow it.' It was only as the words came out of her mouth that she realised why she couldn't take them with her. If someone decided to accost her with their opinion on what she'd done, the way they had in the supermarket earlier, the twins really shouldn't be subjected to it.

'You're an utter disgrace,' an old man had spat at her. 'We pays our taxes for the likes of you to do the right thing by our kids, not to go running off with them. I hope they makes an example of you, and sends you down for the maximum they can, or

361

we're going to have everyone thinking they can make off with a kid any time they like.'

'Hear, hear,' the woman behind him had chipped in. 'You should be ashamed of yourself, that's what I say.'

Knowing she couldn't put the twins through anything like that, Charlotte told them, 'Actually, I'd quite like to buy a TV as well and I probably won't have time to do both, so maybe you could go and help Mummy and Daddy choose one for me, while I do all the boring stuff with the computer.'

'Yeah! Yeah!' they cheered. 'We're really good at TVs, aren't we, Jacks?' Phoebe toasted. 'We chose the one in our playroom and Daddy's always saying it's better than his.' How easy it was to distract them, and how good they'd be for Chloe.

'OK, order's in,' Maggie declared, coming back from the kitchen, 'and I've just . . .' She jumped as a loud buzzer went off somewhere over her head. 'What on earth was that?' she demanded, looking up for the offending ringer.

Laughing, Charlotte said, 'I'm guessing the doorbell?'

Rolling her eyes, Maggie said, 'I thought for a minute we were on fire. Is there an entryphone, or do we have to go down and answer it?'

'I think I spotted something by the front door,' Martin announced. 'I'll go and check.'

Going to the window to find out if the front door was visible from here, Charlotte found it wasn't, but she had no difficulty seeing the carousel Chloe had loved across the street, or the donkeys she'd occasionally ridden up and down the sands.

'There is an entryphone,' Martin informed them, coming back into the room, 'and unless it was someone having me on, a great big bunch of flowers is on its way up.'

Gabby's eyes immediately shone. 'I wonder who they're from?' she cried, all intrigue.

'You!' Phoebe and Jackson shouted. 'We ordered them yesterday,' Phoebe informed Charlotte, 'and I helped choose them.'

Shaking his head in dismay, Martin made to give them both the chop before going back down the hall to open the door.

'We don't have any vases yet,' Maggie pointed out, 'but M&S is only round the corner, so I can easily run out and get one.'

'They should already be in one,' Gabby assured her, glancing curiously at Charlotte. 'Are you OK?' she asked.

Charlotte quickly smiled. 'Of course,' she lied. 'Just a bit overwhelmed, I suppose,' *and absolutely furious with myself for even thinking they might have been from Anthony.* What the hell was the matter with her? She had to get a grip. 'We can put them in the fireplace,' she suggested, 'to brighten it up.'

'Actually, that reminds me,' Gabby said, reaching for her bag, 'I brought a few photos for you to put up, if you want to. I thought it might make it seem a bit homelier if you had some familiar faces around.' Digging out a small parcel she handed it to Charlotte, and came to look as Charlotte went through the contents. 'They're mostly of the twins,' she confessed, 'but there's one there of us two, and oh yes, I thought you'd like this one of you and Millie.'

'Who's Millie?' Phoebe wanted to know.

'She's an old lady who used to live next door to us when we were growing up,' Gabby explained. 'Auntie Lotte was always her favourite.'

As Charlotte gazed at the photo a whole slew of memories were flipping across her heart like old postcards, many of which were of the last time she'd seen dear Millie, at a care home, here in Kesterly.

'Do you ever hear from her family?' Gabby asked. 'Is she still in York?'

'I'm not sure,' Charlotte replied. 'I'll have to try and find out.' She was thinking of the day the ambulance had driven off with Millie, who'd thought she was going to Mexico, and how certain she'd felt then that she'd never see Millie again.

She hoped and prayed that she was wrong about that, not only because she'd always felt so attached to Millie and would truly love to see her, but because she'd started to have the same feelings about Chloe, that she might never see her again.

By eight o'clock that night Charlotte was back at the flat, surrounded by her purchases of the day. The windows were open, letting in the sound of gulls and Saturday night revelry and cars with drivers who had somewhere to go. Maggie and Ron had offered to take her for a drink, or stay and keep her company a while longer, but she'd already put on them enough these last few days. She would have to get used to being on her own, and when better to start than now?

Since she couldn't be connected to the Internet or a landline until Monday, she was using the mobile Gabby had registered in her own name, given that she, Charlotte, hadn't been at her address long enough to qualify for a contract, to call her mother.

'I feel as though I'm starting all over again,' she was saying, after giving Anna an account of what she'd been doing that day, 'except this is only temporary, or that's what I keep telling myself anyway.'

'It is,' Anna assured her. 'You'll be back here before you know it, and Chloe will be with you, you just wait and see.'

Clinging to the words in spite of knowing that her mother was no more certain of that than she was, Charlotte said, 'Gabby gave me some photos today. They're lovely, but there's one of Chloe I'd love to have. It's one you took, do you remember, with us both wearing the daisy chains we'd made?'

'Of course I remember. I'll email it as soon as we've finished talking. I'll send a few others as well; I just hope it's not going to upset you too much to see them.'

'It probably will, but I'd like to have them anyway. It feels wrong to have nothing of her here at all.'

'I'm sure. Have you heard anything about her yet?'

'No, not really. Tommy kind of lets me know she's all right, but he wouldn't want to tell me if she wasn't, so I'm not sure how reliable that is. He didn't mention anything about it being her birthday yesterday, and I can't decide whether it would be a good or a bad thing if no one picked up on it. I guess it depends on who she's with, but she won't have forgotten all her plans for the day and it just about breaks my heart to think of her wondering why none of it's happening.'

'Mine too,' Anna murmured. 'If only we could send her a card, or a little message of some kind, but maybe that would make things harder for her?'

'It would probably confuse her, and as none of

us knows how this is going to turn out . . .' There it was again, the feeling she was never going to see Chloe again, and she just couldn't bear it.

'Do you think she's somewhere nearby?' Anna asked.

'Probably not,' Charlotte answered, pushing past the choking knot of dread as she wandered to the window. 'She'll still be under Kesterly Social Services, but they'll almost certainly have put her with someone outside the area. They have to in order to avoid the risk of us running into each other.' How wretched it was to think of anyone striving to keep them apart; that it was the system, inexorable and impregnable, was hardly bearable at all.

'Are you still there?' Anna asked.

'Yes, I'm here.' She was gazing down at the carousel and the Pumpkin playgroup a few metres behind it. Her memories were like ghosts riding the golden carriages and double-decker buses, drifting in and out of the nursery, getting into her car and driving away with Chloe tucked safely into the seat behind her. 'Sorry, what did you say?'

'That you're sounding quite low. Is there anyone you can invite over to keep you company for the evening?'

'I'm fine,' Charlotte assured her. 'I've a lot of sorting out to do, setting up of TVs and things. What's the weather like over there?'

Sighing, Anna said, 'Right now it's howling a masterful gale, as Bob likes to put it. He's just gone down to the beach to make sure the boats are secure, then we're popping into Kerikeri to run a few errands.'

Seeing herself and Chloe as ghosts again, going

about their day in Kerikeri, collecting Fly Buys at the supermarket, choosing a book at Paper Plus, ordering a fluffy at the Fishbone, Charlotte asked, 'How's Rick? Is he back for the weekend?'

'Actually no, he's stayed in Auckland to work on some big presentation his agency's involved in. I'm afraid he and Bob are still pretty tense with each other. Bob keeps saying he doesn't have a problem with Rick being gay, but Rick knows his father's disappointed and so it makes him defensive. They'll get over it. Shelley says they need their heads banging together and I'm inclined to agree.'

How uncomplicated it all sounded when compared to what she was facing, but it wasn't a contest and she felt sorry that Rick and Bob were going through a tricky time. 'Please send everyone my love,' she said. 'I miss you all so much.'

'Oh darling, we miss you too. Rick and Shelley will want to have your new number, so I hope it's OK if I pass it on?'

'Of course. I'd love to hear from them. I should be able to Skype from Monday, if Virgin manage to get me connected. It's a lovely flat, Mum, even nicer than the one we saw upstairs. I'll be able to use my new laptop to take you on a little tour.'

'That'll be lovely, I only wish I could be there in person. Bob's due to speak to Don Thackeray again on Monday to find out if there's any more news about me being able to come. If it goes on much longer like this Bob's saying he'll take the risk and fly over on his own. He thinks they'll be less interested in him, given that he wasn't in England when we decided to bring Chloe to New Zealand.'

'Oh no, please tell him not to chance it.'

'I'll try, but he's determined that you don't go through a trial without at least one of us there, and so am I. How are things with the lawyers? When are you due to see them again?'

Going to slump into the sofa, Charlotte said, 'Actually, nothing's been arranged, but I'm sure I'll speak to one or other of them sometime during the week.' Anthony obviously wasn't coming to Kesterly this weekend, and though he'd told her to call him any time, she didn't feel she could with no good reason.

'So what plans do you have for the next few days?' Anna asked.

Charlotte grimaced. 'I'm trying to come up with some, but this tag round my ankle won't let me go far, or I'd probably get a bus down to Gabby's, or out to Mulgrove. I guess I'm kind of a prisoner again, though believe me, I'd much rather be here than where I was, and if things don't end up going well in the long run and I'm sent back to prison . . . Actually, I'm trying not to think about that, so let's change the subject. Tell me about Katie, is she still feeling terrible about contacting the police?'

'Mm, very much so. Sarah says she's thinking of closing the salon and moving over to Sydney so none of us will have to see her again, and to be honest I wouldn't be sorry to see her go. I think her being here was all about Rick anyway, and now she knows that's never going to happen there's no point to her staying. What's that noise?'

'The front doorbell,' Charlotte replied, her nerves jangling as hope flared. *It won't be Anthony, don't be such a fool.* 'Stay on the line, I'll go and find out who it is.'

At the entryphone she said, 'Hello, can I help you?'

'Oh hi,' a male voice said at the other end. 'Sorry to bother you. I'm looking for Max Wilton. He told me to meet him here, but I don't know the flat number.'

Having spotted some of her neighbour's mail that morning, Charlotte replied, 'I think he's number four.'

'Great, thanks. Who are you, by the way? You sound kind of cute.'

Putting the entryphone down again, Charlotte returned to the living room and said to her mother, 'Tell me, have you given your statement yet?'

'No, but Don Thackeray reckons we'll probably be contacted sometime next week, now that a date's been set for the prosecution to serve their papers. I can't bear the fact that they're using me as a witness against you. Well, it's not going to happen. If need be I'll say all the decisions were mine . . .'

'No, don't do that, Mum. Just tell the truth. It's the only way we stand a chance of getting through this without both of us ending up in prison.'

'But it was my idea to bring her here.'

'Believe me, I'd thought of it long before you suggested it. No, please don't let's get into an argument about who's responsible. I'm here now, the process has begun and whether we like it or not we have to put our trust in the lawyers, because without them I really wouldn't stand a chance.'

'Well, I guess that's the truth, and I can't tell you how relieved I am that Maggie's brother has taken you on. Bob and I have been looking him up online and he's been involved in some pretty big trials, so he has plenty of experience.'

'He would have, being a QC.'

'Of course. Actually, I was surprised by how young he is. I mean forty isn't that old to have got as far as he has, so he must be very good. He's also quite good-looking and I couldn't find any mention of a wife in his biogr—'

'Mum! That's not what this is about.'

'No, of course not. I was only thinking, if something did develop between you . . .'

'*It won't*, so please stop trying to go there.'

'OK, sorry. I was only going to say that if you ended up deciding to stay in England . . .'

'Oh for God's sake, I hardly even know the man, and considering the situation I'm in, trying to pair me off with him is so totally out of order that I can't quite believe you're doing it. So can we please either change the subject or end the call?'

'OK, we'll change the subject, but before we do I want to say something that I know you're not going to like; however, I'm afraid it has to be said. You can't make your whole life about Chloe. I understand that you love her, God knows, so do I – no one, apart from you, wants her back here more than I do. But we have to face up to the fact that we have no legal claim on her. She's not ours. If we could change that, we would, all of us, but she was born into another family and though she feels in every way as though she belongs to us, in the eyes of the law she simply doesn't.'

Charlotte's eyes were closed. Her heart was so tight it had virtually stopped beating. How could her mother be saying those words when she had to know how devastating they were?

'What I'm trying to get across to you,' Anna went on gently, 'is that months, possibly even years could go by before you're able to see her again, and in that time she could very easily grow close to somebody else, become a part of another family who'll love her as much as we do. At her age it won't be difficult to form new attachments . . . I understand how difficult this is for you to hear, but you have to admit it would be better for her if she did.'

Unable to listen to any more, Charlotte ended the call with a single click and put the phone down on the sofa beside her. She couldn't give up on Chloe, she just couldn't; moreover she wasn't even going to try. Her mother, of all people, should understand that, considering how hard it had been for her, all those years ago, when she'd had to relinquish her own child. She'd never been able to give up on Charlotte, in spite of all the years that had passed, and though they had their difficulties now there was no doubt that the bond between them still existed. True, it was between a real mother and daughter, but what she and Chloe shared might go beyond the ties of birth and blood; it might be something even more special than that, considering the way they'd been brought together at the start, and the fact that until she'd come along Chloe hadn't been properly loved at all.

Now Chloe might be back in that situation, not mattering as much as she should, being moved from one foster family to the next, perhaps put up for adoption and finding herself rejected at the last. Charlotte had seen children experience that, and had felt her heart breaking along with theirs.

She simply couldn't bear that to happen to Chloe, and there was no reason why it should when there was someone who already loved and wanted her more than anything or anyone else in the world.

Chloe was sitting quietly on the wet sand, her legs stretched out in front of her and Boots snuggled deeply into her lap. She was watching the frothy edges of the waves as they crept closer and closer to her shoes, and wishing Danni was there so that they could play running from the tide the way they did in the cove. Chloe wanted to dance for pipis, or to catch fish with sticks that Mummy could cook on a big roaring fire outside the bach.

On the way down the beach she had spotted marks in the sand where horses had walked, but she couldn't see where the horses were now. She wondered if someone had swum them out to sea. She wanted to swim Diesel through the surf with Danni, or help Mummy row the boat round to Nanna's beach. Grandpa was usually there waiting for them, ready to pull the boat out of the waves. He always said hello to her, but she never said hello back.

Was that why they'd sent her away? Because she wouldn't say hello to Grandpa?

Sitting just a few yards away, Carrie Jones was watching her little charge and feeling so sad for her that it was taking a very big effort not to go and sit with her. She'd do it in an instant if she didn't already know that as soon as she sat next to Chloe, Chloe would get up and move away.

'If she knew how,' Carrie had said to the psychologist who'd visited them that morning, 'I'm sure she'd run away.'

'How much does she talk about Charlotte Nicholls and her time in New Zealand?' the psychologist had asked.

'All she ever says is that she wants to go to Mummy,' Carrie replied.

Carrie had hoped the psychologist would give her some advice on how to draw the child out more, but all the woman had said was that this was simply an initial assessment, and she'd be in touch again soon to organise a follow-up visit. Before she'd left there had been lots of form-filling and explanations of charts that Carrie had to keep, but so far Carrie had learned nothing that might prove helpful for her day-to-day dealings with the child. Such as how to get her to eat more, or to engage with her when she was speaking. Not that Carrie was intending to give up on the sweet little thing, she just wanted to hear someone validate her own methods of dealing with troubled children.

Maybe her little tricks would work for Chloe. Certainly her first couple of attempts had yielded some hopeful signs. All she'd done was remove the bear while the child was sleeping and put him on the floor next to her bed. The panic on Chloe's face when she'd woken and realised he wasn't there had not been easy to watch. However, the relief at finding him had encouraged Chloe to tell her his name.

Boots.

Carrie presumed he'd had some once, but that was hardly relevant. What mattered was the fact that she, Carrie, had coaxed something other than 'want Mummy' out of the child. She could also now call the cherished bear by its name.

The other little experiment she'd begun hadn't yet yielded any rewards, but *everything in its time* was Carrie's motto, and given how long she'd been told to expect Chloe to stay, there really wasn't any rush.

Chapter Twenty

'Mm,' Anthony commented in a way that made Charlotte want to laugh, in spite of how useless she was feeling. 'This is it?'

'So far,' she replied, trying to make it sound as though she had lots more in store for the statement. She did, however writing everything down in a way that might encourage the reader to understand, and ultimately forgive her for taking Chloe, was proving far more difficult than she'd expected.

Once she'd explained that, he said, 'I see. So in other words you're trying to do my job for me? Very kind of you, but honestly not necessary.'

'But I want it to come across as believable and heartfelt.'

His eyes widened in protest. 'And you think I'd do otherwise?' he challenged.

This time she did laugh. 'No, no, of course not,' she assured him, 'I just think that if I can convey it to you in a way that's meaningful as well as open and honest, you'll have a better understanding of why I did it. Anyway, it's not your job to take my statement, it's my solicitor's.'

'Indeed, and I'm more than happy to hand the honours over to Kim if you'd prefer, but as I'm here and you're still only ten lines into it, I'm offering to help.'

She appreciated it, she really did, but she was still trying to get her head round the fact that he'd turned up out of the blue about half an hour ago and had managed, in less than five minutes, to make her feel as though he was in and out all the time. She could only wish it were true, given how lonely she'd felt all week – and anxious, and increasingly certain she was going to wind up in prison and never see Chloe again.

'I'm waiting,' he prompted.

'I won't be able to write anything with you looking over my shoulder,' she told him bluntly.

'OK, so how about you *tell* me what happened? We can easily record it and I'll arrange for it to be transcribed later.'

Charlotte pulled a face, which made him sit back in his chair, fold his arms and stretch his long legs out in front of him.

'You're really not the easiest person to talk to,' she informed him.

'Rubbish. I'm the best listener you've ever come across, you just don't know it yet.'

She felt herself bubbling with laughter again. 'How about I make us another coffee – while I try to get my thoughts in order,' she rushed on as he started to object.

He nodded slowly. 'OK, that sounds reasonable. In fact, I'm starving, so why don't I run out for some sandwiches while you're doing that? Ham, cheese, chicken, egg . . . What do you fancy?'

'If you go to the deli on the corner I'll have a tomato and mozzarella wrap.'

'Then I shall go to the deli on the corner. Anything else you need while I'm out?'

'Not that I can think of, thank you.'

For several moments after the door closed behind him Charlotte remained where she was, in the middle of the room, hugging to herself her delight in seeing him. Since he'd announced himself over the entryphone her usual companions of dread and fear seemed to have shrunk back into the shadows as though unsure of their place, now there was such a forceful presence to contend with. They didn't even appear to be trying to steal back again now he'd popped out, for as she went through to the kitchen she was aware of feeling as close to light-hearted as she was able, given the darkness of the cloud she was under.

All in all it had been a strange sort of week, seeming to speed past at times, while at others each minute had felt like an hour. The highlight of her days, if such it could be termed, and she didn't think it could, was the twenty-minute walk to the police station and back to comply with the terms of her bail. Occasionally she saw someone she knew, but she never subjected them to the awkwardness of having to acknowledge her unless they spoke first. A few had wished her well and even invited her to be in touch if she'd like to, while others had gracelessly avoided her eyes. Or, in one case, had pointedly steered her toddler across the street so she wouldn't have to pass her.

Had the woman seriously thought she'd try to spirit the child away?

The worst encounter had happened yesterday morning, when she'd been told by a woman from the Temple Fields estate, whose family she'd had dealings with in the past, to 'do the world a favour and fuck off and die.'

Ironically, that particular woman would probably have given her the exact same advice whether she was on a charge of child abduction or not, but the people around them at Tesco hadn't known that. All they'd known, if they hadn't before, was that the child-snatching social worker Alex Lake was in their midst and buying groceries just like she was one of them.

'You should be ashamed of yourself for all the trouble you've caused,' one woman had informed her. 'Fancy lying to the police and letting them carry out that search when you knew all along where the child was. I was a part of that search and I can tell you, I've got better things to do with my time than to be given the runaround by the likes of you.'

'A bloody waste of taxpayers' money,' the man with her grunted. 'As if the police don't have enough to do without being led up the garden path by people who should know better.'

'She's a disgrace.'

'I wonder she's got the nerve to show her face.'

'Poor kiddie, I wonder what's happened to her now.'

'Here you are, love,' the cashier had said quietly, handing over her change. 'Take no notice of them. You did what you felt you had to, and there's nothing wrong with that.'

What had happened at Tesco was reflected on most of the social media sites, she was finding. It seemed everyone had an opinion, and no one was backward in expressing it, often flagrantly disregarding the law. Sometimes they wrote in terms that made Charlotte want to hide away for ever, or rage back at them to mind their own damned business, or at least get informed, given how many lies and concoctions were littering the pages. At least there had been no more postings from Heather Hancock, who presumably had decided to pull back from the risk of being charged with contempt of court.

In the end, Charlotte had taken Kim's advice and closed down her Facebook and Twitter accounts – there was nothing to be gained from putting herself through the spleen, or even the support, of strangers when none of them really knew what had happened, nor would they until the trial began.

'Much better,' Kim had said, 'to stick to the people you know you can trust, like your sister and Maggie, and if you can possibly help it, don't do any more online research into your charge. Every case is individual, so there's honestly no point in scaring yourself with stories of what's happened to other people in your situation.'

Though Charlotte knew it was sensible advice, she couldn't just wipe from her mind the fact that her crime could send her to prison for up to seven years. And even if she turned out to be one of the lucky ones whose mitigating circumstances had allowed their sentences to be suspended, she'd still have a criminal record, which would completely rule out her ever being able to apply for custody of Chloe, and might possibly prevent her from returning to New Zealand.

So acquittal was the only option, and since the evidence of her crime was totally irrefutable there was no way in the world that was going to happen.

'Try to have faith,' Anthony told her when she confessed, over their coffee and sandwiches, how hopeless she was feeling.

'But in what?' she cried. 'Everyone knows I hid her from the police and took her out of the country . . .'

His hand was up. 'You need to trust me on this, Charlotte. We can get an acquittal. True, it might not be easy, nor can I guarantee it . . .'

'I swear I do trust you, but I don't understand how you can pull it off when everyone knows I took her.'

'Believe me, yours wouldn't be the first case to go in front of a jury with everyone certain of a guilty verdict beforehand. Have you ever heard of someone called Clive Ponting?'

She frowned. 'The name rings a bell.'

'Look him up online. He's a good example of someone everyone knew had done it, but the jury still came back with a not guilty verdict.'

'I don't think he abducted a child, did he? Wasn't his case something to do with breaking the Official Secrets Act?'

'It was, and I know what you're going to say, that in the public's mind taking a child is going to be seen as a much more serious offence than exposing a government secret. My point is, if the jury's on your side then they can, and do, return verdicts of not guilty in spite of the prosecution's case, or the judge's direction.'

With an unsteady sigh, she pushed her half-eaten wrap aside and gazed at it forlornly as she said, 'Which is why it's important for me to convince you that what I did was in Chloe's best interests.'

'Actually, I'm already convinced of that, but it'll be extremely helpful to hear it in your words, before I put it into mine.'

Liking the sense of collaboration, she looked into his eyes and smiled. 'OK, so where would you like me to begin?'

He cocked an eyebrow as he said, 'How about

the first time you and Chloe met. Where was it? What happened? What was said?'

Remembering it as clearly as if it had happened only yesterday, Charlotte's eyes drifted towards the window where raindrops were running ragged paths down over the panes. She and Chloe used to sit in the car sometimes, right here on the front, choosing a raindrop each as they waited for a storm to pass, urging it down the windscreen and cheering when one of them got to the bottom.

There had been no rain that first day in the park; it had been warm and sunny, with not even the hint of a cloud in the sky.

'Hello. And who are you?' she'd asked the little girl on the swing, and as the memories of it all came flooding back to her, from the unease she'd felt about Chloe's father that day, to her first visit to the house on North Hill, to the time Chloe had stowed herself away in the back of Charlotte's car so as not to be left with her father; to the night she'd grabbed Chloe from the house where her mother had lain dead in the kitchen, right through to the day she'd flown her out to New Zealand, she found herself reliving each emotion, each decision, as though it were happening now.

By the time she'd finished the sun was starting to sink over the estuary, and Anthony had moved from the table to the other end of the sofa. She felt exhausted, and yet oddly elated. Jumbled and tangential though her story had been, it was liberating to have spoken it all out loud.

Anthony's dark eyes were regarding her intently as he said, 'Are you all right?'

She nodded. 'I think so.'

'Well, it's quite a story,' he told her, 'and one that

proves to me that my initial instincts about you were right.'

She gave him a quizzical look. 'You had such things about me?' she teased to cover her disquiet.

He smiled. 'I did, and they were that you really are someone I would like to know.'

Feeling herself starting to colour, she said, 'I expect it was my joke about the fish that did it.'

He frowned as he laughed. 'You might have to remind me what it was.'

'Tell you what, why don't I not humiliate myself all over again?'

His eyes were still shining with mirth as he spot-checked the recording he'd made of her statement, before tossing his iPhone on to the seat beside him. 'We'll get it transcribed,' he told her, 'and then we'll work on it together between now and the start of the trial. I'm assuming you don't have a problem with taking the stand?'

She shook her head. 'Of course, I'd rather be playing the Palladium,' she informed him, 'but if that's the only venue you can get me . . .'

Laughing again, he glanced at his watch and said, 'I don't know about you, but I could do with a drink. So, what do you say we stretch our legs, take in some sea air, and stroll along to one of the wine bars in the harbour?'

Every night before going to sleep Chloe whispered her secret to Boots. 'We're going to be nice to Grandpa,' she'd tell him, 'and then Mummy will come for us.' She had no idea how she was going to see Grandpa yet, but she was sure, if she kept her promise to be nice to him, that Mummy would love her again.

'We'll play ride the tiger with him,' she went on bleakly, 'and do everything he tells us to make him happy.'

Boots never answered because he couldn't, but she knew that he didn't like to play ride the tiger any more than she did, but if it was what she'd decided to do he would do it too.

From outside the bedroom door Carrie listened to the whispers, and tried to decipher them, but they were too soft, too broken for her to make out any more than 'Mummy' or 'Grandpa'. So all she could say for certain was that her little charge continued to pine for the woman who'd rescued her from her evil father and taken her to New Zealand, where she'd made her part of a family she would probably never see again.

How tough the world could be on children, Carrie often reflected over a TV dinner for one, or a soak in a nice hot bath, or a trip down her own memory lane. Heaven knew she'd had a great many of the battered and broken ones coming through her door, and though she'd like to think that they left her in slightly better shape than when they'd arrived, she knew that the repair was probably only superficial. The damage inflicted could run so deep that it would never heal.

She had no idea how lasting Chloe's injuries might be, she only knew that she'd been with her for almost three weeks now and still hadn't uttered a single voluntary word, unless it was to Tracy asking to be taken to Mummy. Apparently she hadn't spoken at all when she'd first come under the care of social services, and it was Charlotte Nicholls who'd finally coaxed her to open up.

Carrie wanted to do the same for her, so she was

hoping to assist the speech therapist with one of her own little methods.

'I have to admit, I'm sorry to see you go,' Wendy was saying to Tommy as they wandered from the detritus of his leaving bash out to the Centre's over-crowded car park. The others were still drowning the loss of their beloved team leader in the wine the department had laid on, but Tommy had to leave in order to be somewhere else this evening. 'It's been a real pleasure working with you over the years,' Wendy told him, as they reached his Nissan. 'You're going to be sorely missed. Well, you could see that from how reluctant they all were to let you out of the door.'

Smiling at the way some of the girls had cried, declaring themselves to be in utter despair, he fingered the streamers round his neck as he said, 'People come and go, it's a part of life, and in our line of work we see it more than most.'

'Indeed.' She sighed heavily and watched the clouds swirling overhead as he loaded his parting gifts into the boot. 'I expect your wife'll be glad to see you,' she commented. 'Is the new house all sorted out now?'

'And ready to move into the week after next. We're staying with my brother till then.' He gave an awkward sort of smile. He'd known this woman for a good many years, and though they hadn't always seen eye to eye – in fact she'd driven him to distraction more often than not – it was hard to get through so many ups and downs without developing some kind of rapport, even affection. 'Well, I guess that's it then,' he said, wondering if he ought to hug her.

'Yes, I guess it is,' she agreed, sounding brittle as

she tried to suppress a few tears. 'I hope you'll stay in touch. It'll be nice to know how you're getting on.'

'Thanks, I will,' he promised. 'And good luck with the promotion. I reckon you're in with a pretty good chance of getting it.'

She gave a half-hearted sort of laugh. 'We both know I wouldn't have got even this far if you'd wanted the job,' she said. 'You could have gone right to the top here in Dean Valley.'

'Spare me,' he shuddered. 'All that bureaucracy, all those idiots . . . No thanks, not my cup of tea. You're far better at dealing with them than I could ever be.'

She nodded and kept her eyes on his. 'Before you go,' she said, 'can I ask you a question?'

'Shoot.'

She took a moment to choose her words. 'Have you gone over my head about anything lately?'

His eyes widened in surprise.

'I'm talking about Ottilie Wade.'

Less surprised now, he said, 'If you're asking have I tried to exert some influence on the plans for adoption, the answer's no, I haven't, at least not directly, but I do believe Charlotte's lawyers have taken an interest.'

She nodded, clearly having expected as much. 'Then I imagine you know I've received a directive to hold things up until the court case has been resolved,' she told him.

His eyes narrowed as he regarded her. 'Actually, I didn't know that, but I admit I'm glad to hear it. I know she doesn't stand much chance of getting off the charge, and even less of being able to have the child back, but that still doesn't make it right to fast-track an adoption.'

She didn't argue, but he could tell she wasn't pleased.

'I can say this to you now,' he went on, 'because you're no longer my boss. Actually, I've said it to you before, but I don't think you've listened. You're in danger of having a blind spot where Charlotte Nicholls is concerned.'

'Tommy, please . . .'

'No, I want you to hear me out. I understand that you have to play everything by the book where this case is concerned, that the powers that be are watching you closely, but it doesn't mean you have to run scared from allowing your heart to rule your head once in a while. I know you care about what happens to the child, and that you're doing everything in your power to make sure her future is secure; you just don't have to rush things, OK?'

Wendy only looked at him.

He glanced at his watch. 'I should go,' he said, 'or I won't have time to shower before dinner.'

Accepting his rough embrace with an awkward one of her own, she stepped back and watched him get into the car. 'Are you seeing Charlotte this evening?' she asked evenly.

'Yes, I am,' he replied.

Her expression stiffened around a smile. 'Then please tell her from me that none of my decisions are based on my personal feelings towards her,' and before he could reply she turned to walk back into the building.

'Are you ready yet?' Anthony shouted, drying his hands on a towel as he came out of the kitchen.

'Coming,' Charlotte called back. 'I just can't get this necklace done up,' and appearing from the bedroom she almost collided with him as he headed for the sitting room.

'Let me,' he insisted, and taking the peridot pendant he turned her around and told her to lift her hair.

'You really didn't have to come and collect me,' she informed him, trying to distract herself from the feel of his fingers on the nape of her neck. 'I'm a big girl, I could have walked to the restaurant on my own.'

'There,' he said, patting the chain into place, 'and if you want to walk alone I'll be happy to follow three paces behind.'

'In a hijab?'

'Ha ha. Are you ready now? You look it to me.'

'Shoes,' she declared, pointing at her bare feet, and zooming back into the bedroom she shook a pair of nude slingbacks from their box, allowing the tissue to cascade to the floor as she slipped into them and gave herself a final once-over in the mirror. Everything was new, from the coffee-coloured jacket and cream linen trousers, to the sparkly silk top, the shoes, necklace, bracelet and fake designer bag. Even the perfume she was wearing had come from today's spree, as had the make-up and nail polish, and she was thrilled with the way a hairdresser, picked at random, had trimmed and styled her hair into a loose waterfall of waves.

How Chloe would have loved the day out. She'd kept trying not to think of how Chloe might be spending the time, who she might be with, where she was, but it hadn't been easy. It wasn't easy now, either, mainly because it never was. The love, the fear, the longing were always there, tugging at her heart and her spirits as though to drag them away from any feelings of joy or hope. She wasn't even sure she wanted to feel those things unless Chloe was there to share them.

'OK, shall we go?' she said, walking into the sitting room.

Anthony's hand came up as he said into the phone, 'Yeah, I got the call earlier, thanks. No, I haven't seen the email yet, but . . . All right, I'll take a look at it tomorrow. What about the other matter? That's the one. OK, I'll chase it on Monday. Have a good weekend. Sure, I will too.' Ringing off, he was about to stuff the mobile in his pocket when it rang again.

'Nothing that can't wait,' he decided, and letting the call go to voicemail, his sleepy eyes narrowed as he said, 'Well, now you're standing still long enough for me to see you, I can say that you look absolutely stunning.'

Thrilled, Charlotte gave him a twirl. 'I thought I should make an effort for Tommy's last night,' she explained. 'I don't think we should let him pay the bill though, do you?'

'Certainly not.'

'He's insisting, but with Maggie and Ron on our side, he's not going to win. So, are we set?'

With an ironic raise of an eyebrow, he said, 'I think so,' and gesturing for her to go ahead of him, he remembered to unhook the keys as they passed before closing the front door behind them.

As they joined the strollers and commuters on the seafront and headed towards the old town, Charlotte couldn't help feeling thankful for the sense of freedom stealing over her. The press was having to leave her alone since her case was *sub judice*, and if Anthony wasn't concerned about them being seen together then there was no need for her to be either. In fact, she was probably feeling as close to light-hearted as she could manage, given the situation she was in.

The dark clouds that had come to crowd the horizon earlier seemed to have vanished completely now, leaving a pale blue sky tipping gently over the estuary and sun-sparkled pools of mud on the beach. Thankfully there was almost no wind to bedraggle her new hairstyle, and since it hadn't rained for the past few days there was no dampness in the air either to flatten it. Given how warm it was, it could have been the perfect spring evening, were it not for Tommy's imminent departure making her feel as though a vital link to Chloe was being lost.

She must try not to see it like that though, especially when he hadn't really been able to tell her anything anyway, and besides tonight wasn't about her and her problems. It was all about Tommy, and wishing him well with his return to the north. She suspected the team at Kesterly Social Services was going to miss him a great deal more than he would them, though he'd made some good friends during his time as team leader, so there were probably a few he'd be sorry to leave behind. Whether Wendy was amongst them only he could say, and Charlotte wasn't going to ask, since the subject of Wendy was always one to be avoided.

Aware of the way Anthony was deliberately slowing his pace so she could keep up in her heels, she felt tempted to link his arm, or even take hold of his hand. She didn't quite dare though, in case he looked at her in astonishment, or politely detached himself. He did occasionally take her arm when they were crossing a road, though, or, as had happened yesterday on their daily walk to the police station, when someone decided to share their opinion of her. Fortunately, yesterday's accoster had had only friendly words to impart. Nevertheless, Anthony had kept a firm grip on her elbow until the tattooed youth with his Mohican and piercings had eventually moved on.

It was still completely incredible to her that they were spending just about every day together now, the afternoons anyway, and sometimes part of the evenings too. Without having made any particular plan in advance he simply turned up in time to walk her to the police station, and after she'd been cleared for another day they'd go to a café, or pick up some fish and chips or a sandwich for lunch. It seemed they had an endless amount of things to chat about besides her case, flitting from one subject to the next to the next with the kind of ease and humour that she'd never shared with anyone before.

'No, no, there's definitely nothing to it,' she'd assured Gabby on the phone that morning, while wishing there was, 'or not in the way you're thinking. We just get along really well, and actually, most of our time is spent preparing for the trial.'

'Yes, but when you're not discussing that, does he ever talk about himself?'

'Of course. He tells me about the various cases he's handled, which I find totally fascinating, and hilarious sometimes.' She'd rattled off a few examples, which Gabby had seemed to find entertaining too (as had her mother when she'd related them to her the night before). 'Or he talks about how he always wanted to be a musician, or a carpenter, or a farmer,' she continued, 'anything but a lawyer, because it was what was expected of him. I didn't tell him that my real father had been a carpenter, but it's quite a coincidence that, isn't it? Anyway, he says he's become pretty jaded with the law, which is why he's taken a sabbatical to find out if he really wants to carry on with it.'

'And what about his personal life? Does he ever mention that?'

'Not really. I mean, I know he has a house in Holland Park and that he belongs to a couple of clubs, mainly for sport. He plays a lot of tennis, and likes to fish and sail, and he's quite into wine.'

'And is he with someone?'

'If he is he never mentions her, and he's in Kesterly such a lot . . .'

'Because he's got a thing for you.'

'Oh Gabby, don't be ridiculous. He's just spending time with me because neither of us is working at the moment, apart from trying to get me out of the mess I'm in.'

'And he should care about that because?'

'Because he's like his sister. Kindness obviously runs in the family, and he's definitely that.'

'Plus good-looking, rich, I expect . . .'

'I've no idea.'

'Bound to be with a job like that. Anyway, what really matters to me is that you've got someone to keep you company while you're going through all this, and who better than him when he can actually do something about it? You know, I was really dreading you having to spend too much time on your own, working yourself up into a state, but now it's not happening I can sleep more easily at night.'

Charlotte had to admit she'd also been dreading having too much time on her hands, but apart from the mornings which Anthony spent catching up with emails, or sorting out other business, she was almost always with him. They'd even hired bicycles the day before to explore the extent of her court-imposed boundaries, and next Monday they were going to the first half of a concert at Breston Hall where one of his favourite bands was playing. They'd have to leave at the interval in order for her to avoid breaking her curfew, but when the time came she was going to insist he stayed so he wouldn't have to miss out on the best songs because of her.

'Mm, looks like we're last,' he commented as they approached the Hudson, Tommy's favourite grill, and spotted Tommy and the others already at a circular window table.

Giving them a wave, Charlotte said, 'I hope no one minds eating this early.'

'Faced with a choice of you being here, or not, I imagine everyone's happy to dine at six,' he responded, pulling open the door for her to go in first.

Loving how he always managed to say the right thing, she cast a playful look over her shoulder and went to wrap her arms around Tommy, before doing the same with Maggie and Ron.

'You look an absolute picture,' Tommy declared, holding out a chair for her to sit next to him.

'Doesn't she?' Maggie agreed.

'I think I'm looking pretty good too,' Anthony piped up.

With shining eyes, Charlotte said, 'You were turning heads all the way here.'

Maggie's expression was so comically arch that even Anthony had to laugh, and not for the first time Charlotte felt the pleasure of his humour stealing all the way through her.

'Excellent, here we go,' Ron declared, rubbing his

hands as a waiter arrived with a bottle of wine and five glasses. 'Shame your wife can't be here to help us toast you on your way,' he said to Tommy, 'we would have liked to meet her.'

'Oh, I'm sure you will one of these days,' Tommy smiled. 'We've got too many friends in these parts not to come back on visits.'

'So what are you going to be doing when you've completed the move?' Maggie asked, steadying her glass as the waiter filled it.

'I'm weighing up a couple of options,' he replied, 'but I reckon I'm done with local government.'

'They say it burns you out,' Ron commented, 'especially in your line.'

'Anyone who gets him will be extremely lucky,' Charlotte told them, 'because he's very definitely the best boss I've ever had.'

'She's only had one,' Tommy murmured, making the others laugh.

'To Tommy,' Anthony announced when all the glasses were full, 'may you have a great future in the north and plenty of visits down south.'

Wondering if some of them might be to a prison, Charlotte deliberately kept her smile sunny as they clinked glasses and sipped the delicious Shiraz Mourvèdre. 'How was your send-off at the office today?' she asked. 'Did everyone get smashed?'

'A few did,' he admitted. 'They were very generous with their gifts: a smart new leather holdall and a Newcastle United shirt.'

'You're a footballing man?' Ron leapt in. 'I'm an Arsenal man myself, and my sad case of a brother-in-law here shouts for Liverpool.'

'That's where my mother's from, originally,' Charlotte informed them.

'Our parents too,' Maggie said, 'though they were living in London by the time I was born.'

'Are they still around?' Tommy asked.

'Sadly no. They died quite young, so we were mainly brought up by our grandparents – at least Anthony was, I was already at college by the time Mum died.'

'So how old were you when she went?' Charlotte asked Anthony, concerned for the small boy whose world had been shattered by the loss of his mother.

'Eight,' he replied, 'but I have some memories of her, which is good. Shame I can't say the same about Dad, but I was only three when we lost him.'

'Oh my gosh, you were so young.'

His expression was droll as he said, 'I think I've managed to come through it. Anyway, tonight's supposed to be about Tommy, not me, so . . .'

'No, no, no,' Tommy protested. 'Let's not talk about me. Oh, all right then, if you insist.'

Laughing as she was handed a menu, Charlotte was about to open it when she glanced up at the sound of some newcomers arriving. At first she only registered them as a young family with a toddler and a baby in a stroller, but then the little girl turned around and her heart caught on the suddenness of shock. It wasn't that the child looked especially like Chloe, but her dark hair was similar, and she was definitely the same age, since she was holding a balloon that said *I am four*.

Returning to the menu, she kept her head down as she tried to collect herself. It wasn't as though this was the first time she'd seen a child that made her think of Chloe; it was happening all the time. Even little boys, or older children, or babies, made her long to hold Chloe again. She couldn't pass a toyshop or a children's clothing store, or a sweet counter without wanting to search out a special treat for her precious little girl. Nor could she walk along the street without feeling the urge to reach for her hand, or cross the road without mentally checking that she was safely with her.

Where was she now? Was someone taking good care of her?

By the time a waiter had taken their orders and the child and her parents and sibling had disappeared upstairs to the family room, Charlotte had her emotions back in control, and was able to return to the easy banter between Anthony and Ron as they selected the next wine. She was so lucky to have such loyal and supportive friends. She'd feel, if they weren't there, that she had no one, with her mother being so far away, Gabby in Devon and Chloe all but lost to her.

But Chloe wasn't lost, she *wasn't*. She was simply being taken care of by someone else for a while, someone who loved her and was making her feel safe and special until it was possible for Charlotte to have her back again. She had to tell herself this or she'd go out of her mind with worry, and it could easily be true, so why keep fearing the worst?

'You seem to have gone quiet on us,' Anthony commented as the first course was served.

'Me?' she asked, feigning surprise. 'I was just listening to you, as I always do, with rapt attention and awe, and wondering . . .' she laughed and ducked as he made to throw a cork at her, 'and wondering,' she pressed on, 'if Maggie and Ron have any children with them at the moment.'

To her surprise Maggie seemed a little discomfited

as she picked up her wine and started to mumble an answer.

'Actually, we've decided to take a break from it for a while,' Ron informed her.

Charlotte blinked. 'Really?' she said. 'Well, I guess it can be pretty taxing at times . . .' She stopped as the penny suddenly dropped. 'Is it . . . ? Does it have something to do with me?' she asked, feeling a prickle of unease creeping over her.

Maggie's eyes went to her brother, as though wondering how to reply.

As Anthony started to explain, Tommy said, 'It was felt in the office that with Maggie and Ron being friends of yours it would be best not to place any kids with them until . . . well, everything's resolved.'

A beat of horror struck in Charlotte's chest. 'Do they think I'm a danger to them, or something?' she demanded.

'I don't think that's the case,' Tommy responded. 'You know how these things work.'

'But to deprive kids of the privilege of being with Maggie and Ron . . . What if I said I would never go there? Would that make a difference?'

'Not really,' Anthony told her, 'because, as your lawyer and their part-time lodger, I'm also a bit of a problem.'

'So we decided,' Ron continued, 'that for the time being we'd take ourselves off the register and carry on enjoying having Anthony – and you – as our guests.'

Charlotte hardly knew what to say. While on the one hand she couldn't be anything but relieved – even honoured – to have Maggie and Ron's support, to think of the needy children who were missing out on their care – *because of her* – was absolutely mortifying. This wasn't what she was about at all, depriving kids of one of the best foster families in the region. These defenceless, powerless little individuals, some of them so badly neglected, even damaged, that they were close to breaking, had to come first.

'We can discuss it later,' Anthony said, as though sensing an explosion, 'but try to bear in mind that you matter too.'

'Hear, hear,' Tommy declared, holding up his glass. 'You can't rule the world, much as I know you'd like to, and in this instance I think you have to accept that your needs count as much as the kids', especially when your goal is to get Chloe back.'

Unable to be anything but silenced by that, Charlotte dropped her eyes to her plate as she took in this new status of hers, the needy, care-depriving ex-social worker who was throwing everyone else's lives out of kilter. Yet Tommy was right, she had to put Chloe first – and be thankful for the way she was being helped to do so.

Steering them out of stormy waters, Anthony began extolling the virtues of the excellent Shiraz he'd chosen, while Maggie rolled her eyes and Ron insisted the next bottle, of his choosing, would be far superior. Tommy soon joined in, and by the time the subject changed again, to what options he was considering up north, Charlotte was back in the conversation.

'So when do you think you might make your next trip to Kesterly?' Ron was asking Tommy as the dessert menu arrived.

Tommy glanced at Anthony and Charlotte. 'I guess that depends on these guys,' he replied. 'Do we have a start date yet for the trial?'

As Charlotte's insides lurched, Anthony said, 'The papers are being served the Friday after next, then we'll have the Plea and Case Management hearing, and I'm hoping the trial will begin no more than a month after that.'

Signalling for a waiter, Tommy said, 'Well, whenever it is, I'll be there, you don't want to worry about that.'

'You'll always have a place to stay with us if you need it,' Maggie informed him as Anthony got up to sort out the bill before anyone else could. 'So, who'd like to come back for a nightcap?' Maggie asked, once they were outside. Realising what she'd said as soon as the words left her lips, she looked at Charlotte in dismay.

'Don't worry,' Charlotte told her. 'I don't mind. I'd like to call Mum anyway.' She was feeling foolish for it, but right now, with the prospect of saying goodbye to Tommy on such a close horizon, she'd have given almost anything for her mother to be there when she got home. It seemed so long since she'd seen her, and being as emotionally frayed as she was at the moment, she really needed to be with her.

'Now, I'm not going to make a big deal out of this,' Tommy said to Charlotte when they were outside on the cobbled street. 'I'll be seeing you again in a few weeks, and I'll be at the end of the phone or Skype any time you want to chat. So come on, be giving us a nice big hug and none of your sentimental stuff.'

'Me! Sentimental!' she protested with a tearful laugh. 'And I thought you knew me.'

Wrapping her up in his arms, he gave her the longest, most affectionate hug he could muster. 'You're going to be all right,' he told her gruffly.

'And so's Chloe. She's in good hands, not as good as yours, it's true, but I've got plenty of faith in Tracy so I know if something wasn't right, she'd take care of it in a heartbeat.'

It was long past bedtime, but Chloe was running frantically around Carrie's house searching for Boots. Carrie had hidden him and wouldn't tell her where. All she did was watch and let her know whether she was hot or cold, or tell her to stop worrying because she'd definitely find him in the end.

Running back into the sitting room, sweat dampening her hair and real fear shining in her eyes, Chloe began tearing at the cushions again, throwing them on to the floor, and stuffing her hands into the back of the sofa and chairs. Still not finding him she turned to Carrie, tears of desperation falling on to her cheeks.

Carrie lifted her eyes.

Chloe didn't understand. She hadn't been naughty, so why was Carrie doing this?

Carrie lifted her eyes again, and this time, realising Carrie was encouraging her to look up, Chloe did so, and gave a gasp when she saw Boots sitting right on the top of a bookcase amongst Carrie's fluffy animals.

'There you are, I told you you'd find him,' Carrie smiled proudly. 'Now all you have to do is say, "Please may I have Boots?"'

Without any hesitation Chloe whispered, 'Please may I have Boots?'

Clapping her hands in praise, Carrie said, 'You see, you can speak, and it really wasn't so difficult, was it?'

Chloe looked at her beseechingly.

'All right, all right,' Carrie chuckled. 'I'll fetch him down now and then we can go up to bed and have a little chat.'

Chloe was still panting for breath as she watched Carrie prop a ladder against the shelves and start to climb. Her arms went up ready to catch Boots in case he fell.

'There we are,' Carrie declared, passing him down to her. 'Ah, ah, don't snatch now, there's a good girl.'

Chloe quickly pulled back her hands. Her eyes were fixed on Boots. She wanted him so much it was hurting.

She didn't notice the ladder starting to slide, barely even registered Carrie scrabbling for a hold; she only saw Boots falling towards her, and catching him she hugged him tightly. Then a book hit her, and another and another. Carrie screamed, and as she and the ladder crashed to the floor Chloe pressed her face even harder into Boots.

It was almost the curfew hour by the time Charlotte and Anthony arrived at her front door, the salted night air clinging to their clothes, the thump of disco beats leaping from arcades and wine bars still ringing in their ears.

'Oh no,' she gasped, turning to him, having realised what she'd forgotten.

He was already holding up the keys. 'Are you going to be all right?' he asked.

She nodded awkwardly. *Oh God, she was going to start crying. What was the matter with her tonight?*

Tilting her chin up, he said, 'If you invited me in, I'd accept.'

With a mangled sort of laugh, she turned to open the door and led the way up to the first floor. 'I'm afraid I don't have any brandy, or whisky,' she told him, 'but I can offer you more wine.'

'I have to drive,' he reminded her. 'So coffee will be fine.'

A few minutes later she carried two cups through to the sitting room, to find him standing at the window gazing absently at the distant lights of a ship heading along the estuary for the docks at Avonmouth.

'Thanks,' he said. Then after taking a sip, 'I had some news today that I think I should share with you.'

As her insides turned to liquid all kinds of horror struck through her mind. Something had happened to Chloe. They were going to revoke her bail. Extra charges were being heaped on her.

'Don't look so scared,' he said gently, 'it's not that bad, I promise. It's just that I've been trying to get your case thrown out on the grounds that there was no malicious intent involved, or family being deprived of their child, in that the father has lost all rights to custody.' He sighed. 'It was always a long shot,' he admitted, 'and I'm afraid it failed.'

She took a breath as she nodded. She tried to speak, but the words wouldn't come.

Taking her coffee he put it on the table and folded her into his arms. 'I'm sorry,' he whispered into her hair. 'I wish it could have been better news, but we've still got a long way to go, so there's absolutely no reason to give up hope yet.'

She still couldn't speak. She was sobbing too hard and couldn't make herself stop.

'It's good to let it out,' he told her softly. 'You've

been holding back all night, I could tell. It was seeing the little girl, wasn't it?'

'Yes,' she spluttered, 'and saying goodbye to Tommy and . . . Oh God, I'm sorry . . .'

'Sssh, don't apologise.' He cupped her face in his hands and gazed down into her eyes.

As she looked back at him she could feel the need for him tangling her emotions and starting to over-whelm her. What was he thinking? Was he feeling anything of the sensations that were coursing through her? Please God, don't let her do or say something to disgrace herself even more than she already had. But she wanted him so much, so very, very much . . .

It seemed to take an eternity for the space to close between them, for his mouth to cover hers. She couldn't even be sure it was really happening, or if she was dreaming, until he pulled her against him and as his tenderness and desire fused with her own, nothing else seemed to matter quite so much any more.

Chapter Twenty-One

'So where is she now?' Tracy demanded, her face flushing dark with frustration.

'Who? Chloe or Carrie?' Wendy replied, not bothering to glance up from her computer.

'*Chloe!*' Tracy cried. 'And Carrie. But Chloe.'

Clicking to open another email, Wendy said, 'I'm still waiting to hear. All I can tell you is that no one knew who she was when they got to the house last night, she wouldn't tell anyone her name, so the police, naturally, handed her over to the local social services.'

'And you've already spoken to someone there?' Tracy persisted.

'It's Saturday, I'm having some difficulty getting through to them, but I'm sure someone will call me back soon.'

'So how do you know Carrie Jones had an accident?'

'Because Carrie herself rang from the hospital this morning, wanting to make sure the child was all right.'

'Why didn't she ring me?'

'I don't know. Maybe she didn't have your number with her. Anyway, she told me what had happened, so I contacted the local police, who referred me to West Somerset.'

It was making sense so far, kind of. 'So what did happen to Carrie?' Tracy asked.

'Apparently she fell off a ladder. Her right shoulder is broken and the wrist badly sprained, which means, of course, that she's completely unable to take care of a child.'

'So she's in emergency care? Does everyone realise who she is, how sensitively this has to be handled?'

'How can I possibly answer that until I've spoken to someone?' Wendy snapped. 'And she's no more special a case than any of our other children.'

'So the answer's no, no one does know, which means the poor little mite could be somewhere totally unsuitable with people who have no idea what she's been through, or how to cope with her issues.'

'Carers aren't just selected at random,' Wendy reminded her sharply. 'Now, if you don't mind . . .'

'They are when it's an emergency,' Tracy interrupted. 'Did Carrie give you a number? Which hospital is she in?'

'The Weston General, and her number's there, on that pad.'

Quickly jotting it down, Tracy said, 'If you like, I'll chase up West Somerset myself to try and find out where Chloe is.'

Going to dump her bags on the nearest empty desk, Tracy picked up the phone. 'Carrie, it's Tracy Barrall. I'm sorry to hear about your accident,' she said as soon as Carrie answered.

'Not as sorry as I am,' Carrie groaned weakly. 'I should have made sure the ladder was anchored properly. Just lucky I didn't come down on top of little Chloe, that's all I can say. Do you know how, or where she is yet?'

404

'I'm about to try and find out. What happened after the fall? Who called the ambulance?'

With a tired sort of chuckle, Carrie said, 'Would you believe, Chloe did it? I had to tell her what to do, of course, but she picked up the phone, good as gold, and dialled 999. She even whispered ambulance, but I don't think they heard so I shouted it as best I could and next thing I knew, well, about ten minutes later, it was like a circus in my house. Police, ambulance, even the fire brigade came, I suppose in case I was trapped. Anyway, they shipped me off to the General and I'm guessing one of the coppers stayed with Chloe until social services turned up.'

'Why on earth didn't you give them my number? I'd have come straight away.'

'Oh, Tracy, I was in that much pain . . . I only thought of it after. She'll be all right though, won't she? I mean, the police know what to do in these situations.'

'Yes, of course, I'd just like to know where she is. Do you have the name of the social worker . . . No, because you didn't see anyone. What about the police? Did you get any of their names?'

'No, I'm afraid not, but if you ring up they're bound to know who came.'

'Of course. I'll do it now.'

'Please let me know how you get on,' Carrie insisted as Tracy started to hang up.

'I will,' Tracy promised, and turning on the computer she quickly downloaded the details of West Somerset Council and Avon and Somerset Police.

Charlotte was lying on her side, gazing at Anthony's face as he slept. He looked so peaceful, so at ease with his surroundings, if he even knew where he was given how deeply he was breathing. Beneath the white cotton sheet he was as naked as she was. She wondered if, like her, he would feel a bruising ache in his muscles when he woke up.

Simply to think of the way he'd made love to her, so tenderly and yet with such passion, caused her heart to catch and more desire to shoot sharply through her. She wanted to feel him covering her body again, pressing the length of his legs over hers, pushing between them and sliding slowly, exquisitely into her. No one had ever brought her to a climax before, but he had, repeatedly through the night, making her cry out and cling to him in helpless ecstasy while his own release shuddered silently, explosively between them.

She wondered how it was going to be when he woke up and remembered where he was, and what had happened. Would he regret it, feel angry with himself for taking such an impulsive and fateful step?

Had it been impulsive?

'I've wanted to do that for some time,' he'd told her after their first kiss last night.

'Would you mind,' she'd whispered, her lips still very close to his, 'doing it again?'

And so he'd swept her against him, pushing his tongue into her mouth and letting her whole body know how powerfully he desired her.

It had all felt so natural, so necessary and fraught with the need to be as close as their bodies would allow. Their clothes were strewn across the floor like stepping stones into the bedroom; the wine he'd poured later was still in glasses each side of the bed – they'd been too eager to make love again to drink it.

She wanted to put a hand on his chest, to rub her cheek over the stubble on his chin, to wrap her legs around him and feel him entering her again.

So why didn't she?

What was it about morning that turned lovers into strangers and stole courage and confidence away?

Flipping back the sheet she rose carefully from the bed, not wanting to disturb him, and taking her robe from behind the door she crossed the hall into the main bathroom. There were few supplies in the cabinet, but enough for her to rinse her mouth with toothpaste and run a comb through her knotted hair. Her eyes looked almost feverishly bright, she realised, as she peered at herself in the mirror, and the creamy texture of her cheeks seemed to glow, as though the feelings inside her were burning through her skin. She thought of his hands on her body, and gave a gasp as the pleasure of it shot forcefully through her.

Please don't let him regret it.

Please don't let this turn into the biggest mistake of my life.

It didn't feel wrong; it felt like the most beautiful thing that had ever happened to her, but how were they to go forward from here? Was it possible for him to remain as her lawyer? She was depending on him to keep her out of prison, even to get Chloe back for her . . .

Chloe.

Her heart seemed to collapse around the name. What had been happening to her through the night while she, Charlotte, had forgotten all about her? *Please let her have been sleeping peacefully; let her never know that there had been even a minute when she wasn't uppermost in my mind.*

'You can't make your whole life about Chloe.' Her mother's words came back to her like a lost echo finding its way home.

Going to the kitchen she made a pot of coffee and carried a mug through to the sitting room where she stood at the window, gazing down at the empty carousel. She was like a bereaved mother longing for her lost child, but at least she had the comfort of knowing Chloe was alive, small though that comfort felt at times. Had she let her down by doing what she had last night? Had she allowed an overwhelming physical desire to put their future in jeopardy?

It was a relationship that couldn't possibly go anywhere, so what did she expect to happen now? The truth was, she expected, or at least longed for, so many things that the euphoria and trepidation of her dreams was too tangled to allow her happiness to last, or her fears to take root. She wanted Anthony to come and put his arms around her and tell her that nothing had changed, but how could he do that when everything had?

Hearing him enter the room she turned to look at him, and her breath caught around her heart. He was naked and semi-aroused, and looking at her in a way that increased the turbulence inside her.

Coming to her he took the mug from her hand, put it on the table, and unbelted her robe. 'What are you thinking about?' he whispered, sliding his hands on to her hips.

Her desire was so intense it wasn't easy to speak. 'I hardly know where to begin,' she replied shakily.

'Are you sorry? Upset?'

She shook her head. 'I don't think so. Just afraid that you'll have to stop being my lawyer, and I . . .'

'It's not going to happen,' he told her. 'We'll have to keep it to ourselves, of course, but we don't need to discuss it now,' and easing the robe from her shoulders, he pressed his mouth to hers and began making love to her all over again.

Chloe was curled up on a bed with Boots, facing a wall that had big flowers splashed all over it and words she didn't understand scribbled all over them. She thought the words had been written on with biros and pencils, but the flowers were part of the paper that was peeling back at the top and scuffed and broken all down the edges.

The bed didn't smell very nice, not like her bed at the bach, which had smelled of soap and Mummy and other good things.

Was it her fault Carrie had fallen off the ladder?

It had scared her so much when it happened that she'd run and hidden under the stairs, but then Carrie had told her she had to come and help, so she'd done as she was told and pressed some numbers into the phone.

It had scared her again when lots of people had come crowding into the house. She'd kept looking for Mummy, but she hadn't been with them. Carrie had been crying, she was hurting so much.

If Carrie hadn't put Boots up on the bookcase it wouldn't have happened, but Chloe hadn't told anyone that because she didn't want to get Carrie, or Boots, into trouble. Nor did she want to talk to anyone except Mummy and Nanna – and Grandpa, because she had to be nice to him.

The lady who'd brought her here to this house

was called Alice. She'd said that she didn't really like being called out in the middle of the night, but someone had to do it, and it was her turn.

'We've found a place to tide you over,' she'd told her, 'it shouldn't be for long.'

Chloe had hung her head. She didn't want to go with the lady, or talk to her, or do anything except find Mummy, but Mummy was feeling such a long way away now that she was beginning to think she wouldn't ever come.

'You blubbing again?' the girl on the other bed snapped. 'Can't you shut up for five minutes?'

The girl's name was Carla and she was *fourteen for God's sake*. That was what she'd shouted down the stairs to the man and lady who lived in the house, who were called Dave and Mel. There was a boy here too called Ashley who was about the same age as Danni, but he had a different colour skin and spoke in a way Chloe didn't understand. He had his own bedroom along the landing and Carla said he hardly ever came out of it.

'Thank God, mouthy little shit,' she'd added.

Chloe didn't want to go out of the bedroom either, because Dave was downstairs and he had a computer and looked a bit like Daddy and she didn't want to play ride the tiger ever again. Except with Grandpa, if it would make Mummy love her and take her back to the bach.

Mel said she had to stay in this room till she found her manners and told them her name.

'Tell her to fuck off next time,' Carla had advised. 'She's just a sad, fat old cow who's only doing this for the money, because that lazy arsehole she's married to can't be bothered to get a job.'

Chloe hadn't understood very much of that, but

she did understand that Carla didn't want to be stared at, so she was doing as she was told and lying with her face to the wall while Carla crayoned in her eyes and rubbed something over her skin to turn it the same colour as Ashley's.

'I don't give a fuck what they say,' Carla suddenly spat angrily, 'I'm going out to meet me mates and that's that. Have you got any money?'

Chloe wasn't sure if Carla was talking to her so she stayed as she was, clinging on to Boots.

'Oi, you,' Carla shouted, 'I said have you got any money?' and grabbing Chloe she spun her on to her back to search the pockets of her jeans. 'Should have known,' she snorted when she found they were empty. 'They don't never let you have nothing once they takes you into care.' She picked up a file and began rubbing it around her nails, the way Mummy and Nanna sometimes did theirs.

Feeling another sob rising up in her throat Chloe turned back to the wall, afraid Carla would see she was crying and shout at her again.

'So where's your old lady then?' Carla demanded. 'Or was it your dad who dumped you on the street? That's what mine did to me, the fucker. I'm so going to damage him when I get back there. He's taking it out on me because my old lady run off with some muppet from Birmingham. Don't blame her meself, cos all my bastard dad ever did was knock her about and take all her cash. Fucking men, I hate 'em. Total waste of skin if you ask me.'

Chloe kept her face to the wall and jumped as Carla banged abruptly out of the room and thundered down the stairs.

'Oi! Where do you think you're going?' Chloe heard someone shout.

'Mind your own fucking business,' Carla shouted back.

The door slammed and for a long time there was nothing to hear, apart from the TV downstairs and the roar of traffic outside.

Chloe was hungry, but she couldn't tell anyone because it would mean having to speak and if she said something wrong, like she used to with Daddy, she'd have to be punished, and then she might wet herself and she'd have to be punished again. So she stayed curled up in a ball with Boots, hoping Mel and Dave would forget she was there and that Carla would come back with some biscuits or sweets she was willing to share.

Or Mummy would come to find her.

She wanted to go to the toilet now, so badly that she couldn't wait any longer, so getting up from the bed she crept out to the landing, taking Boots with her, because he was brave, and tried to remember which door was the bathroom. Finding the right one she went inside, pulled down her jeans and pants and tried to get up on the toilet. It was too high, she kept sliding off and then she was weeing all over her legs and the floor and couldn't make herself stop.

'What the bloody hell's going on here?' Mel demanded, coming in with her hand on her chest as she coughed and retched and sounded as though she was going to be sick. 'Oh for God's sake, look at the mess you're in,' she wheezed, hauling Chloe up by one arm and standing her on her feet.

'No, no, don't pull hair,' Chloe cried, cowering away. 'Please don't pull hair.'

'What?' Mel snorted. 'What's the matter with you? I'm not going to pull your hair, you stupid child.

Come here! Look at the state of you, peeing all over yourself. You're old enough to know better. How old are you?'

Chloe put her head down and tried to struggle up her jeans.

'No, no, no, they'll have to go in the wash now,' Mel snapped. 'Take 'em off. Have you got any clean pants in the bag you came with? You better have, or you'll be going without until these dry. Oh, for the love of God, who's that knocking at the door now? *Dave*, can you get that?' and sitting Chloe on the cold tiled floor she began tugging off her trainers so she could start sorting her out.

A couple of minutes later Dave shouted from the bottom of the stairs, 'It's someone from social services about the new kid.'

'Just who we need,' Mel muttered with a cough. 'Is it Alice? Tell her to come up.'

By the time the bathroom door opened Chloe was standing in an empty bath wearing only her vest.

'Oh dear, oh dear, what's happened?' Tracy murmured, going straight to her as she saw how hard she was crying. 'What's the matter, my love? Did you have a bit of an accident?'

As Chloe nodded, Mel eyed Tracy with some suspicion. 'Are you new?' she asked. 'Don't think I've seen you before.'

'That's because I'm with Dean Valley,' Tracy explained. 'Chloe here is one of my girls, aren't you sweetie? Oh now, don't get yourself into a state, everything's going to be all right.'

'So if she's with you, what the bloomin' heck's she doing all the way up here with me?' Mel wanted to know.

413

Dabbing Chloe's cheeks with a towel, Tracy said, 'Why don't we get her cleaned up, then we can talk? Does she have any fresh clothes?'

'I'm hoping so. I'll go and check the bag she came with.'

Left alone with Chloe, Tracy said, 'You poor little thing. What an awful weekend you've had, what with Carrie falling over and all those policemen and paramedics coming to the house. Then you had to go off with someone you didn't know. It was all a bit of an emergency, I'm afraid, so it couldn't be helped, but you don't have to worry. I've found a lovely place for you to go next. It's not all that far from here with a very nice lady called Jane. Unfortunately, she won't be ready to take you until Thursday, which is three days from now, so you'll have to stay here till then, but when you get there you'll have your own bedroom and lots of toys to play with and a garden with a swing. You'll like that, won't you?'

'Go to Mummy?' Chloe gasped through her sobs.

'Sssh, sssh,' Tracy soothed, lifting her up. 'I'm going to give you a nice little wash now, and I've brought some biscuits and orange juice with me which you can have when you're dressed.'

By the time she had Chloe sitting on the bed with a biscuit and carton of orange, Mel was in the midst of a coughing fit that would have alarmed Tracy greatly if she'd cared enough. 'Are you OK?' she asked, as Mel panted her way out to the landing.

'Yeah, yeah, I'll be all right,' Mel rasped, dabbing the tears from her eyes. 'So what's going on then? How long's she going to be here?'

'Until Thursday if that's OK,' Tracy replied. 'She

shouldn't have been brought here in the first place, actually, because she's supposed to be with a single woman who has no other children in residence, but the local authority wasn't to know that, with her being under our care . . .'

Mel waved a hand as she started to cough again. 'Well, it all sounds cock-eyed to me,' she finally managed, 'but as long as I get what I'm due . . .'

'Of course you will. I'm just sorry I can't take her with me today, but I'll be back first thing on Thursday. Meantime, do you have a kiddie seat for the toilet and a step to get up there?'

'There's something around here somewhere,' Mel replied, glancing about the gloom. Tracy shuddered to think what might be lurking there. When had this place last had a hygiene check? Not in a while, that was for sure.

'Well, if you could look it out that should help to avoid any more accidents,' she said, 'and if it turns out you need a new one I'm sure Alice will see that you're reimbursed.' She hadn't actually met Alice, the local social worker, and wasn't in much of a hurry to either, given how short she'd been on the phone. However, they were all overworked and underpaid, and the stress got to most in the end. 'I'll just pop back in and say cheerio to Chloe. Is someone sharing her room at present?'

With a roll of her eyes, Mel said, 'Let's put it this way, there was up until an hour ago. Whether she'll come back is anyone's guess. I'd say probably not until she's hungry or can't find anywhere else to spend the night, which is when she usually shows up.'

Knowing this was a fairly typical story with emergency carers, but never particularly enjoying hearing it, Tracy asked, 'How old is the girl? How long has she been here?'

'She's fourteen, and Alice brought her a couple of days ago, but it's not the first time we've had her. She's in and out of here as often as the bloody postman, and right little tramp she is too, but obviously no fault of her own. You have to blame the parents, don't you, or rents as they call 'em these days. And the boy we've got's no better. He's only ten and I'm telling you he'd stab you as soon as look at you, which is why his old man's been shipped off to jail. Got done for sticking the missus, who's still in hospital recovering. Should be out tomorrow or the next day, he can go home again then. So what's your girl's story? Anything I should know about?'

'It's complicated,' Tracy hedged, 'but she's definitely not going to stab you, or run off and not come back.'

Mel nodded and coughed again. 'No, well, she's a bit small for all that, in't she? The cute mute is what Dave's calling her, and I suppose it about fits. All I've heard her say so far is "don't pull my hair" like I was going to do that.'

'Why did she say it?' Tracy asked cautiously.

'I don't bloody well know, you'll have to ask her.'

Wondering if Chloe had reacted to a fear from her past, Tracy said, 'She's still in a state of trauma at the moment, so you need to go gently with her and don't press her too hard to speak. The psychologists and therapists have everything in hand, they'll be starting work with her as soon as their assessments are done,' and leaving Mel to a fresh bronchial attack, she returned to the bedroom to find Chloe

416

with crumbs down her front and an empty carton of orange clutched in one hand.

'Was that nice?' she asked, taking the carton away. 'Would you like some more?' Though the additional supplies were for the little boy she was due to see on her return to Kesterly, she gave them up readily when Chloe nodded. She could always stop at a garage to pick up something else. 'OK, so you eat that nicely now,' she said, unwrapping another Jaffa cake, 'and like I said, I'll be back for you on Thursday.'

She'd be all right until then, she reassured herself, as she waved from the door. It was only three days, and then she'd be off to . . . Well, to someone else Tracy didn't know called Jane, but that was what happened when they had to place children out of the area.

What was going on with the adoption proceedings? Tracy wondered as she got into her car. Had Tommy managed to exert some influence on high to get them delayed? She hadn't had a chance to ask him before he left; if she had, she'd have told him that she was now firmly of the opinion that finding a good adoptive family for Chloe would be the best way to go.

She'd have a chat with Wendy as soon as she found the time. Maybe together they could persuade them upstairs that the best interests of the child were not being served by this delay.

Coming up behind Charlotte at the kitchen sink, Anthony slipped his arms around her and bent to kiss her neck.

'Mm,' she murmured, leaning back into him. 'Are you sure you want to keep doing that? You know what happened the last time, and I thought you wanted to be on the four o'clock train.'

Laughing, he straightened up and turned her to face him. 'I should be back by tomorrow evening, Saturday at the latest,' he reminded her.

'And then you're going fishing with Ron and a couple of other friends, so I won't actually see you until Sunday. It's OK, I'll survive.'

'Ah, but will I?' he countered, touching his mouth to hers.

As the kiss deepened and their seemingly unquenchable desire flared all over again, he said, 'You're making this very difficult, you know.'

'Really? It feels pretty easy to me,' she murmured back.

With a droll raise of his eyebrows he finally let her go, and forced himself back to the sitting room to pack up the laptop and papers he'd spread out over the much larger table they'd bought earlier in the week. As yet there were still only two dining chairs, but they'd ordered four more, due to arrive next Tuesday, in time for Ron and Maggie to come for dinner.

'No point trying to keep anything secret from my sister,' he'd said, after inviting them, 'of course she'd guessed anyway and is as thrilled as I thought she'd be. So now,' he'd continued teasingly, 'provided we can behave ourselves in company, I think we should follow up with an invitation for your sister and brother-in-law. Have you told them about us yet?'

The question alone had made Charlotte's heart leap with all kinds of excitement, while its implications sent her hopes, her dreams into total chaos. She loved the way he spoke so easily, so confidently of their relationship, in spite of having to keep it a secret from the world at large. It was as if he'd already made up his mind that it was exactly what they both wanted, and God knew she did, how could she not when she was already completely mad about him? She just couldn't help being mindful of all the reasons why, in the long term, it simply couldn't work. He wasn't blind to them either, obviously, but try as she might she couldn't persuade him to discuss them.

'I'm insane,' she'd told Gabby only yesterday on the phone, while he was out buying the papers. 'I should never have let this happen. I hardly know what I'm thinking from one minute to the next, and if he tells me one more time to *stop thinking* I'm going to flippin' well crown him.'

Laughing, Gabby said, 'I think I might be in love with him myself, if he's managing to boss you around. Honestly, you really need to ease up. OK, everything feels in crisis to you right now . . .'

'How can it not be when my freedom and a little girl's life are at stake?'

'But Chloe's life isn't at stake. No one's going to kill her, or abuse her, or in any way neglect her while she's in care . . .'

'Which just goes to show how much you know!' Charlotte cried. 'Oh God, I hardly know what to do I'm so worried about her, and even if I did my hands are tied, or my ankle is braceleted, and then I start doubting myself in a way that drives me out of my mind. Am I really the person she should be with? Would someone else be better for her? Do I have any idea about what children need?'

'Will you stop,' her mother had commanded when she'd poured out the same stream of fears to her. (Anthony had been in the bath then, listening to the radio news with the door closed.) 'Darling, I understand how anxious you feel about Chloe . . .'

'It's not only that, Mum. What if I end up in prison? I can't expect him to wait for me or come and visit. Oh my God, even to think of it . . .'

'He's not exactly ignorant of the situation you're in,' her mother pointed out. 'Now, please try to calm down and think more rationally. Your worst nightmares are not coming true today, they might not even come true in the future, so the important thing is to enjoy what's happening now and try to trust to the fact that everything is meant to be, and that on a level we can't actually see, or even understand, it is all working out perfectly.'

Her mother's favourite mantra, *everything is meant to be. It is all working out perfectly* was a new one on Charlotte. To her surprise it had kind of had the desired effect, because she'd definitely been a bit calmer since their chat.

She just felt so damned guilty about being happy with Anthony, when Chloe might be missing her and longing for her in a way she could do nothing about.

'You're frowning,' Anthony informed her.

Turning to find him leaning against the door frame, she felt her heart lurch pleasurably simply to look at him. 'Actually I was thinking about how much I'm going to miss you,' she sighed, coming to put her arms around him. 'And wondering how on earth I'm going to fill the time.'

Sliding his hands to her bottom to pull her in closer, he said, 'I thought Gabby was coming up for the day tomorrow?'

'She is, and I'm meeting Maggie on Saturday while you're flinging your rods about, and I was thinking I should probably have another look at my statement.'

'Not a bad idea,' he said, pressing a kiss to her forehead, 'it'll be good for you to have everything straight in your mind.'

'The papers are due to be served next Friday,' she stated flatly, as if he didn't already know.

'Indeed they are, so we'll know then how the prosecution's shaping up its case. I'm not worried, and I promise, you don't need to be either – unless there's something you haven't told me.'

She managed a smile at the tease in his voice. 'You know everything there is to know about me,' she assured him. 'Which,' she added playfully, 'is more than I can say about you.'

'Wow, is that the time already?' he replied, glancing at his watch.

She eyed him meaningfully.

'I've never been much good at talking about myself,' he confessed, 'but I'm sure Maggie's told you all the juicy stuff.'

'Possibly, but it's the deepest, darkest secrets I'm after.'

His eyebrows shot up. 'Are you kidding? I want you to fall madly in love with me, not go running scared to the other side of the world,' and before she could respond to that, he kissed her full on her open mouth, picked up his overnight bag and left.

'Mum! I'm sorry to wake you,' Charlotte whispered into the phone, 'but I need to know, do you think it's possible to fall in love in less than a week?'

Laughing sleepily, Anna said, 'Darling, it can take

less than a heartbeat and you know it, so what's happened?'

'Nothing. I mean, it was something Anthony said . . . He's gone to London now, but he's left me in a bit of a spin.'

'So what did he say?'

After repeating it, Charlotte said, 'So was he saying he doesn't want me to go back to New Zealand once it's all over – I mean, if I'm not in prison?'

'I'm not sure,' Anna replied. 'I guess it sounds that way, but he could have just been teasing, because it's what you did the last time he showed an interest in you.'

'Mm, I did, didn't I, but the circumstances were a bit different then.'

'True. Why don't you ask him?'

'No! No, I can't do that. If it was just a throwaway line, and I'm sure it was, he'll think I'm getting too serious.'

'But you are serious.'

'Am I?'

'Aren't you?'

'Yes, I suppose so, but he might not be . . .'

'Darling, he's postponed his round-the-world trip for you; he's taken on your case, and he's practically moved in with you. So exactly what part of that doesn't sound serious to you?'

Charlotte's insides were fluttering wildly as she broke into a smile. 'When you put it like that . . .'

'I can't think of any other way to put it, but given time I'm sure you'll find a problem in there somewhere.'

'Well, the problem's pretty obvious, really. What's going to happen when the trial's over and he has a

422

convicted criminal for a partner who he might only get to see every other Sunday for the next seven years?'

'There you go again, writing your own future when life might have other plans completely. Just let things happen, darling. You're not in the driving seat over this, whether you like it or not, so my advice is to take a deep breath, think of how happy he's making you and let him do what he has to to to get you through this. Remember, he's as keen for a positive outcome as you are.'

Faintly dizzied by how wonderful that made her feel, Charlotte said, 'Of course. And he keeps saying he's not worried, so there's no reason for me to be either, except it's my freedom, my life, that's at stake here. And Chloe's. She's who really matters, and I keep feeling as though she's getting lost in all this . . .'

'Just because you're not thinking about her every minute of every day doesn't mean she's getting lost.'

'No, I realise that, but not seeing her, not knowing anything about her . . . It's hard to put into words . . .'

'Then stop trying,' her mother chided gently. 'And try to remember that Chloe's life journey is her own. I know that's hard to deal with, especially when it's proving so harsh; believe me, I don't find it easy either, but whatever she's been put on this earth to experience is a part of her karma, her destiny. Just as it was mine to lose my family the way I did, and yours to be brought up by the rector and his wife. I've no idea why things happen the way they do, but I do know that if I hadn't lost everyone I love I'd never have met Bob. And if I'd brought you up the way I should have, you might never have gone into social work. And if you hadn't chosen that path Chloe wouldn't have come into your life.'

'So there has to be a reason for *why* she did. It can't just have been to make her feel safe and loved for such a short time, only to have it snatched away again. That would be too cruel. How could she possibly deserve that?'

'I'm not sure it's about deserving, unless, as some people believe, we're paying for mistakes from a past life. If that is the case, then some of us have to pay higher prices than others.'

'So you don't think we're masters of our own destinies? You believe that no matter what we say or do, there's some greater force at work that has it all mapped out and so we might as well stop pretending we can change anything, because we can't?' Charlotte sounded sceptical.

'I'm afraid I don't have all the answers, but I can tell you this: we are able to change the way we think about things, or how we deal with them, and one of the most harmful traits in our characters is resistance. That's not to say we should just roll over and let things happen to us, because sometimes we can make a difference. But there are always going to be situations that are beyond our control, and to resist what's happening can cause so much more anger and pain. As much, if not more, than letting our imaginations run away with us, the way you so often do with Chloe.'

'And you didn't with me, after you'd given me up?'

'Of course I did, but eventually I learned what I'm telling you now, that accepting what is, and letting go of what might be, is a far easier way of getting to the end of a difficult road than seeing obstacles that aren't even there.'

With a sigh of understanding as well as longing, Charlotte said, 'I so wish you were here. I really miss you.'

'I miss you too, but how about this? If I had been able to come when all this blew up would things have taken off the way they have with Anthony?'

Charlotte didn't have to consider it for long. 'No, probably not,' she conceded. 'So now you not being here is a good thing? I'm not sure I can quite make myself see it like that, but I take your point. Is your lawyer still trying to get it cleared for you to come?'

'Yes, he is, but he hasn't received the cast-iron reassurance he's looking for yet.'

'I wonder if Anthony can help.'

'I think you'll find he and Don Thackeray are in touch, so if there is anything he can do he's already on to it.'

Surprised, Charlotte said, 'Really? He hasn't mentioned it to me.'

'Maybe because he doesn't want to get your hopes up until he has something positive to tell you.' Anna stifled a yawn. 'Sorry, you know it's three thirty in the morning here.'

'Oh God, of course, sorry, I should let you go. Thanks for the chat and please tell Bob I'm sorry if I woke him up too.'

'He's dead to the world,' Anna assured her.

A few moments ticked by with neither of them ringing off. In the end Charlotte said, 'She'll be all right, won't she?'

'I'm sure she will,' Anna replied softly. 'And so will you.'

Feeling slightly reassured by the words, Charlotte

put the phone down and went to pick up one of the photos of Chloe that her mother had emailed and she'd had printed and framed. It was a big close-up of Chloe laughing, with sand stuck to her cheeks and the light of pure happiness in her eyes. Charlotte remembered taking it; they'd been playing on the beach swing and for the very first time Chloe had found the courage to leap off into the waves. She'd been so flustered when she'd come up for air, gasping and trying to find her feet, that it had taken a moment for total euphoria to kick in.

She'd done it!

Charlotte hadn't been able to get her off the swing for the rest of the day. Everyone had to come and watch, Nanna, Danni, Craig, Auntie Shelley, even Grandpa had been invited, or at least Chloe hadn't shaken her head when Charlotte had suggested it.

It had been a happy, proud day to be cherished along with so many others: the first time she'd ridden a horse with Danni; the day she'd found the confidence to speak to the other children at Aroha; the little part she'd played in the Christmas pageant; the first time one of her cakes had risen; the recognition of a kiwi call; the naming of wild flowers as they drove into town.

So many memories, floating in from the past like leaves to lie gently upon one another with Chloe's face, her little world on every one of them. If only it were possible to pick them up and hold them, to somehow transform them back to reality.

'I don't know where you are now, my angel,' she whispered to the photo as tears blurred her eyes, 'but I hope you can hear me in your heart when I tell you that I love you and I miss you and I'm not giving up hope of getting you back. Not yet. I can't, because seeing you again, hearing you and loving you means the whole world to me. And now,' she added more softly than ever, 'there's someone else I want you to meet who I just know will love you too, given the chance.'

Chapter Twenty-Two

It was hard to believe how quickly the next few weeks passed. It seemed no sooner had the papers been served than the Plea and Case Management hearing was upon them, and Charlotte was standing in front of a judge pleading not guilty to a crime the whole world knew she'd committed.

'It happens all the time,' Anthony had reassured her after, 'and you're not under oath so you don't have to feel squeamish about upsetting God, or anyone else upstairs.'

'I was actually more concerned about my conscience, and how I'm being given such a hard time in the press again.'

'They'll get over it, and the only people we have to worry about are the twelve who'll be sitting on the jury and they won't be coming to a decision until they've heard you tell what happened in your own words, a privilege no one else has been afforded.'

It was true, they hadn't, but was it really going to make all the difference? She guessed she wouldn't know until the day, but what she did know now was that rumours of their relationship had started up on Twitter.

'Someone's obviously been watching us,' she told

him, unnerved by the thought of it. 'I'd guess at Heather Hancock, but it could have been anyone. God, I couldn't bear it if another barrister had to step in now.'

'Don't worry, I'm not going to let that happen. Maybe we haven't been as careful as we should have, but there's no proof we're actually having a relationship, just that we're spending a lot of time together, and as your lawyer why shouldn't I be spending time with you?'

'But someone's added the fact that you were supposed to be on a sabbatical when you took the case on.'

Looking genuinely annoyed by that, he said, 'Well, that was very obliging of them, but we don't have to explain ourselves to anyone, and nor are we going to try. We'll just simply deny it if anyone asks us outright, otherwise we'll ignore it. Now, my darling, my love,' (this was what he called her these days and she had to admit she quite liked both, together she loved it) 'prepare yourself for some good news.'

Her heart skipped a beat as a hundred thoughts tripped over each other in the rush to guess what it could be. The case was being thrown out after all. The prosecution had decided to drop it. He'd heard something about Chloe.

'We've finally received an assurance from the police that they are not looking to make any more arrests in this case,' he declared, 'which means your mother is able to be here for the trial.'

Charlotte gasped as tears suddenly filled her eyes. 'Oh Anthony,' she cried, running to throw her arms around him. 'This is fantastic, I mean if there *has* to be a trial, and I suppose there has.'

'I'm afraid so, but having your mother and

stepfather here won't only be a great support for you, it could make a big impact on the jury to see the family Chloe was a part of during the time she was with you. Not that we can make this about Chloe, you understand, it's a criminal trial, not a custody hearing. But it's a vital part of the defence to make sure the jury understands and is impressed by the fact that she had a far better life with you than she ever did with her parents.'

'That shouldn't be hard when it's true,' Charlotte murmured. Thinking of Chloe with her abusive father and demented mother always dimmed the light inside her, but the fact that her mother was coming was a joy that, for the moment at least, couldn't be put down.

'We'll have to get a bed for the other room,' she declared, 'and more linen and crockery and . . .'

'Wait, wait,' he laughed. 'We can do that, for sure, but when I spoke to Bob earlier . . .'

'You've already spoken to Bob?'

'About an hour ago.'

'But it was the middle of the night there.'

'I'd had strict instructions to call, whatever the time, if I heard the way was clear for them to come.'

'So you told them before you told me?'

'Because I wanted to tell you in person.'

She smiled, and gazed at him adoringly. 'I'm glad you did,' she whispered.

'Keep looking at me like that and the rest of my news will have to wait,' he warned.

Quickly pulling a straight face, while keeping her hips pressed to his, she waited for him to continue.

'Bob and your mother will be arriving this weekend . . .'

'*This weekend!*'

'. . . and they feel that four of us in this apartment will make it a little overcrowded. Obviously, I offered to move back to Maggie's . . .'

Her eyes widened in protest.

'. . . but they're insisting we book them into a hotel nearby, so can I suggest, once we've dealt with the situation that seems to be arising between us at the moment, that we take a stroll along to the Grand to check out their rooms?'

'You may suggest it, and I accept, but definitely only after we've taken care of the situation you mention.'

'God, I've missed you,' he laughed, and pressing his mouth to hers he began walking her backwards towards the bedroom.

It was incredible, almost bizarre, how happy she was at a time when she'd never been so afraid. Having Anthony in her life had changed so much: he'd become the centre of her world, as she seemed to be of his, and she couldn't, *wouldn't*, allow herself to think of being taken from him. Occasionally she'd watch him from the window as he crossed the street to his car, or while he lay asleep in bed beside her, and her heart would overflow with so much feeling she hardly knew how to keep it in. The only time they spent apart now was when he was in London or Bristol having meetings with the other lawyers on her case, and even then barely an hour would pass without the exchange of a text or email.

They'd done so much together over the last two months that she'd started to keep a diary of it, something to treasure later, she told herself, though where and when she refused to contemplate. It was Anthony's plan, she knew, to try and take her mind off the trial and Chloe, and what the future might have in store. And often it worked, as they walked on the beach in all winds and weathers, talking about everything from the holidays they'd had as children to his love of sailing and good wines and fishing, and hers of amateur theatre, children and interior design. Not that she'd had much experience in the latter, but it was an interest she'd decided to pursue once this was all over, though whether that was going to be seven weeks or seven years from now only time would tell.

'You won't get the maximum sentence,' he'd told her firmly and repeatedly. 'There are no aggravating circumstances and absolutely no harm came to Chloe while she was with you. Quite the reverse, in fact. Nor was anyone deprived of their child, given that her father was already in jail, and no one's ever going to want to see her returned to him. So please put the seven years out of your mind.'

'And replace it with what?'

'Trust. Now, let's change the subject and discuss what we're going to have for dinner.' Or breakfast, or lunch, depending on the time of day the conversation took place.

He was resolute in his refusal to enter into a guessing game, or a series of what-ifs, or even a review of similar cases and how they'd worked out. As far as he was concerned the legal team had everything in hand, and as they were regularly feeding him information his command of the case, at this stage, was absolute.

So their time was spent in ways that were making her fall more deeply in love with him than ever, mainly because of how sensitive and intuitive he seemed to be to her needs and how to distract her.

It would never have occurred to her that a visit to her family's grave at St Mark's churchyard in Temple Fields could mean so much at this time, but it had. Probably, she realised later, because Anthony had been with her, and had listened quietly as she'd told him what little she knew of her grandmother, grandfather, aunt and half-brother, Hugo. Her father's burial place was too far distant for them to visit while she was tagged, but they'd talked about him anyway. The only memory she had of him felt more like a dream: a tall, fair-haired man catching her up in his arms and swinging her round and round until she was too dizzy to see.

A week after the visit to the cemetery Anthony had managed to get her a pass for the day, and had driven her to York to visit Millie in her care home. She'd shed an ocean of tears while there, and on the way back, for dear old Millie hadn't known who she was; she hadn't even seemed to register anyone was there. Her eyes were no more than vacant blue discs sinking to the sides of their sockets, her hands bunched like claws in front of her pallid face. It was the longest, cruellest wait for death, and Charlotte could only wish it would hurry up and come, because the Millie she'd known, spiky, loving and fiercely independent, would never have wanted to wither away like this. Still, at least she'd been able to kiss her goodbye, and take heart from the fact that visiting Millie had made a nonsense of the feeling she'd had the day the old lady had been taken to York, that she would never see her again.

Please, please let the feeling she'd never see Chloe again be equally wrong.

*   *   *

'I thought you was never coming back for her,' Mel Beacher grumbled as she let Tracy in out of the rain. 'Three days you told me when you was last here.'

'I know, I'm sorry, it all got complicated, the person she was supposed to go to had a problem crop up, then I got the flu and no one else was available to come . . . Anyway, how is she?'

'Silent as ever, and in disgrace if you must know.'

Tracy frowned. Chloe wasn't naughty, at least not the Chloe she knew.

'She's been sneaking out at night with that bloody Carla,' Mel rasped, starting to cough.

Not sure she'd heard that right, Tracy said, 'Sneaking out at night? With Carla? Who's Carla?'

'The girl what was here before. Well, she's still here and trying my patience till I'm ready to swing for her, that's for sure.'

Tracy's eyes widened.

'Don't worry, I don't never lay a hand on 'em that way, though half of 'em would be better off for a good clip round the ear, I don't mind telling you.'

'What do you mean, Chloe's been going out at night?' Tracy demanded, bringing them back to the point.

'What I said. I puts her to bed, good as gold with that tatty old bear of hers, and next thing I know she's gone. God knows what those girls want with a kid that age out there on the streets with 'em, cos that's where they'm hanging out, got nowhere else to go, have they? Went bloody mental I did first time the police brought 'em back.'

Tracy was stunned. 'Why on earth was I never told about this?' she cried. She'd have had Chloe out of here faster than she could say her own name if she'd known what was happening, even if it had meant putting her into residential care.

'I don't know,' Mel grunted. 'Social services was told, because obviously they'm both under age, so the police had to contact them. I suppose, cos they'm both already in care, there wasn't much else they could do. I'm telling you though, someone's got to get that Carla in hand, because she's a right bloody nightmare, she is. I've told 'em, she's too much for me with my chest, they have to find someone else, but they're taking their bloody time over it. Can you have a word with someone?'

'I'm not with your authority,' Tracy reminded her, 'but yes, I'll make some calls. Can I see Chloe now? Is her bag packed?'

'Yep, she's all ready to go. Don't take no notice of the bruises on her face now, will you, she got them thanks to some little bastard at playgroup pushing her over. Don't worry, I had her checked out to make sure she hadn't cracked her skull, or anything, and the doctor said she was fine.'

More eager than ever to get to Chloe now, Tracy hurried through to the sitting room to find Chloe standing behind the couch where Mel's husband, Dave, was sprawled out in a mountain of flab watching the Jeremy Kyle show. 'Hello sweetie,' she smiled, going straight to lift Chloe in her arms. 'I'm sorry I haven't seen you for a while, but I'm here now and you're coming with me. Is that nice?'

Chloe's body was limp, her head stayed down and she neither nodded nor shook it.

'And how's Boots?' Tracy prompted. 'Has he been eating all his meals?'

Still Chloe didn't respond, simply held on to the

bear that was dangling raggedly from her right hand.

Turning to Mel as she joined them, Tracy said, 'Has the psychologist seen her lately?'

'Not for a couple of weeks,' Mel replied, trying to stifle another cough. 'I had a call cancelling one appointment, then I couldn't take her last Thursday because my chest was that bad.'

'When's she due to go again?'

'Tomorrow, I think. Or it might be the next day. I'll get her paperwork. Is she staying in this area? I suppose she'll have to change doctors if she's not.'

Unfortunately, a change of psychologist was going to be necessary, but Tracy would deal with that later. For now, she needed to focus on getting Chloe out of here and into the new foster home that had been found for her. It was in the Kesterly area since Family Placements had been unable to find anywhere else, and unfortunately it was on the notorious Temple Fields estate. However, the references for the carer were leaving Tracy in no doubt that Chloe was going to be way better off there than she was here.

It was only when they were in the car and on the way out of Minehead that she realised Chloe hadn't asked to go to Mummy. For some reason this upset Tracy far more than she might have expected. It meant, of course, that the child was giving up, which wasn't unusual, Tracy saw it all the time with children who'd been abandoned, or removed from their parents, even when the parents had been abusing them. Sadly, it was a process that had to be gone through, like grief, in order for them to move on. However, in Chloe's case there was this added worry of what might have happened to her out there on the streets with a gang of teenage girls, and for all she knew boys too. It hardly bore thinking about, yet it was often what happened to small children in care: they became corrupted by older children who'd been in the system for far too long, and there was little that could be done to prevent it.

She'd give Wendy a call as soon as she'd dropped Chloe off, to discuss what could be done about restarting the adoption process. She'd been meaning to do it for ages, but just hadn't had time to get round to it. She would now though, because with the way things were it really, *really* couldn't happen soon enough.

After all the excitement of her mother and Bob arriving and checking into their sea-view room at the Grand hotel, Charlotte wasn't in the least bit prepared for yet more celebrations, especially as she'd intended her thirtieth birthday to be a low-key affair. However, here she was being steered along the hallway of the flat, blindfolded, with Anthony and her mother insisting she didn't peep while the twins gasped and giggled as they dodged her outstretched hands. She knew, because Anthony had told her, that in spite of her instructions everyone had insisted on coming today, so Gabby and Martin, her mother and Bob, Maggie and Ron were all now gathered in the sitting room, while the twins ran in and out. What she didn't know, yet, but was presumably about to find out, was what the big surprise was. She hadn't been allowed into the flat all morning; Anthony had told her that it was because he'd needed Bob's help to get her present upstairs and he didn't want her to see it until it was completely ready. She wasn't sure whether to be taken in by this or not, since it could simply have been a ruse to throw her off the scent of something small, whatever that might be.

So, straight after breakfast her mother and Maggie had turned up to whisk her off to the mall where they'd attempted to spoil her rotten (and largely succeeded, though her mother had stopped when she'd realised how sad it was making her not to be buying for Chloe). Then, when it had come time for her to show herself at the police station, her mother, instead of Anthony, had accompanied her, while Maggie had returned to the flat to check on progress.

Now, Charlotte was reminding herself that what-ever the surprise turned out to be, she must rid herself of the hope that they'd somehow managed to engineer a visit from Chloe. It really wasn't going to happen; she knew that as surely as she knew that her trial was only a week away. Besides, one tiny little girl hardly needed two grown men to carry her up one flight of stairs (presuming this hadn't been said to throw her off the scent); so she was completely at a loss as to what it could be.

'Don't worry, you're going to love it,' Anthony had assured her, when he'd told her last night that she was to make herself scarce while he organised the delivery.

'It's more special than you can possibly imagine,' Gabby had told her on the phone, first thing, and to Charlotte's amazement her sister's voice had been choked with emotion.

'I know it's something you're going to treasure, always,' her mother had assured her, seeming quite misty-eyed too. 'To be honest, I can't wait to see it myself.'

'It's exquisite,' Maggie had sighed. 'My brother's

always been good at presents, but this time I think he's surpassed even himself.'

No big build-up there then, Charlotte was commenting to herself as Anthony kept her on track down the hallway, and what on earth was she going to do if she didn't find herself quite as blown away as everyone else?

She could pretend, of course, but actually, she wouldn't have to, because one of the best parts of being in love, maybe it was even the proof of being in love, was the joy of making the other person happy. And Anthony was happy, she could hear it in his voice, feel it in the way he was holding her, and if it meant this much to him, it was going to mean that much to her too.

It was, it really was.

'Are you ready?' he whispered in her ear.

For a passing moment she wished they were alone, but as she heard the twins begin bouncing up and down, and she sensed the excitement in the air, she gave a wry grin as she said, 'I hope so.'

As everyone laughed, he removed the blindfold and watched as she took in the group of eager faces before realising that her present was right in front of them and it was . . . A bench. A lovely bench, to be sure, with exquisitely shaped arms and legs, and flowers carved into the back panels . . . But it was still a bench, and though she instantly admired and even loved it, she couldn't understand why everyone thought she'd be so enthralled by it.

'Your father made it,' Anthony said softly.

It took less than a moment for Charlotte to gasp and clasp her hands to her face. 'Oh my God, oh my God,' she choked. 'Oh Anthony, how did you find it?'

'I made a little search of the Internet,' he replied, 'and finally tracked someone down who was willing to sell.'

'They're collectors' items now,' her mother told her, running a hand over the wood as lovingly as if the man who'd carved it could feel her touch. There were tears on her cheeks too as the twins looked on, clearly mystified by so much emotion over a *bench*.

Turning to Anthony again, Charlotte put her arms around him and said, so no one else could hear, 'Would this be a good time to tell you I love you for this, and for everything else, actually just for being you?'

His eyes were shining roguishly into hers as he replied, 'Would this be a good time to tell you that Bob and I are going fishing tomorrow?'

With a splutter of laughter, she went to embrace her mother. This present was clearly meaning as much to her as it was to Charlotte, perhaps in some ways more. 'Do you remember him making it?' she asked quietly.

Anna nodded. 'Yes, I do. I was pregnant with you at the time and Hugo was so keen to help.' Her smile faltered as she spoke of the son she'd lost. 'When Anthony told me he'd tracked it down . . .' She had to stop and take a breath. 'He said that he felt your father always seemed to be missing, and he wanted to try and bring him in somehow.' Lifting a hand to Charlotte's face, she said, 'He's a very special man, my darling. I'm so glad you've found him. I know your father would approve, and so do I.'

Turning to where Anthony was helping Martin and Bob with the champagne, while Maggie rustled up a focaccia in the kitchen, Charlotte noticed how shy

Gabby seemed about coming forward. Realising she wasn't sure how she fitted into this, given that she'd always considered her father to be Charlotte's too, Charlotte held out a hand to her. 'The rector will always have a special place in my heart,' she told her, 'you know that. He was impossible not to love.'

Smiling and seeming more at ease, Gabby said, 'He was, wasn't he? And I think he'd really like this bench. It's beautiful. Where are you going to put it?'

Thinking of how perfect it would look outside the bach, Charlotte's eyes went to Anthony's as he brought them a glass of champagne each. 'Well, for as long as we're in this flat, I think it should stay right here, in this room, don't you?' she said.

'Absolutely,' he agreed.

'Auntie Lotte, who's this?' Phoebe asked.

Looking up, Charlotte's heart contracted to see her niece holding a photograph of Chloe. Her eyes shot to her mother, then Gabby, as she tried to think what to say, but they'd been caught off guard too.

'I'll tell you who it is,' Anthony replied, going to look at the photo with her, 'it's a little girl who Auntie Lotte took care of, you know the way she does with children, but this one is special, a bit like you.'

Phoebe's eyes were fixed on this man she hadn't yet got to know. 'What's her name?' she whispered.

'Her name's Chloe.'

Phoebe looked at the picture again. 'Is she my cousin?'

'Well, not exactly, but you make it sound as though you'd like a cousin?'

She nodded eagerly. 'I don't have any girl cousins,'

she told him, 'or a sister, and I don't like being the only girl. Boys are just silly and loud and do stupid things.'

'I know,' he said sympathetically, 'and sadly some of us don't grow out of it, but we do our best.'

Phoebe regarded him approvingly, then putting the picture back on the mantelpiece she skipped off to the kitchen to make sure her brother wasn't wolfing everything down before anyone else got a look-in.

'I had no idea you were so good with children,' Charlotte murmured, moving into the circle of his arm.

'Nor did I,' he replied. 'I think I just got lucky for a minute. So you like the bench?'

Turning to it, she said, 'I absolutely love it. It's the first thing I've ever owned of my father's, and that you gave it to me makes it more precious than ever.' She lifted her face to his. 'Thank you,' she whispered.

'You're welcome,' he whispered back, but as he kissed her his eyes were crossing the room to where Maggie was entering with a large tray of food. 'I think our more private celebration is going to have to wait,' he said softly, 'but an early night's a good idea now I'm having to be up early to go fishing.'

'You really are going fishing?' she cried in surprise.

He nodded. 'I really am, with Bob and Ron. Why, would you like to come?'

Shuddering at the very thought, she said, 'No, thanks, I think I'll spend the day with Mum. She's just the person to help choose a silk seat pad and some cushions for my new bench.' She didn't add that it might be the last chance they'd have to be alone together for longer than she wanted to

442

consider, but the thought was in her mind, and as everyone began tucking into Maggie's delicious frittata Charlotte felt her own appetite fading away.

Charlotte was lying on the sofa with Anthony listening to some old jazz tunes on the iPod system, with rain running down the windows outside and dread gathering in her heart. The trial was due to begin tomorrow; by the end of the following day she might know her fate, and given how much she had to lose she couldn't imagine how she was going to cope if the verdict, when it came, went against her.

Rick and Shelley had flown in yesterday, feeling it important to show support for their stepsister by being there in person, even though their statements, like Bob's and Anna's, could have been read out in their absence. None of them were happy about being called by the prosecution, but Anthony had assured them it was perfectly normal in the circumstances, and since they'd said nothing to give him any cause for concern they had no reason to be worried either.

After hours and hours of preparing Charlotte for her time on the stand, he'd spent most of today in conference with Kim and her boss, Jolyon Crane, who was going to act as Anthony's junior for the next two days. As Kim had put it when she'd rung earlier, 'You've got a crack team supporting you, and the judge we've got tends towards leniency where sentencing's concerned, but I expect Anthony's already told you that.'

He had, but since any sentence at all could mean the end of so much for Charlotte, it was hard to take comfort from the words. Harder still was imagining how awful Anthony was going to feel if things didn't go the way he hoped. He was feeling the responsibility keenly, she knew that, but he was still refusing to discuss what might happen after the trial. Although tonight, when they'd been at dinner with both their families at the Grand, he'd said to her mother, 'There are so many different ways this could go that I don't think it'll be helpful to get into my plans until we know which ones are appropriate.'

'But you do have plans?' Charlotte had challenged.

He'd smiled into her eyes. 'Yes, I have plans,' he confirmed, and that was as far as he'd allowed himself to be drawn.

'Don't worry,' Rick had said, when they'd walked on ahead of the others to say goodnight, 'you'll like the plans once you know what they are.'

Stunned, Charlotte asked, 'You mean he's confided in you and not me?'

'No, no,' he laughed, 'but I think Dad might have an inkling of what they are, which fills me with confidence. Don't quote me, because he hasn't said anything, it's just an impression I got when I saw them chatting earlier. You know what Dad's like, always into everything, and those two seem to get along pretty well.'

'And how are you two getting along these days?' she asked, turning to take both his hands in hers.

'Not bad. He's met Hamish a couple of times now, and he's invited him out to Te Puna when we get back.'

Thinking more longingly than ever of Te Puna, she smiled as she went on tiptoe to kiss him goodnight. 'Thanks for coming,' she whispered, 'it means so much.'

'We had to,' he responded, hugging her close. 'Try

to get some sleep tonight, and if you can, *eat something*. I saw the miserable effort you made over dinner, not that I don't understand, but we don't want you fainting on us tomorrow.'

Thinking now that fainting would be the least of her problems, since she'd been on the verge of throwing up all day, Charlotte linked her fingers round Anthony's as she said, 'If it does turn out that I have to spend time in prison, will you carry on with your plans to travel? I mean, I'd want you to, obviously, I just . . .'

Stopping her with a finger over her lips, he replaced it with his own lips, but this time she pushed him away.

'Anthony, please,' she cried, sitting up, 'I have to know at least something of what's going on in your mind. You're so cool about it all, so uncommunicative that it's driving me nuts. Don't you feel just a little bit worried, because I know I do and I can't go on pretending I don't.'

'Of course I'm worried,' he replied, 'but my way of dealing with it isn't the same as yours. I tend to internalise things more, which I understand can be maddening, but I'm afraid it's the way I am.'

'OK, then just tell me, what worries you most? Is it that I might go to prison? Or that I won't be able to get over losing Chloe for good? Or that you'll be stuck with me if you get me off . . .'

Laughing, he said, 'Stuck with you? I'd hardly put it like that, my darling.'

'Well, however you want to put it. What's going on in your mind, Anthony? Please talk to me, tell me something of what you're thinking.'

'OK,' he said slowly. 'I'm thinking that whatever the outcome is, we will deal with it together and no, I won't go travelling until you're able to come with me. That's not to say,' he went on, seeing the panic in her eyes, 'that I think you're going to receive a custodial sentence, but it could be that we'll need to spend some time in the family courts trying to get Chloe back.'

Merely hearing the words filled her with so much angst and hope that she could only cover her face and pray. There was so much at stake here, so very much, that they hadn't even touched on the fact that a guilty verdict could mean she'd be unable to return to New Zealand. Maybe she wouldn't want to go without Chloe, but what about her mother? After spending so many years apart, they were only just beginning to form the relationship they'd been denied.

And then there was Anthony. She couldn't leave him, couldn't even bear to think of it, but his life was here, whether he continued with the law or not. He'd never said he wanted to leave the country, apart from to travel, and why would he when his family was just down the road and his home and all his friends, his contacts, were in London?

'I know this isn't going to be easy,' he said, 'but I think we should try to change the subject. We need to do something, or talk about something else to distract you from all the craziness going on inside your head.'

Though she didn't disagree, she couldn't begin to imagine what could distract her tonight. She didn't even want to make love, which was most unusual, and unless she was misreading him she didn't think he was much in the mood, either. 'Should we go over my statement again?' she suggested.

'No, we'll do it tomorrow night, when we can adapt it if we need to.'

Accepting the sense of that, she said, 'OK, so what do you usually do the night before a trial? How do you make yourself relax?'

After giving it some thought, he replied, 'To be honest, I don't have any set rituals, I guess because each case is different and some require more input than others.'

With a small, sad smile, she said, 'If it weren't me on trial tomorrow I'd be getting pretty excited by now about seeing you in action for the first time, wearing your wig and gown, objecting, sustaining . . .'

'That's American,' he reminded her.

'Actually, a part of me is excited,' she realised. 'I'm going to feel so proud of you . . .' Turning to look at him, she felt elated all over again by how much he'd come to mean to her. 'You know, you might look like a lawyer,' she said softly, 'and even be a lawyer, but you're nothing like I imagined someone in your position to be.'

He regarded her warily. 'Do I want to know what that is?' he countered.

'Well, you're not stuffy and humourless, or pompous and arrogant. In fact you're one of the kindest, most thoughtful people I know, and that alone would never have fitted with my idea of a barrister before.'

'Ah, I see, you were taken in by the stereotype.'

'I guess I was. Although you have to admit you don't hear of many barristers coming down off their pedestals to get into relationships with social workers, do you?'

His eyebrows rose comically. 'I admit I don't know

of any personally, but you might find there are more than you think.'

'Mm, maybe, but I expect a lot more have partners who are also lawyers, or business tycoons, or high-flying successes of some kind. I was only remarking to Mum today that you must have been leading quite a glamorous life up to now, always off to some cocktail party or fancy dinner, all those opening nights, charity balls and weird rituals you barristers go in for. I'm guessing you do all the big events like Wimbledon and Glyndebourne . . .'

'Wimbledon, yes,' he conceded, 'and the salmon fishing, but I don't go to many of the others.'

'Did you used to, when you were with Anthea?' This was the first time his dead fiancée had been mentioned between them, and she was anxious now about how he might react.

'Let's put it this way,' he replied, after a moment, 'we were often on the guest lists, but we didn't attend every event.'

Knowing it was ridiculous to feel jealous of someone who couldn't possibly be a threat now, she tried to push it aside as she asked, 'What was she like? Why don't you tell me about her?'

A few tense moments ticked by before he finally said, 'OK, well, she was a hat designer, and an excellent tennis player; someone who loved life, wanting to live it to the full, which was why it was so shocking, so hard to grasp when she was taken so suddenly.'

'How old was she when it happened?'

'Thirty-five. She'd just had a birthday. I'd given her a course of flying lessons . . . She was so excited, she'd always wanted to learn to fly, she said, ever since she was a child.'

Knowing that this was how she'd died, Charlotte tightened her grip on his hand as she wondered what kind of guilt he'd tormented himself with since the accident had shattered his world.

'We were due to get married a couple of months later,' he went on, almost to himself. 'She had everything planned, the invitations had gone out, the flowers had been chosen, her dress was ready . . . It was going to be a big event, three hundred people in the gardens of the Inner Temple. All I had to do was organise the honeymoon. I still hadn't come to a decision when I got the news, and the ridiculous thing is, for a long time after I used to think that if I'd already booked somewhere the accident might never have happened. You tell yourself crazy things when you're grieving, or at least I found I did.'

'You obviously loved her very much.'

'Yes, I did, sometimes I thought too much, because I was prepared to marry her even though I knew she didn't want children and I did. I suppose I thought I'd be able to talk her round, though she made it very clear the day she accepted my proposal that she wouldn't change her mind.'

Finding herself struggling with his sadness, she said, 'Was it losing her that made you want to take a break from the law?'

He smiled distantly. 'Yes, it was, though I'd been aware for a while that something was missing, or I wanted more, or . . . I don't know, it's hard to put into words when it's just a gut feeling. Anthea could never understand my doubts, I suppose because I was successful and we were having a great life, so what was the point in trying to change things? The trouble was, she enjoyed the social whirl and the status far more than I did; she was comfortable with it, had more or less grown up with it, whereas I found it all a bit superficial and pointless. I was sure there had to be more to life than having the right address or being seen at the right places with the right people, whoever they might be, on any given day. And when you add to that the skulduggery behind the scenes in my profession . . . Well, let's not even get started on that. Suffice it to say it can be an ugly business, and once this trial is over I won't be sorry to turn my back on it.'

She blinked. 'You mean for a while.'

He sighed and stretched. 'We'll see. Time changes a lot of things, and falling in love again, this soon, wasn't something I was expecting, that's for sure.' He put a hand to her face and gazed into her eyes as he said, 'But I'm very happy I have, even if you have presented me with a bit of a challenge to keep you.'

Chapter Twenty-Three

'Charlotte Nicholls, you are charged with the abduction of Ottilie Wade, also known as Chloe, under Section 2 of the Child Abduction Act. It is alleged that on the evening of 6th October 2011 you took Ottilie Wade, also known as Chloe, from her home on North Hill, Kesterly-on-Sea and removed her to your own residence in the village of Mulgrove. You proceeded to keep her there for a period of five weeks until you removed her to New Zealand. Are you guilty or not guilty?'

The court was so still that Charlotte could hear herself breathing as she said, quietly but clearly, 'Not guilty.'

A murmur of surprise, disapproval, burbled around the room.

What were the jury thinking now? How much did they already know about her and what had happened? She'd watched them file in and had noticed that not one had been able to meet her eyes. Did that mean their minds were already made up?

'I'm bound to tell you this,' Anthony had said when she'd arrived at the court earlier (he'd been wearing his wig and gown by then and had looked so official, so remote, that she'd felt utterly disconcerted). 'I've spoken to the judge and she'll give no more than a suspended sentence for a guilty plea.' His dark eyes, seeming more intense than ever, had increased her shakiness and panic.

'This means you won't go to prison,' Kim had explained unnecessarily. 'There'll be no trial, as such, and when it's over you can be sure of going home.'

Home: the word itself had felt like a sanctuary.

Charlotte's eyes had remained on Anthony's. Was this what he wanted, for her to give up any chance of ever having Chloe back? She'd retain her freedom, they could be together, build a new life somewhere away from here, and eventually, one day, she could maybe put all this behind her.

She'd never be able to do that.

Drawing her aside, he'd told her, 'The decision has to be yours, but whatever it is, I want you to know I'll support you.'

Her response hadn't been easy to get past the lump in her throat. 'I have to know I tried,' she'd said hoarsely. 'For her sake as well as my own.'

His expression had softened, as though he'd known it was what she would say, and looking past her to Kim he'd given a brief shake of his head.

There was to be no guilty plea.

So now, here she was, alone in the dock with rows of black-robed and curled-wig lawyers in the well between her and the Honourable Mrs Justice Caroline Oswald. Justice Oswald's assignment to the case had come out of the blue that morning; as yet no one was clear about what had happened to the judge who should have been sitting. It was hardly relevant, since Justice Oswald was there, in her red robes and ill-fitting horsehair, gazing over the court with a benign sort of severity. What was she thinking? She would surely already have had an opinion by now.

Everyone always brings their past to a party, she remembered her adoptive father once telling her, *whether they intend to or not.*

Even a judge? They weren't supposed to.

Why was she thinking about the rector now? Because, she realised, if there was a God Douglas would certainly be with Him, and maybe he'd put in a word.

Anthony was seated in the front row with Jolyon Crane and someone she hadn't seen before, also in robes. Behind them were Kim and the paralegal team, and behind them a handful of plain-clothed policemen. No sign of Terence Gould. Of course, there wouldn't be. He was being called as a witness.

The press benches were full, as was the public gallery, though Charlotte couldn't see either without turning around and she had no intention of doing that. Gabby, Martin, Maggie and Ron were seated along a side wall beneath the church-like windows, and Charlotte could almost feel their support coming across the room in waves. Her mother, Bob, Rick, Shelley and Tommy were outside in the corridor with the other witnesses waiting to be called.

Charlotte wondered how nervous her mother was, but knew it could never be measured against the turmoil churning inside her.

She wanted to look at the jury some more, but was afraid it would offend them. There were five women, only one of whom appeared around her own age; the seven males seemed mostly in their fifties or sixties, and the ethnic mix had been immediately evident.

She thought that was good, but on reflection how would she know?

Were they looking at her now, as court procedures were explained? If so, what were they seeing? A thirty-year-old woman who'd done the wrong thing for the right reasons? Or an arrogant ex-social worker who'd abused her position, broken the public's trust, and stolen a child? They obviously knew something of her case already; it wasn't possible to be alive in Britain, or New Zealand, and not know. She wished there was a way for them to see, or sense who she really was.

Looking at Anthony as he lent an ear to whatever Jolyon was saying, she wondered how he was managing to appear so relaxed. He seemed as detached from her, and as unreachable, as the opposing team at the other end of the lawyers' benches.

She had never felt so bizarrely cut off from the world around her.

'My Lady, members of the jury.' Simon Kentley, the lead prosecutor, was rising to his feet. He wasn't a tall man, nor was he especially well built, but his voice, his whole demeanour resonated with the kind of authority that made Charlotte tense with unease. She was recalling the dark look that had come over Anthony's face when he'd learned that Kentley was going to be his adversary, and the comment he'd made: 'They're obviously not quite so sure of a win if they've decided to wheel out the big guns.' Words that should have been reassuring, but somehow weren't.

'You're going to hear a lot of talk over the next two days,' Kentley was informing the jury, 'about how the defendant provided a loving home for little

Ottilie Wade, also known as Chloe, and I think it will soon become evident that the defendant did indeed provide a loving home for the little girl who once lived on North Road with a father who was a paedophile, and a mentally unstable mother.'

Let the jury understand, Charlotte was thinking, *that the prosecution fully recognised the tragedy of Chloe's beginnings.* Anthony had told her to expect it, and there it was, right at the start.

'The father has since been convicted of his crimes,' Kentley continued, 'which include the murder of his wife, Chloe's mother, and he's currently serving two life sentences. I feel it important to mention this now, as it will explain why Chloe has no family here in court. Her parents were only children, as was she.

'It would be inappropriate for me to dwell any further on the father's grisly career, as justice has already been served in his case. We are here to deliberate the actions of Charlotte Nicholls, the social worker whose job it was to protect that little girl from her father's abuse and get her out of harm's way. Which she did – *in the end* – but what we need to examine is just how long it took her to remove the child, and the way in which she did so. It was clear from her own initial assessment of the family that the mother was in need of a mental-health check and the father, I quote from her report, left her with an uneasy feeling. So what caused the delay?'

Charlotte could feel the jury's eyes boring into her now and wished she could stand up to tell them how it had really been, that those few words didn't even begin to encapsulate the reality, but the court wouldn't allow it. The prosecution got to make their case first, in the way they saw fit, and only later would she be allowed to speak.

How much damage would have been done by then?

'We will hear from colleagues of Ms Nicholls',' Kentley continued, 'that, at the outset, the defendant adhered to all the proper procedures – paediatricians, psychologists and psychiatrists were all consulted, reports were written up – but what we don't yet have is a clear explanation of *why* it took so long to get Chloe out of harm's way. Of course the system is overloaded, and I'm absolutely sure that my learned friend, Mr Goodman, will describe for us just how overloaded when he comes to speak to you later. However, in the case of an emergency, measures can be taken to remove a child from its home at any time the child is felt to be in danger. And you will learn during the course of this trial that Chloe's case could certainly have qualified as an emergency. Yet Ms Nicholls kept her with the father who continued to abuse her, and heaven only knows what kind of relationship the poor child had with her mother. Certainly, according to Ms Nicholls's own reports, there were no signs of a healthy bond there.

'I believe we will demonstrate that Ms Nicholls's plan to keep the child for herself was already well under way by the time the alleged abduction took place. Indeed, had events not worked against her on the night of 6th October 2011, causing her to act in a very hasty and irrational way, I believe she would have left the child in that house until such time as she, Ms Nicholls, was fully ready to take her to New Zealand.

'In other words, we will learn that this crime was wholly premeditated with small regard for the child's welfare prior to the abduction, and a blatant disregard of the law and the system Ms Nicholls herself represents following the abduction. It will become evident that she seized the child, kept her hidden during a massive police hunt, and then smuggled her out of the country, because she wanted the child for herself.

'Ladies and gentlemen of the jury, it is my job to prove beyond a reasonable doubt that a crime has been committed – and I think in this instance it will be hard to prove otherwise. However, that will be for you to determine after you have heard from the manager of the child protection unit at Kesterly social services; the team leader to whom Ms Nicholls reported directly at the time the alleged crime took place; and Janet Gordon, who runs the nursery school to which Ms Nicholls took Chloe on a regular basis. You will also hear from the police officers who carried out the search for Chloe after she went missing from the family home. The accused's mother and stepfather will also take the stand with their own counsel here to represent them, as will her stepbrother and stepsister. Statements by those unable to be with us in the court today will be read out by the clerk.

'I am confident, members of the jury, that my colleagues and I will prove, beyond a reasonable doubt, that the defendant is guilty as charged, and now, with your leave, I will call the first witness to the stand.'

Wendy Fraser was the first to be sworn in. As Charlotte watched and listened, she couldn't help wondering how Wendy was feeling about this. Given the history of antipathy between them, she might even be enjoying it. Although Wendy would know that she'd never meant Chloe any harm, so did she really feel that she, Charlotte, deserved to be punished with a prison term?

There was a lot of preamble, mainly about how long Wendy had held her position, and whether she had been involved in employing Charlotte in the first place, which she had. Then Kentley was asking, 'Have you ever had occasion to speak to Ms Nicholls about her conduct?'

'Yes, frequently,' Wendy replied, keeping her eyes on the lawyer.

'Can you give us some examples of why this became necessary?' Kentley prompted.

Wendy's lack of hesitation showed she'd been rehearsing for this. 'Well, she's always been headstrong, and given to her own opinions,' she stated, 'which make her argumentative and not, how can I say, as helpful to the rest of the team as someone in her position needs to be.'

Kentley nodded for her to continue.

'To be honest,' she ran on, 'she seemed to consider herself a cut above the rest of us, as though normal rules didn't apply to her. She liked to do things *her* way, and while I'm not suggesting she wasn't good with the children, because in general she was, she had other interests outside of work, such as her theatre group, that often distracted her, or even sometimes came first.'

Charlotte could feel how bloodless her face was as she stared at Wendy. Though Wendy might not have the intention of lying, she was twisting the truth so shamefully that Charlotte couldn't bear to think of how it must be playing with the jury.

It wasn't long before Kentley sat down and Jolyon Crane rose to his feet. 'Can I ask, Ms Fraser,' he began, 'how closely you monitored the defendant's day-to-day running of Chloe's case?'

Wendy instantly flushed. 'As the manager of the department I don't involve myself in the minutiae of a case,' she replied. 'It's my job to make sure that proper liaison is carried out . . .'

'Thank you,' he said, cutting her off. 'Were you aware that the Wade family were a part of Ms Nicholls's caseload?'

Again Wendy seemed awkward. 'Not specifically,' she managed to wrench out, 'but I had heard that . . .'

'A simple yes or no will suffice.'

In the tight voice Charlotte knew so well, Wendy said, 'No.'

Jolyon hadn't finished. 'Regarding the occasions on which you were forced to speak to Ms Nicholls about what you called *normal rules*,' he said, 'we didn't hear exactly what these rules might be and how she broke them. Can you give us an example, perhaps?'

Wendy was looking increasingly uncomfortable. 'I was forever having to chase her up about paperwork,' she said crisply. 'She behaved as if it wasn't important, that it was just getting in the way for her . . . OK, I understand that paperwork is boring, *no one* likes it, but it's the only way we can keep a record of what's happening in the department, and she isn't a special case that can get around it.'

Jolyon nodded agreeably. 'So is there anything missing from your files, specifically regarding the Wade family, from the time Ms Nicholls took the case?' he asked.

Wendy's eyes shot to Kentley. 'I – well, I haven't actually checked, but . . .' She stopped when she saw Jolyon was talking quietly with Anthony.

'Ms Fraser,' Jolyon said, standing straight again, 'do you have a personal axe to grind with Ms Nicholls?'

'Relevance?' Kentley piped up.

The judge looked at Jolyon, who didn't bother to respond, simply thanked Wendy for her time and sat down again.

His point had been made.

Next on the stand was Tommy, in a navy suit and snazzy red tie. Charlotte knew it was going right against the grain with him to be called by the prosecution, which would account for why he was looking both belligerent and uncomfortable. However, it wasn't as though he'd never appeared in court before, and as she and Anthony had reminded him several times over the last few days, all he had to do was tell the truth.

Which was all he did, though the prosecution had little trouble managing to make his answers sound more critical than supportive, and any positive comments he made ended up seeming either biased or improbable.

By the time Jolyon stood up sweat was breaking out on Tommy's face, and his antagonism towards Kentley was still hanging like a cloud in the air. 'As team leader,' Jolyon began, 'were you aware that Ms Nicholls was becoming attached to the child, Chloe?'

'Yes, I was,' Tommy replied.

'Were you concerned?'

'Yes, but I always am when one of the team gets more emotionally involved than is usual.'

'Does it happen often?'

'All the time. It's a hazard of the job.'

'How highly did you rate Ms Nicholls's skills as a social worker?'

'She was one of the best on the team.'

'Was she ever neglectful in her work?'

'Never.'

'Did anything in Ms Nicholls's behaviour, at any time, suggest to you that she might be planning to abduct the little girl she was becoming so attached to?'

'Nothing at all.'

'Thank you, Mr Burgess.'

The next witness on the stand was Janet Gordon, who told of how it was always Charlotte who'd brought Chloe to the Pumpkin playgroup, never Chloe's mother or father.

'Could you characterise for us,' Kentley asked, 'the relationship between the defendant and Chloe?'

'I'd say it was a close relationship.'

'Closer than you're used to seeing between a social worker and child, or about the same?'

'Probably closer, given that Chloe didn't really have anyone else, so I think Charlotte felt extra protective of her.'

'Protective enough to want to keep her?'

'You're leading the witness,' Jolyon interrupted.

Moving on, Kentley said, 'Did you ever, at any time, have reason to believe that Ms Nicholls was having a different kind of relationship with the child from the one her profession dictated?'

Janet Gordon seemed perplexed.

'Were you aware of what the child called Ms Nicholls?' he asked. 'For instance, did you ever hear her call Ms Nicholls Mummy?'

'My Lady, could we have the jury out?' Jolyon barked angrily.

'It won't be necessary,' the judge told him. To the jury she said, 'You'll disregard the last question.' Her steely gaze moved to Kentley, but before she

461

could administer a rebuke for such a blatantly leading question he said, 'I apologise, My Lady,' and turning back to Janet, he asked, 'When Ms Nicholls brought Chloe to your playgroup, did she usually stay, or drop her off and come back later to collect her?'

'At first she used to stay, but then as Chloe gained some confidence she was able to leave her for a while. Much like any parent.'

Kentley nodded. 'Much like any parent,' he repeated, just in case the jury had missed it. 'So in your opinion, that was how she behaved, like a parent?'

Janet was losing her composure. 'I didn't mean . . . I wasn't . . .'

'Thank you, Mrs Gordon,' Kentley cut in, and leaving her to Jolyon he sat down again.

'I have just one question for you,' Jolyon said, getting to his feet. 'In your experience, is it unusual to see a social worker taking on the role of temporary parent or guardian?'

'No, it's not,' Janet replied. 'Sometimes the social worker is the only person the child has . . .'

'Thank you, that's all,' Jolyon interrupted, and turning to Anthony he spoke with him quietly while Janet was released from the stand.

'I think that seems a good place to break for lunch,' the judge announced, and after reminding the jury they were to discuss the case with no one, not even amongst themselves, she recalled the court for one forty-five and left.

'Am I allowed to ask how it's going?' Charlotte said to Anthony when he came to find her and the others in the foyer.

'About as well as we expected at this stage,' he

462

replied, nodding to another lawyer who was passing. 'No one's given any evidence to suggest you were planning an abduction, which is where the prosecution's hoping to go with this.'

'It's this afternoon that we're more worried about,' Kim informed her.

Charlotte didn't miss the flash of irritation that crossed Anthony's face.

'Why?' Shelley demanded, sounding alarmed.

'It's when the police take the stand,' Charlotte told her, still looking at Anthony. 'When are Mum and Bob likely to be called?' she asked.

'Probably straight after that,' he replied, glancing at his watch. 'Have you eaten?'

Her stomach churned at the mere thought of it.

'Send out for some sandwiches,' he said to Kim, and taking Charlotte's hand he drew her out of earshot. 'I'm going to talk to Jolyon now,' he said quietly, 'but I promise, everything's going fine.'

'When are you going to take over?' she asked.

'There's no need for me to yet. Jolyon's more than capable of handling the cross-examinations, and he'll carry on with them unless something happens with the police that we're not expecting.'

'Such as?'

'I can't answer that until, or unless it happens, but they're not supposed to spring any surprises on us so I'm really not worried.'

'And if you're not, I shouldn't be either?' she responded, trying to tease.

'Precisely,' and squeezing her hand more tightly he disappeared back into the depths of the court.

It didn't take long after the lunch break for the mood of the court to start shifting. Whereas an air of curiosity and settling into proceedings had been prevalent before, a sense of suspicion and unease began descending as it became evident that Charlotte herself had made the 999 call alerting the police to an incident at the Wades' home on North Hill.

'And at what time did this call come in?' Kentley asked the officer who'd been first on the scene.

'Just after seven in the evening,' he replied, his round, puppyish face radiating as much youth as honesty.

'By which time Ms Nicholls had already removed the child from the house?' Kentley suggested.

'I can only assume so, as there was no sign of the child when I arrived.'

'When did you find out that it was Ms Nicholls who'd made the call?'

'The following day, after Detective Constable Fields interviewed her.'

'Ms Nicholls admitted to raising the alarm?'

'That's right.'

'But she made no mention of the child when she rang?'

'Not that I'm aware of.'

'Did she make the call from the house?'

'I don't know.'

'Do you know if she ever told anyone why she was at the house that night? We're accepting that she was?' This question was directed towards Anthony, who simply gave a nod.

Kentley turned back to the constable.

'I think DC Fields will be better able to answer the question,' came the reply.

'Of course. Did you interview Ms Nicholls at any time yourself?'

'No.'

After turning a page Kentley moved on. 'Can you tell us what happened when you arrived at the house that night?'

'All the lights were on and the front door was open. As I got out of the car a man came running towards me shouting that he couldn't find his daughter.'

'This man you later learned was Brian Wade?'

'Yes. He was distraught. He kept urging me to find his little girl. I tried to calm him down, but he insisted that she'd gone and he needed to find her. I asked when he'd last seen her and he became confused. So I asked where his wife was, or the mother of the child. At that point he clutched his hands to his head and started to wail. I led him inside, aware that he was telling me his wife had killed herself, but I assumed it was something that had happened a while ago. Then he took me into the kitchen and I immediately radioed for backup.'

'His wife was there?'

'Yes. She'd been stabbed and Mr Wade was insistent that she'd done it herself. It was only later, after he'd been taken to the station, that he admitted he'd stabbed her.'

'I see. Did he at any time claim to have seen Ms Nicholls at the house that night?'

'He never mentioned her to me.'

'Did the search for the child begin right away?'

'Yes, it did.'

'OK, thank you Officer Pollock. You've been most helpful.'

To Charlotte's surprise Jolyon didn't get up to cross; nor did he question the two uniformed officers who followed Pollock on to the stand. However, neither of them seemed to add much to what Pollock had said, and if Anthony, or Jolyon, had felt that something needed to be challenged she was sure they'd never have let it pass. Nevertheless, she could tell that the jury were unsettled by what they'd heard, and when the detectives were called in turn to the stand no one could escape the fact that a far more sinister picture was emerging.

It didn't surprise her that the most damning evidence of all came from DCI Gould; she'd seen his statement so knew what to expect. However, hearing him describing to the court how she'd lied, cheated and stolen her way to motherhood was soon unnerving her badly.

'Tell me, how many times did you interview Ms Nicholls during the search for the child?' Kentley wanted to know.

'In all a dozen,' Gould replied, his superior rank seeming to ooze from every pore.

'And was she helpful?'

'She always appeared to be.'

'But you know now that she consistently lied?'

'Yes.'

'Where did these interviews take place?'

'Some were at her home, others at the station.'

'So is it your belief that while you were at her home talking to her she had the child secreted away somewhere upstairs perhaps, in . . . what? A cupboard, an attic . . .'

'Leading,' Jolyon cut in.

'Where do you assume the child was when you were at the defendant's home?' Kentley rephrased.

'At the time I didn't assume she was in the house at all. Now I believe she must have been upstairs, perhaps in a cupboard, or maybe the attic.'

'With, presumably, strict instructions to stay silent?'

'Presumably.'

Flowers in the Attic.

'And what do you think happened to the child while Ms Nicholls was at the police station? Was anyone there to take care of her?'

'Not that I'm aware of. I didn't see anyone else at the house while I was coming and going, until Ms Nicholls's mother arrived from New Zealand, which was about a week after the child had disappeared.'

'So during that week, as far as you know, whenever Ms Nicholls came to the station to help with inquiries she was leaving the child – *the child you were looking for* – in the house alone?'

'As far as I know, that's correct.'

'And the child was three years old?'

'That's right.'

Kentley gave that a moment to sink in, before saying, 'How long, on average, would you say Ms Nicholls was away from the house during these visits to the station?'

'Anything up to three or four hours.'

Charlotte winced at the murmured shock from the gallery.

'And did Ms Nicholls suggest to you at any time that the child might be safe?' Kentley asked.

'No, never.'

'Can you tell us the sort of things she did say to you concerning the child?'

'That she was very worried about her. That she was as sickened as the rest of us by the father's abuse . . .'

'Which had become public by now?'

467

'Indeed.'

'How did it become public?'

'Ms Nicholls had video footage of the abuse on her computer, which she emailed to us at the station.'

'And do you know how she came by this footage?'

'Apparently it was sent to her by Erica Wade, the child's mother.'

'I see. And when did Ms Nicholls forward it to you?'

'The day after the child supposedly went missing.'

'Do you know how long she'd had the footage before she sent it to you?'

'I'm afraid I don't.'

'So it could have been a few days, a week, perhaps even longer?'

'The witness has already said he doesn't know,' Jolyon jumped in.

Directing a meaningful look Kentley's way, the judge nodded for him to continue.

'Presumably there are dates on Ms Nicholls's computer to show when she first received the footage?' Kentley pressed on.

'If there were I doubt they're there now,' Gould replied. 'You see, as the child's social worker, we never suspected her, so her computer wasn't seized.'

A massive mistake, was how Anthony had described that, *to add to all their other massive mistakes*, and how could anyone disagree? However, Kentley was more interested in the dates than the bungling.

'So you have no idea how long she might have been holding on to this footage?' he asked.

'None.'

'My Lady,' Jolyon protested.

'Yes, quite,' she responded. 'Mr Kentley, please move on.'

468

Nodding agreeably, Kentley said, 'During the time you were conducting the search for Chloe, was Ms Nicholls aware it was happening?'

'She was.'

'So she understood how concerned you and your fellow officers were for the child's safety?'

'She did.'

'Was she also aware of how involved the public became in the search?'

'Yes, she was.'

'Did she ever express an opinion on it?'

'I think she said once or twice that it was lovely to see how much people cared.'

'Did she appear at all concerned by the fact that so many people were giving up their time to find a child she knew was perfectly safe?'

'Not that I ever saw.'

'Did she on any occasion join in the search?'

'No.'

'Did you find that surprising?'

'Not really. The press were giving her quite a hard time, making it difficult for her to go anywhere without being accused of not doing her job properly.'

Kentley turned to the jury, his face as expressive as the words he left unspoken: that the press had been right, she had indeed failed to carry out her professional obligations.

'One final question, DCI Gould,' he said, turning back again. 'Can you give us an idea how much this unnecessary search ended up costing the taxpayer?'

Gould cleared his throat as he replied, 'To date, just under two million pounds, but that doesn't include the cost of bringing Ms Nicholls and the child back from New Zealand, or the investigation that's followed.'

'Goodness. I wonder how many police officers' jobs could have been saved during this time of cutbacks and recession if that enormous sum of money had been directed their way? Thank you DCI Gould, I'm sure Mr Crane will have some questions for you now.'

Feeling every bit as ashamed as Kentley had intended her to feel, Charlotte watched Jolyon get to his feet. Though she'd half expected Anthony to conduct this cross, it didn't seem he was going to, and she wondered if she should take heart from the fact that he didn't feel that matters had become serious enough.

Yet.

'Going back to the video footage that Mrs Wade sent to Ms Nicholls,' Jolyon said, looking down at the notes in front of him. 'Can we just be clear about this: you say you don't know how long Ms Nicholls had the footage before she emailed it to the police. Is that correct?'

'That's correct.'

'So she could have forwarded it immediately she received it?'

Gould didn't reply.

'Couldn't she?' Jolyon prompted.

'Yes,' came the reply.

'Have you any reason to suppose she didn't?'

'Not . . . I guess not exactly, no.'

'Did you ever check Mrs Wade's computer to find out when she'd sent it to Ms Nicholls?'

Gould's colour deepened. 'I'm afraid I don't have that information to hand,' he replied.

Jolyon threw out his hands, as if asking whether

there was no end to police incompetence. 'Presumably it was checked, though,' he prompted. 'She'd been murdered, after all, so you'd want to find out what could have led to it.'

'Her husband confessed,' Gould reminded him. 'Once that had happened there was no reason to look any further.'

'But her daughter was missing,' Jolyon cried incredulously. 'Might there not have been some information on her computer to suggest where the child could be?'

There wasn't much doubt heads would roll after this, Charlotte was reflecting, and one of them was likely to be Gould's.

'Again, I'm afraid I don't have that information to hand,' Gould said tightly.

Clearly unimpressed, Jolyon returned to his notes. 'In retrospect, DCI Gould,' he continued, 'do you feel it was something of an oversight not to suspect Ms Nicholls's involvement in the child's disappearance?'

Gould flushed angrily. 'How could I not, knowing what I know now?' he retorted.

'So you wouldn't claim that all avenues were rigorously explored at the time they should have been?'

'No, I wouldn't.'

'Would it be correct to say that the child might have been found earlier if they had been?'

'I imagine so.'

'And therefore the cost of the search would have been greatly reduced?'

Looking like he wanted to bang a fist on the bench, or even on Jolyon, Gould said, 'Yes, that would be correct.'

'So it could be said that lazy policing has as big a part to play in how these costs were arrived at as anything else?'

Gould seemed about to explode. 'If you're trying to suggest . . .'

'That'll be all, thank you,' Jolyon interrupted, and with a glance at the jury he retook his seat.

Knowing, at least sensing, that any sympathy there might have been for her had still not materialised, Charlotte could only hope that her mother's or Bob's evidence would start to turn things around.

However, the fact that their lawyer, Larry Clark, consistently refused to let them answer questions on the grounds they were likely to incriminate themselves, and proceeded to do the same with Rick and Shelley, only seemed to make matters worse.

'It's not going well, is it?' Charlotte said to Anthony when they were back at the flat that night.

'Everything always looks bleak when the prosecution's having their say,' he replied, pushing a hand through his hair. He looked tired and strained and as though he'd like everyone to leave.

'I wish I could have said more,' Anna groaned. 'I wanted to let them know how special you are, and how much better off Chloe was with us, but that blinking lawyer . . .'

'He had to do his job,' Anthony told her, 'and with the mood the police are in they're likely to arrest anyone as soon as look at them if they're connected to this case.'

'Was humiliating Gould really the right way to go?' Charlotte asked, taking the drink Bob was passing her.

'I'm afraid it had to be done,' Anthony assured her, taking a drink too. 'His police work was abysmal

472

and he was making assumptions all over the place that he had no way of backing up.'

'I'm not sure the jury liked it though.'

He didn't disagree, and seeing his frown deepen as he checked who was calling his mobile sent her nerves into freefall.

Things clearly weren't going the way he'd hoped.

'It'll be your turn tomorrow,' Rick reminded her gently. 'Once they've heard from you it'll all change.'

'They'll understand then how happy Chloe has been with you,' Shelley added.

'They'll also know that I took her,' Charlotte pointed out, 'and that my not guilty plea is a nonsense and that this whole trial is a further waste of taxpayers' money. Kentley's bound to make a big deal of that . . .'

'You have the right to a fair trial,' Bob reminded her. 'We all do.'

'Is it fair to plead not guilty to a crime I know I committed?' She was looking at Anthony as he came back into the room. Her heart turned over at the grim expression in his eyes. She knew he wanted her to trust him, but how confident was he feeling after today?

'The offer's still on the table,' he said quietly. 'A suspended sentence for a guilty plea.'

Her eyes closed as she turned away. She could feel everyone watching her, no doubt thanking God they weren't in her shoes, while wishing they could think how to advise her. She knew whatever she decided they'd support her, but she simply couldn't make this only about her. There was still Chloe to consider, and even if they could forget her she knew she never could.

Yet almost six months had gone by since she'd

last seen her. In that time Chloe could have bonded with someone else, and was by now feeling safe and settled with them. So maybe it would be cruel to disrupt her all over again.

'And these shiny little yellow ones are called buttercups,' Sally Raynes was explaining to Chloe. 'If you hold one under your chin and it glows on your skin that means you like butter.'

Chloe simply looked at her. Then lowering her head she tucked Boots back under her arm and carried on picking daisies.

Enchanted by the pretty picture she made, a fairy-tale vision in the woods at dusk, Sally Raynes sighed quietly as she perched on a boulder to watch the child. It seemed nothing would persuade her to put the bear down, even though trying to grab the flowers with one hand wasn't easy.

She was such a sweetheart, a little dream of a girl with her wispy dark curls and adorable heart-shaped face. If only she would speak, or laugh, or show some signs of being happy to be where she was, Sally knew she'd probably fall head over heels in love with her.

She probably had anyway.

'She will speak, eventually,' Tracy had assured Sally on her last visit. 'As you know, the psychologist is confident of it.'

'Is there anything I can do to encourage her?' Sally had asked both Tracy and the psychologist.

'Just keep talking to her and let her know that she's safe with you,' she'd been told.

'And what about her previous family? Should I ever mention them?'

'For now I wouldn't bring it up unless she does,'

the psychologist had advised. 'I'm working on it myself, but remember she has two families, her real parents and the social worker who took her. She was very attached to the social worker. As far as we know she's the only one who was able to get her to speak.'

Sally felt sure she would manage it too, over time, because in general children liked her and she adored them, especially the little ones. The older kids were often too damaged for her to handle on her own, and sadly her twenty-six-year-old brother, Bobby, couldn't cope with them either. There had been too many occasions when older kids had been mean to him, thinking it hilarious to tease and torment him just because he was fat and not as quick at learning as they were. What they didn't understand, because they never took the time to, was that behind his moon face and lumbering gait he was the dearest, sweetest soul ever to walk the earth.

Sally loved him, and he loved Sally. They'd always been close, even before their mother had died; now they were the whole world to each other, and because they had so much love to give it made sense for them to share it with those in need. Bobby particularly adored the babies who came, those born with addictions or diseases passed on by their mothers. He was so tender with them, so fascinated by their tiny limbs and grasping hands that he'd sit watching them for hours. If one happened to smile he'd break into a delighted laugh, and turn excitedly to Sally, whose heart swelled to see how happy they made him. There was no doubt he had a natural gift with children, possibly because he was still so very like one himself.

He was at home now, painting a picture for Chloe

who'd painted one for him earlier in the day. She hadn't smiled when she'd given it to him, instead she'd put her hands on her knees and gazed up at him as though she were the adult and he the child. He had a knack for painting and would probably teach Chloe some of his techniques, just as he'd taught the other children who'd come into their home. He was so patient with them, so careful never to make them feel inadequate or incapable. She wished everyone could see how wonderful he was.

And harmless.

Please don't let any of the neighbours beat him up again.

This was what happened on the Temple Fields estate. People were rough and cruel and often committed to lives of crime. Sally and Bobby had grown up on one of the better streets, but it was still a part of the infamous estate where outsiders rarely came.

It was ironic, Sally felt, that Charlotte Nicholls had started out life in Temple Fields and now Chloe was here. Not that Charlotte had been born on the estate – it was only just being built when she was a child. However, according to the story Sally had seen on the Internet, Charlotte's family had known all about violence even then, and Sally's heart could easily have broken for what they'd been through.

Still, every story had a happy ending, or so she liked to believe, because Charlotte and her mother had eventually found each other, and even if Charlotte ended up in prison for what she'd done Sally felt sure her mother would never desert her again.

It would be a pity for Charlotte if she was found guilty, but it was hard to see how the jury could come up with any other verdict when everyone knew she'd taken the child. What a daft thing for her to have done, when she'd been in a position to make a difference in Chloe's life without all this fuss. Sally really didn't understand people at times, but she'd learned that it was usually best not to try. Not everyone was like her and Bobby, more was the pity, because if they were many more needy children would have a place to go and someone to care for them in a way their own families couldn't manage.

'Oh, sweetheart, what a lovely bunch of flowers,' she smiled, as Chloe came through the long grass towards her. She looked like a little angel with the rosy glow of the sunset behind her, so sweet, so perfect, as though these woods were exactly where she belonged. Sally inhaled deeply, loving the fragrance of the grass, like happy memories floating by on a breeze. It was gloriously peaceful out here at the end of the day, no one to bother them, nothing to spoil the sounds and colours of nature in its purest form.

'Are they for me?' she asked as Chloe reached her.

Chloe looked down at the mangled daisies in her hand. As her head came up again she whispered, 'Mummy.'

Sally's heart turned over with joy. 'Oh what a lovely thing to say,' she cried, entranced by the mere thought of meaning so much to this little girl, but as she went to take the flowers Chloe moved them away.

'Mummy,' Chloe whispered again.

Sally's smile froze. Clearly she'd misunderstood.

Leaning forward, she took Chloe by the arm as she said, 'But you don't have a mummy, sweetheart, you know that. She's dead.'

Chloe's eyes widened as she looked at her.

'Do you understand what dead means?' Sally asked her.

Chloe didn't reply.

'It means,' Sally said, reminding herself that she was only speaking the truth, for Chloe's natural mother really was dead, 'that she's gone up to heaven and she's never coming back.'

Chloe's eyes filled with tears.

'But you don't need to worry,' Sally told her, mindful of the fact that Charlotte Nicholls would probably be in prison by this time tomorrow, 'because I'm here to take care of you and that's lovely, isn't it? We have each other and Bobby, and do you know what, I think I'm going to talk to Tracy about being able to keep you for ever.'

Chapter Twenty-Four

As Charlotte took her place in the dock a wave of nausea threatened to overwhelm her. She'd barely slept all night, and the breakfast her mother and Anthony had urged her to eat had refused to stay down. She had never felt so afraid, or unsure of herself, but her decision had been made, and she wouldn't go back on it now in spite of knowing that if she did she would be certain to go home tonight.

Seeing Anthony at the front of the court was causing so much emotional turmoil that she had to close her eyes and hold her breath. What did he really think of her decision? That she was insane to stake so much on the small chance of being able to get Chloe back? Or that she was stronger, braver and more deserving of a child than most people he knew, for taking that chance? It was what he'd said last night, and she had no reason to disbelieve him, but he must surely wonder where he, and their relationship, featured in her priorities. He hadn't asked, so she hadn't mentioned it either, but she was finding it as hard to imagine being without him as it was to think of giving up on Chloe.

Aware of everyone watching him as he came to the dock to speak to her, she kept her eyes on his as he said, 'You're going to be fine. I'll be with you, every step of the way.'

Wishing she could touch his face, she simply nodded, too tense right now to utter a word.

Moments later they were being asked to rise, and for one awful moment as the judge came in, Charlotte felt sure she was going to be sick. A cold sweat was breaking out all over her, and her head was spinning so fast she feared she might faint.

Struggling to keep control, she sat down again, pressing her nails into her palms as the sounds of the court seemed to slur into slow motion, or sink down below her. Then Kim was there with a hand on her arm, offering her some water.

Taking it Charlotte drank deeply, as though to drown the maelstrom inside her.

'Are you OK?' Kim whispered.

Charlotte nodded, though she wasn't sure. When she looked up she saw that the judge was watching her, so she nodded again to say she was ready to continue. She wasn't, because she would never be, but there was no way back from this now. She had to go forward and pray to God that refusing the second offer of a suspended sentence didn't turn into the biggest mistake of her life.

As Anthony rose to his feet the court was so silent, so charged with anticipation that Charlotte could only wonder what the press and public were expecting to happen. She knew Heather Hancock would be there, scrutinising her and Anthony's every move, dying to burst forth with everything she knew or suspected as soon as the trial was over.

For Anthony all that would matter now was the opening statement he'd decided upon during the early hours of the morning.

'My Lady, ladies and gentlemen of the jury,' he began, turning to the jury, 'I'm sure you must be wondering by now why on earth my client has entered a plea of not guilty when everyone knows she took the child from the house on North Hill on the night of 6th October 2011. She's never denied it, and I'm not about to either. What I am going to do is point out to you that she *took* the child. Or to be even more accurate, she *rescued* the child from a situation that was so awful most of us don't even want to think of it.

'There was no abduction involved, because the child had no fit parents to be abducted from. Her mother was already dead, and the father was under investigation for serious and serial abuse. So, I am failing to see where a crime has actually been committed. No one had any other claim to the child, apart from the state, and as my client represented the state how was it wrong for her to get the child out of harm's way?

'You might say that after taking the child from the house Ms Nicholls should then have turned her over to the proper authorities, but again, she was a proper authority, and the child knew her, felt safe with her, and was never going to come to any harm in her care. Nor did she *ever* come to harm in Ms Nicholls's care for the entire time she was with her. Quite the reverse in fact, as you will find out when Ms Nicholls herself takes the stand to tell you how she came to know Chloe, how the bond between them developed and of course what really happened the night she took her.

'Before she does so, I would ask you to keep in mind that she has only one driving force behind her now – a force that is making her risk the possibility of a guilty verdict and all that would flow from that, when she might otherwise have avoided it – and that is her love of the child.'

Though he spoke quietly, the power of his delivery resonated around the room and remained with a current of its own as Charlotte was escorted from the dock to the witness stand. She could feel the intrigue from the galleries as if it were physical, while the interest of the jury was making her light-headed with nerves.

After taking the oath she looked at Anthony and her heart contracted at the way he met her eyes. Whether anyone noticed she neither knew nor cared; all that mattered was feeling their connection at this most crucial of moments.

She knew what his first question would be, because they'd rehearsed it many times; however hearing it in this environment felt slightly surreal, as if it were coming from a dream.

'Charlotte, can you describe for us how and where you first met Chloe?'

Before Charlotte could answer Kentley was asking for the relevance.

'My Lady,' Anthony said to the judge, 'my client's relationship with the child is crucial to this case . . .'

'Indeed, Mr Goodman,' and frowning at Kentley she turned her attention back to Charlotte. 'You may continue,' she said.

'The first time I saw her,' Charlotte began softly, 'was at a park, here in Kesterly. I was with my sister and niece and nephew who were playing on the slide, when I noticed a little girl sitting alone on a swing. She was watching me, and because I couldn't tell if she was with someone I went over to make sure she was all right. She didn't appear to be afraid when I spoke to her, but when I asked her her name she didn't answer. She just kept looking at me, and I remember wondering if she knew me. I tried to remember if I'd seen her before – I come across so many children – but I just knew that if we had met I wouldn't have forgotten her.'

'Where were her parents at this point, do you know?' Anthony asked.

'There didn't seem to be anyone around at first, but then a man appeared telling me she was shy and seeming in a bit of a hurry to lift her out of the swing. She didn't call him Daddy, and there didn't seem to be much of a connection between them, but on the other hand, she didn't act as though he was a stranger, and when he led her away she seemed to go willingly enough. I just couldn't help feeling uneasy. Something wasn't right, I felt sure of it, but he hadn't done anything wrong so I could only stand there and watch them walk away.'

'Did you see her again that day?'

'No, it was a few weeks later that our paths crossed again, but during that time I couldn't get her out of my mind. I kept thinking of how troubled I'd felt when she'd been led away, and seeing her face in my mind's eye when she'd glanced over her shoulder to see if I was still there. I began connecting it with how I'd waited for my mother to come and rescue me when I was about the same age as the little girl, and how she never had. I was too young to realise at the time that my mother had been badly injured in an attack so had been unable to come, I just remember trying to reach a door handle to let myself out so I could get to her, but it was too high. For some reason I kept thinking it was the same for the little girl, that she needed rescuing and no one was responding.'

'So how did you meet her again?'

'An anonymous call came into the office asking us to check on a child on North Hill. I had no idea at the time that it was the little girl from the park, but when I finally managed to set up a meeting at the house – her father kept resisting and her mother wouldn't answer the phone – I recognised the child straight away.'

'Who else was present at this meeting?'

'Both her parents. I don't think her father had any memory of me, but I felt sure that she knew we'd met before. She didn't say so, because she didn't speak, not then, but she almost never took her eyes off me. Her father insisted she was a bit of a chatterbox when no one else was around, but I found that very hard to believe. Chatty children are usually that way with everyone, and this little girl was speaking to no one, not even her mother.'

'Tell us something about the mother. What were your initial thoughts about her?'

'That she was very detached and seemed to have no natural warmth towards the child. It was sad to see, because she was such a lovable little girl. In fact, I was worried enough to suggest in my initial assessment that the mother should undergo a mental-health check, because something obviously wasn't right with her.'

'And did she go for this check?'

'No. Her husband kept putting it off and putting it off until . . . Well, until it was too late.'

Anthony nodded gravely. 'We'll come to that later. For now I'd like you to continue telling us about your first visit to the house on North Hill. Did anything happen while you were there to make you think the child was at risk?'

'Nothing specific, but I was as uneasy about the father as I'd been that day in the park, more so now I was seeing them at home, especially when Chloe, or Ottilie as we knew her then, kept pulling her lips between her teeth. I suspected he'd told her I was a wicked witch who'd steal her tongue if she spoke. This is a common threat used by adults who are abusing children, and sucking their lips between their teeth is a common reaction, particularly with the very young.'

Anthony allowed a murmur of revulsion to fade from the room. 'Go on,' he prompted.

'While she was doing this with her lips,' Charlotte said, 'she was showing me how good she was at jigsaws, and for her age she was good. With her father being a primary-school teacher I suspected she could probably read and write a little by now, though he'd already admitted that she didn't attend a nursery. Nor did she have any other family or friends. I felt very worried to think of her shut up in that house with only her parents for company, and her teddy bear who she told me that day was called Boots.'

'So she did speak?'

'Just that one word, but I was sure she could say more than that. She didn't get the opportunity though, not that day, because her father came into the room before I could encourage her to go further and as soon as he was there she clammed up again.'

Looking distinctly unimpressed, Anthony asked, 'So what happened as a result of this first meeting?'

'Well, obviously I wrote up my initial assessment which included recommendations for the child to be enrolled at a nursery school with no further delay, and to see a speech therapist. I contacted a health visitor to set those visits in motion, and I also made an appointment for her to be examined by the community paediatrician.'

'In fact, you did everything someone in your position is supposed to do when it's felt a child is at risk?'

'That's correct.'

'So what happened next?'

'Once he was over his initial anger at having his daughter declared at risk Mr Wade agreed to the health visitor and speech therapist, but he wasn't helpful in finding a nursery placement. It was either too expensive, not good enough, already full . . . So I found one myself, and ended up taking her, because her mother, I then discovered, never left the house.'

'She was an agoraphobic?'

'I believe so.'

'And the father was working?'

'That's right.'

'Was the mother happy for you to take her?'

'I'm not sure Erica Wade was ever happy, but she always had her daughter ready to go when I got there, and even suggested I leave Chloe's car seat in my car so I wouldn't have to keep getting it from the garage.'

'So as far as she was concerned it was now your job to take Chloe to nursery?'

'It certainly seemed that way, and I didn't object because I was afraid Chloe would never get the social stimulation she needed if she didn't go.'

'What had happened about the appointment with the community paediatrician by then?'

'As I said, one had been arranged, but there was

a nine-week wait and since Chloe's GP had checked her over and declared her to be in good health, I couldn't get her in as an emergency.'

'I see. OK, continue if you will with how the relationship then developed between you and Chloe.'

'Well, I could sense right from the start that she was becoming attached to me, and I admit it didn't take long for me to become very fond of her. She's the sweetest, gentlest little soul and she seemed to love being with me, no matter where we went or what we were doing. Though she remained reluctant to speak to others, she began opening up to me, only in small ways, but as I saw her blossom I knew in my heart I had to be there for her, because she so desperately needed someone to love her and at that time I was all she had.

'So I took her to the Pumpkin playgroup three times a week, where she made her first friend and started to gain some confidence. She didn't like me to leave her, she got very upset when I did, but over time she learned to trust the fact that I would be back. It was very touching to see the way her little face lit up whenever she saw me; she'd run straight over and take hold of my hand. She'd even let me hold her precious bear for her sometimes, a very great honour indeed.'

As she swallowed the lump in her throat, Anthony said, 'So was nursery the only place you took her?'

'No, we used to go for rides on the carousel near the Pumpkin, before I took her home. It wasn't difficult to tell that she'd never been on one before and she absolutely loved it. Round and round and round we'd go, and she was so happy it was impossible not to give in when she wanted more. Not that she ever asked for more, she didn't have the courage for that, but I could sense it and so round we'd go again until eventually I'd tell her we had to go home. It was as though a light inside her went out whenever I said that, so after a while I began stretching things out, taking her for a glass of milk and a brownie at a seafront café, or for a ride on the donkeys if the weather was good. Actually, I took her to lots of places, the aquarium, the zoo, walks on the pier, to the park, and whenever we were together I could see how much it was all meaning to her. So much that she once smuggled herself into the back of my car and I didn't realise she was there until I got home.'

Anthony waited a moment as she smothered another rise of emotion.

'I've never seen her cry so hard as she did when I tried to explain that I had to take her back,' she finally continued. 'My mother was there at the time, so she saw too just how desperate she was to stay with me. It upset us a lot to see the state she got into, but obviously I had to take her home. Her father had called me by then demanding to know where she was, so faced with no alternative I put her back in the car and drove her to North Hill. It was honestly one of the most difficult things I've ever done. She sobbed and sobbed the entire way there, and I did all the way back.'

'Yet you'd dealt with traumatised children before, so doing the difficult thing wasn't new to you?'

'No, it wasn't, but believe me it's never easy, and because I'd become so attached to Chloe . . . I really can't explain why it was different with her, it just was. She wanted to be with me all the time, and I admit I wanted to be with her. It wasn't that I thought

I was the only one who could help her, but there was a connection between us. I knew I was the only one she trusted, and so to try to hand her over to someone else, another social worker I mean, would have seemed cruel when I knew how much it would upset her.'

'And when you discussed this with Tommy Burgess, your team leader, he agreed that she should remain in your caseload?'

'Yes, he did. By then we weren't far off an appointment with the community paediatrician, so it made sense for me to see it through.'

'And during this time were there any signs of abuse that you noticed?'

'Yes, there were, but Brian Wade always had an explanation ready – she'd either fallen off the bed, or had an infection that had been diagnosed by their doctor . . .'

Anthony put up a hand. 'I think it's important for the jury to note that the GP that's been referred to twice now was later found to be a member of the same paedophile ring as Brian Wade. At the time Ms Nicholls had no way of knowing that, so she had no reason to distrust his diagnosis.' To Charlotte he said, 'Please continue.'

'Actually, I wasn't happy with the doctor's diagnosis,' she told the jury, 'but as the paediatrician's assessment was imminent I decided I should wait for that.'

'What were you expecting from this assessment?'

'I was hoping he would tell me that Chloe was still intact.'

'And did he, after the appointment took place?'

'No, he didn't.'

'Meaning she wasn't intact?'

'No.'

'So at the age of three she was no longer a virgin?'

Charlotte's eyes were closed as she said, 'No.'

The horror of a child so young being subjected to any kind of act that would deprive her of her virginity spread another murmur of revulsion through the court.

'So what happened next?' Anthony prompted.

Taking a breath, Charlotte said, 'Brian Wade insisted that her hymen had been ruptured in a fall from a tyre swing. Disproving that was almost impossible. It wasn't helped by the fact that Chloe would sometimes say to me what sounded like "not tyre, not tyre". I only realised later that what she was actually saying was "not tiger." Tiger was the euphemism her father used for his genitalia. One of his commands while raping her was, "Ride the tiger."'

As more disgust reverberated around the room the judge looked sickened too.

'When did it become clear to you that she was saying "not tiger"?' Anthony asked.

Trying to blank the images from her mind, Charlotte said, 'When I saw the video footage Erica Wade sent me.'

'Because this footage contained . . . ?'

'Graphic images of the rape and what he was telling her to do.'

'He was saying, "Ride the tiger"?'

Remembering the agony on Chloe's face, the tears, the sobbing and violent jerking as she was forced to obey her father, Charlotte could barely manage a yes.

Anthony's head went down.

The court was so silent it was as though no one was breathing.

'And when,' Anthony asked, looking up again, 'did Erica Wade send the footage?'

'It was sent on the night of 6th October, but as it was a Sunday I didn't actually open the email until the following morning.'

'And why do you think she sent it to you?'

'Because she wanted me to help her daughter.'

'Did she say so in an accompanying message?'

'Yes.'

'What did the message say?'

'She told me to get Chloe away from him.'

'Anything else?'

'She said, "My daughter needs a mother. It can't be me, but it can be you. Watch what I've sent you and don't let her down."'

'Where is this message now?'

'I deleted it along with the footage.'

'But only after forwarding it to the police?'

'That's right.'

'And you didn't actually see the message, or the video, until the morning of 7th October?'

'No.'

'So it wasn't Mrs Wade's request, or the video, that led you to remove Chloe from the house on the night of 6th October?'

'No.'

'Then why did you take her that night? Please talk us through what happened.'

As he stood aside, so as not to distract the jury, Charlotte felt herself starting to tremble as she allowed her mind to return to that fateful Sunday. 'My mother had just returned to New Zealand,' she began hoarsely. She cleared her throat. 'We'd spent two weeks together, for the first time in over twenty-five years, so I was feeling quite emotional about that, and I was worried about Chloe, because I was always worried about Chloe. I'd driven myself down to the seafront, because I sometimes find it calming to watch the waves, but for some reason that day I couldn't shake my gloom. I didn't know if or when I was going to see my mother again, and having just found out that Chloe was no longer a virgin . . . It was tearing me apart, because I *knew* her father was responsible, but I didn't have a way of proving it. He was clever, manipulative, and being who he was no one was going to want to believe he was capable of doing something like that to his own child, especially not when he had so many children from the South Kesterly community in his care. Yet somehow I had to get to the truth so I could get her out of that house on North Hill. Leaving her behind after playgroup had become so hard by then that I almost dreaded going to pick her up, although nothing in me, not a single shred of me, would ever have let her down.

'I just wished I could find an answer, but there didn't seem to be one. I had no idea that Erica Wade had already sent her email by then, I only knew that when I got back into my car I felt impelled to turn in the direction of the Wades' house just in case Chloe was at the window, looking out for me. She used to do that sometimes, and it would break my heart to see how lonely she looked as she waved.

'When I reached the house all the lights were on and though I had no idea why, I suddenly felt scared. I immediately turned into the drive, got out of the car and ran to the front door. It was open so

I went inside, but no one answered when I called out. I carried on through to the kitchen and saw the back door was open and a light was on in the shed Brian Wade used as a studio. I don't recall making a conscious decision to move quietly – I guess on some level I suspected I could be about to catch him with Chloe. Though I desperately didn't want to see it, at least if I did I'd be able to get her away from him and make sure he never went near her again. So I crossed the garden as silently as I could. I was able to see the back of his head through the shed window, but he didn't turn round. By the time I was close enough to look inside I could sense the panic around him. He was working so frantically at his computer that he had no idea I was there. Something was horribly wrong, I knew it; I noticed then that a massive hole had been dug in the garden, but there didn't seem to be anything in it. Terrified it was meant for Chloe I ran back to the house, and as I went into the kitchen I saw a pool of blood seeping out from behind the centre island. Praying it wasn't Chloe, I forced myself to look and saw that it was Erica Wade. She'd obviously been stabbed, and from the amount of blood and the way her eyes were open I could tell straight away she was dead.

'Desperate to find Chloe I tore upstairs to her room, trying not to scream her name in case her father heard. At first I thought she wasn't there. Then I heard a scraping on the cupboard door in her room. I couldn't get it open, someone had obviously locked her in, but then I spotted a key on the floor . . . I wrenched the door open and there she was, shaking with terror . . . I didn't know how much she'd seen of what had happened downstairs,

I only knew I had to get her away from there. As I scooped her up her arms and legs went round me so tightly it was difficult to move, but I made myself run. As I went I kept getting flashbacks to when I'd been shut in a cupboard at her age and how I'd waited for my mother to come . . . I started to feel confused about who I was, who she was . . . It was like she was me as a child and I was my mother . . . I know it sounds crazy, but it's how it was.

'It seemed to take an eternity to get outside to my car, then she remembered Boots, her bear, so I put her in the passenger seat and ran back inside. I was sure Brian Wade was going to walk in any minute. I had no idea what I'd do if I saw him, but thank God I didn't.

'I was already drawing up outside my own house, about half an hour later, before I fully realised it was where I was going. All I'd been thinking till then was that I had to get as far away from Brian Wade as I could, and make sure Chloe was safe. She was so traumatised; she was still shaking as I lifted her out of the car and when we got inside she wouldn't let me put her down. To be honest, I didn't want to. Holding her reassured me she was all right, alive. That we both were. After what had happened to her mother and how crazed her father had seemed, it felt almost untrue.'

She paused for a moment, putting a hand to her mouth as the memory of it all shook through her.

'At what point did you call the police?' Anthony asked, gently bringing her back on track.

'About then,' she answered, the words coming out in a gasp. 'I rang and said I was worried because I couldn't get an answer from the Wades' home, so could someone go and check everything was OK.'

'So you'd decided by then to keep the child with you?'

'In so far as I was thinking about anything clearly, which I wasn't, I guess the answer has to be yes, at least for that night, because it would only have traumatised her further to be handed over to strangers.

'It was about an hour later that the police came knocking on my door. She was asleep by then, upstairs on my bed, and because I knew that as soon as they saw her everything would have to go into motion to take her into emergency care, I decided to leave her there.'

'Did the police ask you if you knew where she was?'

'No, actually, they didn't. They just told me that they'd responded to my call and that Mrs Wade was dead and Mr Wade had been arrested on suspicion of murder.'

'Did anyone mention the child at all?'

'Yes, they said that Mr Wade was claiming not to know where she was, but they were afraid that he knew exactly where she was.'

'The implication being that they thought he'd done the same to his daughter as he had to his wife?'

'That's right.'

'Do you know if they had any reason to suspect foul play where his daughter was concerned?'

'I didn't know then, but I was told later that photographs had been found in the shed of him and his daughter that were . . . Well, I guess that told their own story.'

Anthony nodded understandingly. 'So was there an actual moment when you decided to yourself that you weren't going to hand Chloe over?' he asked bluntly.

She shook her head. 'No, not really,' she replied, 'it just seemed to happen as it became harder and harder to think of how devastated she'd be if I did give her up, especially when I could see how happy she was to be with me. For her it was like a dream come true, and I just couldn't bring myself to crush that dream.'

'So what did you think you were going to do with her? There you were, a single woman, known in the community to be childless. How did you imagine you were going to pass her off as yours – if indeed that was what you intended?'

Swallowing dryly, she said, 'My mother had already talked to me about visiting New Zealand, possibly even moving there, and from what I knew of it I couldn't think of a better place for Chloe to be after all she'd suffered. I wanted to go anyway to be with my mother, but I didn't feel I had the right to go away and be happy as if I was the only one who mattered, because Chloe mattered too. I just couldn't leave her behind. She had no one, whereas with me she'd be able to have a loving home and family, cousins, animals, adventures, *friends*, and most of all the abuse would be so far away she might one day be able to forget it.'

'And you didn't think anyone else could give her that?'

'Maybe someone could have, but I know what the care system can do to a child, and there was a chance she'd have had to go through many carers before a suitable adoptive parent could be found. Even then there'd be no guarantee that the adopters would go through with it – I've seen the way children can be crushed by eleventh-hour rejections, and I couldn't bear the thought of that happening to her. I knew what it could turn her into, and it didn't seem right even to risk it when I already loved her so much and she was so happy with me.'

'However, you were successfully adopted yourself and brought up in a loving home?'

Had Gabby not been in court, Charlotte knew she'd have explained how lonely it could be knowing you didn't quite belong in a family, and that your sister always mattered more. Since Gabby was there, she said, 'I was, but it doesn't always turn out that way, and as Chloe and I were already so close it seemed to make sense for us to stay together.'

'So you kept her with you throughout the entire time you knew everyone was looking for her?'

'Yes, I did. I felt terrible about it, but I had to put her first. I also knew that after the first few days had gone by, if they found out I had her, I could be charged with a criminal offence that might end me up in prison. Certainly they'd have taken her from me, and then I'd lose my job, never be able to work with children again, and I just couldn't see what purpose that would serve for anyone.'

'So you took her to New Zealand, where she was introduced to a life we will hear more about when the statements from the owner of Aroha Daycare and local policeman Grant Romney are read out for the court. In the meantime, I'd like to thank you for giving us such a full and frank account of how you came to rescue Chloe from the abusive home that had all but devastated the first years of her life.'

As Anthony retook his seat, Charlotte's tension began beating through her skull like a drum. Kentley was going to cross-examine her now and though Anthony and Jolyon had done their best to prepare her for it, she knew this was going to be the hardest part to get through. Not because she'd lied about anything, but because of how he was likely to twist it.

'Mr Kentley?' the judge prompted.

Still listening to the lawyer next to him Kentley rose to his feet, cleared his throat and said, 'Thank you, My Lady. No questions.'

As Anthony glanced up in shock, Charlotte felt herself reeling.

Seeming equally stunned, the judge said to Charlotte, 'Well, Ms Nicholls, it would seem you can stand down, and this, ladies and gentlemen, would be a good time to break for lunch.'

'I can't believe he didn't question you,' Kim declared, as Charlotte joined the legal team in an anteroom. 'What's he up to?' she demanded of Anthony. 'Does he know something we don't?'

Anthony's expression was grim as Jolyon said, 'He'll be planning something, that's for sure, but he can't call any more witnesses without notifying us – unless he's about to.'

'Even if he does,' Charlotte said, 'there's nothing anyone can say to disprove my testimony, because I didn't lie or even bend the truth. It was the way it happened . . .' She turned suddenly cold as a horrible thought occurred to her. 'Oh my God, do you think they're about to call Brian Wade?' she gasped.

Anthony shook his head. 'We'd know if they

were, and anyway, even if they did, what would it change?'

'Potentially everything if he lied,' Charlotte pointed out.

Though unable to argue with that, he continued to shake his head. 'Using a convicted paedophile to try and win their case would be nothing short of madness.'

'So what's going on?' Kim implored.

'My guess,' he replied, looking at Jolyon, 'is that he sensed he'd lose the jury if he started pulling Charlotte apart.'

Jolyon's eyes narrowed as he thought. 'I'll buy that,' he responded. 'She came across as completely credible, someone who obviously loves the child, and no one's ever going to damn her for that.'

'Especially given the abuse she described,' Kim added.

Charlotte was still watching Anthony.

'I'm thinking about the statements from New Zealand,' he said. 'They're going to be read out straight after lunch . . .'

'And,' Jolyon picked up, visibly brightening, 'when the jury hears how well the child was doing over there, they're going to be paying for her flight back themselves.'

To Charlotte's dismay Anthony didn't appear as encouraged.

'You could be right, Jolyon,' he said, 'but I'm asking myself what I'd do in Kentley's shoes to get around that, and I know I'd be relying on my closing statement to remind the jury that this isn't about the child. It's about Charlotte, and the fact that in the eyes of the law she has committed a crime.'

As Charlotte's insides churned, Kim put in, 'But

you have a closing statement too, Anthony, and yours is the last they'll hear before they go to deliberate.'

Anthony's eyes came to Charlotte as with the merest trace of irony he said, 'Then I guess I'd better make it a memorable one.'

Chapter Twenty-Five

It didn't take long for Grant Romney's and Celia Bradley's statements to be read out after lunch, and it was apparent from both that their admiration for the way Charlotte had made such a difference to Chloe's life was affecting the jury just as Jolyon had predicted.

However, Charlotte was in no doubt that Kentley's closing was going to be far more relevant to the afternoon's proceedings than these character references, and knowing how concerned Anthony was, she could feel the jagged edges of panic digging into her unease as Kentley rose to begin.

'My Lady, ladies and gentlemen of the jury,' he pronounced through a sigh, 'there is no doubt we have heard some very touching testimony in the court today, from the defendant herself, and from her friends in New Zealand. I don't imagine there is one amongst us who seeks to damn her for loving the child. To the contrary, it is what we would hope for when a small child is as vulnerable as Chloe, that those whose job it is to remove her from harm's way would care for her not only because it's their job, but because the child really matters to them. Clearly Chloe mattered a great deal to Ms Nicholls. However, the question we have to ask ourselves is, can we say it's all right for a social worker to take a child and keep it as though it were her own?

'You know, I know and the defendant knows very well that things don't work that way. Nor can they, because if they did we'd have social workers all over the place helping themselves to any child that might take their fancy, and who knows, giving them back when it's no longer convenient to keep them. And what would happen then to the wretched little souls who no one felt a strong enough attachment to?

'No, we can't allow the very people we trust to do what's right for our children to pick and choose which ones they might want to keep and bring up as their own. We have a system, albeit flawed, but a system nonetheless, to protect our children from those who neglect and abuse them – and from those who seek to steal them. Ms Nicholls was a part of that system and she has abused it in a way that, I'm sorry to say, led her to commit a serious crime.

'We all heard my learned friend, Mr Goodman, try to pass his client's actions off as a rescue, and on the night Ms Nicholls took the child it was most certainly that. We would hope that no one, least of all someone working in child protection, would leave a child in a house where a murder had already been committed. What concerns me, members of the jury, is not what happened that night, but what happened afterwards. She could, at any point, have handed the child over to a foster carer, she might even have had some say in who the child went to, but rather than do the right thing – *and she knew what the right thing was* – she hung on to the child, while allowing the police to mount a search that she knew was an appalling waste of their time and resources.

'I'm sure, like me, you wish little Chloe well for her future, and I don't imagine any of us wishes otherwise for the defendant. She certainly didn't seem to have a malicious intent when she kept the child, and we've heard today how well she took care of her. However, nothing can get us away from the fact that we have laws in this country which apply to every one of us, including social workers, and if we break any of those laws the consequences must be met. I understand it might seem hard to punish a woman for loving a child, but I ask you to put your emotions aside as you consider the crime she has committed. It is a very serious crime, and just so we're clear about what the law says, let me read it out to you: the abduction of a child under Section Two of the Child Abduction Act of 1984 is when a person *without lawful authority or reasonable excuse takes or detains a child under the age of sixteen so as to remove him or her from the lawful control of any person having lawful control of the child, or so as to keep him or her out of the lawful control of any person entitled to lawful control . . .*

'In the first instance it could be argued that Charlotte Nicholls had both the lawful authority and a reasonable excuse to take the child from the house on North Hill on the night of 6th October. But she had neither lawful authority nor reasonable excuse to *detain* the child after that – and she most certainly did not have the right to take the child out of the country to the other side of the world.

'So I'm afraid, ladies and gentlemen of the jury, no matter how else we might want to look at this, and I understand it can be difficult when our emotions are engaged, the law is very clear. Ms Nicholls knowingly broke that law and so she must meet the consequences. I ask you to return a verdict of guilty not only for justice to be done, but to send a clear message to everyone everywhere that no one, even for what they might consider to be the right reasons, can take a child that isn't theirs and try to make it their own.'

As he retook his seat, Charlotte couldn't bear to look at the jury. His argument had been so short, yet powerful and *right*, that she could already feel their decision forming as though it was crystallising the air between them.

To her surprise Anthony appeared unperturbed, possibly even relaxed as he got to his feet and addressed the court with the usual formalities. 'I would like you, for a moment,' he began, 'to recall the many connections you have made in your lives. The first might have been with a teacher or a friend, or an older boy or girl at school. For many the teenage years would have brought your first love, followed in some cases by the second, third and fourth.' As everyone smiled, he smiled too. 'Falling in love is one of the most profoundly powerful experiences we have in our lives; and yet most of us are at a loss to explain what it means, how it feels, exactly, much less have any idea of how or when it might strike. Nor can we say what it is about him or her that works for me when my friend can't see the attraction at all. Or let's hope they can't, anyway.'

After the smiles died down he continued. 'Love is delivered at random, bringing the greatest joys in our lives, and sometimes the greatest pain. We all know how irrational someone can be when in the throes of it, behaving in ways they might never even dream of otherwise, while the rest of us, being temporarily unafflicted and therefore in possession of our marbles, can only sit back and wait for the storm to pass. I'm referring mainly, of course, to adult love, but I'm sure you can see where I'm going. Connections are made on a visceral, or instinctive level that half the time we cannot anticipate.

'Now I want you to consider the love for a child, because it's my belief, and I feel sure you'll agree, that this is the most powerful love of all. There are no words to describe how deeply a child can bury itself in our hearts, or how it's done, it simply happens. For many of us, there are no lengths we won't go to to make a child happy, to keep it safe and give it the very best we can. Children can often make us far better people than we were before they came along. As parents we're most of us proud of our children, and make it an enormous part of our life's work to bring them up and set them on the right path.

'Sadly, not every child has parents like that, and this is why Ms Nicholls, with her great love of children, went into the profession she did. They are the reason she gets up in the morning, and why she is so passionate about protecting them. You heard her team leader, Tommy Burgess, tell us how becoming attached to a child can be one of the hazards of the job. The emotional wear and tear on social workers cannot be quantified; the heartbreak many of them suffer at the end of the day, most days, happens in private and hardly ever gets discussed. We all just take these people for granted, hoping they'll be there for a child in need, and ready to blame them if something goes wrong that more often than not couldn't have been foreseen. They receive very little praise, or indeed respect for what they do, and yet they continue to do it because they know that if they don't the most vulnerable children in our society will have no one.

'Chloe was one of those children, and the only thing that set her apart from the others was the depth of the connection that formed, almost instantly, between her and Ms Nicholls. Love can, and frequently does, take us by surprise, but Chloe, at her age, had no way of understanding, much less coping with what was happening to her. All she knew was that she wanted to be with Ms Nicholls all the time, because she'd never known what it was to be properly loved before. And Ms Nicholls, even with all her experience of working with children, was totally unprepared for the overwhelming love she felt for Chloe. We've heard her describe in the best way she could how it was between them, and no one who knows them has contradicted her. From the moment they met in the park, to the instinct that took Ms Nicholls to the house on North Hill on 6th October, to the way in which nothing intervened over the following weeks to prevent their journey to New Zealand, it was as though a greater force was at work to keep them together.

'If that's correct, then why is she standing before us now? The reason, I believe, is because the relationship she has with Chloe needs to be formalised. You might feel this is a strange way for it to happen, but you don't need me to tell you that fate can behave in some very strange ways – and in the grand scheme of things this probably isn't the most bizarre.

'So, ladies and gentlemen of the jury, does Ms Nicholls really deserve to be punished for what she did? I say what she deserves is to be able to go on loving and caring for the little girl whose world was shattered the day she was snatched from Aroha Daycare by total strangers. Since then she's been allowed no contact with Ms Nicholls, and Ms Nicholls has not been able to find out how or where Chloe is. If you imagine for a moment how hard that has been, then I'm sure you'll realise that this brutal separation has been punishment enough. Should you still be in any doubt of how much this woman and child mean to each other then I'm sure, when you look at the photograph my colleague is about to hand each of you, you will see for yourselves just how close and happy they were.'

'Let it be noted,' the judge said, looking at her own copy as Kim passed a set around the jury, 'that the photograph shows the defendant holding the child in the air.'

'And they are laughing delightedly into one another's faces,' Anthony added for the record, 'wearing the daisy chains they'd made for each other. A picture of pure happiness, of deep and very tender love.

'Where is Chloe now?' he continued after a moment. 'We don't know, but what I can tell you, members of the jury, is that she is somewhere in the care system with people who may or may not be connecting with her needs; who might have other children from difficult backgrounds with far more pressing problems; who could be in neighbourhoods where other children will try to corrupt her; who could be taking in children more for the money the state gives them than for the love of children. Some of you may have caught the news just this morning; if you did you will have heard about the shocking increase in the numbers of children in care, and how

507

poorly they fare. And the story that followed told us of how concerned social workers are by the limited time they are able to spend with children due to cutbacks, and the danger this is putting children in.

'We thought this was all being sorted out, didn't we? After the case of Baby Peter we were promised that swingeing changes would be made to make sure nothing like it ever happened again, and yet social workers, just today, are warning us that it still could.

'Ms Nicholls was well aware of the pressures the system is under when she decided she couldn't let Chloe go into care. This child who'd become so uniquely special to her needed her in a way the others didn't. This wasn't to say she in any way neglected the other children in her caseload, because no one, not even her manager who was critical in other ways, could fault her when it came to her dealings with the children.'

Pausing to glance down at his notes, he allowed several moments to pass before he looked up again.

'Ladies and gentlemen of the jury, Ms Nicholls isn't a criminal, she's quite simply someone who took the law into her own hands and gave a little girl all the love she could wish for, a family, friends and a safe and loving home. I ask you what purpose it would serve to prevent her from ever seeing Chloe again, because that is what would happen if you were to find her guilty. It won't make society a safer place, or right the wrong a parent might feel has been done to them, because Chloe has no parents – at least none who will ever be able to have custody of her again. It's my belief that the only people in this room who really want to see Ms Nicholls punished belong to the Kesterly division of Dean Valley Police, and not for abducting a child, but for the humiliation they have suffered due to their own ineptitude.

'I say let them look to themselves, while we turn our minds to a little girl who's out there somewhere in care, facing a future fraught with all kinds of dangers, when where she ought to be is with the woman who loves her and who will make sure she never comes to any harm.

'Ladies and gentlemen of the jury, I thank you for your time. I know you will give this matter your careful consideration, and I am confident you will agree that the only way justice can be humanely and properly served is to return a verdict of not guilty.'

As Anthony sat down and picked up a glass of water, the court remained silent. It was as though no one wanted to break the moment, to do anything at all to start unravelling the delicate yet compelling argument he'd made. He didn't have the law on his side and everyone knew it, but his question still resonated in the air: what purpose was there to depriving a little girl of the safe home and wonderful life he'd described?

Charlotte was hardly daring to think as the judge began explaining the jury's duties, what was now expected of them, and the procedures they could take should they require assistance of any kind. 'You've heard a most persuasive argument from Mr Goodman for the defence,' Charlotte suddenly registered, 'but I would urge you, members of the jury, to keep in mind during your deliberations the fact that a crime *has* been committed. It is why we are here, because a child, no matter how deeply she was loved, was abducted by the defendant. You will be provided with a copy of the relevant law to assist with your deliberations.'

Charlotte could feel the world falling away from her. The judge had just instructed the jury to find her guilty, so what chance was she going to stand now? She could hardly believe it had happened, and from the look on Anthony's face as he turned to her, he couldn't either.

An hour later Charlotte was alone in the ladies' room on the next floor up from the court. She'd had to come here to escape the nightmare of waiting with Anthony and her mother, Bob, Gabby, Martin . . . Everyone was crowded into the room Kim had found for them, and everyone was still trying to put a brave face on things in spite of how hopeless they now knew it to be.

'Surely the judge can't get away with that,' Bob had protested as soon as Anthony and Jolyon had come into the room.

'She can, because we haven't tried to deny that Charlotte took Chloe and held on to her,' Jolyon replied.

Anthony had said nothing at that point, but Charlotte had been able to sense how angry he was with the judge's summing up.

'She's barely said a word for the past two days,' Kim snapped irritably, 'so to go and do something like that is bloody outrageous. Surely it has to give us grounds for appeal?'

'An appeal will only be necessary if there's a guilty verdict,' Anthony had reminded her, 'so let's cross that bridge when we come to it.'

Pressing cold water to her face as though it might

wash away the images of Walworth and Nola and the threat of Molly Buck, Charlotte tried to focus only on Chloe. Never had she felt such an over-whelming need to hold her, to hear and smell her and tell her how much she loved her. She wanted to touch her hair, as dark as coffee, as soft as petals; to kiss her cheeks, as tender as a baby's. Why, she wondered, now she was on the very brink of losing her for good, was she seeming so real, so near?

'All I can hope,' she whispered to her tormented reflection as though it was Chloe, 'is that you forget me, because that will be the easiest thing for you, my darling – but I know I'll never, ever forget you.'

Chloe was sitting on the bottom step of a tombstone in a cemetery that was on the side of a hill looking down over the sea. She didn't know that the grave she was on belonged to Andy and Peggy Nicholls, their daughter Yvonne and Hugo, aged five, and that they were Mummy's family. Sally didn't know that, either. All Sally knew was that it had seemed right to bring Chloe here to show her where people went when they were dead. Had she been able to find out where Erica Wade's ashes were she'd probably have taken Chloe there, but no one had seemed to know or care about Erica Wade. So they'd come here instead, because it wasn't far from Sally's home, and was where Sally's mother had been buried, in one of the newer plots the other side of the church.

'I know how sad it is to lose your mummy,' she said softly to Chloe. 'I was very sad when I lost mine.'

Chloe's eyes were wide with confusion as tears welled from them and rolled on to her cheeks.

Why wasn't Mummy coming back? She didn't understand.

'I'm sorry,' Sally whispered, 'if I could make your mummy come back I would, but I can't.'

'She's not thinking about that woman what died,' Bobby said, ambling up to join them. 'She's thinking about t'other one.'

'I know,' Sally murmured, 'but she's not coming back either, is she?'

Bobby's pale eyes drifted down towards the sea. 'No, I s'pose not,' he grunted after a while. 'Not if she's going to prison.'

'She is,' Sally hissed, 'I already heard it on the news, that there's no way she's going to get off.'

It was strange and awful, Charlotte was thinking as the jury filed back into the court, how the last little shred of hope would never quite die. Even though she knew the press were already forecasting anything from a suspended sentence to a possible five-year term, and she knew instinctively they were right, she wasn't going to be able to accept it fully until she heard the actual words.

Perhaps not until a guard came to escort her from the dock.

Please, please don't let me ever have to go in that Reliance van again.

God, if you exist, please take care of Chloe. Let her go to some good people. It wouldn't be fair to hurt her any more; she's already been through too much.

Knowing that some children went through even worse wasn't a thought she could hold on to now. She wouldn't be in a position to help them again after this, and right now it was hard enough trying to cope with what was going on around her.

512

'Whatever happens next,' Anthony had whispered to her before they'd returned, 'it won't be the end.'

In a bizarre effort to keep herself steady, she was trying to work out what that meant; that he was intending to appeal if – when – the verdict went against them? That it wouldn't be the end for them? Maybe he'd been trying to tell her that she still shouldn't give up on Chloe . . . Oh God, there was that irrepressible shred of hope again, her tormentor and Chloe's only champion.

Chloe, I love you.

'Will the defendant please rise?'

She started to move and was suddenly so light-headed that for a horrible moment she was afraid she wouldn't be able to get up. But then she was on her feet, swallowing the bitter taste of bile in her throat and staring straight at the judge while the jury were asked if they'd reached a unanimous verdict.

'We have,' came the reply.

So not a hung jury. The very idea that everyone would want to acquit her was plain madness.

'Will you please tell the court, do you find the defendant guilty or not guilty?'

More bile rose to Charlotte's mouth as the foreman said, 'We find the defendant . . . guilty.'

The room dipped away from her as she swayed; she was being crushed from within. She didn't understand why there was so much noise. The judge was speaking, but Charlotte couldn't hear what she was saying. The jury were leaving; she wanted to scream at them to come back, but she couldn't force out the words.

Then Gabby was there, pulling her into her arms and laughing as she cried, 'Thank God, thank God.'

Charlotte blinked uncomprehendingly.

'Are you OK?' Gabby asked, ignoring the fuss going on around them.

'I – what . . .' She stumbled. 'They said guilty.'

Gabby laughed. 'No! Not guilty! It's over, Charlotte, you can go home.' She hugged her again.

Certain she was dreaming, Charlotte searched the crowd for Anthony. When their eyes met she could tell from his expression that it was true, she had misheard. They'd found her not guilty.

Minutes later Charlotte was in the corridor surrounded by her family, her legal team, Tommy and half a dozen of her former colleagues. She was still sobbing as everyone fought to get to her, wanting to hug and congratulate her, and Anthony too.

In the end Anthony said, 'The press will want a statement. Kim's already drafted something and she'll read it out if you don't want to.'

Charlotte could hardly think. Did she want to go out there and face all those cameras, the questions, opinions, censure and whatever else the world at large was needing to express?

'Let Kim,' Anthony said, sensing her reluctance. 'There'll be time to talk to them later, if you want to. For now, I think we should go and get that charming little bracelet removed from your ankle. Then, if you're up to it, Maggie wants to host a celebration.'

Maggie had already planned a party?

'What – what time is it?' she asked, searching for a clock.

'Four fifteen,' Bob told her.

Charlotte's eyes went to her mother and as they seemed to read each other's minds, Anna came to wrap her arms around her.

'Is it too late to do it today?' Anna asked huskily.

'I don't think so,' Charlotte replied, and turning to Anthony she said, 'Before we do anything else, I need to prepare an application for a residence order.'

With an ironic raise of an eyebrow he turned to Tommy, who waved an envelope in the air.

'We've got the forms right here,' Tommy told her.

Charlotte gave a sob of laughter.

'We've tried to stay positive,' Anthony smiled.

Feeling herself welling up again, she said, 'We're going to get her back, aren't we?'

'That's certainly our next goal.'

Still gazing into his eyes, she said, 'We do need to talk about us.'

'All in good time,' he promised, and stood aside as Tommy handed her the forms that, please God, would see Chloe returned to her within days.

Chapter Twenty-Six

'Wendy, you cannot block this,' Tommy declared fiercely the following morning. 'First of all you have no damned good reason to, and second if you do you'll make a serious enemy out of me.'

'Me too,' Saffy piped up.

'And me,' Tracy added. 'If you could see what it's doing to that child, being separated from the only mother she's ever really had, you'd be rushing this through so fast they'd be together by the end of today.'

Wendy's face was pinched and pale as she looked up at them. Tommy didn't even have the right to be there, but such was his affection for Charlotte that he'd stayed on to make sure that she, Wendy, didn't stand in the way of what Charlotte wanted. She wasn't surprised to see Saffy in here; Saffy and Charlotte had always got along, and Tracy, who rarely took sides, had obviously been persuaded that Charlotte was the only parent for Chloe too. They clearly weren't alone either, since the door was open and the rest of the team weren't even pretending to work as they watched and waited for her response.

'Wendy, you can do this,' Tommy told her firmly. 'You have to.'

She could no longer look at him. She hated being harangued like this, and didn't see why she should take it, especially from someone who didn't even work here any more. He was just making her want to dig her heels even deeper. 'Actually,' she finally managed, looking directly at Tracy, 'I would appreciate it if you and I could speak alone. Certain things have come up that we need to discuss and as they are no concern of anyone else's I'll thank you, Tommy and Saffy, to leave the room.'

Avoiding Tommy's glare as he left, she didn't speak again until the door was closed.

As she listened Tracy's face flushed. 'I'm sorry,' she murmured, not knowing what else to say.

Wendy slipped the application for a residence order into a drawer. 'In future it might be a good idea to let me speak before you bring your colleagues in here to attack me,' she declared, and getting to her feet she went to open the door for Tracy to leave.

Tommy caught up with Tracy as she was getting into her car. 'What's happening? Where are you going?' he demanded.

Wondering if Wendy was watching from her window, Tracy said, 'To the court.'

His eyebrows shot up. 'Does that mean she signed the order?'

Tracy shook her head. 'Not yet,' she replied. 'I'm going for another case.'

'So?'

'So, she reminded me that no one's inspected where Charlotte lives yet to make sure it's suitable.'

Tommy's jaw dropped. 'You're kidding me.'

''Fraid not. She's also worried, she says, about the fact that she's heard there's a man living there, or visiting often, and if it's true he'll need to be checked out too.'

Tommy was incredulous. 'She knows we're talking about Anthony Goodman,' he stated.

'Presumably, it's all over the press today, though she didn't mention him by name. Anyway, we can't argue with her because she's right, the proper procedures have to be gone through, and, wait for this, she's only going to carry them out herself.'

Tommy's eyes widened with shock. 'I'll call Charlotte,' he said, 'at least forewarned is forearmed, but I dread to think what's going to happen when those two come face to face. If Wendy's going to try to stand in the way of Charlotte getting Chloe back, well all I can say is Wendy's a braver soul than I took her for.'

Charlotte was with her mother and Shelley, strolling through the sprawl of deckchairs and sun worshippers on the beach, when she heard someone shouting, 'Hey! Alex! Alex!'

Hoping it wasn't anyone from the press, she turned around and shielded her eyes from the sun as she tried to spot who it was. For the moment she couldn't tell.

'It's me, Gemma,' one of a trio of teenagers announced, as she ploughed through the sand towards her.

Recognising her behind the badly applied fake tan and outrageous eyelashes, Charlotte's expression softened with affection. 'Gemma, what a lovely surprise,' she cried, giving her a hug. What had happened to the plain, shy little girl from her caseload? 'How are you? You look so grown up.'

'I'm going to be fourteen next month,' Gemma

beamed, showing a mouthful of teeth that were neither clean nor straight.

Though Charlotte knew that couldn't be true, since the girl had been only twelve this time last year, she gave a dutiful gasp of awe. 'Amazing! 'Doesn't time fly? So how are things? No, let me introduce you first. This is my mother, Anna, and my stepsister Shelley. Mum, Shel, Gemma used to be one of my star charges.'

'Hello, Gemma,' Anna said warmly. 'It's lovely to meet you.'

'Yes, lovely,' Shelley echoed. 'And who are your friends?'

Gemma spun round to where the other two were huddled over a mobile phone. 'Oh, that's just Molly and Pia,' she replied with a dismissive wave. 'We like, go to the same school, and hang out together and stuff. Obviously we're on holidays now.'

'Are you still with the Brownings?' Charlotte wanted to know, referring to the carers who'd taken Gemma into their home after her mother died.

'Oh yeah,' Gemma replied airily, 'but I'm going to be moving on in a couple of months. We've kind of like had enough of each other. They're a bit, you know, old and stuff and Linda, who's my social worker now, said it would be good if we could find someone younger.'

Dismayed to hear that, since she knew how kind the Brownings had been to Gemma and her mother during her mother's illness, Charlotte said, 'I'm sure they'll be sad to see you go. They were always very fond of you.'

Though Gemma gave a careless shrug, Charlotte could tell she wasn't quite as indifferent as she was trying to appear. 'Yeah, well, you know,' she sighed, 'they're always on my case about my clothes and my mates and stuff, it's like non-stop. Really does my head in. Anyway, I been hearing all about you on the news and I'm really, really glad you got off. It would have been like mental if you hadn't.'

Charlotte smiled. 'Thank you,' she said softly.

'And all that crap they been writing about you in the papers since, well some papers anyway, it's like sooo obvious they don't know you. It makes me so mad, honest, it does.'

Taking her hand, Charlotte said, 'Don't you worry about me, I can fight my battles, you just need to think of you and what a lovely girl you are.'

'Oh yeah, like right,' Gemma scoffed with a blush.

'I think so, and I know the Brownings do too, so don't give up on them, Gem. They're just doing what they think is best, and not everyone's as sweet and caring as them.'

Gemma pulled a face.

Leaning in to whisper, Charlotte said, 'I think your mum would want you to stay there, don't you?'

As Gemma's colour deepened tears welled in her eyes.

Having guessed that she was still grieving, Charlotte pulled her closer and stroked her hair. 'You're doing really well,' she murmured. 'I think she'd be proud of you.'

Pulling back, Gemma kept her head down as her eyes slid off towards the sea. 'You know what I wanted to ask you,' she said, 'is why you didn't take me? I wanted you to, do you remember? I begged you to, but you didn't.'

As guilt twisted her heart, Charlotte replied, 'The circumstances were very different, Gem, but that doesn't mean you weren't special to me, because you were, you know that, and you still are . . .'

'But my mum had just died, same as hers, so why did you choose her and not me?'

'Oh sweetheart, I promise you it wasn't about choosing between you. That didn't even come into it.'

'So can't you take me now?'

Aching with pity, Charlotte cupped a hand round her chubby face as she told her, 'You're settled here, with the Brownings, and no matter how much they might annoy you at times I know they love you. They won't want to lose you, and I don't think you want to lose them either, not really.'

'I wouldn't care if you said I could come with you.'

Folding her back into an embrace, Charlotte said, 'Yes you would, because I know you've got a very tender little heart in that new big chest of yours . . .'

Gemma giggled.

'. . . and the Brownings mean a lot more to you than you're letting on.'

'Yeah, well, it might be easier if you were still my social worker,' Gemma grumbled. 'I've had about five different ones since you left and not one of them's anything like you. Do you think you'll be coming back now?'

Smiling as she looked down at her, Charlotte said, 'To be honest, I don't think they'd have me, but even if they were willing, it wouldn't be possible.'

As another question formed on Gemma's lips one of her friends shouted, 'Hey! Gem! Come on, we have to go. Everyone's there already.'

Spinning round, Gemma said, 'Don't go without me.' Then to Charlotte, 'It was really cool seeing you. Like I said, I'm really glad you got off, but I still wish it was me you took,' and after giving her a bruising hug she dashed off down the beach after her friends.

Looking from her mother to Shelley as they closed in either side of her to start walking again, Charlotte sighed and linked their arms. She wondered how many of her other charges felt she had let them down by taking Chloe and not them. And how would she explain it to them if they got the chance to ask? She probably wouldn't do any better than she had with Gemma, since there was no easy way – in fact no way at all – to tell one child that they hadn't meant quite as much as another.

Taking out her phone as it beeped with a text she saw there were two, and opened the one from Anthony first. As she read it she smiled past the disquiet her thoughts had aroused. 'Seems the guys are having a successful day,' she told her mother and Shelley. 'Rick's caught two, Bob three and Anthony three, so trout for dinner at Maggie's?'

'Sounds good to me,' Shelley responded, springing up to catch a beach ball and tossing it back to its owner.

'I'll text Maggie to say I'll be over early to help,' Anna declared, taking out her own phone.

Charlotte's second text turned out to be from Tracy. As she opened it she felt a horrible clenching in her stomach and a wave of dizziness passing through her. For a moment the words swam before her eyes, as though dancing in a heat haze, then registering what they said she bit down hard on her frustration and passed the phone to her mother so Anna could read the message too.

* * *

The following day Charlotte waited in the sitting room while Anthony went down to sort out a parking space for Wendy in the residents' bays across the street. If she weren't so anxious, she might actually be able to admire Wendy's nerve in coming here. As it was she could only feel thankful that Anthony was going to be around to keep a lid on the proceedings, otherwise they probably wouldn't even get as far as hello before things took a turn for the worse. Of course she understood that the proper checks had to be carried out, but she also knew that Wendy was perfectly able to fast-track the residence order were she of a mind to. If she had, it might have been granted by now, and preparations would be under way to welcome Chloe home. Instead, Wendy had decided to come and carry out the inspection herself, no doubt already relishing the thought of being able to have a good nose around Charlotte's home, while flaunting her power and making Charlotte grovel.

Remember, you're doing this for Chloe, and humbling yourself to Wendy is a very small price to pay if it all works out in the end. And it will work out, it really will.

She had to believe that, or she'd never get through the next hour.

'Here we are, through here,' Anthony was saying chattily as he led Wendy to the sitting room. 'We've made some coffee, but if you'd prefer tea . . .'

'No, no, coffee's fine,' Wendy assured him, appearing in the doorway with her head tilted up to the ceiling, apparently searching for cobwebs.

Wishing she'd remembered to carry out the search herself, Charlotte said, 'Wendy!' and promptly cringed at the falseness in her tone. Still, at least she was trying.

'How nice to see you,' Wendy responded, with an expression Charlotte couldn't quite read. 'You're looking well.'

Unable to detect any disdain, yet, Charlotte accepted the gloves were still on for the time being and said, 'Thank you, so are you.'

'Milk? Sugar?' Anthony offered, as he poured the coffee.

Wendy pinked slightly as she looked at him. 'Neither for me,' she replied. Her eyes began travelling around the room again, taking in every crack and crevice, stray crumb and wandering hair. 'Well, I must admit, I never expected us to meet again under these circumstances,' she commented, gazing at the open French windows where a thirsty-looking planter of geraniums was hanging from the balcony rails.

'No, me neither,' Charlotte muttered. Was she imagining it, or was Wendy finding it hard to meet her eyes? A painful jolt of unease struck through her. Surely to God Wendy wasn't here to tell her that the residence order couldn't be processed? It wasn't that the possibility hadn't occurred to her, because it had; she just hadn't been able to imagine Wendy finding the courage to come and tell her in person.

'Thank you,' Wendy said to Anthony as he passed her a mug and invited her to sit down.

Having never really seen Wendy at a loss before, Charlotte found herself at one too. What was going on? Why wasn't Wendy stalking around here like a health and safety freak making her feel as though the place wasn't fit for animals, never mind a child *you made off with when you were on my team, and have you given even a moment's consideration to all the stress you've caused me since, not to mention the sleepless nights when I thought I might lose my job, and the humiliation of headlines these past few days such as: It's OK to steal a child in Kesterly.* That particular nastiness had only appeared in the local *Gazette* but it would still have been very damaging for Wendy, who probably didn't know, or had forgotten, that Heather Hancock had always had it in for Charlotte.

Actually, Charlotte realised, she probably hadn't given enough thought to how her actions might have affected Wendy, and sadly it was a bit late now.

'Would you like a biscuit?' Anthony offered, picking up the plate. 'I was going to lie and say I made them myself, but then I thought, under the circumstances that might be going too far.'

To Charlotte's surprise Wendy seemed to find that funny, or at least she got the joke. *New daddy figure, bakes biscuits, must be a good guy.*

Suddenly realising she was frozen like a deer in headlights, Charlotte mentally shook herself and tried for a sprightly tone. 'So how are things going with the new hub? Is it working out well to have both divisions of Kesterly under the same roof? Well, obviously it is, with you running it, how could it not be?' She really wished she hadn't said that, since it sounded even more sarcastic than sycophantic and wasn't supposed to be either. However, if it was what Wendy needed to hear she'd say it again and again and again; she only wished she could make it come across as more believable, and that Anthony wasn't looking at her as though he might laugh.

To Charlotte's surprise Wendy didn't seem to be listening to the compliments. She was looking in the direction of Chloe's photograph on the mantelpiece.

Not sure whether to go and fetch it, or to pretend not to have noticed, Charlotte was about to speak when Anthony put a discreet hand on her arm. Realising he was cautioning her to relax, drink her coffee and let things flow, she tried and failed. She was wondering now if Wendy had seen the picture already, since it was the one Anthony had handed out at the trial, showing Charlotte and Chloe laughing into one another's eyes. It wasn't permissible for the press to reveal Chloe's face, of course, so it had been pixilated in a way that attempted to convey a sense of her joy while not making her recognisable. However, it was patently the shot that had graced many front pages the day after the trial.

How split the nation seemed on whether she should have got off or not! Everyone was talking about it in the papers, on TV, the Internet. Charlotte was doing her best not to engage. All that mattered to her now was getting Chloe back; she'd deal with everything else later.

She wondered if Wendy had ever actually seen Chloe before.

'She's very sweet,' Wendy commented.

'Yes, she is,' Charlotte confirmed. 'Very.'

Anthony shot her a warning look.

Wendy took a sip of her coffee and began studying the bench that was now decorated with pale blue and cream silk pillows and matching seat pad.

'My father made it,' Charlotte blurted. 'I mean the bench.'

Wendy looked surprised. 'The rector made it?'

'No, my real father. Anthony found it online.'

Wendy nodded, and sipped her coffee again.

Trying to keep her tone pleasant, but needing to move things on, Charlotte said, 'Well, I'm sure you know who Anthony is; he's the lawyer who represented me at the trial, but obviously, he understands the need for him to have a criminal record check, so if you haven't already . . .'

'It's been done,' Wendy assured her quietly.

Thrown, Charlotte glanced at Anthony, who simply raised his eyebrows and lifted a foot to rest it on the other knee.

Deciding to continue with her bid to impress, Charlotte told Wendy, 'We have two bedrooms here, and as you can see it's very clean and well taken care of. I'm happy to show you around, or if you'd rather do it alone . . .'

'It's OK,' Wendy said, 'it's not . . . Well, it's not really why I came. I know you can provide a good home for the child and of course I have no doubts about Anthony either. It's just that the formalities need to be gone through and I . . . I thought that maybe this would be a good opportunity for me to come here and try to . . . Well, to have a talk with you.'

Baffled, Charlotte glanced at Anthony again to see if he had any idea where this might be going, but his attention was focused wholly on Wendy.

'This isn't very easy for me to say,' Wendy continued, looking down at her coffee, 'but I'm going to try.'

Charlotte was starting to panic. Either Wendy herself, or someone higher up had decreed that no matter what a jury thought, it was *not* OK to steal a child in Kesterly.

'Ever since you joined the team,' Wendy was saying, 'was it eight or nine years ago . . .'

'Nine,' Charlotte said croakily.

Wendy nodded. 'Well, in all that time I've been

aware of how easily people warm to you. You don't have to go out of your way to make yourself liked, or admired, or loved by the children, it all comes so naturally to you that I . . . Well, I have to confess it's made me jealous of you at times, and because of that I haven't always treated you fairly or kindly.'

Charlotte blinked, not sure she was hearing right.

'Fiery though you can be,' Wendy continued, 'I'm not sure you've got it in you to hurt anyone, at least not deliberately, and knowing that about you . . . Well, it made me more resentful than ever, because I do have it in me and I wish I didn't. People aren't drawn to me the way they are to you, they probably wouldn't even notice me if I weren't their boss.' Her smile was a flat line as she glanced down at her coffee again. 'Anyway, before this turns into a hideously self-pitying rant, I want to apologise for the way I've been with you in the past, for making life difficult when I probably didn't need to, and especially for not allowing you to know anything about Chloe over these last few months. If it's any consolation I truly thought I was doing the right thing, but I realise now how hard that must have been for you, and I know it hasn't been easy for her either. It's OK, she's fine,' she added quickly as Charlotte's eyes widened with alarm, 'but it's clear from every carer she's been with since coming back here that all she really wants is you.'

As emotions began unlocking in Charlotte's chest, she tried to speak and found she couldn't.

'The residence order has been approved,' Wendy continued, putting her mug on the table, 'and I hope, in time, you'll be able to accept my apology.'

Spurred by a surge of unbridled emotion, Charlotte rushed to embrace her. 'Of course I accept it,' she cried, 'and it's me who should be apologising, not you. I was a nightmare at times, especially with you, and there was never any need for it. You were just doing your job, and I should have realised that and been more respectful. I'm sorry, I really am. If there's any way I can make up for it, please just tell me how.'

With an unsteady smile, Wendy replied, 'All you have to do is give that little girl the home she deserves.'

'Yes, oh yes,' Charlotte gasped. 'I will, I promise.'

Taking her hand, Anthony drew her back into the circle of his arm as he asked, 'Can you give us any idea when it's likely to happen?'

Crooking a finger beneath one eye to block a tear, Wendy said, 'If it's not too soon for you, Tracy will bring her on Friday.'

Charlotte spent the next two days in a dizzying state of intense and exhausting emotion, as she shopped with her mother and Shelley for everything they could possibly need for Chloe, aged four. Meanwhile, Anthony and Bob were turning the second bedroom into a little girl's dream, and Rick was calling regularly from London to find out if there was anything he could bring back from his meeting. Over at Maggie and Ron's hurried repairs to the tree house were under way ready for Chloe's visits, and down in Devon the twins were thinking up all kinds of games to play with their new cousin.

'You understand, don't you,' Charlotte had said to them on the phone several times, 'that it might be a bit soon to meet her this weekend? She'll have to get used to us all again and we don't want to overwhelm her, do we?'

'No, definitely not,' they'd agreed with one voice. 'But we will be able to meet her, won't we?'

'Of course you will, just as soon as she's had a chance to settle in. And I'm sure, once I've told her about you, she'll want to meet you straight away.'

The truth was, she had no idea how Chloe was going to react to anything or anyone after being away for so long, and the fear that she'd gone so deeply inside herself that it might take weeks, even months to reach her, was growing each day. She knew from her chats with Tracy that Chloe hadn't spoken in the past six months, other than to ask for her, and while it just about broke her heart to think of it, it was unnerving her too. How on earth was she going to persuade her that it was safe to trust Mummy again, after Mummy had let her down so badly? She was too young to understand what had happened, too emotionally fragile to be able to cope with much more.

'All you can do is take one day at a time,' her mother repeatedly advised, 'and remember how well she survived what happened to her before. In other words, she might look as delicate as a flower, but even when she's been crushed her little spirit seems to survive.'

Please, please, let her little spirit bring her through again. Don't let this time in care, the fear and confusion of why Mummy disappeared, turn out to be what's finally broken her.

'You'll have plenty of help,' Tracy reminded her. 'She's already seeing a psychologist, and we're hopeful she'll start responding more favourably to him if you're there too.'

Him? Charlotte had wanted to say. Didn't they realise, after everything Chloe had suffered at the hands of her father, how hard she'd find it to open up to a man? She guessed they did know, but with so many children in the system it wasn't always possible to make a special case of an individual, though where they'd been able, she'd discovered, they had placed her with a single woman. Tracy hadn't yet told her much detail about any of the carers, but Charlotte would be quizzing her on it soon, since it was going to be vital for her to know as much as she could about what Chloe had been through as she tried to settle her back in.

With so much to do and make plans for, Thursday evening was suddenly upon them, and while she was a hundred times more agitated than a teenager preparing for a first date, she knew she had to set it aside for at least a few hours. This was going to be the last night she and Anthony would spend together for a while, and she wasn't sure exactly when they'd see each other next. They'd agreed it wouldn't be right for him to come to the flat until Charlotte felt Chloe was ready to meet him – and before that she'd have to explain who he was.

That might be easier if she had an idea of who he wanted to be in Chloe's world, presuming he wanted to be in it at all. He hadn't said he didn't, and given how readily he'd thrown himself into the preparations for her return, not to mention into achieving it, Charlotte had to believe that he had at least some sort of plan for staying in their lives. On the other hand, he might be viewing tonight as the perfect time for them to go their separate ways.

Watching him as he stood at the table pouring two glasses of wine, the sun streaming in through the open windows either side of him and the cry of seagulls swooping through the air outside, she couldn't help thinking of her mother's words: *Sometimes people come into our lives for the time they're needed and then they go again.*

She was desperate for that not to be the case with Anthony, but maybe it was why he'd never been willing to discuss the future; he'd always known in his mind that once the trial was over and Chloe's custody was sorted, he'd be moving on with his life. Was that what he was preparing to tell her now, as he brought her drink to the sofa and sat at the opposite end?

He usually sat with her, so why the distance?

She had no right to expect him to delay his plans any longer than he already had; six months had passed since the start of his sabbatical, and thanks to her he'd had virtually no time off at all. He'd intended to travel, to take time to think about his future and whether he wanted to go in a new direction or continue with the law. He was such a practised, even natural, barrister that she couldn't help feeling it would be a great loss to the Bar, to the public too, if he decided to give it all up. On the other hand, if he did stay with it she'd have to accept that there could be no future for them at all.

Unable to bear even the thought of that, she forced a smile as they touched glasses and toasted tomorrow.

'I wonder,' he said, lifting a foot on to one knee in his habitual fashion, 'if she has any idea that all her dreams are about to come true?'

Swallowing her nerves, Charlotte replied, 'I doubt it. Tracy thought it was best to leave telling her until she goes to pick her up in the morning.'

Seeming to see the sense of that, he took another sip of his wine and said, 'Do you have anything planned for the rest of the day, once she's back?'

'No, not really.' Having been unable to think much beyond how it was going to be when she actually saw her, and that kept changing by the minute, she'd been unable to focus her mind much beyond it. 'If it feels right I might take her over to the carousel, or for a walk on the beach. They're places she'll recognise from before.' Wanting to close the gap between them, she reached for his hand. 'You understand, don't you . . .'

'Ssh, of course I understand,' he interrupted. 'It would be very confusing for her to have me around at this stage, although I must admit, I'm keen to meet her.'

Loving him for those words, she said, 'I just know you'll fall for her the same way I did. She's so sweet and good and eager to please, though I have to admit I'm hoping she'll learn how to be as naughty as the next child one of these days.'

Smiling, he linked his fingers through hers and drank some more wine.

'What will you do tomorrow?' she asked.

'Actually, I was thinking I'd go up to London for a few days. I ought to check the mail and make sure the house is still standing.'

'Do you realise I've never actually seen where you live?' she reminded him.

He arched a humorous eyebrow and she couldn't help but smile. The only reason she'd never been to London with him was because until last week her bail terms had confined her to Kesterly.

Would he invite her there now?

'Tell me,' he said, 'do you want me to get to know Chloe?'

Her heart leapt with the shock of surprise. 'Yes, of course,' she assured him. 'More than anything. Why on earth would you think otherwise?'

He was watching her closely.

Remembering how well he read her, she seemed to collapse inside as she said, 'OK, I have to admit, I don't want to get her used to you only for you to disappear again, and I know you have plans . . .'

His hand went up. 'My plans are not what you think they are. In fact, they've changed so radically over the last few months that I can barely remember what they used to be.'

Reacting to the humour in his eyes, she asked, 'So are you going to tell me what they are now?'

He appeared thoughtful, apparently debating his reply. 'You know, I'm really not sure this is the right time to get into that,' he told her. 'I think you need to get Chloe home first, settle her in, and then we might have a clearer idea of what we both want to do.'

Though his words were beyond generous, her heart contracted with misgiving. 'You know I want to go for adoption so I can take her back to New Zealand,' she said. 'I've never made a secret of it . . .'

'Actually, you've never spelled it out that clearly before, but obviously I assumed it was what you intended.'

Feeling utterly wretched now, she said, 'Which doesn't fit in with you at all.'

His head went to one side. 'Are you telling me, or asking me?'

Since she wasn't entirely sure, she lowered her eyes as she sought the courage to speak the words that were clambering to the top of her heart.

In the end, clinging to them before they could disappear, she said, 'My mother told me once that I couldn't make my whole life about Chloe. Even though I knew she was right I didn't want to listen. In fact I hated hearing it, mainly because I love Chloe with all my heart and I know I always will.' Her eyes flicked briefly to his. 'The thing is,' she continued, still not quite able to look at him, 'since we've been together, you and me, I've discovered that it doesn't mean I can't feel as strongly for someone else. In fact I clearly can, because I do. But what I need to do for Chloe, and what I want to do for us – and for me and my mother, now we've found each other again . . . I keep trying to reconcile it all in my mind, to sort out what to do for the best, but I never seem able to come up with an answer that can work for everyone.'

Taking her glass from her hand, he put it on the table and drew her to him. 'You've got a big day ahead of you tomorrow,' he said softly, 'and no doubt a few more challenges to overcome before any real decisions can be made. So maybe it's time to relax now, think a little about what we've said, and then concentrate on how happy you're going to make one very lucky little girl in the morning.'

535

Chapter Twenty-Seven

'She's outside in the garden,' Sally was saying as she led Tracy through to the kitchen. 'All her stuff's ready, not that she has much, but I bought her a couple of things, a new toothbrush and a flannel. I'd have got her some toys, but all she ever seems to want is the bear.'

Unsurprised to hear that, Tracy went to the open door where a beaded curtain was fluttering in the breeze. 'Have you told her anything?' she asked, peering through.

'Well no,' Sally said awkwardly. 'You said not to, so I just mentioned that you were coming today.'

Spotting Chloe sitting at the far end of the lawn with her legs outstretched and the bear between them, facing her, Tracy felt captivated all over again by how cute – and horribly lonely – she seemed. Then she frowned. 'She looks as though she's talking,' she remarked, glancing back at Sally.

Peering over Tracy's shoulder, Sally said, 'I expect she is, because she does to the bear. As soon as you get close she clams up again.'

Intrigued, Tracy moved on through the curtain and turned off her mobile as she started across the grass. For the next hour or so she wanted her focus to be wholly on Chloe and returning her to Charlotte. After that she could turn her attention to the three dozen or more children in her caseload who, by then, would be in far greater need of her care.

'Hello you,' she said tenderly as Chloe turned to watch her coming. 'How are you today?'

As usual there was no reply. However, instead of getting to her feet and taking Tracy's hand, the way she normally did in the hope of being taken to Mummy, she stayed sitting on the grass with her bear.

'Were you having a nice little chat with Boots?' Tracy asked, going down to her level.

Chloe's eyes went to the bear, but she neither nodded nor shook her head.

'I've got some good news for you,' Tracy told her in a whisper. 'Do you want to know what it is?'

Still no response.

'How about we go and see Mummy?' Tracy said, thrilled that she was finally able to utter those words.

To her amazement Chloe didn't react to that either.

'Did you hear what I said?' Tracy asked gently. 'We're going to see Mummy.'

Chloe's head stayed down.

Concerned, Tracy said, 'I thought you'd be excited to see Mummy.'

A cracked little whisper broke from Chloe's lips.

'What did you say?' Tracy asked.

'Mummy's dead,' Chloe told her.

Puzzled, Tracy said, 'Mummy isn't dead. Why do you say that?'

'Actually,' Sally piped up from behind her, 'technically speaking her mother is dead.'

Tracy turned to look up at her. She surely hadn't just heard right.

Sally shrugged awkwardly.

Taking her to one side so Chloe wouldn't hear, Tracy said, 'Have you told her her mother's dead?'

Sally swallowed. 'I thought it would be for the best, and it's not a lie, is it, because the woman what gave birth to her, she's not with us any more, is she?'

'But you know she thinks of Charlotte as her mother,' Tracy hissed.

Trying to shrug it off, Sally said, 'Yeah, but it wasn't looking very like Charlotte was coming back for her either, was it? So I thought it would help her to move on if she knew the truth.'

'Except it's not the truth,' Tracy snapped, failing to bite down on her anger. 'You can't take these decisions into your own hands . . .'

'I'm sorry, I didn't mean no harm,' Sally rasped. 'I'd never do anything to hurt her, not intentionally. I've become really fond of her, Bobby has too. We were even talking about seeing if we could adopt her.'

Having dealt with many people whose intelligence wasn't quite what she'd have liked it to be, Tracy knew there was no point remonstrating with the silly woman now. The damage had already been done and all she could do was hope it wasn't lasting.

Returning to Chloe, she lifted her to her feet and lowered herself so she could look into her eyes. 'Mummy's not dead,' she told her softly, 'she's at home waiting for you, and I'm going to take you there now.'

Whether or not Chloe believed her was impossible to tell, for once again she showed no reaction.

Since there was only one way to handle this now, Tracy took Chloe to the car, sat her in, then opened her mobile to call Charlotte.

* * *

538

It's not going to matter, Charlotte kept telling herself, as she paced up and down waiting for Tracy and Chloe to arrive. *As soon as she sees me she'll know it's not true and everything will be fine.*

'Of course it will,' Anthony had reassured her when she'd called to tell him what had happened. 'Does she even really know what dead is?'

'I'm not sure. I wouldn't think so, at her age. I know I've never explained it to her, but heaven only knows what the wretched carer has told her.'

'Whatever it was, you're in a position now to put things straight.'

'Of course. And I will. I mean, how can I not when I'm patently not dead?'

'Take a breath,' he advised.

Doing as she was told, she found it helped. 'Are you still OK with our change of plan?' she asked. Having decided during the night that it wouldn't be a good idea to make a big deal out of introducing him to Chloe, she'd woken him up to suggest that he came with her family as though he was one of them, or at least a friend who was kind of supposed to be there.

'If you think that's the best way to go,' he told her now, 'I'm up for it, but I really will have to go to London on Monday at least for a couple of days.'

'OK, it's fine. I'm sorry I've asked you to put it off, but the more I think about it the more convinced I am that we need to do it this way.' She jumped and almost gasped as the door buzzer blasted down the hall. 'That must be them,' she blurted. 'Wish me luck,' and forgetting to say goodbye she clicked off the line and ran to the entryphone.

'Hi, it's us,' Tracy announced over the intercom. 'I've had to leave the car on a double yellow . . .'

'I'll bring down a permit,' Charlotte told her, wanting to kick herself for not thinking of it sooner.

'No, it's OK, I'll come and get it.'

'Is she . . . Is she with you?'

'Yes, she's here. So's Boots.'

As her heart swelled with an unsteadying rush of relief and joy she quickly released the downstairs door, fumbled to open the one next to her, then ran back down the hall to the sitting room. This was what she'd arranged with Tracy, for Tracy to bring Chloe into the flat rather than have the reunion outside on the street, or on the stairs.

By the time she heard them coming in the front door, putting down bags and Tracy chattering away, her heart was thudding so hard it was making her shake. Her hands were bunched tightly at her mouth as though to hold back the longing, while inside she was repeating over and over, *please let it be all right, please, please.* She could imagine Chloe's little feet coming along the hall tucked neatly into trainers or sandals; she probably had one hand in Tracy's, while the other would be clutching Boots. Her pretty curls would be all wayward and fluffy – *please don't let anyone have cut them off* – and her big eyes would be taking everything in as she wondered where she was. It tore at Charlotte's heart to think she might be afraid.

'Here we are,' Tracy said tenderly, coming into the room first. 'And what did I tell you? I said, didn't I, that Mummy would be here?'

As Chloe came in after her with Boots under one arm, it took every ounce of willpower Charlotte possessed not to run and sweep her into her arms. She'd grown in six months, and it devastated Charlotte to see how sad she looked, but she was still the adorable little girl from Te Puna and Charlotte knew it wasn't possible to love her more.

'Hello, sweetheart,' she whispered shakily.

Chloe only stared at her.

'Aren't you going to say hello?' Tracy asked gently.

Chloe's eyes were still on Charlotte.

'You do remember me, don't you?' Charlotte said, gripped by the fear that Chloe might not.

Then she realised Chloe was trembling, and suddenly huge, wrenching sobs began tearing from her.

'I'm sorry, Mummy,' she gasped. 'I'm sorry. I won't be naughty again.'

'Oh my darling, my love,' Charlotte choked, rushing to scoop her into a crushing embrace. 'You didn't do anything wrong.' The feel of her in her arms was so wonderful, so right, she was in danger of crushing her too tight. 'It's Mummy who should be sorry,' she sobbed, 'and I am, my darling, so, so sorry.' She drew back to look at her, smoothed her hair and kissed her face all over. 'Oh, God, I've missed you so much. Thank God, thank God, thank God you're here.'

Chloe could still hardly speak, she was crying so hard. 'Go home now?' she managed to ask.

'Oh yes, we can go home,' Charlotte laughed, hugging her again. 'Just as soon as we've sorted some things out, but you're going to stay here with me while we do that. You do want to stay, don't you?'

The way Chloe's arms and legs tightened around her was answer enough.

'We're going to be together,' Charlotte told her, 'just like we always were, and I promise no one's ever going to take you away again.'

'No, not again,' Chloe echoed, her little body still jerking with sobs.

'No, no, definitely not.'

Picking up Boots who'd dropped to the floor, Tracy used a finger to dab the tears from her own eyes, and setting him on the bench she whispered, 'Better go move the car.'

'There's a permit next to the front door,' Charlotte told her, her voice muffled by Chloe's embrace, 'and thank you. Thank you so much. I can't tell you how happy I am to have her back.'

Tracy had to laugh. 'I kind of noticed,' she said wryly.

Charlotte laughed too, and began kissing Chloe's hair again. Even if she wanted to, which she definitely didn't, there wasn't much chance of her putting Chloe down any time soon, because they were both holding on so tight it seemed they might never let go.

An hour later, Tracy had gone and Charlotte was sitting at the table with Chloe, watching her eat a brownie that used to be one of her favourites at the café along the road. She wasn't sure if Chloe remembered those days, when they'd go for treats after nursery, and she wasn't going to ask in case a little trip back in time managed to stir up memories of her father. For now it was enough just to sit here with her, watching the colour returning to her cheeks and trying not to keep touching her.

'You've grown so pretty,' she told her, smoothing her hair again. The feel of her, the smell of her, the very essence of her was swelling through Charlotte as insistently as if it had all the power of the tide outside. It was right that she was here, that they were together again, and she could only feel an eternal gratitude to Anthony and to the jury for making it possible. She should feel grateful to life too, she guessed, and its very strange way of doing things.

Chloe didn't seem interested in her compliment as she munched her brownie and swung her legs back and forth. Her eyes came to Charlotte, and she gave a chocolatey smile that just about melted Charlotte's heart.

'I can't tell you how happy I am to see you,' Charlotte whispered. 'And guess who else wants to see you? Nanna and Grandpa; Auntie Shelley and Uncle Wick.'

Chloe blinked as she took this in. 'Uncle Wick,' she repeated with a spray of crumbs. 'Nanna.'

Loving the sound of her voice, while wondering what memories she had of her family and what new ones had settled since they'd been parted, Charlotte had to swallow before she said, 'Yes, they're here. They came all the way from New Zealand to help me find you, and now here you are.'

Chloe's dark eyes stayed on hers. 'Not naughty,' she said earnestly.

'No, no, no,' Charlotte assured her. 'You're not naughty. You're a good girl, and I love you very, very much.'

'Stay with you now.'

'Of course you're staying with me. You'll always be with me from now on, because as soon as we can arrange it I'll be your legal mummy and then we'll be able to go back to New Zealand where we'll have the same surname and you'll have your own passport and a new birth certificate.' She knew this was far too much for Chloe to understand, but she'd needed to say it anyway, and felt sure she'd be saying it often over the coming days and weeks.

'Boots,' Chloe announced, pointing to where he was sitting on the table beside her.

'Yes, and doesn't he look smart.' In fact he was tattier than ever, and an ear seemed to be missing, but it was almost as good to see him as it was to hear Chloe speaking. Whatever had been going on with the carers she clearly hadn't felt confident enough to open up to them, or she simply hadn't wanted to. Either way, she was finding her voice now.

'She's a little girl who knows her own mind, that's for sure,' Tracy had commented before leaving. 'Tenacious, that's what she is. You were all she ever wanted and she never wavered from it once.'

Hearing that had affected Charlotte deeply; how lonely and frightened she must have been, how bewildered by the strangers coming and going from her life. Had anyone been cruel to her? Please God there had been no more abuse. Tracy had assured her there were no signs of it, but Charlotte knew from bitter experience how long it had taken to detect them before.

'Going through that trial the way you did,' Tracy had continued, as they'd walked to the door, 'and pleading not guilty . . . It was a really big chance you took. I know I wouldn't have had your courage if it had been me, but thank God, it paid off in the end.'

Yes, it had paid off, because Chloe was here, right in front of her; it wasn't a dream, and all the threats, the dread of prison, of never being allowed to see her again had gone away.

You're meant to be together, her mother had texted

earlier and Charlotte knew, because she'd always known, that Anna was right. She just had to hope there were no complications with the adoption now, though Wendy had assured her she would lend her support in getting it through as quickly as possible.

'Would you like to see your room again?' she asked, as Chloe downed the last of her squash.

Grabbing Boots, Chloe slid down from the table and took Charlotte's hand to walk along the hall to the princess emporium Bob and Anthony had created. Though it was completely over the top, awash with pink and glitter and stars on the ceiling and lacy pillows on the bed, Chloe seemed delighted with it and that was all that mattered.

They spent the next half an hour unpacking the few belongings she'd brought with her, adding them to the new wardrobe Anna and Charlotte had splashed out on, while Boots watched from his new position inside a cherry-coloured three-wheeler stroller.

'Do you think you'll like to sleep here?' Charlotte asked as they lay together on the bed staring up at the stars.

'Sleep with you,' Chloe answered.

Since she'd expected this and had forewarned Anthony that it might take a while for her to feel OK about sleeping alone, Charlotte simply smiled as she said, 'OK.'

'And Boots.'

'Of course, Boots too.'

A while later Chloe whispered, 'Mum-my.'

Realising it wasn't a question, more a little statement of wonder, Charlotte turned on to her side to look at her. 'Chloe,' she said softly.

Chloe broke into a smile and waved her hands in the air.

Was it really possible to love someone so much?

'Are you tired?' Charlotte asked, 'or would you like to play a game?'

'Do a painting?'

'That's a lovely idea. Shall we do one for Nanna?'

'Yes, for Nanna.' Her voice was quieter as she added, 'And for Grandpa.'

Startled, Charlotte said, 'For Grandpa too? That's lovely. He'll be very pleased. What are you going to make the painting of?'

Chloe shook her head. 'I don't know,' she answered, and her eyes welled with tears.

'Oh, sweetheart,' Charlotte murmured, pulling her close, 'don't worry if you can't think of anything now. Let's do one for Nanna first and see if we can come up with something for Grandpa later.'

They spent the rest of the day just the two of them, painting and watching the world from the window, spotting ships on the horizon and clapping when the donkeys trotted back along the sands with their riders. Since Chloe expressed no desire to go down there, Charlotte didn't suggest it, simply took her into her bedroom and got her ready for the bath.

'Nanna will come tomorrow,' she told her, squeezing a sponge over her back and watching the bubbles swim down over her slippery little limbs. 'She's going to be very happy to see you. Everyone is. I expect you'll be happy to see them too, won't you?'

Chloe nodded and zoomed her toy fish through the foam.

'Mummy's got a new friend who I want you to meet. His name's Anthony.'

Chloe was intent on filling up the fish and squirting the water back into the bath, so Charlotte decided to leave it there. The first seed had been sown; there would be plenty of time to mention him again in the morning.

As it turned out it was the following afternoon, when Charlotte suggested they write everyone's name in icing on the cupcakes they'd made, that the subject came up quite naturally.

Clearly thrilled by the idea of naming the cakes, Chloe said, 'That way everyone will know which one is theirs.' Her face was all powdery with flour, her T-shirt flecked with butter, sugar and practically an entire packet of sprinkles – in fact she was good enough to eat.

'That's right,' Charlotte agreed. 'And it'll make them feel very special.'

By the time they finished the squiggle that was supposed to say Shelley, Chloe realised they had one cake too many. 'Shall we make that one for Boots?' she suggested.

Charlotte had to laugh. 'Which would make it for you really,' she teased, giving her a tickle. 'No, I think we have to make it for Anthony.'

Though Chloe frowned in confusion, instead of asking who he was she simply said, 'Show me how to write it?'

'Of course,' and holding her hand and the stool she was standing on steady, Charlotte guided the nozzle to form an A followed by a Y.

'What does it say?' Chloe asked when they'd finished.

'Well, Anthony is a bit of a long name and it's

547

quite difficult, so I thought we'd just do it like that.'

Chloe nodded agreement, and wiping her hands on her shorts she turned to fall into Charlotte's arms so she could get down.

An hour later, squeaky clean from the bath, and still flushed from the excitement of Nanna, Auntie Shelley and Uncle Wick sweeping her up for giant hugs and kisses, Chloe ran to the table eager to give out the cakes. Though it saddened Charlotte to see the way she'd carefully avoided Bob – and Anthony – it didn't really surprise her, in spite of her having said she wanted to do a painting for Grandpa. Nothing had come of it; in fact she hadn't mentioned it again, so Charlotte hadn't pushed it. Now she was interested to see what might happen when it came time to give Grandpa his cake.

The first ones went to Rick and Shelley, who dutifully gasped with delight, and Nanna's lavish praise when she saw that her own name was actually quite legible set Chloe all aglow. Running back to fetch the cake meant for Anthony, she put it on a plate then stopped and looked up at Charlotte, apparently not quite knowing what to do.

Giving her a playful wink, Charlotte made sure she had the plate in both hands, then turned her around and steered her over to where Anthony was sitting on the bench with Anna. He looked so handsome, Charlotte thought, so relaxed, as though he belonged, and why not when he did?

Sitting forward to rest his elbows on his knees, he said, 'Is this for me?'

Chloe's eyes were huge and cautious as she looked up at him. She held the plate forward and whispered,

'This is for you,' and Charlotte almost sobbed with pride.

Looking very honoured as he took the plate, he said, 'My goodness, this is a fine-looking cake. I think I might have the best one.'

Chloe watched him bite into it.

Going down to her height, Charlotte said, 'Anthony is Mummy's very special friend. He's very kind and lots of fun . . . In fact, he's just like Uncle Wick.' Realising her mistake the instant Rick choked back a laugh and Anthony's eyebrows rose, she said, 'Well, not exactly like Uncle Wick, but he likes doing jigsaws and paintings and going for rides on the carousel. I expect we can do that later, can't we?' She turned to Anthony.

'It would be my pleasure,' Anthony told Chloe, 'but you'll have to show me where to sit, because it's been a long time since I was on one.'

Chloe only blinked.

'I think we should put him on the top of the bus, don't you?' Charlotte suggested.

Whether or not Chloe heard wasn't clear, as she took a noisy breath and turned to hide her face in Charlotte.

Laughing, Charlotte scooped her up and said, 'Shall I tell you a secret about Anthony? He's the one who fought off all the bad people so we could find you and bring you back here.'

Chloe's eyes widened as she turned to him.

Her very own hero, Charlotte hoped. 'So I reckon that makes him your special friend too, don't you?' she continued.

Chloe tilted her head against Charlotte's and twisted her hands around one another.

'I definitely think we're going to be friends,'

Anthony informed her, 'especially now I know you make such good cakes.'

Coming over self-conscious again, Chloe turned her face into Charlotte's neck, and wrapped her arms around her. More than happy with how well the first meeting had gone, Charlotte carried her back to the table, where she whispered a reminder that Grandpa hadn't had his cake yet.

Keeping her back to the room, Chloe reached out a hand as she said, 'Want Boots.'

Knowing she always wanted her bear when she felt insecure, Charlotte lifted him off the table and tucked him under her arm. 'Are you going to give Grandpa his cake now?' she asked, unwilling to force it, but feeling terrible for Bob if it turned out that nothing had changed.

With her face half buried in Boots, Chloe slid to the ground and put the last cake on a plate. As she tottered towards Bob with Boots still trapped under one arm, she kept her eyes down, so didn't see how thrilled he was looking.

'My goodness,' he declared as she reached him, 'it's the best cake I've ever seen and you've spelled my name right too. Not everyone does, you know.'

Chloe's head stayed down.

'Shall I have it?' he asked, when she hung on to it.

Still not looking up, she pushed the plate forward.

'Thank you,' he said warmly. 'I think I'm going to enjoy . . .' He broke off as, to everyone's surprise, she started to climb on to his lap.

Bemused, but quickly setting aside the cake, he lifted her up and settled her on his knee. 'There, how's that?' he smiled, holding her steady and glancing to Charlotte to make sure everything was all right.

Charlotte merely shrugged, as taken aback as he was.

Chloe's words were lost in Boots as she whispered something, so Bob said, 'What was that, sugar? I didn't quite hear.'

Chloe's head came up a fraction. 'Play ride the tiger,' she said.

Horrified, Charlotte quickly went to kneel in front of her and took hold of her hands. 'Grandpa doesn't play those games, sweetheart,' she told her firmly. 'He doesn't like them, and you don't either, do you?'

Chloe shook her head.

'So you don't have to play them, not ever again. OK?'

Chloe looked at her miserably.

'*Not ever again*,' Charlotte repeated.

Chloe's eyes went down. 'I'm a good girl,' she said brokenly.

Smoothing her face, Charlotte said, 'Yes you are, a very, very good girl, and it's only bad men who play that game. And Grandpa isn't a bad man. He's a very good man like Uncle Wick and Anthony.'

Chloe regarded her uncertainly.

'Grandpa's never done anything to hurt you, has he?' Charlotte reminded her.

Chloe shook her head.

'So you see, he's a good man and he only plays games like pass the parcel, or cricket, or hide and seek. And he wants to learn how to do jigsaws. You're very good at them, aren't you?'

Chloe nodded.

'So why don't we eat our cakes and drink our tea, then we can show Grandpa some of your new puzzles.'

'I've got some new puzzles,' Chloe said softly.

'Yes you have, lots of them, and Grandpa would love you to show him how to do them.'

Wriggling down from Bob's lap, Chloe grabbed Charlotte's hand and pulled her towards the door. 'Get them now?' she said.

Deciding that discipline could wait, considering what a breakthrough this might be, Charlotte took her along to her bedroom and returned with an armful of colourful boxes. After laying them out on the floor and settling Chloe in the middle of them, she watched for a while as Bob and her mother helped her to lay out the pieces, then signalled to Anthony to follow her into the kitchen.

'That was amazing,' she commented quietly. 'It's the first time she's ever had anything to do with Bob. It's going to mean so much to him if she starts to accept him.' She smiled at him lovingly as she slipped her arms round his neck. 'So what do you think of her?' she asked, feeling as though she might burst with pride as she recalled the way Chloe had given him a cake.

'Well, she's every bit as cute and adorable as I expected,' he replied, sweeping her face with his eyes. 'Perhaps even more so.'

'I think she liked you,' she said. 'And I'm sure she'll like you even more if you take her on the carousel . . .'

His eyes narrowed dangerously.

'. . . but you might just be off the hook on that, because we're bound to be recognised and I'm not sure any of us wants to face that today.'

'You're right, we don't,' he agreed, 'but we'll have to at some point, so we ought to start thinking about how we want to deal with it.'

With a wry twist to her smile, she said, 'It might

help if we could get Heather Hancock to tone it down a bit.'

'She will,' he assured her, 'once I've had a chat with her editor, because there are negative campaigns, and then there's libel, and I'm afraid she's crossed the line a couple of times this past week.'

Liking the sound of that, Charlotte asked, 'Are we going to sue?'

'We're certainly going to let them think we are,' he replied, 'but in the grand scheme of things she's just a local hack who no one seems to be taking much notice of anyway. And as we can't expect everyone to love you quite as much as Chloe and I do, I think we'll just give her a bit of a scare and get on with our lives. Agreed?'

Charlotte was gazing at him incredulously. 'Do you really love me?'

He appeared surprised. 'You have to ask?'

Laughing, she said, 'Could you say it again, please?'

'Certainly,' he murmured against her lips, 'but right at this moment there's a little person behind you who I think would like you to turn around and notice her.'

Immediately conscious of how disturbing Chloe might find any physical displays of affection between her and Anthony, Charlotte quickly pulled away. 'Hello, my darling,' she said, going to pick her up, 'how's Grandpa getting on with the jigsaws?'

'What you doing?' Chloe asked in a small voice.

'Well,' Charlotte replied, thinking fast, 'I was just giving Anthony a kiss, because that's what people do when they love each other, don't they? Like I kiss you, and you kiss me.'

'And Boots,' Chloe reminded her.

'And Boots, we mustn't forget him, because we love kissing him, don't we?'

Chloe nodded and looked warily at Anthony.

Deciding a change of subject was the best way to go, Anthony said, 'Someone told me you've got a new stroller, and I think I'd like to see it.'

Immediately sliding through Charlotte's arms to the floor, Chloe ran along the hall to her bedroom. Moments later she was wheeling the stroller straight past the kitchen into the sitting room.

'Well, it was brief,' Anthony said drily as Charlotte started to laugh, 'but at least I saw it.'

Chapter Twenty-Eight

Anthony and Charlotte were dancing closely to the romantic sounds of a lazy jazz sax. Though the tourists had long since gone from Kesterly, leaving the beach strewn with random tangles of seaweed and other flotsam, and the leaves on the plane trees had faded to bronze before vanishing on the breeze, a window was open allowing the salty tang of sea air to mingle with the citrus scent of candles. Chloe was fast asleep in her bed, where she'd been sleeping more regularly lately, after a long and sometimes seemingly endless battle to persuade her that Charlotte wasn't going to disappear in the night. Now, it was rare for Charlotte to sleep in with her, though there were still occasions when Charlotte would wake up in her own bed to find Chloe curled up on the floor next to it, sometimes asleep, but just as often awake and clinging to Boots. Charlotte would invariably lift her up and take her back to her room, staying with her until it was time to get up in the morning.

If she and Anthony hadn't slept in the nude it might have been possible to bring Chloe in with them, but wearing clothes in bed was one concession neither of them was willing to make.

What really mattered, though, was that Chloe's

initial shyness with Anthony had evaporated, along with the days and weeks that had helped to bond them. Now she was almost as pleased to see him when he came back after a spell in London as Charlotte was. While he was gone she'd speak to him on the phone telling him about her day, and at weekends she loved nothing more than to go with him to the miniature village, or to play crazy golf, or to climb Milligan's rock. Occasionally he took her fishing and riding. Naturally, Charlotte had to go along too, and she had images from those trips now that she knew would stay with her for ever, such as when Chloe, sitting astride an enormous thoroughbred in front of Anthony, tilted her head back to look up at him and broke into a breathy little smile. And the day she'd caught her first fish at the end of a line (having no idea Anthony had put it there); she'd looked so proud, so important as she held it in her hands to pose for the camera that even Anthony had seemed misty-eyed.

There were so many moments piling up on top of each other to create her little world: a return to the Pumpkin playgroup where Charlotte was helping out part-time; trips to London to stay in Anthony's villa next to the park; hours of fun in the tree house at Maggie's and Ron's and lots of exploring to be done in Devon with her new cousins Phoebe and Jackson. Of course, there was much Skyping with everyone in New Zealand too. Though she'd still only got as far as being jigsaw mates with Bob by the time he'd left, there had been one wonderful morning when Danni and Craig had persuaded her, over Skype, to have a ride on his back the way they often did. It seemed to surprise even her to realise how much she loved it, and she'd clapped her hands with glee as everyone cheered at the end. Since then it had fallen to Anthony to provide the rides, which he often did as a way of getting her to bed, and tonight had been no exception.

As the music faded, and Charlotte went to refill their glasses, he sank into the sofa and stretched luxuriously as he said, 'You know, I've been thinking.'

'Mm?' she prompted, licking a stray drop of Shiraz from her fingers.

'About buying a vineyard.'

Stopping what she was doing, she turned round slowly. Given how close they'd become over the last few months, she couldn't quite believe he'd been contemplating such a big decision without her. 'OK,' she said carefully. 'And this vineyard would be where, exactly?'

'Actually, about five miles from Kerikeri,' he replied. 'Heading north.'

She blinked.

'I'd have mentioned it before,' he went on, 'but I wasn't sure until now that the chap really wanted to sell. If he didn't, and we got our hopes up . . .'

'Stop, stop,' she protested. 'You're planning to become a vintner in *New Zealand* – the Bay of Islands – and you never mentioned it?'

'Well, like I said . . .'

'I heard what you said, but can you imagine what a difference it would have made to me if I'd known you were even thinking about it?'

Grimacing, as it seemed to occur to him now, he said, 'I wanted it to be a surprise.'

She almost had to laugh. 'Well, it's certainly that,' she informed him, still not entirely sure she'd

557

heard him right. 'Can you say again where it is?' she urged.

He repeated it.

Oh my God, he really had said New Zealand. Forcing herself to stay calm, though having no idea why, she said, 'OK, before I start breaking out the champagne or thinking I'm dreaming, please can you remind me what you actually know about running a vineyard – or making wine, or even living in New Zealand, which is a very long way from . . .'

'Your turn to stop,' he objected, holding up a hand. 'This particular vineyard isn't huge, but it's profitable, and my man of business has been vetting it for me . . .'

'Your man of business?'

'Bob.'

'Of course,' she cried, throwing out her hands. How could any of this have been possible without Bob, Anthony's new best friend – sorry, man of business – who he was forever on the phone to, or Skyping, or emailing?

'*And*,' Anthony pressed on, 'there's a small restaurant in the grounds, already established, with a successful chef willing to stay on, plus another property that we thought you might like to make yours for whatever purpose. But only after you've renovated the main house for us to live in, which is large but doable, your mother assures me, and I know you want to put your own stamp on somewhere, so I'm thinking this will work very well provided you're . . . Why are you looking at me like that?' He asked sounding wary.

'Why do you think?' she cried, clasping her hands to her head. 'You're making me the happiest person in the entire world and treating it as though it's just a little something you thought up . . . What about your house? Your life here? Are you really saying you want to move to New Zealand?'

'Of course that's what I'm saying. You didn't think I was going to let you go without me, surely?'

'Well, I don't know. I mean, obviously I knew you were planning to fly back with us when the time comes, and perhaps to stay on for a while, but *buying a vineyard* . . .'

'With a restaurant and a house for you to turn into a home while I'm learning how to make wine. I was thinking of starting a course while we're still here, but now we've got our day in court for the adoption order it seems to make more sense to wait till we get there.'

Charlotte hardly knew what to say. 'The house in Holland Park?' she prompted.

'Will go up for sale.'

'But you've been working as a barrister again lately. I know not as full-on as you were before . . .'

'It's not what I want to do. I'm over it, done, finished. I'm ready to start a new life with you and Chloe, in an environment I know is better than this one. It's where she should grow up, and I know it's where you want to be.'

It was all becoming too much for her now. She tried to speak, but the words wouldn't come. A new home *with him and Chloe* in New Zealand, *a vineyard*, a restaurant, her family nearby . . .

'Oh now, if I knew it was going to upset you that much,' he teased.

Laughing through her sobs, she went to throw her arms around him. 'I love you, Anthony Goodman,' she told him passionately. 'I love you so much I might have to scream, or dance, or sing . . . Oh God, I'm so happy I don't know what to do.'

'You could always try this,' he suggested, and tilting her mouth to his he kissed her so deeply and completely that in spite of all there was still to discuss, she happily set that aside to indulge herself fully in the promise of what was already under way.

'I've been thinking about the other building at the vineyard,' Charlotte said to Anthony over breakfast the following morning, 'the one you said could be mine? I think I'd like to turn it into a children's daycare centre, if it's big enough and there's the right amount of land attached.'

'Great idea,' he commented, wiping egg from Chloe's chin, 'we'll check out the dimensions and do what we can to make it work.'

'I'd also like to pay for the renovation of the main house,' she continued, buttering another slice of toast. 'Actually, how much is it all going to cost? Do you have a budget yet? Maybe this is something we could do together.'

'We are doing it together,' he reminded her, taking the toast and biting into it. 'But once I've sold the house in Holland Park . . .'

'I know it's worth a lot, but I can't let you pay for everything,' she came in determinedly. 'OK, my little nest egg is paltry in comparison to what you can bring to the table, but I need to invest it somewhere and where better than in our home?'

His reply was cut off by the blast of the doorbell.

'Buzz, buzz,' Chloe cried, mimicking the sound.

'That'll be Julia,' Anthony said, referring to the woman the court had appointed as Chloe's guardian during the adoption process. 'I'll go, but don't steal my toast.'

'Huh, like it was yours in the first place.'

Minutes later Julia came bustling into the room, her plump cheeks reddened by the wind, her merry smile appearing from behind a long woollen scarf as she unravelled it. 'My, the temperature's dropped this morning,' she stated in a jovial grumble. 'And there we were just getting used to it warming up again. We never know where we are these days, do we?'

'Would you like some coffee?' Charlotte offered, going to give her a hug.

'Love some,' Julia replied, as though it might save her life. 'And how's our little poppet today?'

'Still in her pyjamas,' Charlotte responded meaningfully.

'They've got kiwis on,' Chloe told Julia, pointing to the cartoonish birds pecking at the fleece. 'Nanna sent them from where the kiwis live.'

'Did she now, and very smart they are too. Are you going to nursery today?'

Chloe looked at Charlotte.

'No, not on Wednesdays,' Charlotte reminded her.

'Not on Wednesdays,' Chloe told Julia.

'Here we are,' Anthony declared, bringing a fresh mug of coffee to the table. 'I have to rush off I'm afraid, but before I go, have you heard from the man on the inside yet?'

Knowing he was referring to Chloe's father, Brian Wade, Charlotte's heart contracted as she looked at Julia.

'Actually, we have,' Julia told them, 'and I don't mind telling you I thought we weren't going to get a

561

favourable response, given how long he's taken to get back to us. However, I'm happy to report that he's raising no objection to the adoption.'

Almost collapsing with relief, Charlotte swept Chloe into her arms and kissed her hard.

'Ouch!' Chloe protested, rubbing her cheek.

'That's what you say when I kiss you,' Anthony told her.

'That's because you're prickly.'

Laughing, he said, 'We could always have contested if he'd refused, and won, but it's better it happens this way.'

'Indeed,' Julia agreed. 'I imagine he decided it would be wiser not to bring any more attention to himself than he's already received, and since no court in the land is ever going to grant him custody again, I guess we can say that for once he's done the right thing by her.'

Deciding merely to feel thankful for that and not think about him any more, Charlotte said to Anthony, 'You're going to miss the train if you don't go now.'

'I am indeed. It was good seeing you, Julia; Chloe, take care of Mummy, Mummy stop stealing all the toast,' and after planting a kiss on Charlotte's and Chloe's cheeks, he grabbed his laptop and briefcase and swept out of the room.

'He's appearing at Bristol Crown Court today,' Charlotte explained as the front door slammed closed behind him. 'He's saying he wants to give up the law, but I fear it's more in his blood than he realises.'

'Is that a bad thing?'

Charlotte shrugged. 'Only if he ends up regretting it.' Her eyes started to shine, and unable to keep the news to herself a moment longer, she filled Julia in on the plan to buy a vineyard.

'Wow!' Julia exclaimed. 'I've never even been to a vineyard, never mind thought about buying one.'

Feeling suddenly awkward in case she'd come across as boastful, Charlotte said, 'Well, this time last year I'd never been to one either, and now look what's happened. I guess you just never know what life's going to throw at you, do you?'

'You certainly don't,' Julia agreed, 'and it hasn't been an easy journey getting here, that's for sure. The important thing is though, you've made it now, and your plans are wonderful. Tell me, is Anthony interested in adopting Chloe too?'

Loving the very idea of it, Charlotte said, 'Actually, we haven't really discussed it yet, except to say it'll probably hold things up for me if he does it now, so we're going to deal with it later.'

'Along with wedding bells?'

Charlotte laughed. 'No mention of those at all, but there's so much else going on. I'm sure it'll happen though, especially if we have more children, and he definitely wants to.'

Though Julia appeared thrilled, she clearly didn't miss anything, because her eyes narrowed with interest as she said, 'And how about you? Is it what you want?'

With a sigh that she hadn't even known was coming, Charlotte replied quietly, 'I always used to think Chloe needed to be an only child, and so I was willing to give up any idea of having one of my own. But knowing how much it means to Anthony, and seeing her with my niece and nephew lately, and with the other kids at playgroup . . . She's come to really enjoy the company of other children, and actually, I think she'd love nothing better than having a little baby to help take care of, provided it can happen.'

Turning to look at her, sprawled out on the carpet with Boots and a few other toys, Julia said, 'Oh, I'm sure it will.'

Since she hadn't even told Anthony about the pregnancy test yet, much less tried it, Charlotte only smiled as she looked at Chloe, and still felt unable to imagine loving a child more.

'Mummy,' Chloe said, rolling on to her back, 'I need the toilet.'

'Well go along then, you know where it is.'

Springing up, Chloe said to Julia, 'Going to the toilet,' and grabbing Boots she scampered off to the bathroom.

After waiting for any bangs or crashes followed by a wail, and thankfully hearing none, Charlotte turned back to Julia. 'Do we know yet,' she asked, 'who the judge is going to be when the order's made?'

Julia's smile was slow, but reassuring. 'You're in luck,' she replied, 'it's Dudley Cross. I know you wanted him, because he's always so good with the kids on their special day.'

Having some lovely memories of Judge Cross sending lucky children into homes they might not otherwise have had, Charlotte couldn't have felt more thrilled. 'Have you told him what we're hoping to do for Chloe?' she asked.

'I have,' Julia confirmed, 'and he's asked me to tell you he's very happy to comply with your wishes, he'll just need some instruction because he's never heard of a jump-off before.'

* * *

The morning had finally arrived for them to appear at the family court to make Chloe's adoption official. Charlotte couldn't imagine Myra, her own adoptive mother, ever feeling as deeply as she did now when it had come time to make Alex, as they'd renamed her, a part of their family. However, Myra had cared for her additional daughter well enough, and if she and the rector hadn't taken her in Charlotte would never have had Gabby as a sister.

All Charlotte could hope for now was that she never *ever* made Chloe feel that she mattered less than any other children she might have, but she knew in her heart that she wouldn't. Loving Chloe as much as she did, it simply wasn't possible. She was the centre of her and Anthony's world, and that was where she would stay, never falling into the shadows even when the new baby joined her.

She wondered whether it would be a boy or a girl, and felt a flutter of joy like a baby's first kick. She gazed down at the narrow white wand with its solid blue line, and tried to decide when to tell Anthony. Not yet, because this time was all about Chloe, but she'd keep the test to show him. They might even keep it to show the baby when he or she was older.

It was sad they wouldn't have one to show Chloe later in life to mark her first days in the womb; however, what she would have was a very special video of her, aged four, jumping off in front of a judge. Since there was strictly no photography of any kind allowed in a family court, it was a bit of a miracle that they'd been given permission for this. However, their sworn assurances to Judge Cross that no recording would be made of the official part of the proceedings had persuaded him to bend the rules, just this once.

Though Chloe knew that everyone from New Zealand – Nanna, Grandpa, Uncle Phil, Auntie Shelley, Danni, Craig, Uncle Wick and his friend Hamish – had arrived a few days ago and were all along the road in a hotel, as yet she had no idea there was such an important reason for their visit. Nor did she know anything about the very special parcel they'd brought with them that, mercifully, had made the journey intact. All Charlotte had told her so far was that she could wear her new dress and coat today, because they were going to a party later at the Pumpkin. To tell her about the jump-off too far in advance would have got her into a state of such wild excitement that she'd never have slept last night, or eaten this morning, or been able to sit still for a single minute of the adoption order being granted.

What Chloe had prepared, however, with the help of her friends at nursery, was a list of the games she wanted to play with her cousins at the party, and the songs she wanted to sing. A copy of the list was waiting at the Pumpkin, while the jump-off ring that Celia at Aroha had so kindly allowed them to borrow, was now at the court.

So everything was more or less set. Gabby, Martin and the twins were meeting them at the court, along with everyone else, and Janet from the Pumpkin had called to say that the kids were already lining up to get on the bus.

'Where is she?' Charlotte asked, as Anthony came to stand behind her in the bathroom.

'Putting her boots on,' he replied, splaying his fingers across her tummy as he caught her reflection in the mirror. 'I offered to help, but she wants to do it herself. You look beautiful.'

She smiled softly. 'Who were you on the phone to just now?' she asked, resting her head on his shoulder, while keeping her eyes on his.

'Oh, just someone else from the press wanting a little chat. I put them on to our new publicity agent.'

Laughing at the absurdity of having such a person in their lives, she closed a hand around the pregnancy test and turned to tilt her face up to his. 'We're doing the right thing, aren't we?' she asked, from the pleasure of his embrace.

He frowned cautiously. 'About what in particular?'

'The statement for the press, and the photograph.'

'Absolutely,' he assured her. 'You worded it perfectly, with a thank you to everyone who supported you at the most difficult time, and an apology to those who felt justice wasn't served. I'm sure even they will change their minds when the publicist releases the photo of the three of us. I know it manages to bring a tear to my eye every time I look at it.'

Recalling how moved she'd been when the photographer had first shown them the selected image of them appearing so relaxed and happy at home, she said, 'It's amazing to think anyone would be interested, really.'

With a wry smile, he replied, 'Interested enough to be paying small fortunes to run it, all of which, thanks to you, will be split between the NSPCC and Save the Children.'

Pleased with her decision, she said, 'It wouldn't have made any sense to do it otherwise, at least not to me.'

'Mummy,' Chloe said from the bedroom. 'I ready.'

Following Anthony through, Charlotte gasped and melted to see how adorable she looked. She was wearing her new dark blue and purple striped woollen dress with a flower on the patch pocket and matching navy tights, and her wayward curls were already struggling to escape the pretty hair bobbles that Anthony loved so much. The fact that her cute little Ugg boots were on the wrong feet and Boots was his usual mess were small issues they'd deal with later. 'You are the most beautiful little girl in the world,' Charlotte declared, scooping her up. 'I'm so proud of you, and today's going to be very, very special, you know, because in front of everyone we know and love the judge is going to make me your mummy for ever and ever and ever.'

'And then we're having a party at the Pumpkin?'

'That's right, but before that something else is going to happen. Shall I tell you what it is?'

Chloe looked at Anthony and held out her arms for him to take her.

'Today,' Charlotte said, when she was settled, 'you are going to have a *jump-off*.'

Chloe's eyes grew round.

'Do you remember what that is?' Charlotte asked.

It took a moment, but suddenly she was bursting with so much excitement that she almost fell out of Anthony's arms as she struggled to get down. 'I'm having a jump-off,' she told Charlotte. 'Mummy, I'm having a jump-off.'

'That's right,' Charlotte laughed. 'We've got everything ready for you, even the jump-off ring that Celia sent from Aroha.'

Chloe gave a leap of pure joy. 'Having a jump-off,' she said to Anthony. 'Want you to come too.'

'Of course I'll be there,' he assured her. 'I wouldn't miss it for the world.'

Loving how readily Chloe had accepted Anthony into their lives, Charlotte scooped her up again and gave her a resounding kiss. One day soon she might be persuaded to call him Daddy, but Charlotte had no intention of pushing it, not when the word alone had such awful connotations for Chloe. She'd find her way to it in time.

Much as Charlotte had expected, Chloe was hardly able to sit still in the court, wanting to run back and forth between her and Nanna and Auntie Maggie and Danni to tell them she was having a jump-off. Before coming inside she'd done her best to explain to Tracy, Tommy, Wendy and Julia the guardian exactly what a jump-off was, though how much they'd understood of her breathless garbling Charlotte wouldn't have liked to guess. On the other hand, her cousins, Phoebe and Jackson, were almost as excited as she was, so presumably, on some level, they understood what was going to happen, even if their parents remained slightly mystified.

Now, still not having quite connected with the fact that the big event was going to take place in this funny room with lots of benches and big tall windows, Chloe whispered to Charlotte, 'When are we going?'

'Ssh,' Charlotte replied, putting a finger to her lips.

Chloe looked up at Anthony. 'Can we go now?' she asked him.

As Anthony started to respond Judge Cross came to the end of his official speech with the words, '. . .

and so I am now in a position to announce that the adoption order has been granted.'

Grabbing Chloe into a bruising embrace, Charlotte jumped up and down with so much relief and joy she might have burst with it. Anthony was laughing as he threw his arms around them, but he was soon making way for the others to crowd in with their own joy and congratulations.

'Is it time to go now?' Chloe asked, bemused by all the fuss.

'Oh, no,' Charlotte whispered. 'We've got the most important bit to come.'

Chloe looked crestfallen. Since she didn't have the courage to argue, she slid down from Charlotte's arms and stood looking dolefully at the floor.

'Chloe Nicholls, are you still here?' Judge Cross asked in a gentle sort of roar.

As the small crowd parted to reveal Chloe in their midst, her head came up, and almost instantly she shrank back behind Anthony's legs, making Charlotte laugh and feel glad that the judge, as requested, hadn't robed up for the occasion. With his frosty wig and flowing gown he'd have appeared even more terrifying to someone as small as Chloe than, with his bushy grey whiskers and eyebrows, he already did. Though it was true some kids loved nothing better than the whole lawyerly regalia for the granting of their adoption orders, they were usually older than Chloe and quite possibly already knew the judge from previous appearances in the family court.

Hoisting Chloe into his arms, Anthony said, 'She's here, My Lord.'

Chloe immediately tried to launch herself at Charlotte.

'It's all right,' Charlotte assured her, 'there's nothing to worry about, I promise.'

The judge's watery blue eyes were twinkling with merriment as he said, 'I do believe we have something very particular planned for you, young Chloe, so shall we begin by . . .' He gave a quick glance at his notes. 'Ah, I believe we should have a throne somewhere . . .'

'It's here,' Janet from the Pumpkin called out, as she came bustling in from a side room with a silver-foil-wrapped high-back chair. After setting it in front of the judge's bench, she held it steady as a maintenance man climbed nimbly on to it and attached a hoop of gaily coloured ribbons, bows and bunting to a pre-installed hook.

Chloe gasped, clasping a hand to her mouth. 'Mummy, it's the jump-off ring,' she whispered loudly.

Laughing, Charlotte said, 'I do believe it is.'

Chloe's eyes were almost bursting from their sockets. 'It's the jump-off ring,' she informed everyone, and thrusting Boots at Anthony she slid to the floor and grabbed Charlotte's hand.

Going down to her level, Charlotte said, 'Janet's going to take you into the other room now where all your friends are waiting to walk to the throne with you.'

'Want you to come,' Chloe said, not exactly shyly, more excitedly.

'I have to wait here with everyone else,' Charlotte reminded her, 'because if you remember, you have to choose who you're going to jump off to.'

Chloe's mouth fell open. Apparently she'd forgotten that part of the ritual. 'But we haven't played any games yet,' she protested. 'Or sung any songs.'

'We're going to do that later, at the Pumpkin. Everyone will be there, and we've got lots of prizes for pass the parcel . . .'

Coming to join them, Judge Cross said, 'Are you ready, Chloe?'

Spotting the huge paw of a hand he was holding out, Charlotte realised it was going to be too much for Chloe to go with him on her own. Together with the judge, she walked her past the lawyers who'd overseen the adoption and who were now appearing highly entertained by the prospect of a closing ceremony, over to the side room. Inside, the kids from the Pumpkin were already kitted out in the hats and costumes they'd been making in secret under Janet's guidance.

Seeing them, Chloe jumped up and down with joy. 'Mummy, look, look,' she cried, almost beside herself.

'And this is for you,' Janet told her, lifting a sparkly crown fit for a fairy-tale princess from a large pink box.

Chloe blinked in awe.

After carefully placing it on her head and telling her she looked beautiful, Charlotte said, 'I'll see you out there, OK?'

Chloe nodded. Her face was so flushed it was almost feverish.

Accepting it was OK for her to go, Charlotte returned to Anthony's side to wait for the ceremony to begin. There was a chance, she realised, that she might actually be as excited as Chloe.

At last, after much shuffling and bumping around offstage, the side door creaked slowly open and a moment later Chloe, looking a little more anxious than important, appeared in her crown and a glittering blue robe that Janet must have made specially.

Hearing Anna choke back a sob, Charlotte had to laugh through one of her own.

'She looks so sweet,' Phoebe whispered.

'Doesn't she?' Gabby agreed.

'We always do this at home,' Danni told them.

If anyone else spoke it was drowned in a sudden deafening noise from Chloe's accompanying band, and as she began walking towards her throne, dutifully followed by her retinue of Pumpkin attendants, the cacophony of drums, trumpets and tambourines became so loud it might almost have raised the roof.

As Anthony dropped his head into one hand, either to disguise a laugh, or wince at the noise, Charlotte leaned in to him saying, 'Has this court ever seen anything like it?'

'I doubt it,' he replied, and clapping along with everyone else he suddenly had to smother another laugh as one little boy blew his trumpet so hard that the boy in front turned round and thumped him.

Eventually the children were gathered in front of the judge, still hooting and banging, until Janet finally persuaded them to stop and sit on the floor. Then taking Chloe's hands, the judge and Janet half lifted, half swung her up on to the throne. Once settled, she looked up at the jump-off ring and promptly lost her crown.

Quickly restoring it, Janet gave her a reassuring smile and stood back as the judge cleared his throat, ready to begin.

'Chloe Nicholls,' he said solemnly as he unfurled the scroll Charlotte had prepared, 'this is a very special jump-off you're having today to mark a very special event indeed. Do you know what the event is?'

Chloe didn't look sure.

Smiling kindly, he said, 'This is the day that you become Chloe Nicholls in the eyes of the law. That might not mean very much to you right now, because I know you're used to being Chloe Nicholls, but in years to come, when you look back on today and watch the video which is being made of it, you will understand its significance and how very much you are loved.

'Though you're only four years old, you have already shown more courage and resilience than most people can manage in forty-four. You have also brought more joy to your mother's heart than she can express, and brightened her world in ways too numerous to mention. Though there have been dark days, times when you were not together, the bond between you was never broken; if anything it simply became stronger.'

Though still appearing slightly mystified, Chloe was hanging on to his every word, and Charlotte wanted to squeeze her so much that she had to take Boots from Anthony and squeeze him instead.

'Some people say we choose our parents,' the judge continued, 'and in your case, Chloe, I don't think there's any doubt of it.'

Charlotte blinked in surprise. She hadn't written those words, so the judge must have added them himself.

'I believe you've made one of the wisest choices of your life, Chloe,' Cross was saying, 'and as the years pass I've no doubt you'll find that it remains the wisest, because you are a little girl who is truly wanted in every way, and couldn't be more loved

574

by your mother, your soon-to-be father and the whole of the rest of your family.'

Cross smiled at Chloe's bemused little face as he said, 'I have heard much talk of you over the past months, and I have no doubt that you are going to grow up to be a most remarkable young lady.'

Just about bursting with pride, Charlotte gripped Boots more tightly than ever as Cross went back to the script. 'Some of your family have travelled from the other side of the world to be with you today,' he read out. 'Nanna and Grandpa Reeves, Auntie Shelley and Uncle Phil, Danni, Craig, Uncle Rick. From Devon we have Auntie Gabby, Uncle Martin and your cousins Phoebe and Jackson; and from Kesterly we have your Auntie Maggie and Uncle Ron. Also from Kesterly we have Tracy Barrall, Tommy Burgess, Wendy Fraser and Julia Minor, and of course all your friends from the Pumpkin playgroup.' Looking at her again, he said, 'I wish all children who had a difficult start in life could find the love you have, Chloe, but sadly it doesn't happen for everyone. You are a very lucky girl indeed.' His smile broadened quite suddenly. 'And now I do believe it's time for you to tell us who you have chosen to jump off to.'

Chloe blinked.

'Have you decided?'

She nodded shyly.

He waited. 'So are you going to tell us who it is?' he prompted.

Chloe turned to search the room, her eyes travelling from Nanna and Grandpa, to Uncle Wick, to Auntie Gabby and Danni, to Auntie Maggie and Anthony, until finally they came to rest on Charlotte. 'Mummy,' she whispered haltingly.

Biting her lip to try and stop her smile from becoming too wide for her face, Charlotte stepped forward. 'Of course Mummy,' she heard Anna murmur, 'it could only ever be Mummy.'

Glancing at her mother, Charlotte gave her a smile.

'And how many claps would you like to take?' the judge asked Chloe, after consulting his script.

'Four,' she replied.

'OK, so are we ready?'

Charlotte leaned in to remind him to ask the children to stand.

'Sorry, yes of course. That's right, everyone up we get and form two straight lines from Chloe to her mummy . . . Very good, wide enough now for Chloe to jump through. Excellent.'

Chloe was standing on the throne now, holding on to Janet's hand to keep herself steady.

'Are you ready, Chloe?' Judge Cross asked.

Her eyes were glittering widely as she nodded.

'Then it's time for you to *jump off*,' he cried, and punched a fist in the air.

'Jump off,' everyone chorused.

Gripping the judge's and Janet's hands so they could swing her down from the throne, Chloe proceeded to make four giant leaps through the columns of her friends, with the last being straight into Charlotte's arms.

'Well done,' the judge praised as everyone cheered and applauded. 'You have performed an excellent jump-off to your mummy, Chloe, and may I be amongst the first to wish you both a very happy and healthy life together.'

'Thank you,' Charlotte murmured, her voice muffled by the enormous hug she was being given.

'Thank you, thank you,' she repeated over and over, as everyone crowded round to congratulate them.

It was almost too much, she wasn't sure she could contain all the emotion, and seeming to sense it Anthony wrapped her and Chloe in his arms as though to hold them together.

It was many hours later that Anthony carried a sleeping Chloe up to the flat and into her bedroom. The jump-off, followed by the party at the Pumpkin when she'd played all her favourite games and sung the songs of her choice, had worn her out completely. She didn't even stir as Charlotte undressed her and tucked her under the duvet with Boots.

'She's my daughter,' she whispered incredulously, as she and Anthony stood looking down at her. 'She's actually mine.'

As he tightened his arm round her shoulders, she turned to him. Though she knew everyone would be arriving soon for the adult celebration of the adoption, she said, 'Do you mind if I sit here with her for a while?'

'Of course not,' he replied, and after kissing her he closed the door quietly behind him.

Lying down on the bed, she turned on to her side to gaze at Chloe's sleeping face. She looked so peaceful, so angelic with her tufty curls and sweeping lashes. Her creamy complexion was softly flushed, and her sweet little mouth was half open as she breathed. Could a child look, or be, more innocent and tender? Was it really possible for one little heart to contain so much courage and hope? She'd never given up on the dream of coming back to Charlotte, and now Charlotte could only wonder at the power of that dream.

Kissing her fingertips, she touched them gently to Chloe's cheek. It would be wonderful to think she could simply erase the trauma of Chloe's early life, and silence the demons for ever, but she knew they'd probably stir up trouble somewhere along the way, because those sorts of demons always did. Her own hadn't really kicked off until she was in her teens; maybe it would be the same for Chloe. Whenever it happened she had a mother now who'd be there for her, making sure she had all the help she needed and that she never doubted how much she was loved.

It was the most she could do, the best she could do.

Smiling as Chloe's eyelids flickered, she began wondering about the journey life had sent them on in order to bring them to today. There was no point trying to understand it, because she would never be able to. Instead, she was simply going to feel thankful over and over again for the way things had turned out. And that Anthony had played such a vital part in it was making it more incredible, more special than ever.

Who could possibly have imagined this time a year ago that she'd be where she was now? Certainly not her. It was proof indeed that life could turn things around, and in ways it was impossible to foresee. Of course she understood that the future was likely to have plenty more challenges in store, but all she was going to think about now was Chloe, Anthony and the new baby inside her who was still her little secret – and the wonderful new home in New Zealand with a vineyard, a restaurant and room for her to create her own business. She'd be close to her mother so they could carry on making up for all the years they'd lost, and now she no longer had anything to hide Gabby and her family could come to stay. In fact, their first trip was already planned for Christmas, just six weeks away.

Hearing the door open, she looked round and smiled as Anthony came in.

'Are you OK?' he asked, coming to sit on the bed beside her.

'Better than that,' she whispered, linking her fingers through his. 'Are you?'

Smoothing a curl from Chloe's brow, he said, 'I'm fine. Though, actually, there is one thing that's bothering me, and I thought it might be a good idea to bring it up now.'

'Oh?' she said, waiting for his eyes to return to hers.

When they did, he seemed perplexed as he told her, 'I've been trying to decide when would be the best time to make honest girls of you, before we go to New Zealand or when we get there.'

Laughing as she wondered if her heart could take any more joy, she asked, 'And have you come to a decision?'

He nodded. 'I think I have.'

'Are you going to share it?' she prompted.

'Well,' he responded slowly, 'it seemed to me, that if Gabby's going to be around for Christmas, we could perhaps persuade Maggie and Ron to come too, and have a family wedding at Te Puna.'

Imagining the vivid red flowers of the pohutu-kawa – pokwa – tree hanging over the beach, with everyone she loved in scant summer clothes and bare feet in the sand, she sat up to put her arms around him. 'That's a wonderful idea,' she whispered, wishing she could tell him about the baby now, but still mindful that this was Chloe's day.

As they kissed, Chloe stirred in her sleep and turned on to her back. 'Mum-my,' she sighed softly.

Gazing down at her, Charlotte whispered, 'Chloe.'

When they were sure she wasn't going to wake up, Anthony said, 'So is that a yes?'

'If it's a proposal it is.'

'Then I guess,' he murmured, his lips already on hers, 'we could make the announcement tonight.'

'Yes, let's tell everyone tonight,' she agreed, thinking of how thrilled they'd all be.

However no one, not a single person in the entire world, could be as happy as she was right now.

And now, as her mother kept reminding her, was all that really mattered.

Acknowledgements

An enormous thank you and much love to my dear friends Vanessa and Richard Owen for making this book possible, and for such a warm welcome to New Zealand. To say the first half of the story couldn't have been written without them is an understatement indeed, particularly the patient and painstaking attention Vanessa gave to the proof read. The Owens have the great good fortune to live in the house I have described herein as Te Puna Lodge, and some of you might be interested to know that the bach is a perfect romantic hideaway. If you'd like to find out more, the web address is: www.driftwoodnz.com

Many warm thanks also go to Fiona Shepherd of Arohanui Early Childhood Learning Centre (especially for introducing me to the Jump Off ring); and to John Roberts for explaining police procedure for the arrest.

Once again I am hugely indebted to my dear friends Ian Kelcey and Gill Hall for guiding me through the legal maze of the criminal case, and the even denser process of family law. If you've already read the book by the time you turn to these acknowledgements you'll be very aware of how vital their input was.

No book of mine can be complete without thanking the incredible team at Cornerstone: my brilliant editor Susan Sandon; the constant and always supportive Georgina Hawtrey-Woore; the wholly inspiring talents of Louise Page, Jen Doyle and Sarah Page; and the wizardry of Robert Waddington and everyone in Sales. Also my thanks go to my good friend and agent, Toby Eady.

Getting to know

Susan Lewis

Read on for an insight into *Don't Let Me Go*,
all about Susan and her links to the charity
Breast Cancer Care

Those who've read *No Child of Mine* will understand why I simply had to write this sequel. Actually, in my mind there were two reasons for doing so, the first because as wonderful as it would be to assume Ottilie (Chloe) was safe, I didn't feel quite right about leaving the situation with a social worker getting away with taking a child. The second reason was because I had completely fallen for Ottilie (Chloe), fictional as she is, and I couldn't bear to think of Alex (Charlotte) living in constant dread of her being taken away. They could never have had a normal life, running from the law, so the only solution was to allow the law to take its course.

Since *No Child of Mine* was published I've heard from many readers about how difficult they found it to read at times. Naturally, I understand this, and I salute and thank those who did stay with it. No one has yet said that they're sorry they did, only that they couldn't wait to find out what happens next. I'm not sure that has been a particularly easy journey either, at times it was certainly quite hard to write, but if you've come this far I'm assuming you made it. (Perhaps not without a tissue or two, but at least in one piece, and hopefully with a sense of completion.)

In creating these stories my aim wasn't only to try and bring home the tragedy of neglect and abuse, but to throw a more positive light on child protection workers and how difficult their jobs are. We most often hear about them when something has gone tragically wrong, at which point blame is heaped upon them by press and public alike. These instances are mercifully rare, the rest of the time we don't hear much about social workers at all; certainly not how harrowing, even dangerous their jobs can be; how the system itself so often works against them; or how emotional burn out is a very real problem for them.

Something else I encountered during the writing of *Don't Let Me Go* was the human side of the family courts; another institution that often gets very bad press. Of course not always undeservedly, but I hope you agree that the view the legal system took at the end of this story was as human as it's possible for the law to be.

Once again, I thank you for choosing to read my books. It matters a great deal to me what you think of them, so if you would like to be in touch please don't hesitate. You can reach me through the contact link on my website: www.susanlewis.com or on the Official Susan Lewis Facebook page: www.facebook/susanlewisbooks

was born in 1956 to a happy, normal family living in a brand new council house on the outskirts of Bristol. My mother, at the age of twenty, and one of thirteen children, persuaded my father to spend his bonus on a ring rather than a motorbike and they never looked back. She was an ambitious woman determined to see her children on the right path: I was signed up for ballet, elocution and piano lessons and my little brother was to succeed in all he set his mind to.

Tragically, at the age of thirty-three, my mother lost the battle against cancer and died. I was nine, my brother was five.

My father was left with two children to bring up on his own. Sending me to boarding school was thought to be 'for the best' but I disagreed. No one listened to my pleas for freedom, so after a while I took it upon myself to get expelled. By the time I was thirteen, I was back in our little council house with my father and brother. The teenage years passed and before I knew it I was eighteen…an adult.

I got a job at HTV in Bristol for a few years before moving to London at the age of twenty-two to work for Thames. I moved up the ranks, from secretary in news and current affairs, to a production assistant in light entertainment and drama. My mother's ambition and a love of drama gave me the courage to knock on the Controller's door to ask what it takes to be a success. I received the reply of 'Oh, go away and write something'. So I did!

Three years into my writing career I left TV and moved to France. At first it was bliss. I was living the dream and even found myself involved in a love affair with one of the FBI's most wanted! Reality soon dawned, however, and I realised that a full time life in France was very different to a two week holiday frolicking around on the sunny Riviera.

So I made the move to California with my beloved dogs Casanova and Floozie. With the rich and famous as my neighbours I was enthralled and inspired by Tinsel Town. The reality, however, was an obstacle course of cowboy agents, big-talking producers and wannabe directors. Hollywood was not waiting for me, but it was a great place to have fun! Romances flourished and faded, dreams were crushed but others came true.

After seven happy years of taking the best of Hollywood and avoiding the rest, I decided it was time for a change. My dogs and I spent a short while in Wiltshire before then settling once again in France. Perched high above the Riviera with glorious views of the sea. It was wonderful to be back amongst old friends, and to make so many new ones. Casanova and Floozie both passed away during our first few years there, but Coco and Lulabelle are doing a valiant job of taking over their places – and my life!

Everything changed again three months after my fiftieth birthday when I met James, my partner, who lives and works in Bristol. For a couple of years we had a very romantic and enjoyable time of flying back and forth to see one another at the weekends, but at the end of 2010 I finally sold my house on the Riviera and am now living in Gloucestershire in a delightful old barn with Coco and Lulabelle. My writing is flourishing and thirty books down the line I couldn't be happier. James is still in Bristol, with his boys, Michael and Luke – a great musician and a champion footballer! – so I believe James and I are what's called very happy LATTES (Living Apart Together – don't quite see how that acronym works but I'm told that's what we are!). I wonder what we'll be called after we get married this year, twice! First time in Bristol, second on the French Riviera.

It's been exhilarating and educational having two teenage boys in my life! Needless to say they know everything, which is very useful (saves me looking things up) and they're incredibly inspiring in ways they probably have no idea about.

Should you be interested to know a little more about my early life, why not try *Just One More Day*, a memoir about me and my mother? The story then continues in *One Day at a Time*, a memoir about me and my father and how we coped with my mother's loss.

1. What made you want to become a writer?

It's something I instinctively felt would happen one day, though I didn't do much about it until I began working in TV drama. Editing scripts, pulling together storylines, dreaming up characters and their backgrounds was something I enjoyed so much that when an agent suggested I turn one of my projects into a book I decided to give it a go. That book was never published, but the bug had bitten and the rest, I guess, is history.

2. Describe your routine for writing and where you like to write, including whether you have any little quirks or funny habits when you are writing.

I have a study at home that overlooks a beautiful spread of lower Cotswold countryside where I aim to be by ten each morning, through until six or seven in the evening. For a long time I wrote seven days a week taking a break only when I was so exhausted I couldn't do any more. Now, I pace myself a little better by doing only five or six days, but even that is pretty gruelling. I don't have any quirks particularly, but I do have a very bad but thoroughly enjoyable habit of drinking a glass or two of wine when I read back over what I've written during the day.

3. What themes are you interested in when you're writing?

I'm always interested in the strange or terrible things fate inflicts on innocent people and how courageously (or not) they strive to overcome it.

4. Where do you get your inspiration from?

The most obvious source of inspiration is life itself. Added to that there are certain authors I find very inspirational in the way they write, such as Lionel Shriver; Jodi Picoult; Anita Shreve; Susan Howatch and Irène Némirovsky whose book, *Suite Française*, played a very big part in my own book, *A French Affair*.

5. How do you manage to get inside the heads of your characters in order to portray them truthfully?

It's all done through imagination, I guess – I can't think that there would be any other way.

6. Do you base your characters on real people? And if not, where does the inspiration come from?

Very occasionally they're based on people I meet, but as a real character is so highly complex it would only ever be one or two aspects of them. I guess you could say that personality traits are perhaps more inspiring than actual characters.

7. What's the most extreme thing you've ever done to research your book?

I once allowed myself to be locked up in a Filipino jail when researching *Last Resort* – that was pretty scary, and it didn't smell too good either!

8. What aspect of writing do you enjoy most?

I enjoy it all, especially when exciting and pivotal things happen that I hadn't seen coming!

. What's the best thing about being an author?

or me it would definitely be doing the second draft when all the
eally hard work is done, and the smoothing out is underway. After
hat comes a lovely freeing time when I hold onto the book before
;iving it to my editor – this is a period when there is no pressure
it all, or anxiety about whether or not she is going to like it. That
>egins the moment I send it from my computer to hers.

10. What advice would you give aspiring writers?

Probably that you have to be serious about writing to make it
work, not simply think 'I'm going to write a bestseller' or 'I'd
write a book if I only had time.' It takes a huge amount of
dedication and belief in yourself; if you have that then I think the
best advice I could give is pay great attention to your characters
and who they are, and don't forget to listen to them. It's uncanny
how often they'll help out when you find yourself stuck.

11. What is your favourite book of all time and why?

There are many books I could list here, but I'm going to settle for
Suite Française, because it's the only book I've ever finished
reading and then gone straight back to the beginning to read it
again.

12. If you could be a character in a book, or live in the world of a book who or where would you be?

I wouldn't mind being one of Georgette Heyer's heroines back
in Georgian times, but as they didn't have much in the way of
anaesthetic then, perhaps I'd rather be Claudine in my own book,
Darkest Longings.

Susan Lewis

and

breast cancer care

I lost my mother to breast cancer when she was thirty-three years old and I was nine. This was back at a time when women, even doctors, spoke in hushed tones about the dreaded Big C. Nothing was discussed, no counselling offered; there was even a kind of shame attached to having fallen victim to this terrible disease.

Luckily, all that has changed. Today someone is always there to offer advice and support to those who need it, or simply to lend an ear if all that's required is to talk. Many of these people are doctors, nurses, or members of the healthcare professions; but just as many are women who selflessly give up their time to be there for those in need. Stephanie Harrison of Breast Cancer Care is one of these very special people, and it is because of her that I have become associated with this extremely worthwhile organisation.

Read on to learn more about Steph in her own words...

In June 2008, I was sitting in my doctor's office hearing the words 'Stephanie, you have breast cancer'. As those words reached my ears I felt like I'd been kicked in the stomach, and for a moment or two I sat in a daze of numbness and shock. I then heard, 'Is there any history of breast cancer in your family?' to which I replied 'No, but trust me to start a new trend'. Everyone in the room laughed, and I decided from that moment on I would try to fight this disease with humour.

At my diagnosis I received all the information I would need about treatment, lifestyle and aftercare, which was provided by Breast Cancer Care. At that time I had no idea just how important this organisation and its staff would become in my life. Subsequently they gave me so much help and support throughout my fight with cancer. I consider myself very fortunate that I was offered their support because now I realise it really is second to none. What I didn't realise at the time is that not everyone is aware of the support they offer. Therefore I decided to help raise awareness for this amazing charity by choosing Breast Cancer Care for my own fundraising activities.

It seems odd to say that my life has got better since being diagnosed with breast cancer, but in a lot of ways it has. It has focused my mind and made me realise life is short – that old cliché 'life is not a dress rehearsal' is so true. Seeing that this disease has no respect for age, colour or creed was a real eye-opener for me and it made me realise I had to do something to help others who would hear this devastating news. So I set out on my path as a fundraiser for BCC. During this time I have been overwhelmed by the love and support of so many people and their willingness to help me, as well as by the support of those at Breast Cancer Care. I have met so many amazing people, many of whom have become good friends and some of them have changed my life in more ways than they will ever know. One of those people is Susan Lewis.

In the spring of 2011 I was given a copy of the first part of Susan's autobiography *Just One More Day* and it changed my life. I wasn't sure reading a book about someone dying from breast cancer as I approached my 3rd annual mammogram would be a fun thing to do, but how wrong could I be. From the very first few lines I was hooked and I spent the next two days laughing and crying as I experienced all the ups and downs of Susan's family's lives; a family being torn apart by illness and secrets. Three things struck me immediately. One was how well written it was. Then I wondered how Susan wrote so effectively from the point of view of a child. I was also overwhelmed by Susan's honesty. By the end of the book I was so moved that I had to speak to Susan and tell her how it affected me. The mother/daughter scenario she described got me thinking about my own mum and just

how important this book is and on so many levels. I have since read many of Susan's novels, and last year the wonderful *One Day at a Time*, the second part to Susan's autobiography. Every book is not only a joy to read but also a learning experience about life. The first time I met Susan I realised I was in the presence of a kind, caring and truly genuine human being and working with her is one of the greatest joys of my life. I am proud to call her my friend and know that we will do wonderful things to help Breast Cancer Care help those who suffer from this life-altering disease.

Being told you have a life-threatening illness totally puts your life into perspective and makes you realise just what is important. It is also one of the scariest things any of us will ever have to face but with the love and support of others we can hopefully make the lives of those diagnosed in the future a little easier. It is a joy and an honour to represent Breast Cancer Care and the wonderful work they do.

There are more than half a million people in the UK
today who have been treated for breast cancer and
every year another 50,000 or so – including around
300 men – hear the devastating news that they have the
disease. They'll probably feel frightened and confused
– and their family and friends might need help too.

Breast Cancer Care is just a phone call or mouse
click away for anyone affected by breast cancer. Their
free helpline and information-packed website offer
a friendly ear and expert guidance to anyone dealing
with the turmoil of this life-threatening illness. Across
the UK, they also provide skilled emotional and
practical support through a range of confidential, face-
to-face services, helping people every step of the way.

Their unique strength lies in the way they combine
their understanding of people's experience of breast
cancer with the clinical expertise of their team of
specialist nurses. They care because they've been
there, and they know how to help.

Breast Cancer Care helpline:
0808 800 6000

Breast Cancer Care website:
www.breastcancercare.org.uk

Read my story...

To find out more about my family's experience with breast cancer then you can read *Just One More Day* and *One Day At A Time* – two memoirs that will hopefully make you laugh as well as cry! For some they may prove entertaining trips down memory lane; for others they will hopefully show how fortunate we are to be living in the times that we are.

Available at your local bookshop or online

Look out for Susan's new novel
out in hardcover 7 November 2013

Lainey Hollingsworth has spent her whole life on the outside
of a secret. Her mother would never discuss the reasons she
abandoned Italy when Lainey was a new born, nor has she
ever stayed in touch with the family she left behind.

Now Lainey's mother is dead, taking the secret with her,
and leaving Lainey free to find out about her roots.

Her husband, Tom, appears supportive, until he hits her
with a bombshell that shatters the very foundations of their
marriage. Another secret Lainey never knew anything about.
Shaken, but more determined than ever to find out who she
really is, Lainey takes her children to Umbria in
search of answers.

What she finds in the sleepy, sunbaked village of her
birth turns her world inside out.

Join

Susan
Lewis

online

Sign up for her newsletter
at www.susanlewis.com

Get in touch via the
Official Susan Lewis Facebook Page:

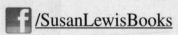 /SusanLewisBooks

Or follow Susan on Twitter:

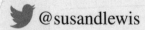 @susandlewis